The PLOT to COOL the PLANET

A Novel

Sam Bleicher

NEWMAN SPRINGS PUBLISHING
320 Broad Street
Red Bank, NJ 07701

First originally published by Newman Springs Publishing 2018

This book is a work of fiction. Except for known public figures, all individuals in this book are fictional, and any resemblance to individuals living or dead is coincidental. All events described occur in a hypothetical future and are a product of the author's imagination.

ISBN 978-1-64096-289-7 (Paperback)
ISBN 978-1-64096-290-3 (Digital)

Printed in the United States of America

To my companion, who suffered through this project with me; my family and close friends who read rough drafts; and the scientists, diplomats, engineers, and government officials who are devoting their lives and careers to saving humanity from the destruction of our only home.

Chapter 1

AT SEA

*T*he excursion to the Buddhist shrine is the perfect opportunity to meet her, he thought. Sri Lanka was the seventh stop on the twenty-one-day cruise, and he was ready. He had noted her well-tailored wardrobe, elegant jewelry, and lighthearted conversations with passengers and crew. He was confident he understood her personality and style.

He caught her eye and tentatively offered a slightly ironic, cynical comment.

"For a mere mortal, the Buddha certainly seems to have acquired some superhuman qualities, don't you think?" The remark was designed to provoke a longer conversation. She took the bait.

"Well, perhaps he actually was more in tune with the universe than the rest of us," she rejoined.

"Maybe so, but I'm not persuaded yet." After a bit more good-natured sparring, he introduced himself.

"I'm Mark O'Mara, from Ireland."

"Ingrid Halvorson, from the Netherlands," she answered carefully.

"Really? I would have expected Halvorson was Swedish."

"It is. My family moved to Amsterdam when I was a child. I still speak some Swedish."

The conversation flowed from there. Ingrid was delighted to talk about something more intellectually stimulating than the weather and the food, though she was enjoying both. Mark was younger, more charming, and more sophisticated than most of the cruise passengers. After a bit, he suggested dinner at La Petit Brasserie, the French dining room aboard the ship. She cheerfully accepted.

The *Royal Asia Explorer* was the world's newest, most exclusive cruise ship. Though registered as a Canadian flag vessel to reassure passengers and minimize taxes, it was conceived, owned, and managed by an Italian line. This trip was the ship's maiden voyage from Dubai to Bali and Singapore, and the June weather was perfect.

The next day was at sea, crossing the Bay of Bengal. Mark and Ingrid spent most of it together, eating and talking. They eased into the subject of world affairs and found similar perspectives on climate change and global politics. She found him intelligent and well-informed, appropriately dressed, and aware of which fork to use at dinner.

They danced that evening around the pool under a full moon as the ship glided toward Myanmar. By dinner the next day, she was entranced, and he seemed equally intoxicated with her.

The forty months since the election of President Donald Trump had been a continuing public policy disaster from her perspective. The paralysis of global climate policy particularly distressed her professionally and personally.

Climate deniers have captured the US Government, she railed to herself. *Since its reversal on the Paris Accords, other governments have been quietly slipping away from their own commitments. Humanity is facing a fatal catastrophe, probably sooner than later, and the world's leaders are in deep denial, pursuing their petty dreams of power and glory.*

The past three years were even more upsetting because industry flacks and certain environmental activists were continually challenging her scientific competence on climate change and scoffing at her highly visible, "alarmist" policy recommendations. She knew the disparaging attacks were fraudulent, but that made them even more distressing. *These people aren't seeking the truth. They're suppressing it. They prefer to manage the planet as a business in liquidation, rather than a going concern,* she raged, sometimes audibly when alone.

Incognito cruises with shipboard romances had become Dr. Ilsa Hartquist's escape from the stress and depression engendered by her daily exposure to the stark scientific realities of damaging climate change. Although she was not in the same class as a Hollywood personality, she appeared in the media often enough that people occasionally recognized her on the street, even in foreign countries where she traveled for speeches and conferences.

The internal and external demands of her work as a Johns Hopkins University professor, climate scientist, conference speaker, and media personality left her almost no opportunity for pursuit of the supportive male relationship she longed for, and increasingly any social life at all.

So she escaped at sea by posing as Ingrid Halvorson, a recently widowed woman of forty-four with money, time, no particular plans or ambitions, and an interest in meeting men. Only the last of these was true.

She was thin for her 5'9" height. Dyed black hair hid her natural dishwater blonde color, further protecting her anonymity. Dressed in a flashy style, quite different from the usual cruise wardrobe. Not strikingly beautiful, but attractive enough to find willing men on ocean voyages.

She had found playmates on earlier cruises, even on this one. Ten days earlier, near Mumbai, she had persuaded Xavier, one of the new ship's waitstaff, to visit her stateroom for a few hours of wine and small talk, followed by energetic sex. He was a solid, handsome, talkative young man from a small village in Kerala, with beautiful dark skin and deep, coal black eyes.

It was what she needed. She invited him back the next two nights and enjoyed their physical liaison immensely. To her, it was obviously just a once-around experience. He hardly knew anything about her and could never understand her world.

Neither did she tell Mark O'Mara anything about her real life. Ingrid had learned long ago to be cautious about expecting anything more than a brief affair. She tried to remind herself they had met only about seventy-two hours earlier. *We hardly know each other's names, much less each other's pasts or future.* This lapse did not strike her as unusual for a brief shipboard romance with no expectation of an encore.

Still, she fantasized that Mark might be more than just an extended hookup. *He seems really attracted to me. Knowledgeable about science and world affairs. Intellectually and psychologically strong enough to cope with a successful, independent woman. Physically attractive as well, with a full head of blond hair, bright blue eyes, and a muscular body. Well-mannered, well dressed, considerate, charming, wry sense of humor.*

No red flags so far, she reflected. *But there is so much more to learn about a potential mate—about temperament, honesty, financial stability, desire for a permanent relationship.*

All that can wait, she concluded with a smile. *There's one crucial fact I can learn right away, is he any good in bed? Happily, I can find that out without a tedious computer background check. A definitive answer will be apparent at once.*

That evening at dinner with Mark, the bouquet of the wine and the tang of the salmon entrée seemed particularly delightful. The Chocolate Volcano dessert was so delicious she thought about having another. After the ship's entertainment, they went to the Panorama Lounge to listen and dance. The Filipino vocalist's sultry voice crooned Sinatra-era love songs with beguiling visions of romance.

Soon her cautionary self-admonitions were no match for the rush of adrenalin at the prospect of days and nights of passionate sex and emotional connection. After another hour of drinking and dancing, Ingrid was more than ready for a tryst. With Mark at her side, her keycard silently unlocked the door to Stateroom 712.

This is going to be easier than I imagined, he sensed, as Ingrid opened the curtains. Reflections from the moon-lit ocean beyond the veranda were the only light—more than enough. Somewhat tipsy, she steadied herself on his arm as she kicked off her shoes and dropped her purse. She reached for one of the chocolates on the turned-down bed, unwrapped it, and touched it to his lips. She felt him becoming physically aroused, and her own body responding enthusiastically.

She undid his tie and slowly unbuttoned his shirt while he softly kissed and caressed her arms and neck. There was no need to speak. Soon they were fully undressed. In the small but elegant quarters, the freshly made queen bed was right beside them.

She playfully pushed him down, then allowed him to take charge of their lovemaking. Their bodies came together gracefully—gently at first, then with greater fervor. She surrendered with passionate intensity, losing herself in the erotic sensations. He responded with equal enthusiasm. After a brief pause, she urged him on a second time. He was reluctant, but with oral stimulation to aid and encourage, he complied energetically.

In time, overcome by the dancing, the wine, and the enervation that comes after copulation, she nestled comfortably in his arms, pleased to know that Mark fully satisfied her needs for a sexual companion. As she drifted into sleep, she dreamed of more intimate times together in the days ahead.

When he was satisfied she was completely asleep, Mark took one of the extra-large pillows and softly closed it over her face. For a few moments, she struggled for air, but finally succumbed to the lack of oxygen. He waited anxiously for her movements to subside completely.

Satisfied that she was dead, he slid out of the bed and rapidly into his clothes. *Sorry, Ilsa,* he said to himself, *you're a delightful person. But the livelihoods of millions of people depend on your radical ideas never gaining public support.*

He carefully opened the stateroom door. Seeing no one, he slipped out and walked as quickly as was seemly to the stairs leading to his own stateroom. Now he was again merely one of the 648 passengers enjoying an Asian cruise adventure.

Barely twenty-five minutes later, Xavier entered Stateroom 712, using the pass key "Ingrid" had given him six nights before. He felt he must talk to her. He could not believe she could discard him after those ecstatic nights. He had seen her together with Mark all day yesterday and today as he served at meals and performed in the staff show. He had hoped to catch Ingrid's eye, but Mark was the sole focus of her attention. Watching them later, dancing so romantically in the Panorama Lounge, was a humiliating torture.

The scene in the room seemed peaceful enough. She was alone, though she had obviously shared the bed with someone. Her clothes and purse were in a pile on the floor, unlike his nights with her, when she had carefully put them aside. *She must have been quite eager,* he realized. A painful revelation. He was still captivated by his desire for her, so close, yet so far beyond reach. He tried waking her by whispering her name, but to no avail.

He was desperate to confront her, to tell her how much he wanted her, to express his anguish at her indifference. Suddenly, he came to his senses. Frightened by his own dereliction in entering the room uninvited, he retreated out the door, hoping no one saw him.

◦○◦

Captain Christian Ricardo, the very model of a cruise ship captain, with over thirty years' experience and the physique and bearing to match, stared at his Chief Service Manager, Angelo Simonie. He was as annoyed by the interruption as by the news that Ingrid Halvorson was dead. Docking the

Royal Asia Explorer for its first visit to Yangon demanded his full concentration. He knew his obligations and priorities.

"Ingrid Halvorson, that attractive, dark haired young woman, is dead? That's unfortunate. We're about to arrive in Yangon, and I need to stay on the bridge and concentrate on docking the vessel. Please follow the standard procedure for handling deaths aboard the ship. Store the body. Notify the authorities in her home country."

Angelo didn't leave. He had more to say. "We may be jumping to conclusions, but she seems to have been murdered." He paused, knowing this information would command the captain's attention.

Ricardo turned to look at Angelo. "What did you say? Murdered? I'm sorry, Angelo, but a possible murder deserves my undivided attention, as does docking the ship. I can only do one thing at a time. Come see me in thirty minutes, after we are secure."

Thirty minutes later, Angelo was waiting for Captain Ricardo in his private office. Ricardo sat down at his desk, fidgeting uncomfortably.

"So, what makes you think Ms. Halvorson was murdered?"

"The Chief Medical Officer called me. He said the condition of her face and skin indicates that most likely she died of asphyxia, by suffocation, but a full autopsy would be necessary to confirm that conclusion."

Captain Ricardo, a fan of Agatha Christie's fictional Inspector Poirot, was intrigued as well as concerned. "What do we know about her?"

Angelo grimaced as if punched in the stomach. He wasn't eager to give the Captain more disconcerting news.

"After I talked to the Medical Examiner, I immediately examined her EU passport. It shows her to be a Dutch citizen. We contacted the Dutch authorities. They have no record of a passport issued to anyone by that name or on that date. On closer examination, the passport name and dates appear to have been professionally altered.

"The valid passport with that number originally belonged to a staff member of the Dutch Ministry of Health who is currently living in Amsterdam. It was stolen eight years ago.

"We don't know who Ingrid Halvorson really is."

He stopped to breathe and allow the Captain to digest this information, then proceeded.

"According to the butler, here's what happened this morning. Ms. Halvorson had a standing order for breakfast in her room at 7:00 am. Today she didn't answer when he knocked on the door. On the assumption she was asleep or in the bathroom, he took the liberty, as he had done before, of opening the door and setting up the breakfast table. As he finished, he saw she was still in bed, but something about her face looked wrong.

"He looked around the room carefully. There was no sign of anything else unusual, though her clothes and purse were on the floor beside the bed. His speculation is that a man had joined her in the evening. The veranda door appeared not to have been opened after he turned down the bed around 8:45 pm, but the curtains had been opened afterward. He decided not to touch anything. He called the infirmary. The Medical Office personnel confirmed that she was dead and took her to our makeshift morgue.

"The butler—"

Captain Ricardo interrupted, his eyes narrowing with intensity, and began a cross-examination. "And do you trust this butler? How long has he been with us? Is his record clean? How much contact did he have with her?

"No one else on board would have had a key to the room, unless she gave it to someone. We can't afford to have anyone think even for a moment that any member of the crew has done anything untoward. It would damage the reputation of my ship and the whole Royal Asia fleet!"

"Yes sir," Angelo answered. "I completely understand your concerns. I have asked every member of the crew to report any contact with her and any activity they saw. So far, only Sylvia, the singer in the Panorama Lounge, thinks she remembers Ms. Halvorson dancing with another passenger last evening. She didn't think there was anything unusual about it, though they were obviously in a romantic frame of mind. She doubts she could identify the man from among the other passengers in the Lounge that evening."

Ricardo threw his hands in the air. "Wonderful! So we have a female passenger traveling alone who has died, probably murdered, and it turns out she was traveling on a forged passport, so we don't even know who she really is. This is starting to sound like fiction! Where's Inspector Poirot when we need him?"

Ricardo instantly caught himself, embarrassed at making a flippant remark amid a calamitous situation. Regaining his authoritative demeanor, he barked his instructions.

"Allow no one in her suite for any reason. Call the Royal Canadian police at once, before some amateur sleuth on board thoroughly botches the investigation. We can't keep this secret for long. We're only in Yangon for thirty-six hours, and we must have this matter under control before the passengers return to the ship from today's excursions. Passengers who knew her will no doubt wonder where she is and start asking questions. Great publicity this will be!"

"Yes, sir. I'll get everyone working on it." Angelo stood and turned toward the door, eager to avoid more of the Captain's displeasure.

Alone, Captain Ricardo sagged in his chair. There would be no hiding this disaster. He had never wanted any other career than cruise ship captain from the time he was a child in Livorno. But he knew that cruise ship captains are routinely relieved of duty even for minor mishaps, and even if they are not found legally responsible. He suddenly realized he needed a career plan B, something he had never contemplated seriously—until now.

—◦◦◦—

On June 20, 2020, Mark Miller checked into the five-star Hotel Ciputra in central Jakarta, a first-rate establishment where Winthrop, his handler, had reserved a room for him. Before flying out of Yangon, he had made use of an airport fitness club to shower, take out his blue-tinted contact lenses, and return his eyes and hair to their natural deep brown. Neither the Mark O'Mara passport nor Mark O'Mara any longer existed.

After discarding his clothes and showering again at the hotel, he wrapped himself in the hotel's plush Turkish cotton robe and called Winthrop.

"The assignment has been completed successfully," he reported.

"Excellent! And you're sure you can't be traced?"

"Traced? Hardly possible. At this point they probably don't even know who Ilsa is, since she was traveling incognito with a forged passport.

"I was one of the first people off the ship after it docked, supposedly intending to visit the Shwedagon Pagoda on my own. I took a taxi to town, reverted to my original identity, and flew to Jakarta this morning.

"They no doubt discovered that passenger Mark O'Mara, who was traveling on a forged Irish EU passport, failed to return to the ship that evening. But I expect they would see that as just a coincidence. And anyway, they'll never find me."

After a slight hesitation, Winthrop responded, "I'm sure you're right, but please be careful. They'll be looking for you. The money is in your bank account. Thank you for your service to a worthy cause. Sleep well."

Mark checked the bank account set up for just this purpose, and the one million euros were indeed there. With any luck, he was fixed for life. Next week, after a few days of relaxation, he would talk to his financial advisor about how to invest the funds.

Satisfied that his assignment was now compete, he called room service for a double Smirnoff vodka and tonic, his favorite drink. He wanted to treat himself well; he felt his successful feat warranted it. He sipped the beverage slowly. It was a satisfying reward, although the flavor of the local tonic water seemed a little off.

Compulsively, he reviewed each step of his "campaign," which he had executed with military precision. His first big problem was finding a way to meet Dr. Hartquist. Getting her vacation schedule was not so difficult; her secretary at the Johns Hopkins Climate Science Department was happy to help him find a date when she would be available for a news interview.

He gleaned the crucial information about Dr. Hartquist's vacation by suggesting he might interview her on her vacation. Then he needed to get his own cabin and the necessary documents. He was surprised when she introduced herself as Ingrid Halvorson, but he knew who she was from photos and news stories, and later from tidbits of their conversation.

His anxieties aboard the ship had revolved around finding a way to get into her room at night and the fear that he would accidentally call her Ilsa instead of "Ingrid." He almost slipped once as they were making love, but he swallowed the sound at the last instant. Not listening carefully, she missed it.

He had coated his hands with a thin layer of wax hours before the crucial evening to obscure his fingerprints. Pretending to acquiesce to Ingrid's insistence, which she took for thoughtfulness, he had worn a condom. It captured bodily fluids that could easily be used for DNA analysis by whoever investigated the death. He had flushed it down the toilet before leaving Ilsa's stateroom.

Feeling proud but exhausted after the adrenaline surge of the last forty-eight hours and a little woozy from the drink, he lay down for a moment, subconsciously fearing a policeman's knock on his door in the night. But rationally, he felt confident no one could track him down.

The only knock on his door was the maid in the morning, and Mark did not answer. The local coroner ruled his death natural, from heart failure, never thinking to test for exotic poisons. His belongings showed no sign of illegal drugs or the presence of any visitors to his suite. Mark Miller never knew the worldwide consequences of his murderous act.

Chapter 2

YSTAD

D r. Ilsa Hartquist, deceased at age forty-seven, was born and raised in the tiny medieval fishing village of Ystad, Sweden. Her parents taught math and science in the upper school. At home, they devoted their energies to supplemental education of their four children. Ilsa was the eldest and by far the most talented. Her parents did everything they could to advance her knowledge and academic skills as she rapidly progressed.

Ystad is the site of author Henning Mankell's novels about detective Kurt Wallander, later made famous by the BBC television series based on his stories. Tourists come from around the world to take "conceptual guided tours," following the rugged policeman's imaginary footsteps along the town's cobblestone streets.

Ilsa's early exposure to the impact of media on her hometown, combined with her wide-ranging knowledge of science, social studies, and the humanities, set her on the path to prominence. After earning a PhD in Climate Science from Harvard University in 2000, followed by post-graduate training at MIT, she joined the faculty of

Johns Hopkins University as a tenure-track Assistant Professor in 2006.

She immediately became an active climate research scholar and a vigorous participant in the deliberations of the United Nations Intergovernmental Panel on Climate Change (IPCC), the committee that speaks most authoritatively on the global scientific consensus about the dangers created by the changing climate.

For several years, she had argued vigorously for prompt, effective regulatory action to reduce methane emissions along with carbon dioxide emissions. This advocacy made her a leader and the hero of environmental activists. The US EPA adopted methane rules as part of its program to satisfy US commitments under the 2015 Paris Accords.

In September 2017, Dr. Hartquist presented a path-breaking paper to the IPCC that stressed the unacceptably high risk of immediate, irreversible consequences from climate change. The paper gained wide notoriety beyond the climate science community.

Shortly thereafter, Judy Woodmont, a nationally-known TV anchor, interviewed Ilsa on her nightly news program. Transcript excerpts went viral on the social networks interested in climate issues.

Woodmont: Dr. Hartquist, thank you for joining us this evening. I'd like to talk with you about your recent presentation to the IPCC. Your paper seems to be quite critical of the IPCC's climate change modeling. What is wrong with their models?

Hartquist: It isn't that the IPCC modeling is wrong. The problem is that it is overlooking the most dangerous, immediate threat from global warming. The IPCC's one hundred-year horizon models project a smooth increase in earth's temperature caused by carbon dioxide emissions that will eventually have a catastrophic effect on all life on earth.

But the IPCC has not given sufficient attention to the immediate effects of other, more potent but short-lived greenhouse gasses, particularly methane and HCFCs, a gas used in air conditioners around the world.

Woodmont: My understanding is that methane and HCFCs are included in the IPCC's models. The IPCC hasn't ignored them. What exactly is the error you see?

Hartquist: The IPCC does recognize that the Global Warming Potential, or GWP, for methane is twenty-eight times that of carbon dioxide over one hundred years. And the IPCC climate models use that GWP ratio for predicting global conditions in 2100. But the one hundred-year model assumes that methane's effects will emerge smoothly over that time period.

That assumption disregards the fact that methane only stays in the atmosphere about twelve years on average. Most of that "28 times more potent" GWP occurs in those first twelve years. Before the methane dissipates, its global warming effect is over 8 times the one hundred-year average, or 224 times the GWP of carbon dioxide. The effects of increased methane emissions are front-loaded. In other words, their most powerful impact occurs in the first few years of their presence in the atmosphere.

HCFCs have an even shorter lifespan in the atmosphere, but they have a far stronger GWP, so their effects are even more front-loaded than methane.

Woodmont: But if the effect of these emissions averages out over the century, do the short-term effects really matter?

Hartquist: Yes, the short-term effects do matter. The fundamental conclusion of my analysis is that the IPCC needs to reverse its focus on the one hundred-year term. It won't matter what the one hundred-year effect of carbon dioxide is, if civilization has already been drastically undermined in 2040 or 2060 by the disruptive effects of increased emissions of methane and HCFCs.

Human civilization as we know it may implode long before we reach the 7^0 Fahrenheit increase by 2100 that the IPCC is warning us about.

Woodmont: I'm not sure I understand how that would happen. Aren't the long-term consequences the most important consideration?

Hartquist: Critical in the long term, but not the most urgent danger. Yes, we must stop emitting carbon dioxide long before 2100, if we are to preserve the planet as we know it. And substantial reductions in methane and HCFC emissions starting now would significantly reduce the one hundred-year average temperature increase, as the models illustrate.

But methane emissions are now 150% above 19th Century levels, and they have risen quite sharply in the last twenty years, as more natural gas wells and pipelines leak methane into the atmosphere. This increase doesn't include the unmeasured emissions from oil fields damaged during the two Iraqi wars and various terrorist attacks on oil industry infrastructure.

I believe this front-loading of additional methane and HCFCs is what is causing the current unpredicted spike in global average temperatures. The world has set new temperature records almost every year since 2000, and that trend will continue as methane and HCFC emissions grow.

This effect is a much more immediate threat than the one hundred-year average. The current spike in earth's temperature is already destroying vital features of our global ecosystem. That damage may be irreversible right now or in the near future if we don't act.

Woodmont: What kinds of effects from this small temperature change, which currently amounts to less than 2^0 Fahrenheit, are you seeing?

Hartquist: The effects are showing up in scientific research results in many fields, from agronomy to oceanography to geology. The current and potential disruptions are of two kinds—secondary effects, and nonlinear irreversible impacts.

The secondary effects are evident everywhere. The current small average global temperature increase is much more extreme in the polar regions, causing the ongoing destruction of the polar ice caps. That loss is causing significant changes in weather and ocean patterns around the world.

We have recently seen the destruction caused by more frequent and more powerful hurricanes. Less dramatic visually, but in many ways more severe, are the long-term droughts in many parts of the world, causing famines and mass refugee migrations.

The shifts in weather patterns everywhere are disrupting agricultural planting and harvesting cycles and facilitating the multiplication of destructive plant pests. Together, these shifts are progressively

reducing crop yields, causing more frequent famines across the globe.

At the same time, ocean acidification and higher ocean water temperatures are causing the decline of sensitive
fisheries around the world. Most of the
world's population depends on fisheries
for protein. The destruction of fish pop-
ulations means even more starvation and
malnutrition.

Woodmont: What are these "nonlinear" threats you mentioned?

Hartquist: The nonlinear, potentially
irreversible effects are even more frightening. Let me list a few of the many disaster possibilities that have recently been
identified:

- Collapse of the Ross Ice Shelf or
  other Antarctic glaciers, which could
  produce a three- to six-foot rise in sea
  level within a few decades,
- Reduction in the freshwater runoff
  from Greenland and Iceland that
  drives global ocean currents, which
  would radically change climate conditions everywhere,

- Massive, irreversible releases of currently frozen natural methane from the Arctic permafrost, which could exceed current industrial methane emissions, and
- Saturation of the oceans with carbon dioxide, so they no longer absorb carbon, but instead release it into the air, accelerating global warming.

Woodmont: You've painted a grim picture of what we can expect if we continue on this path. Is there anything we can do to reduce the risk of these disasters?

Hartquist: That is the most complex question. Scientists in various fields have suggested several potential approaches that would intentionally change the earth's oceanic and atmospheric chemistry. Collectively, they are often lumped together under the term "geoengineering."

Adding iron or other nutrients to the ocean so marine organisms absorb more carbon is one proposal. Another method is solar radiation management, known as SRM, primarily in the form of a tropospheric veil. We could create the veil by dispersing chemicals into the upper atmosphere to reflect more sunlight away from the earth.

The difficulty with these proposals is that we cannot test and calibrate such a large-scale engineering project in the real world without risking adverse consequences. We have no "Planet B" to experiment with. On the other hand, our current situation is equally fraught with dangers.

I tend to think that a physical veil is simpler and less risky than a biological ocean fertilization approach that causes and depends upon the far more complex interactions of live organisms.

The scientific community has not reached consensus on what approach is the most feasible or least risky. But the current threats won't wait.

Woodmont: Well! That's a lot to think about. Thank you, Dr. Hartquist, for your enlightening explanation of this complex problem. I'm sure we will hear other views on this subject in the days ahead, and then we may want to talk with you again.

Hartquist: My pleasure. Thank you for inviting me.

Ilsa was pleased with the interview. She felt that Woodmont's aggressive questioning had allowed her to articulate her disagreements with the IPCC clearly and precisely. She had drawn attention to methane and HCFCs and introduced the concept of a tropospheric veil to a much larger audience. She felt hopeful that her widely-publicized analysis would have a tangible effect on the policies of the US Government.

But the President continued to contend the whole idea of global warming was a hoax, even in the face of the opposite conclusions reached by the Federal Government's November 2017 *Climate Science Special Report*.

That Report, cooperatively produced and reviewed by representatives of all the relevant Federal agencies, reached significantly different conclusions:

1. Global annually averaged surface air temperature has increased by about 1.8°F (1.0°C) over the last 115 years (1901–2016). This period is now the warmest in the history of modern civilization. The last few years have also seen record-breaking climate-related weather extremes, and the last three years have been the warmest years on record for the globe.

2. It is extremely likely that human activities, especially emissions of greenhouse gases, are the dominant cause of the observed warming since the mid-20th century. For the warming over the last century, there is no convincing alternative explanation supported by the extent of the observational evidence.

Dr. Hartquist was outraged that the President was blatantly disregarding the considered judgment of the scientific community in and out of the Federal Government.

———⊃o⊂———

A year later, in desperation, she adopted a more radical position, which she announced in an Opinion column in the *New York Times*. She selected the publication date, October 1, 2018, with an eye toward influencing the upcoming US Congressional elections.

Her column began with a brief statement of the latest scientific consensus:

The natural atmospheric and oceanic systems that have sustained human survival for millennia are breaking down.

These effects will likely disrupt and destabilize contemporary civilization long before the 100-year increase in CO_2 makes the earth uninhabitable.

Her policy recommendations, however, were far more controversial:

> In my view, governments around the world must promptly initiate a variety of active engineering projects that intervene in our climate system to increase the earth's albedo—its reflectivity—and cool the planet.
>
> First, governments must immediately pursue a program of solar radiation management (SRM), creating a chemical veil for the planet to scatter more sunlight back into space.
>
> Second, governments must implement every other imaginable reflectivity mechanism on the earth's surface as quickly as possible. All man-made structures and vehicles should be colored white, including building roofs, streets, and highways. Less valuable forests should be cut down and buried to create more reflective

open land, even though that would reduce the amount of CO_2 the earth's forests will ultimately absorb.

Some will object that SRM or any other intervention must wait until we can resolve the scientific uncertainties about its potential adverse effects. But we no longer have the luxury of time. At this point, only radical steps can save us from the damage being caused by a century of mistaken and shortsighted policies.

When a person is drowning in an icy ocean, you don't debate whether the life preserver or the rope will be most effective to save him. And you don't try just one to see if it works before trying the other. You throw both, fully aware that he might not catch either one, or he might catch one and still freeze before he is rescued, or he might even get tangled in the lines and drown more quickly. Because action is the only hope.

That is the circumstance in which we find our home, planet earth. We must act now with the knowledge and tools we have at hand.

Finally, I must stress that while SRM may work to cool the earth and minimize the risk of immediate catastrophe, we still have only a few decades to end the use of fossil fuels. The most successful tropospheric veil will not affect many of the long-run destructive impacts of increased atmospheric carbon from fossil fuels.

The 2018 elections succeeded in breaking down the climate-denier majority in Congress. But the President didn't reverse his decision to withdraw from the Paris Accords in 2019, which would make the United States the only nation in the world that was not a party. Less visibly, the EPA Administrator continued to nullify all regulations designed to implement the binding commitments the US had accepted in the Paris Accords.

Dr. Hartquist's call to action produced no positive response either in the US or at the international level. At the same time, both back-to-nature environmentalists and reactionary climate deniers attacked her controversial views and her scientific competence.

By March 2020, she was emotionally spent. She continued to work at winning support for her critique of the IPCC and her SRM recommendations, but the only prospect that sustained her from day to day was the fantasy of another ocean cruise as Ingrid Halvorson.

Chapter 3

YANGON

On June 23, 2020, four days after the *Royal Asia Explorer* had left Yangon, two plainclothes investigators from the National Division of the Royal Canadian Mounted Police (RCMP) in Montreal arrived in Kuala Lumpur, the next stop on the *Royal Asia Explorer's* itinerary. Marie Veronique Roy and her junior partner, Jon Martin Wolfe, took a taxi to nearby Port Klang and boarded the *Royal Asia Explorer*. They collected samples of human hair and bed sheet stains from Stateroom 712, then began interviewing passengers and crew members.

Beginning with the ship's photographic records, the RCMP computer wizards in Montreal undertook global facial-recognition searches for "Mark O'Mara" and "Ingrid Halvorson." They rapidly identified "Mark O'Mara" as Mark Miller and "Ingrid Halvorson" as Dr. Ilsa Hartquist.

Using various other surveillance and electronic data search capabilities, they were able to trace Miller to the Hotel Ciputra in Jakarta. They also learned of his death there. Now Marie and Jon were investigating a second death, which raised a new set of possibilities to pursue.

Two months later, the Hartquist and Miller murders seemed likely to end up in the cold case files. Royal Asia Cruise Lines quietly announced the death of "'Ingrid Halvorson,' a passenger on the *Royal Asia Explorer,* perhaps actually Dr. Ilsa Hartquist," without giving any details. The RCMP later confirmed that Dr. Hartquist had been asphyxiated. Neither made any mention of Mark Miller or his death.

The announcement ignited enormous global interest. The Swedish public and the climate science community worldwide were shocked by unconfirmed rumors of her death. They were deeply distressed by the report officially confirming she had been murdered. Media stories about her death ran for days, including tearful interviews with grieving family and sad and angry professional colleagues. The Swedish Government and the public wanted answers and justice.

The internet was soon thick with blog posts about who she was and who would want to murder her. Organizations opposed to her views aired old attacks on her scientific integrity in a final attempt to discredit her views.

Others attacked by personal denigration, implication, and innuendo. The gist of their assertions was that since Dr. Hartquist was traveling incognito, she was surely involved in some criminal venture, perhaps even a treasonous plot. The false passport indicated that her death most likely had nothing to do with climate science at all.

Passport and travel records showed she repeatedly cruised the world under a false name, no doubt looking for drugs or hookups, and who knew what her sexual proclivities were anyway?

Sympathetic scientists, government colleagues, and lay fans rose to her defense. Aside from disputing the merits, some enthusiasts sought to discredit the hostile rumors. They claimed the fossil fuel industry was fomenting them for its own ends, perhaps to hide their involvement. The result was a cacophony of claims and counterclaims that threatened to sully her reputation and taint her call for action.

Faced with these developments, the Government of Sweden officially requested the RCMP to give Dr. Hartquist's murder the level of attention usually reserved for the murder of a senior government official. The RCMP readily agreed, while stressing that the case was a difficult one that could take years to resolve, if ever. Marie and Jon got orders to expand their investigation.

Both were experienced investigators. Marie Veronique Floquet was a native Quebecoise, descended from a long line of fur trappers turned clothing merchants, turned department store owners. She grew up in elegant surroundings in Montreal and attended high-quality private schools. In 1998 she graduated from McGill University Law School, where one of her great-uncles had been a Member of the Board of Governors.

Marie earned degrees in both civil and common law, joined the Montreal office of the Dentons international law firm and married a law school classmate, all in accordance with her family's wishes and expectations. After a few years, however, she tired of corporate work and began looking around for something more exciting.

In 2002, the National Division of the RCMP was recruiting plainclothes investigators to focus on international crimes, mostly of the white-collar variety, but increasingly involving potential terrorists. The job promised international travel, mysteries to solve, and ideally a little intrigue. The pay was not important, as her trust fund and her husband earned more than enough to support her "champagne tastes." She applied and was accepted.

Her husband did not approve, and after it became clear she was more interested in the drama of investigative work than in giving him an heir, he suggested a divorce in 2005. Despite her attachment to him, she agreed in order to escape the strain of his constant dissatisfaction with her chosen career.

After eight years living unhappily alone, Marie found the man she needed and could love—Christopher Matthew Roy, an older coworker and widower with two teenage girls. Their strong relationship helped them survive the hectic years before the girls left for college. Now in her fifties, Marie Roy was enjoying life with Chris, at least when their schedules allowed them to spend time together.

Jon Martin Wolfe also grew up in Quebec, but in a small working-class English-speaking town. His parents, descended from farm hands, labored in the town's one large factory. He was the first in his family to get a college education and earned a JD degree in common law, with a smattering of civil law, from the Université de Montréal Faculté de Droit. He married Linda, his secondary school sweetheart, a primary school teacher, two days after finishing his university studies.

A stoic, risk-averse slogger, Jon had no desire to pursue anything entrepreneurial in a law firm or business. He preferred the Canadian civil service, where he had the security of government employment and a dependable paycheck. The RCMP wasn't what he had in mind, but they were hiring in a year when the government generally was shrinking, so he took advantage of the opportunity. Working on white-collar crime gave him all the challenge he wanted. He had no deep interest in clothes or cars; his only avocation was pick-up soccer, twice a week. Within a few years, he and Linda were living happily together in a modest but roomy apartment with their two young boys.

Marie and Jon had begun working together in 2014, and by now they were a smoothly functioning team. Their physical appearance often evoked ironic smiles. Marie was a scant 5'3" tall, with a slight build that she clothed with elegant suits and shoes. Jon was 6'2" with big bones, large muscles, and indifferent suits that had fit him five years ago. He looked like a night club bouncer; she looked like a sophisticated chanteuse. Neither fit the image of a Sherlock Holmes or Inspector Poirot.

Marie's determination and enthusiasm for finding the culprits nicely offset Jon's innate caution, skepticism, and pessimism. Marie was the senior and clearly in charge, but she loved the adventure inherent in complex cases, as well as the challenge of overcoming Jon's more staid, practical, and defeatist outlook. Jon, in turn, admired her creativity and willingness to pitch in on the mundane chores their work entailed, rather than supervise investigations from a distance.

They were both delighted to be given the chance to take charge of the Hartquist case, with its prominence. Marie particularly enjoyed knowing that their efforts would receive continuing visibility. It meant they would not be constrained by the usual penny-pinching of the budget office.

They set about methodically identifying leads and pursuing ideas that would crack the case. After interviewing the Royal Asia Explorer passengers and crew, they left Kuala Lumpur for Jakarta. Although Mark Miller's body had been cremated, they hoped to retrieve the remains and conduct DNA testing. The ashes still resided at the crematorium. But it would take some time to get through the customs red tape to import them into Canada for first-class analysis and testing. Until they were tested in the RCMP laboratories, it was impossible to say whether they would yield any useful DNA data.

Meanwhile, they asked the US Federal Bureau of Investigation to search Dr. Hartquist's apartment in Baltimore, Maryland, and her office at Johns Hopkins University. Perhaps the FBI would find some useful information among her effects. It reported that it found nothing relevant, beyond receipts for the cruise and some old "hate letters" from a variety of sources, attacking her for believing in climate change or for proposing an active climate modification program.

Her modest finances were in order, and no one other than her parents and some charities would benefit financially from her death. Her secretary did recall talking to someone about interviewing Dr. Hartquist on the cruise, but she was unable to retrieve the name or phone number.

Three weeks later, the lab successfully completed DNA testing on Mark Miller's remains and compared the results with the DNA from Dr. Hartquist's body and the bed linens from her suite. At best, this information would show whether Miller was in Dr. Hartquist's room and had sexual relations with her the night of the murder. But it could not definitively establish his responsibility for the murder. Moreover, Miller's unexplained death just days later raised the obvious possibility of a larger conspiracy.

The Hartquist DNA testing turned up another possibility. The investigation showed semen in and on Dr.

Hartquist's body from two different individuals, but hair from only one. The RCMP forensic experts theorized that the person whose hair and semen were found would have been with her the last night, while the other person probably would have been in her room on some earlier night. That person's hair would have disappeared when the housekeeping crew replaced the sheets two days before the murder, and any of his hairs on her body would have been lost in the shower.

The evidence of intimacy with two different men suggested a more prosaic motive for murder—jealousy. Perhaps after the first man discovered the existence of the second (or vice versa), he murdered Dr. Hartquist in a moment of rage. It would have been someone still on the ship when it docked in Yangon, in addition to Mark Miller. The RCMP began by testing those most readily available: the crew. And it discovered the other matching DNA.

It came from Xavier. They took his fingerprints, which also matched a few of the fingerprints found in the room. Marie and Jon interviewed him again, now with this evidence in hand. He had earlier acknowledged knowing "Ingrid Halvorson" from serving her in the main dining room but denied any personal contact.

When confronted with the fingerprints, he tried at first to profess ignorance. But his emotions and body language contradicted that contention. Under intense interrogation, he admitted going to her stateroom for drinks and ending up in bed with her, at her request, some days before. But he adamantly denied any interest in recent contact with her, claiming he would not dare jeopardize his job.

Marie and Jon confronted him with a carefully conceived "jealous triangle" narrative, "Overwhelmed by your desire for her, you returned to her suite the night before the ship docked in Yangon, hoping to find her willing to continue your liaison. Half asleep, she spurned you. From the conditions in the room you realized that another man had just left the suite. You murdered her in a moment of rage."

After a painful silence, Xavier broke down completely.

"I did go back to Ms. Halvorson's room that night. Yes, it was obvious from the clothes on the floor that a man had been in the room. She seemed to be deeply asleep. I whispered her name, but she did not answer. I suddenly realized the precariousness of my situation. I would not dream of touching her without permission, for fear she would report me. I tiptoed out without disturbing her, angry with myself for such a foolish lack of personal discipline.

"The next day, when I heard she had died, and then later that she was murdered, I was terrified that I would be accused of the crime. But I had nothing to do with any of it."

The investigators didn't give up so easily. "Let's go over this again. What time did you go to her room?"

"Around midnight. Maybe 1:00 am."

"What time did you get off work?"

"At 11 pm."

"What did you do for that hour or more?"

"I was obsessed with her. I kept telling myself to go to sleep, but I couldn't do it. I finally gave in to my fantasy that she would welcome me with open arms, and no one would ever know."

"Had you seen her that evening? What was she wearing? Did she encourage you?"

"No, I didn't see her at all."

"Are you absolutely sure?"

Xavier paused. "Well, I guess I did see her dancing with someone that evening. That was part of my problem. I was so eager to be with her again. She didn't come to the main dining room for dinner at my table. Then I saw her dancing with this other guy in the Panorama Lounge. It drove me crazy."

"Crazy enough to murder her. What weapon did you use?"

"NO! I never touched her! Not that kind of crazy. Ms. Halvorson was so beautiful and kind and wonderful. I knew she would be leaving forever in several days. I would never hurt her. I just wanted to spend a few more hours with her."

"And sleep with her, of course. But she refused you. So you killed her. Where did you go after you left her suite?"

"NO! None of that is true. She never awoke, never moved. I went back to my room, fearing that I had stupidly risked my whole career on that one night. I couldn't sleep, but I was afraid to go anywhere."

Repeated interrogation failed to break Xavier's story. Jon, the skeptic, suspected that Xavier had in fact discovered that Dr. Hartquist was dead and was afraid then to report it and was afraid now to admit failing to report it. But both Marie and Jon came away persuaded that Xavier was not the murderer. Among other things, a man in a jealous rage is unlikely to asphyxiate the object of his anger. That takes time, and it doesn't inflict enough pain to be satisfying. They both believed that overall, he had told them the truth. That left them with Mark O'Mara (or Miller, if that was his real name.)

⸺◦◦◦⸺

Marie and Jon assembled what answers they could find in a first report dated October 6, 2020. The report discreetly omitted any specific reference to Xavier by name, as the report would inevitably become public. But it could not ignore the Captain's failure to track all his passengers from the moment he was notified of the murder, considering that one of them might well be the villain. As a courtesy, and part of their investigation, they gave Captain Ricardo a draft copy, to allow for his additions or corrections. Ricardo read and reread the crucial portions of the report.

Fingerprints and DNA evidence identified the deceased as Dr. Ilsa Hartquist, a Swedish citizen living in the US, traveling under a forged Dutch/EU passport as Ingrid Halvorson. She was a highly respected and highly visible climate scientist with controversial views. No motive has been found for her use of a false passport. Other cruise ship records show that she had traveled as Ingrid Halvorson on previous occasions. The likely reason was simply a desire for anonymity, given her high public profile and the controversies surrounding her views.

The time of death was either late June 17 or very early June 18, 2020. It appears to have been a carefully planned murder, executed with great care, and for reasons that are not likely to be typical. No personal or financial motive is evident.

The investigation found small quantities of semen from two men in Hartquist's body, but their order could not be definitively proven. There is no evidence of a lovers' quarrel, or an angry ex-spouse or professional enemy seeking revenge.

There are no financial circumstances that might provide a motive for murder— no beneficiary from a large life insurance policy, no pension proceeds to anyone other than her parents, no family feuds, no evidence of entanglements with drug dealers or other underworld characters. No money or other property appeared to be missing from her stateroom on the ship, her office, or her apartment.

The search for "Mark O'Mara," also a passenger, who left the ship when it docked in Yangon and never returned, led to his identification as Mark Miller, using facial recognition technology. He was traveling on the cruise ship under a forged Irish/EU passport. He disembarked in Yangon in the morning of June 18.

Two days later, he boarded a flight from Yangon to Jakarta. Indonesian immigration has a record documenting Mark Miller's arrival in Jakarta. Perhaps coincidentally, he was found dead in his room at the Hotel Ciputra in Jakarta on June 21.

The coroner handling Mark Miller's death saw no evidence of anything other than natural heart failure. The body was immediately cremated at the request of someone who claimed to be Miller's uncle, but he cannot be found. Analysis of the alleged uncle's handwriting is underway.

Miller was known to have underworld connections and a record of arrests, but no convictions. Other than his presence on the ship and his unexpected departure, no evidence connects him directly to Dr. Hartquist's murder, although two crew members recognized him as probably the man Dr. Hartquist was dining and dancing with the evening of the 17th.

No identifiable fingerprints, other than those of the deceased and various crew members, were found in the stateroom. Even if Miller did know Dr. Hartquist and was in her room on the night of June 17–18, that would not be enough to demonstrate that he committed the murder.

Captain Ricardo set down the draft report and put his head in his hands. First, the crew had failed to verify every passenger's passport long before the ship arrived in Yangon. That would have found both O'Mara and Halvorson.

Second, to anyone at Royal Asia reading the report, it would be obvious that allowing any passenger to disembark without constant supervision was a mistake. Ricardo was thinking about preserving the quality of the passengers' experience in Yangon, but that was only one consideration.

I'm the one who botched the investigation, he sighed to himself. That fact swirled in his head as he looked for a way to minimize the effect of his errors. *There was no way of ensuring that Mark Miller would not disappear in Yangon unless every passenger was detained aboard the ship, but for how long? The investigators only arrived four days later! Whoever arranged for the elimination of poor Dr. Hartquist, and then Mark Miller after the deed was done, would not have been deterred by anything we did.*

Ricardo paused. *Maybe I'm not thinking enough like Inspector Poirot. What difference does it make if the crime could not have been prevented? The criminal could have been caught!*

Captain Ricardo was by now deeply fearful about his own future. *This one disaster could bring my entire career to an end. I have an unblemished record as a ship's captain, but I'm not a trained investigator. There is nothing in the Captain's Manual or training on how to handle the situation I faced. I did need to concentrate on docking the vessel. I did my best to reassure my passengers and crew that the murderer was not a threat to anyone else, without fabricating stories out of pure supposition and speculation. But there was only so much I could do.*

For the most part, I was successful. Passengers and crew went on with their vacations and their work without fear. One damn passenger, however, filed a complaint to Royal Asia about the way I handled the matter. And the media got the story.

Will Royal Asia blame me for the bad publicity? A claimed lack of security onboard ship, the allegedly dangerous crew member, the failure to secure every passenger? How long could I have sequestered them? Maybe it's time to retire gracefully, before I'm asked, he concluded. He requested retirement as of December 31, 2020. His request was granted. He departed without the usual formalities and celebrations.

———◦○◦———

Having ruled out Xavier, Marie and Jon concluded that Mark Miller was almost certainly Hartquist's murderer, but the trail seemed to end there. These murders were carefully organized and executed, involving extensive preparation and a fair amount of expense. Hartquist's demise was unlikely to have been Miller's own idea. If he was a hired assassin, who hired him? Where did the money come from for him to arrange to be on the same ship with a forged passport, and then fly to Jakarta and stay in the elegant Hotel Ciputra?

Reviewing every scrap of information, Marie and Jon had one other clue, which also pointed to the larger conspiracy. Mark Miller had made a call to a Geneva cell phone from his own cell phone shortly after he went to his hotel room. If they could track down the recipient of that call, they might yet untangle the threads of the larger story.

It would take some time to get the Swiss and Indonesian authorities, and then the cell phone service providers, to release the phone records, but there was still a small hope of finding the truth about Dr. Ilsa Hartquist's death. Marie and Jon were just beginning that search.

Chapter 4

PHUKET

The February 2021 conference of AOSIS, the Alliance Of Small Island States, assembled on the lush tropical resort island of Phuket, Thailand. The 44 AOSIS Member States and observers came from every corner of the globe—Singapore to Trinidad & Tobago, Cuba to Papua-New Guinea, and the Republic of Maldives to the Federated States of Micronesia.

Of the AOSIS entities, 39 are Members of the United Nations, comprising almost 28 percent of the developing countries, and 20 percent of the UN's total membership. Together, AOSIS Member peoples constitute five percent of the world's population, more than the US or Western Europe—all facing a precarious future.

The peaceful, sunny beach weather that made tourists visiting Phuket happy belied the reality of coming changes in the climate. Increasingly destructive monsoons would threaten Phuket and many parts of the world with unlivable, destructive conditions.

Inside the elegant Casa Blanca Hotel and the modern, efficient Phuket Convention Center, the pervasive mood was anxiety and gloom. The delegates had one immediate focus in mind. They must quickly persuade the incoming American President, Edwardo Gonzalez, formerly a Democratic US Senator from Texas, and the rest of the world's governments to take aggressive measures to delay and ultimately minimize the sea-level rise that would otherwise inundate their countries, either entirely or in their most heavily inhabited coastal regions.

Many of the delegates had participated in the Paris Accords negotiations, follow-up meetings, and other climate-related forums. They had known Dr. Ilsa Hartquist well, both in person and through her scientific papers, public advocacy, and media presence. They had looked to her for guidance, believing she was both honest in her analysis and insightful in her advice.

Dr. Hartquist understood in terrifying detail as a scientist what they knew firsthand—that the AOSIS Members' peoples would bear the most immediate and devastating brunt of climate change: rising sea levels inundating their coastal homes, more powerful and frequent typhoons causing destruction and discouraging tourists, ocean acidification decimating their fisheries, and unpredictable weather conditions making their subsistence agriculture increasingly unreliable and inadequate to their needs.

The most low-lying AOSIS States would disappear completely beneath the waves like slowly sinking ships; more would become uninhabitable as a practical matter. Prospects for economic progress and healthy, thriving communities would evaporate. Their citizens, more than 60 million people, would suffer impoverishment and physical dislocation. Whatever their native talents, it was difficult to see how refugees dispersed in other lands would survive economically without their traditional fishing grounds, farmland, and social structures, even if any other government would take them in.

The progressive closing of borders to Syrian refugees and African boat people, and the political backlash against immigration in Europe and the United States since 2015 were ominous. AOSIS government leaders rightly feared that their citizens, mostly dark-skinned and uneducated beyond elementary school, would not be rescued at all.

Dr. Hartquist had addressed several AOSIS Conferences and Work Group meetings, most recently in January 2020. Her presentation reiterated the substance of her 2018 *New York Times* editorial advocating SRM in the form of a tropospheric veil over the Arctic Ocean. The delegates warmly welcomed her remarks.

Member governments large enough to have their own scientific and technical expertise had independently reviewed her scientific analysis and agreed her projections were fundamentally correct. The excess carbon dioxide would be fatal in the long term, but increased releases of methane from expanded natural gas drilling and HCFCs from air conditioners—both much more powerful atmospheric heat-trapping agents—made the possibility of more immediate disaster much higher than the near-term effects from carbon dioxide. These threats demanded urgent attention, but they were largely neglected compared to the focus on carbon emissions in the plodding deliberations of international climate conferences.

To the AOSIS delegates, Dr. Hartquist's concern appeared to go beyond a detached scientific interest in climate change. She obviously understood the structure of the island societies and the life of their people. Her frequent media appearances, as more climate-related disasters struck, had made her sympathies clear.

These appearances were typically circumscribed, explaining the scientific realities in abstract terms. But in occasional in-depth interviews, she recalled with fondness growing up in the small fishing village of Ystad, where people's lives revolved around fishing and farming. Her emotional attachment to their way of life, so like that of the ocean islanders, was profound.

As the delegates exchanged initial greetings, they shared their shock and outrage at the news of Dr. Hartquist's murder. Their concern over its political impact was enhanced by their personal attachment to her. She had been an engaging and delightful personality at AOSIS gatherings predominantly populated by older male diplomats. She was more than commonly friendly, especially with the younger delegates and AOSIS staff. The many delegates who had enjoyed her company felt a strong personal sense of loss at her premature death.

Rumors had circulated that in some cases her flirtatious manner with others in attendance went further, but diplomatic discretion kept such matters secret. Many delegates were surprised, and some dismayed, by the revelation that she was travelling in disguise on the *Royal Asia Explorer* and by rumors she had found sexual companions aboard. Nevertheless, they mourned her absence, both professionally and personally. The Conference would be pallid without her lively presence.

The Official Agenda of the 2021 Conference called for a review of progress under the Paris Accords and sharing of their respective steps toward "adaptation and resilience." The work was preceded by a handful of eulogies in memory of Dr. Hartquist. Some speakers characterized her as a martyr for their cause; others as the victim of a political act by unscrupulous interests conspiring against prompt action on climate issues. Many delegates were visibly moved by the tributes.

Then the Conference turned to business. Charles Christopher, the delegate (and former President) of the Federated States of Micronesia, traced the progress to date under the Paris Accords. Most of the conclusions in his Report were grim:

In response to the US announcement of its intent to withdraw from the Paris Accords, virtually all other governments have vowed to respect their commitments. But signs of widespread backsliding are evident. Despite Dr. Hartquist's call for immediate action, no concrete geoengineering steps are being considered.

Some states take the cynical view that without US leadership and its financial and technical assistance, a climate change catastrophe is unavoidable. Others are simply following the US "America First" example and putting their peoples' immediate economic well-being ahead of preventing long-term disaster. A few theocratically dominated regimes would apparently welcome "the end of days," confident that their God would rescue them.

The most hopeful recent development is that American President Edwardo Gonzalez, who took office just days ago, announced in his Inaugural Address that "climate change is a growing threat that demands immediate attention, and the

United States must once again provide leadership in this effort."

But he is a former Senator from the oil state of Texas. We don't know what specific action he will propose, or whether he will be able to obtain support for his legislative objectives in Congress. Inevitably, climate change is just one of many urgent matters on the President's agenda.

The presentation was met with silence, followed by quiet applause. Delegates absorbed the clear deterioration of political will to address climate problems. Pro forma draft resolutions acknowledged the Report, exhorted the Members to redouble their own efforts, and called upon the US and other governments to take prompt action. No one proposed anything more radical than the programs being pursued under the Paris Accords. Many AOSIS delegates felt that the SRM veil concept recommended by Dr. Hartquist was not sufficiently plausible from a political standpoint to warrant a formal AOSIS resolution.

The Members' presentations of their adaptation and resilience programs were enlightening and sometimes uplifting, but when measured against the predicted disasters, utterly inadequate. Most were uneconomic for widespread application due to their prohibitive cost or were technically appropriate only in response to certain narrow aspects of the threat.

The full Conference recessed for the day. The remainder of the first week was spent in Work Group meetings, debating and adopting draft Resolutions calling for action, and setting up the AOSIS work plan and budget for the coming year. The results of these activities did nothing to dispel the deeply pessimistic feelings of the delegates. The full Conference would reconvene on Monday with the intention of completing its work and adjourning on Thursday.

———◦———

One delegate, attending his third AOSIS Conference, was particularly dismayed and frustrated by Christopher's report and the lack of progress. Mohamed Ibrahim, representing the Republic of Maldives, found himself muttering to his bathroom mirror as he awoke the next morning.

I can't believe I'm the only one who really gets it, he fumed. *My country alone has almost a half million people living and working on a collection of atolls whose average elevation is less than two meters. The median elevation is even less. Thousands have already lost their homes and land. An additional two-meter rise in sea level, which would flood only the coastal periphery of most countries, will put almost all our inhabited land permanently under water. Several other states here will also be inundated, compounding the magnitude of the crisis.*

He continued to seethe as he dressed in his well-tailored British casual clothes for a day of leisure and informal negotiation.

Why isn't anyone fighting for an action program to avoid destruction of our peoples' lives? No one has offered to take in our people. And even if we can go somewhere as refugees, we'll be without our homes, our land, or our fisheries for economic survival. The disruption of our lives, our culture, our traditions will be devastating.

We're exactly the 'drowning man' that Dr. Hartquist talked about, only in a tropical sea. Yet no one is even trying to throw us a life preserver. If the world community is too disorganized to avert this tragedy for AOSIS states, we need to help ourselves. It's time to do something!

Ibrahim was relatively new to the world of diplomacy. He was born in 1981 and reared in Fuvahmulah, a town of thirty thousand on a tropical atoll near the southern end of the Maldives chain, just south of the equator. Its closest neighbors are India and Sri Lanka. His father was a construction engineer; his mother a schoolteacher. Their home was unimpressive, a handful of small rooms in a secluded grove near the beach, but it provided a comfortable, stable environment in which the three children could flourish.

From the time he was ten, Ibrahim, the second child, was marked as a superior student with immense potential for leadership. His alert eyes and wiry build communicated the nimbleness of mind and body that allowed him to excel at surfing as well as academic pursuits.

When he finished secondary school, the Maldivian government awarded him funds to study economics and politics in Delhi, then at Cambridge. While in England, he traveled to Prague, Vienna, Berlin, and Rome. He spent six months in Paris, developing a taste for French food and Baroque and Classical chamber music. He could easily have stayed in London or Frankfurt and made himself wealthy as an investment banker. Instead, in 2005, he abandoned this promising option, choosing to honor the implicit obligation that came with his educational subsidies. He accepted an entry-level position in the Maldivian Foreign Ministry and moved to the national capital, Malé.

The moment he announced his intention to return home, his parents began looking for an intelligent, self-sufficient woman who could manage their son's household and raise his children during the many absences his new position would inevitably entail. They chose Adeela Mansoor from among many eager candidates and arranged the marriage.

Ibrahim first met Adeela, his betrothed, shortly before the wedding. He found her pleasant in appearance and a lively and discerning personality with good practical sense, though only a rudimentary education. He was happy with his parent's choice. The marriage negotiations culminated in a wedding ceremony in January 2007, followed by a two-day celebration in the traditional Maldivian manner.

Ibrahim vowed to extend Adeela's education and expand her personal horizons, but life's other demands quickly intervened. Within a year, Adeela was busy with the arduous chores of recovering from her first pregnancy, managing the household, and rearing their child.

The child was a girl, which satisfied Ibrahim but left his parents and older relatives disappointed. He assured them that the girl was just the first of several children, which would eventually include a boy. When the second child was also a girl, their parents' concern increased. Adeela knew that to Ibrahim the girls were just as enjoyable and valuable as boys, but she felt the stress of disappointing their families.

In the Foreign Ministry, Ibrahim was a star almost from the first day. His deep knowledge of English, his Indian and British training in philosophy and government, his broad knowledge of the perspectives and problems of Europe, and his pleasant, noncombative, but persistent personality put him in a class by himself compared to his contemporaries.

Overseas as well, his British education, elocution, and sophisticated taste in clothes and manners gained him easy acceptance in diplomatic circles. After the standard three-year tours in the Maldivian embassies in Delhi and Sri Lanka, he began serving as his country's Delegate to various UN specialized agency conferences. In these forums, the plight of the Maldives could be argued to a larger audience of diplomats from states that were similarly threatened, though not so immediately and drastically, as well as to others less aware of the threat of global warming.

The more he learned about climate change, the deeper his anger and frustration grew. *Most of the delegates to these conferences are either inexperienced or mediocre. They have no real influence at home, and many are simply enjoying the good life, traveling to beautiful conference venues, staying in four- and five-star hotels, and eating well. They return home with interesting gossip for their home office managers and colleagues. They have no sense of mission or urgency, and little ability to change policy even if they did.*

There were no AOSIS Conference sessions on Friday, Saturday, or Sunday, and Ibrahim had no specific plans or obligations. Many delegates spent the weekend enjoying Phuket's beaches, restaurants, and other pleasures. In between, they used some of their time to draft reports on the meeting activities for the edification of their prime ministers and foreign ministries.

As Ibrahim ate breakfast in his room, he took out his tablet and began struggling to bring an inchoate fantasy to life: designing a strategy to initiate an SRM project— a tropospheric veil that could give some immediate relief from climate change and save at least some of his people from disaster.

As the scheme unfolded in his mind and took shape in black-and-white on his tablet, his mood alternated between exhilaration and despair. One moment he saw his "plan" as creative, bold, and plausible, the next moment as an armchair fantasy, a science fiction dream that would never survive a conversation with the first person he approached for support.

With the rough outline of his scheme in hand, Ibrahim began scouring the list of AOSIS delegates in search of a few trustworthy allies. He found two who might see the necessity and have the courage to proceed in an unorthodox way. The first was Ambassador Kamla Panday, currently UN Ambassador for Trinidad & Tobago, two low-lying islands at the southern tip of the Caribbean archipelago.

Aside from its undeniable exposure to sea level rise, Tobago had been completely flattened by a hurricane in 2019. Tobago residents were evacuated to Trinidad, which fortunately did not suffer the same level of damage. Without that possibility, thousands of lives might have been lost. As it was, the property damage was enormous. It would require years of investment just to restore the infrastructure and moderate quality of life that had existed for the previous decade.

Panday was a senior diplomat and the son of a diplomat, far more experienced than Ibrahim. He had benefitted from education at Yale University and served in his state's diplomatic corps all his life. His family's origins were a mixture of African slaves and South Asian "indentured servants" imported to replace African slaves who rebelled against the backbreaking work on the sugar plantations. His American education had shaped his personality and approach to problems toward practicality and openness, unlike the more formal diplomatic style of most ambassadors.

Still healthy and clearheaded, Panday had nevertheless reached the point where he was comfortable with his present status. He had little expectation of a more demanding or visible leadership role either at home or abroad. His most immediate concern was finding an appropriate husband for his youngest daughter, Nora. He had married children and several grandchildren, but Nora was his favorite. He was determined to ensure a secure future for her.

Ambassador Anarood Doyal of Mauritius was the other possibility. He was also a seasoned diplomat, older than Ibrahim but still young enough to have ambitions and correspondingly, more cautious. Fluent in English, French, and Bhojpuri—all widely spoken in Mauritius—he had earned a first-class diplomat's education at the University of Tokyo, including Japanese and a solid grounding in Asian political history. He pursued a year of postgraduate studies at Tsinghua University in Beijing, learning Chinese and getting a feel for the tensions and disconnects in China's rapidly evolving society. Then he worked for a few years in the Shanghai office of an American bank, evaluating investment opportunities for its clients and learning how the business world works.

When he applied for a diplomatic position in the Foreign Ministry of Mauritius, he was hired at once. A big man with dramatic facial expressions and a forceful personality to match, he rose quickly through the ranks of Mauritius' small diplomatic corps, serving as its Delegate to the UN Educational, Scientific, and Cultural Organization (UNESCO), then as a senior staff member in the Mauritius UN Mission, and eventually as Ambassador to the United States. Now he was back in the world of international organizations as Ambassador of Mauritius to the United Nations and to AOSIS. He displayed great style and presence and an excellent sense of the dramatic. He loved the pomp and circumstance of diplomacy. He looked forward to being the center of attention wherever he went.

Doyal loved the challenge of threading the needle to gain consensus on issues large and small. His ambitions grew with his success. He had persuaded a coalition of island and East African states to nominate him for Director-General of UNESCO, and though this effort seemed likely to fail, other similar opportunities would arise. Meanwhile, if the local political winds blew in the right direction, he might become Deputy Foreign Minister, the highest ranking civil servant in the Mauritius Ministry.

Ibrahim hesitated even to approach either of them. *Why would either one risk tarnishing his record to pursue this fool's errand of a project dreamed up overnight by an inexperienced junior diplomat from another tiny island state?* Ibrahim asked himself. *They both have little to gain, a lot to lose.*

He knew Panday better than Doyal. *Panday is a perceptive senior diplomat,* he reasoned. *He demonstrates a strong concern for future generations, and relatively less concern for his own advancement. Perhaps he would be willing to take a chance with my scheme because it is the right thing to do, despite doubts about its success and a powerful desire to avoid an embarrassing end to his illustrious career.*

He would start with Panday. If Panday seemed interested, they could approach Doyal together. Trying to restrain his enthusiasm, Ibrahim slept on the idea overnight. He recognized he would be rolling the dice by talking to Panday. Even to propose his scheme to one of these "old hand" Ambassadors might create a perception of him as an unrealistic dreamer and damage his own career. But he was determined to embark on this perilous enterprise.

Chapter 5

PHUKET

Ibrahim gathered his courage and called Ambassador Panday. "Are you free for lunch?"

Panday readily accepted, pleased that Ibrahim wanted to consult him. He didn't know Ibrahim well, but he was impressed by the young man's intelligence and drive.

"Certainly. Meet you in the hotel dining room?"

"How about the Rasta Café across the street? I think our conversation would be more private there."

"I guess that's all right," Panday replied, suddenly wary of getting entangled in some kind of compromising activity. He would of course refuse to take part in anything nefarious. He would instantly excuse himself from the table if the circumstances demanded it. He had done so before and was always happy with those decisions in retrospect. But even knowing about an illegal scheme could create unpleasant responsibilities and complications. And it would certainly change his impression of Ibrahim.

The Rasta Café lunch was a mediocre collection of local dishes, not nearly as satisfying as the food in the Casa Blanca dining room, but ample in quantity. Ibrahim began the serious conversation by discussing the urgency of the climate change threat:

"Both our governments recognize that we are facing a genuine threat to our very existence. The sudden disintegration of the rest of the Antarctic Ross Ice Shelf or the more rapid depletion of Greenland's glaciers, either individually or together, could easily cause the near-term destruction of generations of effort by our people to build healthy, economically viable lives.

"The physical and economic chaos as the seas rise will soon undermine the entire social fabric of our communities, washing away governments as surely as it washes away coastal communities and infrastructure. Immediate climate intervention of the kind Dr. Hartquist advocated is not only desirable but essential to our nations' survival.

"Unfortunately, the UN Secretariat and Paris Accords implementation meetings haven't seriously considered SRM or any other geoengineering concept. The slow processes of international consensus building mean that even if AOSIS succeeded in adding SRM to the UN agenda immediately, the outcome would be distant and uncertain. At best, it would be several years before we could expect any action. And then it would likely be a watered-down, timid, half-hearted effort."

Having laid the groundwork, Ibrahim paused before explaining his idea. "I'd like you to keep the rest of this conversation confidential, whether you join forces with me or not. Is that agreeable?"

Panday, his appetite whetted for the rest of the story, signaled his agreement. It wouldn't be the first time he kept a secret, and so far, he did not see anything criminal in the offing.

Ibrahim continued with his prepared outline.

From a technical engineering standpoint, creating a tropospheric veil of reflective chemicals over the Arctic for SRM is neither very challenging nor very costly. It doesn't take massive resources. A veil project is no more difficult or expensive than some of the weather modification programs that various countries already operate. The failure of the UN to consider such a program reflects two realities:

First, not enough scientific data exists to ensure good results or avoid potential bad outcomes. That's a "chicken and egg" problem since the only way to get valid data is to run some experiments in the real world. To create an effective veil, the chemicals must be released into the upper tropospheric margin, a very thin outer layer separating nearly all of earth's atmosphere from the true emptiness of space, about seventy thousand feet above earth's surface.

Scientists are still learning how the troposphere behaves. We do know that the temperature and gravitational balance between the warmth of earth's lower atmosphere and the near-absolute zero of outer space minimizes convection currents that would carry the chemicals either upward into outer space or downward to the earth's surface. But at this point we have no precise data on how long any released chemical compound would stay in the troposphere or how it would react with ozone, methane, carbon dioxide, and other substances also present in the atmosphere.

Second, there is strong emotional and political opposition from both the left and the right to the idea of 'reengineering the planet,' as if we have not irreversibly transformed the planet with our artificial, technologically-based agriculture, fishing equipment and techniques, and modern communications, manufacturing, and transport systems.

There are theoretical dangers from an experimental SRM project. The first tests might have a far more dramatic effect than predicted. Ultimately worse, the adverse effects might initially appear minimal, but later turn out to be much greater. Before the miscalculation became evident, the experimenters might decide to increase the quantities of chemicals used, only to discover later that the longer-term effects were far more severe than anticipated.

For AOSIS States that are drowning, however, these risks are outweighed by the certainty that inaction will bring destruction. If this small project has only marginal impact, as we would hope, the experiment will still provide invaluable data and visibility to the concept.

My argument is that we, as representatives of our endangered States, should begin an effort in secret, without seeking or obtaining approval from any international institution, to create an experimental tropospheric veil. I am hopeful that we can find a few other states that will cooperate and make the project feasible.

Ibrahim paused to gauge Panday's reaction, which was instantly clear. Panday's face revealed the depth of his discomfort. The suggestion of acting in secret without international approval contradicted the framework of his whole life's work, just as acutely as if Ibrahim had actually suggested they start smuggling illicit drugs or weapons.

To himself, Panday said, *Doing anything without a high degree of international consensus is dangerous, especially for small states, who are fortunate even to have seats at the table in the UN and other organizations. Besides, the idea is completely impractical. We'll never get anyone to provide the financial resources or the location from which to run this "modest experiment." The whole concept verges on absurdity.*

Being a diplomat, what Panday said to Ibrahim was more nuanced. "I share your frustration, Ibrahim, but aside from the fundamental danger to small states of undermining the rule of law and international order, it's impractical. Neither your country nor mine even begins to have the financial resources, the technical expertise, or the physical facilities to initiate such a project. Why are you even talking to me about this idea?"

Ibrahim seized the opportunity to give a positive answer. "You are right, of course. I didn't come to you to get financial or territorial resources from your government. What I want is your help to find the necessary resources from others. If you are willing to help, I think it's possible we can find what we need. But I need your knowledge, experience, and support to proceed."

Intrigued by the idea, relieved that Ibrahim was not asking for financial or other material support, and flattered to have his capabilities appreciated, Panday leaned back in his chair and took a sip of water, gathering his thoughts.

I need to analyze this proposal from several angles, he mused. *The chances of this extraordinary scheme succeeding, or even getting off the ground, are exceedingly small. But if it did, it would be a dramatic step forward in protecting my country, my children and grandchildren, and the entire world.*

If it fails to get the necessary resources, as is almost certainly the case, I'm no worse off for having tried. At least I can say to myself and report to my government and my children that I explored this possibility to address our fundamental problem of survival.

Cementing a working relationship with Ibrahim, who will clearly be a force in AOSIS and the UN for many years to come, can only be good for Trinidad & Tobago. If we can recruit others to help us, that would make me more comfortable. It may even provide the occasion to build some new diplomatic relationships.

He turned to Ibrahim. "I'll need to think about whether this is a rational gamble for me and my country. Who else would you propose to help us? And where would the money and physical resources come from?"

Ibrahim was unwilling to share all his speculations without a clear commitment from Panday. "I don't have answers to your second question. I think we need to feel our way forward, identifying possibilities and probing for support. If you are agreeable, I suggest the next step might be to recruit Ambassador Doyal into our circle."

Panday was pleased to discern Ibrahim's realism, though a little apprehensive about being characterized as part of Ibrahim's "circle" at this stage. He still had reservations. But he reassured himself, *At least Ibrahim realizes that carefully exploring the possibilities for this wild idea is not the same thing as rushing headlong into it. "Circle" sounds too much like a conspiracy to me. I'll need to make sure I have opportunities to call a halt if it seems to be getting too dangerous.*

"Do you know Doyal?" Panday asked.

"Not well. But Mauritius is as endangered as our countries, and he has lots of connections around the world. I think he would be valuable to the effort."

"Yes, he has contacts everywhere," Panday replied. "but you should be aware that he has great ambitions, perhaps UNESCO Director-General or Deputy Foreign Minister back home. He's unlikely to risk those possibilities to promote your unorthodox scheme."

"That's why I need your help," Ibrahim responded. "Can we meet with him to discuss this matter at dinner this evening? Would you like to invite him, or should I?"

Panday saw through Ibrahim's effort to tie him into advocating the project. "I think you should call him. I'm not entirely committed yet myself."

"That's fine. I'll propose 7 p.m. at Lotus, around the corner."

Panday nodded, still uncomfortable. They finished the last of their tea, paid for lunch, and ambled back to their hotel chatting about inconsequential matters and enjoying the pleasant sunny weather and the panorama of green hills, white beaches, and blue-green ocean waters.

Chapter 6

PHUKET

Doyal accepted Ibrahim's invitation for dinner with him and Panday without hesitation. He liked and respected them both. Reinforcing connections with other AOSIS delegates was always worthwhile. Besides, he was looking for votes in UNESCO. And he was intrigued by Ibrahim's call, which somehow seemed formal and premeditated, despite the short notice.

At this moment, global warming was a high priority for Doyal. Rising seas threatened both his country and his career, as he knew well. He had been Mauritius' Delegate to the biennial meetings of the Conference of Parties under the UN Kyoto Protocol on Climate Change for over a decade before the 2015 Paris Conference, and he played an instrumental role in securing the adoption of the Paris Accords.

But saving his country required much more, especially given the damage done by the US withdrawal from the Accords in 2019. He was looking for innovative ideas to reverse the deteriorating political will to act.

At dinner, Ibrahim obtained Doyal's commitment to secrecy, repeated the arguments for secret, unilateral action, and sketched the scheme he had presented to Panday. Doyal was more openly resistant than Panday. "Wouldn't this secret SRM project be a violation of the UN Charter and general principles of international law?" he asked. "You can't expect me to help you with anything that runs contrary to international law. Our small states exist in reliance on it."

Ibrahim had already quickly researched the legal questions, and he offered his answers.

> I appreciate your concerns. Let me respond to that question on several levels. I believe Article 51 of the United Nations Charter, which recognizes "the inherent right of individual or collective self-defence" justifies unilateral action in our situation. While Article 51 speaks to defense against an "armed attack," this "inherent right" surely includes the right to act when the very existence of a group of states is being threatened by the increasingly destructive environmental behavior of the world's advanced powers.

> Many states are taking modest defensive steps unilaterally. For example, the Netherlands is building more sea walls to protect Amsterdam and other valuable coastal areas. No other state objects on legal grounds, even though the construc-

tion may have adverse impacts on breeding grounds for shared fisheries. And many countries conduct weather modification programs that inevitably affect other states without seeking any international approval or supervision, or even reporting the activities or results.

I concede that there are some international agreements and pronouncements that seem to point in the opposite direction. The 1977 Convention on the Prohibition of Military or Any Other Hostile Use of Environmental Modification Techniques prohibits damaging climate manipulation for military or hostile purposes. Various International Court of Justice decisions and other pronouncements assert international legal liability for transboundary environmental harm. And the Conventions on ocean pollution provide an analogy to atmospheric pollution.

But the reality is that our people are the victims of violation of these concepts by others right now, and this action on our part would in fact be a form of remediation in response to the damage done by them.

"I see your point," Doyal responded. He conceded to himself that Ibrahim's legal argument was plausible as a theoretical matter. But he also knew that opponents of the project would vehemently disagree, arguing that unilaterally creating an SRM veil, whatever its purpose or goals, is an intentional invasion of their sovereignty that would justify their own unilateral action in response.

"So, forgetting the legal arguments, what makes you think you can find money or physical support for this effort? Our countries don't have the resources. And what about our disregard for international due process and consensus? We're not exactly Great Powers who can throw their weight around, thanks to their economic and military capabilities. Hardly a week goes by that we aren't admonishing some Great Power for acting unilaterally in disregard of international rules and procedures."

Panday remained silent, leaving Ibrahim to address this question as well. He had supported Ibrahim's arguments on the desperate need for the project, but that was as far as he was willing to go at this point. He was not convinced about the legality of unilateral action. He was still reserving his decision on the viability of Ibrahim's plan.

Ibrahim, fully aware that he alone must defend the rationale for this project, responded carefully to Doyal's objection. "I don't know if we can find the resources, but I believe we must try. Some AOSIS Members, and some other threatened States, have either the financial resources or the physical capabilities, or both, to implement this plan. It's actually quite small-scale in the grand scheme of things, certainly less than $10 billion, involving about a dozen ordinary commercial planes, modified to carry out the mission. Some large countries spend that much on defense every month.

"The obstacle is political will, not resources. I share your commitments to consensus, law, and due process in international relations. It's the only security for our tiny States. But the danger of irreversible climate change is too urgent to ignore. Dr. Hartquist explained the realities in her speech to the AOSIS Conference last year. That's why I'm asking you and Panday to join me. I need the judgment and gravitas you two would bring to the effort to obtain the necessary resources.

"As I see it, our first task is to identify the right targets and generate the political willingness to try something real, to get beyond the hand-wringing and ineffectual warnings. The first step is to find the money, then the logistical base. Is there a better way to proceed?"

Ibrahim was trying not to sound inflexible. He really did welcome their insights, and he hoped to focus their thinking on specific next steps, rather than the feasibility of the whole effort.

Doyal had listened carefully to the arguments, weighing the merits of the idea in the abstract. His mind rapidly evaluated the risks and benefits to his country and to his own career.

Whatever the law, he realized, *it would be dangerous to get entangled in a subversive conspiracy that could affect the entire world without some sort of international approval. The last thing Mauritius, and I personally, need is a scandal that involves bypassing all the established global mechanisms for transparency and consensus. Why would a diplomat willing to take such a step be an acceptable candidate for a high-ranking position in an international organization like UNESCO?*

Nevertheless, he recognized that Ibrahim's and Panday's argument for urgent action was persuasive. They had all been present last year when Dr. Hartquist argued so passionately for immediate action, and her nefarious murder had added widespread notoriety and emotional depth to that advice.

To Ibrahim and Panday he said, "Successfully leading consensus-building efforts has been the hallmark of my career and Mauritius's reputation. My involvement in this secret effort, even if successful, could permanently damage my credibility and my government's if the facts ever emerged. I need to think over this proposal."

Doyal remained deeply doubtful. His judgment was that their three small countries could not accomplish anything beyond talk. *Ibrahim is too young to recognize the extremely low probability of success,* he thought, *and the unavoidable danger in having conspired to set up this secret, unauthorized project, whether or not it succeeds.*

At the same time, working with them, and inevitably a few others if we can recruit them in the attempt, would have the political advantage of earning me some markers for future use. And if by chance the effort is productive, it could show the kind of bold leadership that would help propel me upward as a leadership candidate.

Through his participation in AOSIS, Doyal had learned a great deal about the theoretical research into climate intervention and SRM. He agreed that a chemical tropospheric veil was the only reversible geoengineering technique that could plausibly be undertaken by a small number of states acting unilaterally.

He also agreed with what Ibrahim described as the inherent "chicken-and-egg" dilemma: The most ideal quantities and types of chemicals for these purposes have not been determined, but as Dr. Hartquist's articles and speeches explained, the general effect of various materials can be predicted. She believed existing knowledge is sufficient to minimize the risks of unanticipated and irreversible climate damage. She was convinced that humanity must begin large-scale experiments, leading directly to an operational program in the immediate future. Her metaphor of the drowning man was compelling. The combination of research and action in otherwise hopeless cases is what medical doctors have done for centuries.

Professor Feith, a climate expert at Stanford University, had also concluded that with a handful of planes, a base from which to fly, and the necessary materials, the learning process could begin. At the same time, it might in some small degree reduce the pace of global warming. Creating a planetary veil isn't a fantasy like CCS (carbon capture and sequestration), which at best would require many billions in infrastructure investments to upgrade thousands of carbon-generating industrial facilities.

The consensus in the knowledgeable scientific community was that the only way to learn more is to begin seeding the troposphere with experimental levels of various candidate chemicals and measuring the effects. Any experiment entails the risk that well-intentioned but mistaken actions will do harm. But many island peoples are facing certain destruction from the current trajectory.

The practical obstacle was to find and mobilize sufficient resources to execute a coherent SRM program.

Setting aside these larger policy issues, the three diplomats proceeded to a discussion of the intrinsic risks of broaching the subject with representatives of other states.

Panday remained very nervous about the danger of involving more diplomats in the project. "Rather than just saying 'no, not interested,' someone might reveal our effort prematurely, undermining it before it can get off the ground. Worse, we might lose control of the project to others who would skew it to favor their own interests. These are very real hazards."

But without sufficient financial or physical resources of their own, they saw no choice but to take this risk if the project were to go forward. Keeping those consider-ations in mind, they carefully reviewed the list of other AOSIS members to see who might be persuaded, capable, and trusted to contribute money or other resources to the effort.

Ibrahim, of course, had already given this matter some thought. "Only a handful of AOSIS states have even some of the financial, technical, and logistical resources to con-tribute meaningfully to the project. The primary candidates for financial support are the members with larger econ-omies—Singapore, Cuba, Bahamas, and the Dominican Republic."

"Singapore is the most obvious source of funding," Ibrahim observed. "They can afford it most easily, and they could quietly provide the funds without public knowl-edge or protest. I suggest we start there. I'm not sure either the Bahamas or the Dominican Republic actually have the ability to provide the necessary financial resources on a confidential basis."

Panday stared uneasily into the distance. "I don't know. Singapore is becoming an unstable democracy these days, with an election in two years that could change everything there. I wonder if the government could hide this activity from the aggressive new opposition party. If the transac-tions are disguised as some sort of economic development project, the opposition might stumble across it and start looking around for corruption and self-dealing. Once they find out where the money went, even if there's no evidence of anyone lining their pockets, they will attack Prime Minister Li for this risky, unauthorized use of government funds.

"Although I find the current Cuban regime distasteful, my neighbor has a history of providing both funds and military equipment for its revolutionary projects around the world without accounting to anyone. That's my suggestion."

Fearing his plan would be derailed, Ibrahim interjected, "Do either of you know anyone from Cuba we could approach? I don't."

Panday slumped in his chair. He had never cultivated any relationship with anyone in the Cuban government. The US would never have approved Trinidad & Tobago building a close relationship with its communist neighbor.

Doyal sat silent through this discussion. At this point, he was unwilling to get more deeply involved in this plot. Reading his impassive face, Ibrahim didn't even ask.

After what seemed like an interminable silence, Ibrahim spoke. "I don't know anyone from Cuba either. So that leaves us with Singapore. I do know Wang Shu, the AOSIS Delegate from Singapore. I worked with her when she served as Singapore's UNESCO Delegate," he added, hoping that fact would arouse Doyal's interest in meeting her. "She knows our issues and shares our strong views on addressing global warming. I suggest we meet with her tomorrow, here in Phuket."

Panday suddenly felt rushed. "How do we know that this woman will keep your idea secret? If she tells the media about our rogue initiative, it will be buried in UN reviews and die a slow, painful death over the next five years!"

"And so will we renegades," Doyal added with a smile.

Ibrahim responded calmly, despite his growing frustration with his colleagues. "I agree the risks you see are real, but there's no way to avoid them if we want to go forward. We will face the same risk of exposure from anyone we talk to. Right now, we are all here, and Wang is too. I think she's an honorable diplomat and civil servant. If we ask her to keep our conversation secret, I'm confident she will. If she says no, we'll just have to start over."

Panday tried again. "So are we left with Singapore and this young woman, Wang Shu? That's it? No other suggestions?" He paused, looking at Doyal, who still had not spoken.

Doyal still remained silent, declining the implicit invitation to take part in any decision.

"What about Brunei?" Panday offered, grasping at straws. "The Sultan has more money than he knows what to do with, and there is no public governmental process to entangle him or us."

Ibrahim quickly dispatched that possibility. "Brunei's wealth depends solely on its oil and gas resources, generating about $10 billion annually. That's a lot for its five hundred thousand people, but the $10 billion we need would take a big bite out of Brunei's wealth. And I haven't seen Brunei expressing any concern about climate change, beyond signing the Paris Accords along with everyone else. I think the sultan is a sure no."

Lacking any alternative except to abandon the effort, Panday conceded. "Well, Ibrahim, I guess we'll try your Singapore friend. I hope you are right about her reliability."

"I'm as confident as one can ever be about such matters. I've worked with her at various conferences over the last decade. Doyal, can we meet in your suite tomorrow morning?"

Doyal silently acquiesced. Ibrahim immediately excused himself to call Wang Shu, not wanting to risk a change of heart by either Ambassador.

Panday and Doyal looked at each other, wondering if they had already gone too far. Ibrahim's confidence about Wang seemed to satisfy them, though they still worried that he was a bit too rash. More experienced, with more professional wounds, Panday and Doyal understood that this effort could easily be disastrous for their careers.

The two senior Ambassadors would pay a higher price than Ibrahim, because they had earned higher professional status. Moreover, being older, they would have less time to recover from a career setback. Probably they would be finished, with no future opportunities, if this crazy scheme exploded in their faces.

"So far, Ibrahim has managed to avoid getting tarnished by some no-win personal or political controversy that damaged his reputation and career," Doyal pointed out, "and he's never suffered through the repeated policy setbacks that would chasten his enthusiasm for this high-risk strategy. I wonder whether we should follow him down this primrose path.

"By the way, he seems to know this Wang Shu quite well, and to have unlimited confidence in her. Do you think that is more than a purely professional judgment?"

Panday shrugged. "Who knows? Look, Doyal, the chances of this ever getting anywhere are very small. Do we really think Singapore will give us $10 billion? Or that some other State will allow us to use its territory as a base for these experiments? I don't, but so far, I think we should give it a try. It's a moral and professional responsibility to our people."

They remained anxious, but in the end, they had let Ibrahim proceed. Ultimately, they saw no alternative that could save their countries.

Chapter 7

PHUKET

Ibrahim rushed back to his room and telephoned Wang Shu. It was a short, businesslike conversation.

"Good afternoon, Wang. This is Ibrahim. I trust you are finding the AOSIS meeting worth attending.

"I'd like you to meet informally with Ambassadors Panday and Doyal and me to discuss a special project we are hoping to get started, with Singapore's help. Can you meet with us some time tomorrow?"

"I would be happy to meet with those distinguished Ambassadors," Wang instinctively replied, recognizing the value of the opportunity.

"Excellent. Ambassador Doyal has a suite suitable for our discussion. Number 501 in the Casa Blanca Hotel. How about 11:00 am tomorrow?"

"That should be fine. See you there," she replied, and quickly ended the call. Wang had many questions, but they could come later.

The meeting began with introductions and coffee. Wang deferentially acknowledged the honor of meeting the two senior Ambassadors. They reciprocated the kind words, expressing their pleasure that she was willing to meet with them on a Sunday morning.

The substantive conversation opened with a request from Ibrahim that the discussion stay completely confidential, whether she agreed with or approved of what the three were about to reveal, or not. Wang found it an unusual request to precede an informal discussion. She responded cautiously, but lightly, "I guess if it's not nuclear war or a program to accelerate global warming and rising seas, I can keep a secret for as long as you can. That will have to do."

Ibrahim glanced at his colleagues to gauge their reactions, then continued, "Thank you. We trust your word. You heard Dr. Hartquist's speech at the AOSIS Conference last year, so you understand what our countries and the world are facing. The difference is that our countries are desperate. We're already the drowning man that Dr. Hartquist has described in her speeches and writings. If we don't begin taking real, physical action now, our lands and people may all may be irreversibly lost before the end of the decade.

"We believe Dr. Hartquist gave us the only possible answer: physical intervention in the earth's climate system now to delay the potential for disruptive, catastrophic climate changes. We believe that the initiation of an SRM project creating a chemical veil in the troposphere is essential and urgent. We are aware of the environmental and political risks, and we will proceed as carefully as possible.

But we cannot wait to obtain an international consensus, which may never emerge.

"The cost of the project is small by comparison to defense expenditures around the world, but our three developing countries cannot afford the ongoing expenses of this kind of operation. Equally important, we could not spend such sums, which are large compared to our national budgets, without a public discussion in our parliaments. That would be the death of the entire effort. We need the help of Singapore, and your assistance to get that help."

Wang Shu sat up in her chair, her almond eyes wide. "Are you saying you would conduct this whole project in secret? Is that even possible? Won't creating a veil require constant flights into the troposphere? What happens when the US, or China or Russia, discovers unknown planes buzzing around the troposphere, releasing unknown substances?"

As quickly as Wang asked these questions, she realized there could be no satisfactory answers. Ibrahim offered a sanguine hope: "I expect that a small additional number of commercial aircraft flying from a remote location at a very high altitude will simply be ignored by military personnel focused on instantaneous response to a massive surprise attack. They'll just be hidden in plain sight," he suggested.

Wang appeared doubtful.

Panday joined in gently, seeking to calm her fears. "We fully understand the risk you have identified so perceptively, but our islands are drowning right now. As you know, AOSIS has tried publicly and vigorously to get action through the standard international processes, without success. We can't even get a small-scale international research program underway. If we try to proceed publicly, we'll be pushed by the opponents right back to the Kyoto Protocol Conference of Parties, which means paralysis."

Wang Shu remained profoundly skeptical, but she wanted to know more before saying anything. "How much money are you talking about?"

Ibrahim replied, "We think no more than US$10 billion over the first three years, which would get the project far enough along to have useful data to show. We hope it will provide some degree of cooling as well. Professor Feith wrote a decade ago that he thought US $3 billion would be enough, but an upward adjustment for inflation and some contingency reserve would be prudent.

"We can promise you that we will work with you to disguise the sources of the money. Singapore won't be the only contributor, though we expect it would be the largest. We'll set up appropriately anonymous shell entities to give, receive, and spend the project money. We personally pledge our best efforts to ensure that the arrangements preserve Singapore's deniability. Our own careers are on the line as well if this effort becomes public prematurely."

Wang stopped to think, evaluating both the overall project's diplomatic risks and possible mechanisms by which the transfer of funds could evade detection. She also considered whether she had legal or policy authority to make any commitment. The three "conspirators" held their breath in the silence. Wang's answer could be the make-or-break moment for this fantasy.

Finally, she spoke. "I don't have authority to make any financial commitment at all. My instructions for this meeting only address AOSIS policy matters that are coming up for a vote. I question whether my government would be willing to get wrapped up in this irregular venture at any price. But I can tell you this. I will recommend that Singapore either provide all the money or none. Singapore won't want any financial partners.

"The more parties involved in this process, the greater the uncertainty whether other partners will all ante up their shares. Worse, the more partners, the greater the risk that we will all read about this 'evil conspiracy' in the *New York Times*, with names and dates and bank accounts. A secret widely shared rarely stays a secret...

"Speaking of which, who are the nonfinancial partners? Who will be providing the air bases and planes and scientists? I will need to know."

Ibrahim started to explain that those answers would be worked out later after they had the money, but Panday cut him off.

"We cannot reveal the names of other parties we are approaching. They will be as interested in secrecy and deniability as you are. We can only say that the project will require the involvement of at least one State that has the logistic capability to conduct the missions, as well as the territorial character to camouflage them without arousing suspicions. We don't believe Singapore can help on that score.

"The other party will be trusting us that the money will be forthcoming without knowing its origin. You will need to trust us that the mission will be handled professionally and without any side payments or other corruption. And this secrecy will help preserve Singapore's deniability."

Wang paused, absorbing the implications of Panday's comments. She wondered whether the three had anyone else in mind at all. Then she faced Ibrahim directly and spoke with uncharacteristic intensity,

"Ibrahim, I have known you for several years, and I have always found you to keep your professional promises. If I become a party to this secret plot, I will be staking my entire career on your integrity, discretion, and judgment. It's a risk I would be taking by even trying to persuade Singapore to participate."

Wang took a breath, trying to retain her composure. "I'm eager to know a lot more, but maybe the less I know, the better. I hope your plan works, for your sake and the sake of humanity.

"Now if you will excuse me, I have another meeting soon. I'll let you know as soon as I can whether Singapore's involvement is even a possibility."

Wang stood and bowed her head slightly toward each of them, avoiding the awkward possibility that one of them might refuse to touch a woman other than his wife, at least where others could see. She didn't want to embarrass them or herself by offering to shake hands. She walked out of the room almost too hurriedly, without saying another word or waiting for any reply.

Ibrahim turned to his colleagues, hoping they were not terrified by the result of the conversation with Wang. "Well, we've taken the first step. Ms. Wang didn't say no, and she left the distinct impression that she would consider the matter. I don't think we could have hoped for anything more at this point."

Panday and Doyal were relieved that the meeting ended without an outright refusal, an explosion of outrage, or a threat to expose the cabal. But at this moment they almost hoped that Singapore would say no and bring an end to their continuing anxieties.

Rather than wait for a response from Singapore, Ibrahim suggested they begin evaluating the AOSIS States to see who could handle the physical operation if the money were forthcoming.

Ibrahim outlined what he saw as the relevant parameters. "Only a few large Member States have small remote airbases from which to operate without immediate detection, and a functioning logistic capacity to acquire the necessary fuel and chemicals for the airbase. We want to avoid the necessity to create new, visible commercial and transportation channels."

"If the operation is to be secret, basing it in a small, open State like Singapore is unworkable," Doyal reiterated. "Singapore has more than enough military and logistic capacity, but its intensely watched commercial markets leave no way to hide the acquisition of the planes or materials, or disguise the flights. Cuba has the capabilities and remote areas that could more easily hide these activities."

This time Panday nixed even speaking to Cuba. "Cuba is still afraid to do anything that would give the US Congress or the new President an excuse to end their fragile relationship. It's one thing to provide funds secretly. I'm certain they would say no to continuing flights and the resulting risk of military retaliation. They might even feel it advantageous to tell the US about our project immediately."

None of the other AOSIS Members fit the requirements very well. Doyal didn't volunteer Mauritius, which would be marginally capable of meeting their requirements, and Panday and Ibrahim were sensitive enough not to ask.

The diplomats began evaluating friendly States outside AOSIS. The two best candidates appeared to be the Philippines and Indonesia. "Both countries have literally thousands of islands, habitable and uninhabited, that would be inundated in rising seas, so they should have an interest in helping," Doyal noted.

"Moreover, these sprawling archipelagoes have dozens of major but largely uninhabited islands that could easily host a few flights a day from small, remote airfields. That would be the best chance of escaping the attention of US, Russian, and Chinese surveillance operations."

Ibrahim ruled out The Philippines. "The government is too unpredictable. President-for-life Duterte's erratic behavior and declining popularity could sink the whole project in an instant if he changed his mind, carelessly tweeted something, or let some oil company crony twist his arm—"

"That leaves only President Kartawijaya of Indonesia. Does anyone know Wijaya?" Panday interjected.

"I do," answered Doyal, finally shedding his cloak of silence when the opportunity arose to show his unique value to the effort. "I helped him resolve some Asian Development Bank issues not too long ago. Indonesia needed some exceptions from the ADB rules for a loan it wanted. It succeeded with my help.

"The President's an unusually open-minded and thoughtful person. Likes innovative ideas and real solutions to problems. If Singapore says yes, I will call him. I'm pretty sure Wijaya would take my call. But I can't promise he would agree to help!"

The next day was Monday, and the four delegates returned to their second-week Conference tasks, going through the motions as the committees recommended various official resolutions calling for immediate international action. Most of these substantive resolutions were passed by the plenary session, but the delegates had no expectation they would be implemented.

The week passed slowly for Panday, Doyal, and Ibrahim. They felt the fate of their countries and their peoples hanging on Singapore's response.

The Committee and Plenary sessions were particularly awkward for Ibrahim and Wang. He made sure their paths crossed at least once each day in the hallway outside the main meeting room, in the hope she might impart some hint of progress, or even merely what she was thinking. She smiled pleasantly and said hello but did not stop to say more.

The Conference adjourned Thursday at noon; still nothing. Panday, Ibrahim, and Doyal met in a small bar several blocks from the Phuket Convention Center. Panday immediately turned to the matter of overriding importance in each of their minds. "Well, Ibrahim my friend, do you think we have our answer from our new young friend? Or is the delay to be expected?"

Ibrahim tried to be optimistic. "I can't imagine that she would consider silence a sufficient answer. I'm supposing the decision requires a personal conversation with someone at home. Maybe that can't be handled from a distance. But I confess that with every passing day, my fear that we will not have a favorable answer increases. On reflection, she may not think it safe even to raise the subject with anyone at home or ever meet with us again."

Doyal inquired more pointedly, "Has anyone spoken even a word with the esteemed Delegate?" Silence around the table. Ibrahim acknowledged they had said hello in the hallways in passing, but nothing more.

"Well then," Panday concluded with obvious relief, "I guess we stand down until we're satisfied we've learned what we need to know, one way or the other. No point in pursuing further steps without knowing if we have any money. We'll talk again when we know more."

Chapter 8

LANGLEY

As soon as the results of the 2020 presidential election were final, CIA Director Harold Williamson asked his staff for a background report on climate change issues and the political significance of Dr. Hartquist's murder on national security and foreign policy. He anticipated the new President would want a report on the subject, and he wanted to demonstrate that he was on top of current developments. *That is the CIA's job, after all,* he reflected with a smile.

No one following climate change and energy issues needed an intelligence report to know who Dr. Ilsa Hartquist was. She had a talent for presenting complex scientific concepts and her own controversial policy perspectives in articulate, succinct language. Her telegenic appearance and straightforward speaking style had made her a darling of the media in a field dominated by boring old white men. The public liked and believed her.

The cable media commentary on Dr. Hartquist's murder made her a climate change martyr, but for what cause exactly? Methane emissions reduction, immediate initiation of a tropospheric veil, other forms of climate intervention, or some or all simultaneously? Or was she simply a role model, a fearless female crusader for the cause she believed in, regardless of the merits?

In the social media, new conspiracy theories about the murder appeared daily. They ranged from claims Dr. Hartquist was an agent of Satan who deserved to die, to her being secretly in collusion with the defense and construction industries. Other bloggers confidently identified various generic culprits, from the oil industry to oil-dependent Middle Eastern governments to Greenpeace or "environmental radicals." Many rumors were in turn alleged by others to be intentional disinformation campaigns by foreign governments or special interest groups.

Dr. Hartquist's dramatic and inevitably simplified analysis of climate issues generated distain among some mainstream climate scientists, who were put off by what they saw as her "grandstanding" and "hysterical" tone. They particularly objected to her insistent certainty about the likelihood of near-term disaster, a breach of the scientific community's ethos of perpetual uncertainty and skepticism.

As part of the process of preparing the briefing paper for the new President, Director Williamson asked the relevant Cabinet Departments and Agencies for their views. Despite the official US hostility to the concept of global warming over the last President's four years, the government's career bureaucrats, scientists, diplomats, and intelligence analysts had continued to study the matter thoroughly. They recognized climate change as a real threat to civilization.

The various Cabinet Departments offered conflicting views on Dr. Hartquist's scientific analysis and policy conclusions. Taken together, they sounded like the proverbial blind men describing an elephant.

The Department of Natural Resources (a recent combination of the Interior Department, EPA, and National Oceanic & Atmospheric Administration) viewed Dr. Hartquist's analysis sympathetically. It did not support implementation of an SRM program, but it agreed with her assessment of the risks, and it had no other alternative to recommend.

The Department of Energy was skeptical on both theoretical and practical grounds, arguing that disruption of the existing fossil fuel energy systems would cause major adverse economic consequences in the US and many major economies around the world.

The State Department Memorandum, while acknowledging the inadequacy of current action worldwide, emphasized the international political risks of SRM. "No matter what governments may say, initiation of an SRM project will provide an easy excuse to delay the decarbonization process in both oil-dependent consumer nations and oil-exporting nations. Control of carbon dioxide emissions is more likely to be put off until too late."

The Defense Department Memorandum emphasized the potential for political and military conflict over any SRM program. "The climate effects around the world would vary radically, resulting in sharply different economic and social impacts. If an SRM program caused some State significant harm or threatened its national ambitions, it might initiate a military response."

The significant international powers—Russia, China, the EU, Japan, and the US—joined Sweden in a call for prompt investigation of Dr. Hartquist's death and more studies of her analysis. But that action masked their inability to agree on decisive action.

Opinions were similarly diverse in the nongovernmental world for a wide range of reasons. Some climate scientists believed that once they tried to translate Dr. Hartquist's SRM recommendation into a concrete program, the unacceptably high risks involved would become obvious, to the embarrassment of all proponents. They pointed to the gaping inadequacies in the available data, the heroic assumptions behind all the climate models, and the even more heroic physical and chemical guesswork inherent in the SRM schemes. They stressed the potential for doing greater damage to the global ecosystem and invoked the Precautionary Principle and the credo of the medical profession—"First, do no harm."

Other scientists advocated SRM, pointing out that when a patient is dying, physicians routinely and appropriately apply untested remedies—the greater the risks from doing nothing, the stronger the arguments for trying anything.

Some industries dependent on fossil fuel saw SRM as a less threatening alternative than the regulations the new US President would likely impose on their facilities. They faced the prospect of losing their immense "sunk investment costs" in transportation, oil refining, and electric generating facilities that would be shuttered long before their intended lifespan. A "talking points" paper from the natural gas producers welcomed SRM to provide "breathing room" for continued use of fossil fuels while national economies transitioned toward sustainability.

Some industry leaders were willing to support a "climate tax" on their products or fossil-fuel inputs as part of a compromise package, but the widespread anti-government, anti-tax ethos among corporate CEOs undermined their efforts to build a consensus for taxes of any kind. The defense and construction industries saw possibilities for massive infrastructure repair and replacement. Their support for SRM especially enraged many environmentalist and anti-corporate activists.

The environmental community also split wide open. Many citizen-based organizations condemned on principle the idea of intentionally modifying the entire planet. They argued that the only solution is to leave oil and natural gas in the ground, move immediately to exclusive reliance on renewable energy, and take radical steps to preserve the earth's pristine beauty and complex naturally-evolved ecosystems.

More "professional" environmental organizations voiced practical concerns that experimenting with SRM might well have dangerous unintended consequences. The attempt might overshoot or undershoot the desired level of sunlight reflected back into space. If successful, a veil might create a false sense of security, delaying problematic decisions on energy transformation. An SRM program would also entail hidden trade-offs that would most likely favor humans over all other species, and rich business interests over poorer societies and individuals.

Many environmentalists agreed with Dr. Hartquist's judgment that without immediate action, the entire planet could quickly become irreversibly unfit for human habitation, so an SRM veil was urgently needed. Overall, however, the disarray in the environmental community, like the divisions in the government and among industrial leaders, limited its ability to demand action.

Meanwhile, the SRM idea, which previously only had the attention of a small group of enthusiastic scientists, suddenly became a highly visible topic for new scientific investigation and discussion in a variety of national and international forums.

Director Williamson and his staff did their best to reconcile the conflicting internal positions within the US government and neutrally analyze the outside world's views without antagonizing anyone or undermining the incoming President's campaign positions. It was a hopeless task, but the President nevertheless found the CIA Memorandum enlightening.

Chapter 9

SINGAPORE

Back home in Singapore, Wang was still amazed at the audacity of Ibrahim's proposition. *Maybe this is the way things really get done in the international system,* she speculated. Her first hurdle in seeking approval for Ibrahim's request was simply scheduling a meeting alone with Singapore's Prime Minister, Li Hongyi, without explaining the reason for it. His first open time for a one-on-one meeting was in mid-March, almost a month after her return from Phuket.

Wang managed to avoid giving a reason for the meeting by letting the Prime Minister's staff assume it would be about promoting her to an ambassadorship. *That meeting would have been easy,* she mused ironically. *It will take a lot more persuading to get past Prime Minister Li's fear of entangling himself and Singapore in this risky adventure. He has to protect his political career and his family's legacy and future.*

Wang's history was perfect for the Singapore diplomatic service. She had left Hong Kong for Singapore as a child in 1995 with her parents, in anticipation of the 1997 reversion of Hong Kong to Mainland Chinese control. They had seen enough of the brutality of Mao's communism to harbor a deep distrust of the Mainland's promises to keep Hong Kong's capitalistic, democratic, cultural, social, and political order.

They preferred a Chinese society dedicated to the ancient Confucian precepts—justice, humaneness, respect for family and community tradition, and devotion to education. They believed that Singapore would show the world a different face of the Chinese people, one they could be proud of. And they wanted the best opportunities for their three children.

They were determined that Wang, their eldest, should excel as a student and gave her private tutors and year-round schooling. She was six years old when they moved. She grew up to be an attractive woman with a classic Han Chinese face; tall, thin frame; cooperative personality; and great proficiency in math and languages. She was among the highest-ranking students at the National University of Singapore. Then she studied at the Sorbonne in Paris for a year, learning French, improving her English, and absorbing European culture.

Wang's only goal in life was to live up to her parents' ambition for her: a career in the Singapore Diplomatic Service, where she and Singapore could help make the world a better place. Within a few years, she had distinguished herself from her Foreign Service contemporaries by her insightful analyses and graceful manner. Her prospects for becoming an ambassador soon, and eventually an ambassador to a Great Power, were excellent.

Her parents' forward-looking attitude toward their daughter's professional ambitions contrasted with their much more traditional notions about marriage and family life. Most of Wang's female classmates had found their first male companions well before graduating college and married them as soon as possible. Perhaps because of their inexperience with the opposite sex, the divorce rate among these successful professional women was quite high, but not until after they had a child.

More dedicated to her schooling than others, Wang never found "the one" in her college years. Still single and now over thirty, she saw eligible men socially on rare occasions, at their initiative. Most men her age were either married and raising their children, or divorced and looking for a younger mate.

Wang was hesitant about proceeding with Ibrahim's project. *He is gambling his career on the success of this effort. He and the two Ambassadors might be able to afford that risk, though I would say that's crazy. Anyway, for me, it risks everything my life is about. My career is my whole life*, she reflected.

The two Ambassadors are older and perhaps wiser, but Panday is in the twilight of his career, and both have already accumulated successes in many diplomatic efforts. They will disavow this whole effort if it collapses. All three come from tiny countries where they face little internal competition. I don't have family wealth or status to fall back on, and at my age I could literally lose everything. In Singapore, the number of highly talented competitors for my job is huge. I admire these men's desire to save the world, even if the approach is unorthodox, and I agree there are no workable alternatives. Logically, this approach deserves a try. But I will be gambling my life to promote this wild scheme. In the end, however, Wang felt she had given her word that she would try.

Thinking it over, she realized the issue wasn't really the cost. Singapore could easily fund the US$10 billion SRM project over three years from the US$200 billion Asian International Development Aid Fund it had created and supported for several years. She had worked at the Fund for a few years, and she knew how to arrange the transfer of funds with minimal oversight.

No, it was about the international and domestic political risks. The only person who could approve this project was Prime Minister Li, the second son of Lee Hsien Loong and a grandson of the late Prime Minister Lee Kwan Yew—the third generation of the Lee family (now "Li" in the Mainland Chinese Hanyu pinyin) to lead Singapore's government since before its independence from Malaysia in 1965. Though Singapore was nominally a democratic State governed by a president and a parliament, in practice, the Li family had the first and last word on everything of consequence, despite a rising chorus of dissatisfaction over the nepotism in Singapore's government leadership.

Singapore had joined Malaysia at the time of its independence from Great Britain in 1963, but the dominant Chinese population of Singapore quickly discovered the disadvantages of subordination to the Malay-dominated Government in Kuala Lumpur. The Malaysian Government in turn feared that Malaysia's ambitious Chinese and Indian minorities would one day band together to take control of the Malaysian Parliament, leaving the Malays without access to governmental power. The two entities quickly agreed to an amicable separation. They formally announced Singapore's independence from Malaysia just two years later, in August 1965.

The day of Wang's meeting with Prime Minister Li finally arrived. After the usual formalities, Wang began explaining the SRM project and its importance. As soon as the Prime Minister understood what she was talking about, he was visibly dismayed. He impatiently laid out the dangers to Singapore of any involvement in this scheme:

"I assumed you wanted to see me to discuss giving you an ambassadorship, which I would view favorably. You are superbly qualified. I had no idea what you had in mind, or I would have refused even to meet with you. Do you realize that there is a significant chance that your island diplomat friends will just line their pockets with our money? Even if they don't just disappear entirely, they will certainly take a "commission" off the top, either directly or through kickbacks. What happens when that is discovered?

"More important, what will it do to Singapore's politically neutral status when the world discovers that we have funded a clandestine experiment on the global climate? We have a reputation as a city-state that respects all points of view, avoids entanglement in controversial issues, and welcomes investors from around the world. We take pride in being the Switzerland of Asia, only better.

"We depend entirely on the United Nations, the WTO, and the broad network of international institutions and international law and customs for our survival. If they are weakened or we are suddenly viewed with suspicion or hostility, we are in great danger. As a result, foreign investment would dwindle to a trickle, and banks would see net outflows of liquid assets.

"We wouldn't last a week against any modern foreign army or opportunistic terrorist organization that chose to plunder our island, unless the world came to our support. Despite our first-class military machine, we have no more real defense than Crimea.

"Besides, there is no reason to believe that this pie-in-the-sky veil project will work. It's a crazy idea, and we can't afford to gamble on it. I'm sorry, but the answer is no."

Wang Shu paused to allow Prime Minister Li to settle down after his passionate diatribe. Then she methodically responded to each of his concerns.

"Thank you for those kind words about my qualifications. I truly believe this project is more important than my future career as an ambassador. It's about the survival of human civilization here in Singapore and around the planet."

Then she quickly pivoted to her carefully prepared positive arguments.

It's important to remember that Singapore is not a disinterested bystander in this unfolding climate disaster. We are surrounded by ocean. Increasingly frequent and powerful monsoons will destroy a large part of our beautiful city sooner or later.

While we may be able to build sea walls at great expense to protect parts of our coastline, the necessary diversion of human and material resources will drag down our real wealth as surely as if we were physically throwing gold into the ocean. It may make the GDP and employment numbers look good, but such defensive mitigation spending doesn't produce any useful goods or services for our people.

We will certainly survive longer than most other island states, but many of our trading partners will suffer much greater losses. Low-lying coastal cities like

Shanghai, Kolkata, and Miami will lose a large part of their useful land area, with economic consequences that will significantly weaken the entire global economy on which we depend. Indonesia and The Philippines will lose many of their smaller islands, creating refugees and disruptive diplomatic controversies over international land and sea boundaries.

Monsoons, unpredictable weather, and the loss of many beneficial animal and insect species will decimate agricultural production around the world, even on higher ground. Hundreds of thousands of fishermen and farmers in coastal areas in Bangladesh will lose everything. Many thousands of people have already lost everything in low-lying island states like Seychelles and the Maldives.

These developments will create massive refugee outflows that will make the exodus from famine-plagued and war-torn countries like Syria and Somalia look like small problems. Many refugees will try to come to Singapore, probably more than any other developed state in the region.

The international community will pressure us to take in more refugees than our public will want to absorb. We have seen what that issue has done to the political balance in the US, the UK, France, and Germany.

If successful, this SRM project could postpone and mitigate these disasters. By the time the world's governments find out about it and track down the source of the funds—if they ever do—its beneficial effects will be evident to all.

You will be recognized as a visionary leader who demonstrated the kind of long-range focus and imaginative planning that the Li family has been so proud of. Ignorant, shortsighted politicians in the US and elsewhere will be exposed as the fools they are.

If you do give your approval, I propose to be watching where the money goes myself. I know the Development Fund's systems well. The money can be funneled to the project through a secondary bank in Taipei in ways that will not reveal its origin and would be disbursed only when needed.

The best way to keep close track of the project's physical progress is for me to join the staff of our embassy in the country where the operations are conducted, ideally on "special assignment" as a midlevel environmental officer with miscellaneous, undefined responsibilities. That may look to others like a demotion from my present position, but I'm willing to take that step.

As for the threat of corruption, I can't promise that every penny will be spent in the most efficient manner, but I am proposing to put the funds all in the hands of just one individual, Ambassador Mohamed Ibrahim of the Maldives. I have worked with him for many years now at a variety of international meetings, sometimes as an ally, other times as an opponent. I trust him. He has always done what he said he would do, no tricks, no shading the truth, no last-minute switches or 'extras.'

Wang Shu was gilding the lily on Ibrahim's behalf. Her professional experience with him was not that deep. She did trust his professionalism, however, and the Prime Minister needed comfort on that point.

Prime Minister Li sat back in his chair. His desire to prove he was not simply the grandson of the late Lee Kwan Yew enticed him to consider this risky, yet dramatic and humanitarian step. He was egotistical enough to want to be recognized as a bold leader in his own right who deserved public support. And he was impressed by Wang's willingness to put her own career on the line.

"I can see your arguments. I will sleep on it and give you an answer. But I can't afford to be reckless with Singapore's finances or infatuated with a frivolous pet project whose purpose is to make me look important. Don't get your hopes up."

He paused, seeing Wang's disappointment. "I'm sorry. I was expecting a much happier ending for this meeting."

Wang left the Prime Minister's office utterly dejected. *My first high-level diplomatic challenge, and I've failed,* she concluded, painfully. *I gave it my best effort. But the outcome is inevitable. He will say no. The more he thinks about this project, the more of an irrational gamble he'll realize it is. So all I have done is jeopardize my career and probably dash my prospects for ever becoming an ambassador.*

Four days later, to her surprise, the Prime Minister called Wang back to his office.

"Good afternoon, Ms. Wang. Please sit down. I've thought a lot about your plan. I want you to understand that we can't just write a blank check. You will need to be informed and involved at every step in the project. If it appears to be getting off track, I will need to know at once, and you must be able to cut off all funding and shut the operation down instantly, even if the money has not run out.

"Your colleague Mohamed Ibrahim needs to understand our rules at the outset and promise to honor them. No one can know that anyone from Singapore is involved except you two. If the project goes badly, I will disown you as a miscreant, entirely on a frolic of your own. I may even say you profited from your corruption.

"Finally, you are right that I must assign you to the embassy in the country where the project is being carried out. It certainly will look like a demotion. I can't make any promises about your future even if the project succeeds."

Wang's intense pleasure at his decision prompted Li to wonder if she was hiding some personal interest in this risky project. Instinctively cautious, he added,

"Please remember that any personal relationship with anyone involved in this project would be a conflict of interest and probably destroy your career."

Wang Shu nodded, afraid to say another word, lest she jeopardize the authorization she had just received. Though she had almost completely given up hope, she had prepared for the slim possibility of success. Reaching into her briefcase, she presented the Prime Minister the one essential document.

"I do need one document, which I will show to as few people as possible: your written approval to allow me to access unspecified amounts up to $20 billion for 'miscellaneous environmental projects' from the Asian International Development Fund."

The prime minister looked over the unexpected document. Absorbing the significance of its contents, he smiled and signed it. "You have just demonstrated why you deserve to be an ambassador."

The prime minister's enemies, if they ever saw his signature on this unusual document, would denounce it as a misuse of government funds, a reward to a "female favorite," or even an attempt to buy silence. He was fully aware of the risks he was taking.

"Thank you, sir. I will do everything I can to ensure that you never regret this decision."

"I hope you succeed."

Walking out of the prime minister's office, Wang was giddy with excitement, but deeply anxious.

He's warned me. He will not hesitate for one moment before claiming he never authorized anything like a climate intervention project when he signed my vague and ambiguous document. He will stand aside and see me prosecuted for misuse of public funds if the circumstances warrant, to ensure his own and his family's political survival.

The risks were enormous for her—and for everyone involved, including the Prime Minister. But now they were all committed to the project, for better or for worse.

Chapter 10

PARIS

Wang was also burdened with a more specific worry. It was far too late to avoid "any personal relationship with anyone involved in the project."

She had first met Ibrahim in Paris seven years earlier. Still a neophyte in the world of international organizations, she was part of Singapore's Delegation to the March 2014 UNESCO General Assembly. Her specific assignment was to obtain expanded funding for implementation of the 1970 UNESCO Convention on the Means of Prohibiting and Preventing the Illicit Import, Export and Transfer of Ownership of Cultural Property—particularly Chinese antiques, which are often smuggled through Singapore.

Wang called on Delegate Mohamed Ibrahim to obtain his support for Singapore's budget request. He was seeking more funds for UNESCO's International Oceanographic Commission, to accelerate its studies of rising sea levels. They agreed to support each other's efforts and talked frequently to discuss tactics and progress.

They often met at the end of the day, which allowed a more relaxed conversation. Such conversations among diplomats from diverse cultures are useful; they build the personal rapport that allows one to request help "as a personal favor," beyond just immediate reciprocity. That ability to obtain a favor when needed is an important part of the diplomat's stock in trade.

Wang's diplomatic skill and acumen impressed Ibrahim. He saw her as a rising star who would be a valuable connection. He had also learned that she hoped to be her country's regular Delegate to AOSIS, an ambition he shared.

Ibrahim also had larger ambitions. Perhaps inevitably, as the challenges and pleasures of his overseas assignments grew, life in the remote tropical community of Malé grew pale in comparison to the excitement of life in the great capitals of the world. Ibrahim found himself restless at home, recalling the cultural pleasures of his youthful life in Delhi, London, and Europe. He was determined to obtain a permanent assignment in Europe or North America.

When the third weekend approached, Ibrahim invited Wang to dinner. They dined at La Piscine, one of several small cafés by that name scattered around Paris. This one was more formal than most. It boasted more space between tables, linen tablecloths, a wide selection of individually prepared entrees, and impeccable service.

They quickly discovered many interests in common— their love of life in Paris, where they had both been students enjoying sophisticated cuisine and chamber music;

deep concerns about global warming and its inevitably destructive impact on contemporary civilization, especially in their island countries; frustration with the virtual paralysis of internally divided national governments and plodding international institutions in addressing this problem; and an urgent desire to overcome these obstacles.

As they relaxed over the sauvignon blanc and chilled *scallop ceviche* hors d'oeuvres, they imagined themselves on vacation in Paris, taking full advantage of the city's museums and concerts, not locked in endless budget discussions in windowless conference rooms. They joked that had they met as students, they could have enjoyed Paris together, disregarding the realities that his student days were several years before hers, and she had hardly looked up from her books while studying in Paris.

As the dinner conversation continued, Ibrahim was mesmerized. Here was a woman he could enjoy talking with every day, working with on issues of importance, explaining his innermost dreams and ambitions, and sharing the rich experiences life had to offer. She seemed equally enthusiastic about their new friendship.

Wang was indeed enthralled with Ibrahim. She found in him exactly the intelligent, good, foresighted, and determined diplomat she was looking for as a colleague and confidante to build a better world. She was flattered that he clearly enjoyed working with her.

Eventually the wine and Ibrahim's desires overrode his better judgment, and he put his hand on hers. The touch of his hand ran like an electric pulse through her body. There was no mistaking its meaning. It had been months, actually years, since she felt this level of arousal. The sign he found her physically desirable unleashed urges she had subconsciously repressed in her past meetings with him.

After a moment of internal elation, Wang withdrew her hand. To Ibrahim, the meaning of her action was at best ambiguous, at worst a polite but firm rejection. But he could not bring himself to quench his desire. He changed the subject, then later asked a superficially innocuous question. "Do you have time for dinner tomorrow night?"

Wang's heart raced. She understood the inquiry's probable meaning and tried to think what to say. But at that moment her whirling mind found it impossible to say anything but "Yes. That would be nice."

The next evening, after another wonderful Paris dinner, they went to Ibrahim's hotel room. He took her hand. They kissed. The warmth of his body and the intensity of his desire stripped away whatever constraints she would normally have felt. Soon they were passionately coupled for what seemed like an eternity but was only an hour. Their energy spent, Wang quickly rose, dressed, and departed, afraid to say anything that might shatter the mood. She refused to let herself hope they would ever meet this way again.

Far from home, Ibrahim imagined that a brief affair would be manageable and unthreatening. The next morning, he sent Wang a warm but unrevealing text message. They were soon exchanging emails and texts every day—sharing personal feelings, small secrets, and playful chatter along with the useful information about the day's work. He quickly became the heart of Wang's emotional life and a source of comfort that balanced the daily stress of discovering how difficult it is to accomplish anything in the diplomatic world.

Though they were rarely in the same place at the same time for work, they continued their daily communications long after they left Paris. Six months later, they created an opportunity to meet in London for three days. Ibrahim relished the opportunity to share the wonders of London's theater, music, and museums.

By this time, there was no doubt about the depth of their feelings toward each other. The pleasures of their physical and emotional connection were undiluted by the trepidations of that first night together in Paris.

Wang felt the relationship was more than wonderful; it opened her eyes to the joy of an all-consuming personal tie to a lover. Their intimate moments were relaxed and exhilarating. He was an accomplished consort, and she was a quick study. She was pleasantly surprised to discover the strength of her own erotic needs, sometimes even overpowering his. If he had any complaints about their physical relationship, they were unspoken. She had none.

They met again in Tokyo in the fall of 2015, a place neither had previously explored, and their relationship was as fresh and intense as before. They continued to communicate daily, whether discussing their minor diplomatic triumphs and defeats or simply sharing their emotions of the moment. To Wang, the days and nights together were never enough to satiate her emotional or physical desires. She wished they would last a lifetime.

Ibrahim, however, soon found himself too entangled with Wang for his own peace of mind. He missed her when they were apart, and that longing undermined his relationship with Adeela and his patience with his children. His wife was charming, intelligent, increasingly aware of the demands of his world, and devoted to him and the children. But she was no intellectual competition for the brilliant and creative Wang. Too often Ibrahim found himself feeling his family was an obstacle to sharing time and emotions with Wang. The triangle was tearing him apart.

In late 2017 they spent a blissful weekend in Hong Kong—their third extended rendezvous—where she introduced Ibrahim to the diverse aromas and tastes of Chinese cuisine, the ornate designs of Chinese temples, and the subtleties of Chinese painting and traditional opera. He was amazed at the depth and complexity of traditional Chinese culture and Wang's knowledge of its many facets.

He savored every minute with her. But on the last day, he painfully informed her that their personal relationship must end. Fighting against his own instincts and wishes, he carefully articulated the overwhelming arguments against continuing their intermittent rendezvous.

"The risks of someone discovering our relationship are too great, and the potential consequences are too destructive. For me to have a known relationship with a Chinese woman from Singapore, Confucian and at least culturally Buddhist, certainly not Muslim, would doom my career. The Maldives Constitution makes Sunni Islam the State religion, and all voting citizens and officials must be Muslim. The emphasis on religious correctness is still rising in Muslim countries. I would forfeit any hope of holding a public position, including my current position.

"You know I have a wife and two daughters, and there must be at least one more child to meet my parents' and older relatives' need for a boy. Divorce would destroy me and my family. The days of plural wives are long gone. My parents would disown me. It is out of the question.

"The discovery of our relationship would be destructive for your career as well. A continuing, unreported liaison with a diplomat from another country would cast a shadow on all your past and future advice. Your Ministry would view it as one step below treason. It would never give you a significant diplomatic post.

"Please believe me. I understand how painful this separation will be for you, and I assure you it will be equally painful for me. The void left by your absence will be impossible to fill. I can only hope time will heal our wounds. But we really have no choice."

Wang recognized Ibrahim was entirely right about the risks and consequences of continuing. The inevitable conflicts of interest and the disgrace of their illicit relationship certainly would end her career. She would be forced out of the diplomatic life she loved and was pursuing so successfully. She could not argue with him on that.

But the shock of parting, cutting off all communication, was too depressing to contemplate. They hardly spoke for the rest of their time together and said goodbye at the airport in a state of gloom and misery that neither would ever forget.

Wang's next few weeks were enveloped in a fog of reveries and recollections, and a deep yearning to be reunited with Ibrahim, emotionally and physically, whatever the cost. She reread his emails and texts, looked at old photos, recalled thrilling intimate moments.

Two months later, Wang was still depressed, mourning as if Ibrahim had died. No matter how rational the decision, it left her completely at sea emotionally. Her practical, rational, clearheaded Chinese mind, which had been her path to success from the time she was five years old, refused to function effectively when she thought about him.

Some days her mind was captivated by imaginary schemes that would result in their being reunited, but she knew they were all fantasies. None made any sense.

Without Ibrahim's encouraging support, Wang lacked the energy to pursue her work vigorously. She was alone. She still had her aging parents, but no one else aside from her professional colleagues. Life without Ibrahim's daily communication felt barren and dull. She had never before experienced such an intimate partner and lover. Before, that absence was an abstraction; now she knew specifically what was missing from her life.

At first, she rehearsed Ibrahim's reasons for their parting every day. She tried to reassure herself that they were the real ones, not just a persuasive speech to end a relationship he was tired of.

He honestly seemed to have been miserably unhappy at cutting off all future personal contact. Clearly, he cares more for me than just as a convenient, part-time playmate.

Pausing to focus on that point three months later, Wang caught herself. *To be honest*, she acknowledged, *our relationship was all a romantic fantasy. Play and sex were the essence of our trysts. We only met on vacation! We slept late, ate leisurely meals at good restaurants, took in the local sights, window-shopped for antique jade and collectibles, attended concerts and plays, or went to bed early and enjoyed sex together. We had no chores, no responsibilities.*

Suddenly, she recognized another obvious motivation driving Ibrahim's expression of concern for her. *"Of course he wants me to believe he cared deeply for me and would miss me terribly. Public knowledge of the existence of our relationship, past or current, would jeopardize his family and his career. I know too much. He needs to ingratiate himself enough to ensure that I would never expose him.*

Not that I ever would.

But she no longer entirely trusted that his words and professed emotions had been genuine. *Maybe he doesn't even know himself,* she thought, still trying to give him the benefit of the doubt.

With that realization, she was able to set him aside and turn to other, more abstract sources of support—books, family, reunions with college friends, and the pleasures of art and music. But the void remained.

For Ibrahim, ending the relationship with Wang was far more difficult than he had imagined. The time he had spent with her was in many ways a highlight of his personal life, a few brief opportunities for complete freedom to say and do anything, whether it was food or Western contemporary literature or sexual experimentation. Free from the whole network of family and religious rules and customs. Free from the conventions that made his emotional and physical relationship with Adeela entirely formal and scripted—what he could do or say and how Adeela would respond.

He sometimes wondered whether Adeela shared his dissatisfaction and desired a more open, relaxed, and spontaneous relationship. Given her sheltered upbringing and domestic life, what would make her even think of these things? In any case, with all his travel and long hours at the office for work, he had not found the time for the careful exploration that this subject would need. Meanwhile, he wasted too much emotional energy reliving his days with Wang.

After the February meeting in Phuket with Panday, Doyal, and Ibrahim, Wang's mind and emotions were again in turmoil. This new connection to Ibrahim had fallen into her lap, and she had no idea how to come to grips with it. The idea of a purely professional relationship with Ibrahim seemed simply inconceivable. She could never fully submerge her feelings for him when hearing his voice or reading his emails.

She wondered whether this new project said anything about Ibrahim's feelings. *Has he engineered this whole plan to justify more contact with me? Is he still attracted to me? Is there still reason to hope, or is that just the path to more misery? Is the fact that this crazy scheme of his depends on Singapore all just a coincidence?*

And what about my own motivation? Did I agree to take on this task to save the planet, or to make him happy? Create an excuse to talk with him again? Make him indebted to me? Show the depth of my love?

It was too much to untangle.

Nevertheless, the prospect of regular conversations with Ibrahim, and the glimmer of hope that accompanied it, brought Wang more comfort than she had felt about anything in three years. Whatever it meant, she looked forward to simply hearing his voice on the phone and exchanging e-mails.

Wang returned to her office with Prime Minister Li's signed authorization in her hand. She called Ibrahim immediately. "I got the money. Singapore will be the sole source of funds, and you will be the sole conduit to the project managers. He expects utmost secrecy. I will be disowned if it goes badly or there is any graft or corruption.

"I'll be stationed as an environmental officer to keep track of the project, wherever it is conducted. I'll be reporting to you and him regularly. No one else.

"I should tell you that the PM followed up with a specific warning that any personal relationship with anyone involved in the project would destroy my career. I'm taking this gamble for you as much as for the world. My future is entirely in your hands."

Ibrahim drew a slow breath. He was afraid to make any promise he would be unable or unwilling to fulfill. He didn't know what to say. A vague "You know how I feel about you" seemed worse than nothing. On the other hand, he didn't want to lead her on. All he could manage was a brief, impersonal reply. "Thank you. I fully appreciate the risks you are taking, and I am honored by your continued trust in me. I'll do my best to ensure that neither of us ever suffers from this decision." They avoided any more discussion of their relationship.

Wang wasn't sure what to think of his response. It was certainly not "I love you" or "I promise to protect you" or even "I understand. We are in this together." Not what she had hoped for. But maybe she was reading too much into, or out of, his few words.

Wang consoled herself with the knowledge that there was no point in worrying now. Whatever the personal or professional outcome of this decision, it was a *fait accompli*.

She was committed. She had promised to try to get the funds, and for better or worse, she had succeeded. The PM had said yes, do it. They were all taking the gamble. Happiness, disaster, or neither or both, might lie ahead.

—◦—

After pausing to catch his breath and regain his composure, Ibrahim thought for a moment about the Prime Minister's insistence on complete secrecy about the project. Inevitably, many others would need to know about the project as it went forward.

He could only do so much to shield the identity of the source of funds if the effort was to succeed. Success must be the Prime Minister's objective, or he would have refused to supply the funds. But the tension between secrecy and success made it more dangerous for all of them.

He called Panday and Doyal to give them the good news. "Our first friend explained that it took a lot more selling than originally expected. I'm not exactly sure whose approval was necessary, though my understanding of the government structure gives me a good idea.

"A sufficient line of credit for the entire project will shortly be available in the Second Bank of Taipei. I alone will be able to draw on it when necessary. The source reiterated that he wants no partners. He prefers the greater likelihood of true secrecy.

"Our first friend will be assigned as an environmental officer in whatever country we persuade to carry out the operations. Her presence will allow close oversight of the work, which was a condition of the grant. It's nominally a demotion for her. She is making a significant professional sacrifice for this effort.

"Finally, I should warn you that any corruption, even the most common sorts of skimming, kickbacks, or bribes, will result in the end of the project and whatever punishment her source is able to impose on all of us."

Panday and Doyal were both surprised and thrilled. Maybe this improbable scheme could actually come together! But their anxiety level rose as they realized that now the project was more real, involving billions of dollars, and they were exposed more deeply than ever to the attendant risks.

Doyal was uncomfortable for another reason. *Ibrahim has delivered the money*, he muttered to himself. *Now I'm on the spot to deliver a meeting with Wijaya. I bragged that I knew him well and implied he owed me a favor. But can I really get us a date on his calendar? I hope my connection with him is as strong as I claimed.*

Doyal's next call was to the office of President Kartawijaya of Indonesia.

Chapter 11

JAKARTA

"Panday, this is Doyal. Can you come to Jakarta on Thursday, May 20, and stay for a Sunday meeting with the man in Jakarta? I know it's short notice, but that's when he is available. After several tries, I finally got my foot in the door yesterday."

Doyal waited, letting the news sink in. A meeting with a foreign president is not so frequent or easily arranged, especially without even revealing the subject matter. He was still congratulating himself on his excellent work.

Panday, after a moment's disbelief, was ecstatic, but once again anxious. He had never expected the project to get this far, and he was ambivalent about pursuing it further. He examined his calendar, though it would be hard to imagine anything that would take precedence over being in Jakarta on May 20, 2021.

"That's excellent news! I'll make my travel arrangements today. I have a hundred questions, but this is not the time or place to discuss them. Anyway, it will take me a while to fully absorb what you've told me and sort out what I really want to know.

"But I do know two things—we have overcome the first great obstacle, and we have an even greater obstacle ahead before the project can even begin. We need to think about how we will sell this idea to our next best friend."

Doyal smiled. "Wonderful. You're right, we still need the second right answer. We need to be fully prepared. The big meeting will be Sunday, May 23. See you in Jakarta on the 20th, at the Westin Hotel!"

"Inshallah! God willing!" Panday replied jokingly.

Doyal replied with a somber "Inshallah" and ended the call.

Next, Doyal sent an email to Ibrahim:

> Panday and I are ready to meet our next best friend in Jakarta Sunday, May 23. We need you to join us on the 20th to prepare. I hope we can see you there!

Doyal had no doubt that young Ibrahim would come, whatever the conflicts on his calendar. This whole project was his idea, after all. Especially if it failed.

⌒◦⌒

Arriving in the evening on Thursday, May 20, as planned, Panday found the Westin lobby mostly deserted. Many Muslim travelers would already be at their destinations to observe Friday, which begins at sunset Thursday in most Muslim traditions and at sunrise Friday in others, as a full day of rest and prayer. Devout Muslims preferred to leave work early on Thursday. The staff on duty was mostly Buddhists or other non-Muslims.

Doyal and Ibrahim had arrived earlier in the day. Panday would have done the same, but he had been obliged to attend a high-level Foreign Ministry staff meeting on Tuesday afternoon. He had compressed his travel schedule to arrive on time. It still took thirty-one hours to travel from his home in Port of Spain to Jakarta. Even flying in business class, it took a toll on the body.

The Westin Jakarta is certainly luxurious, he noted to himself. It is situated on the top twenty floors of the tallest building in the city, at a height of almost one thousand feet. Its premier restaurant, located on the top floor, features "Nikkei Cuisine infused with exotic Peruvian flavors prepared by Chef Hajime Kasuga." It is among the very best in Indonesia and offers a breathtaking 360-degree view of the nearby embassies and offices, and the city beyond.

Panday checked into his room and admired the view. He unpacked, still a little disoriented from the flights and the eleven-hour time difference, but savoring the rewards of being a senior diplomat. At least he would eat well and sleep comfortably here. After checking his email and texting his wife that he'd arrived safely, he called Doyal.

"I'm finally here. The taxi driver mistakenly took me to the Sheraton Jakarta, not the Westin Jakarta. Then we were trapped in the city's three-hour 'rush hour' for an extra hour and a half. I'm told the traffic is always this way. So when and where will we meet?"

"Ibrahim and I are in my room waiting for you. I booked a suite, so we could meet without being seen or heard. We've had some halal food delivered. Come on up. Suite 4542."

For Panday, the whole adventure was still completely unreal. His private evaluation remained pessimistic. *I've seen schemes that were far better planned, organized, and executed than this one collapse after years of effort. It had been barely plausible that we would get the money from Singapore, even though that unbeliev-ably wealthy city-state's entire existence depends on the oceans and on global physical, political, and economic stability.*

But providing disguised money is one thing. Hosting physical operations is quite another. It's entirely implausible that Indonesia, or any government, will allow its territory and equipment to be used in such a risky enterprise. How long could the effort be kept secret, especially if it progressed well?

How many other countries would be outraged by this maneuver, fearing short-term economic losses or differing in principle about SRM? Could any government risk being held responsible for conducting the project if some of its effects were undesirable for even a few major states?

Nevertheless, the project, if successful, will be in Trinidad & Tobago's best interest. And there's another upside to involvement in the effort. Working together with Ibrahim and Doyal is creating a bond of reciprocity that will surely be useful in other contexts. There is every reason to help make the project go forward, especially given the small prospect of success. It might even make an interesting chapter in my book, if I ever find time to write it.

Panday proceeded to Doyal's suite. In a few minutes, the three diplomats were enjoying the exotic flavors of the room service repast. Avoiding business, they shared stories of their travel to Jakarta. Panday revealed the good news that his youngest daughter was now engaged to a rising political personality from a wealthy family in a nearby village. Congratulations and good wishes followed.

After dinner, the discussion focused on the crucial meeting that lay ahead. Panday began reading out a list of logistical questions he had assembled on the plane:

"Will we meet with Wijaya himself? How do we address him? Who else will be present? How much time will we have to lay the groundwork? Does he speak English well enough to fully understand what we are saying? Will he need an interpreter, or claim to?"

Doyal had some answers.

"We'll meet Wijaya at the National Museum at 10:00 o'clock Sunday morning. The Museum will be closed at that hour, but someone will meet us at the front entrance and take us to a private conference room that Wijaya can enter and exit without being seen.

"I asked for two hours, because if he is interested he might have lots of questions. But I don't know what else is on his schedule. In any case, he'll end the meeting whenever he likes. We need to get his attention immediately, explain the project succinctly, and answer questions for as long as he is interested.

"I don't think he'll invite us to call him Wijaya, so he should be addressed as 'Your Excellency.' Fortunately, he traveled widely in Europe over a decade ago to promote his family's apparel manufacturing business, and he spoke English to everyone there. After several years as Governor of Jakarta, and more than five years as President, he has remained quite fluent.

"I suppose I will open the discussion, but we should have assigned topics in advance, and I will turn to you when the time comes to address them."

The others indicated their assent. Then came the more complex and delicate questions. Ibrahim began reciting his list, encouraging the others to enlarge and refine it:

"Are we asking for confidentiality, and suppose he won't agree until he hears what we are proposing? How can the project be effectively disguised, so the Indonesian government can disclaim any knowledge or responsibility if it is discovered? We have the money, but we can't tell him where it's coming from, so how can we satisfy him that it's real? Without Dr. Hartquist, can we name any reputable scientists who will endorse this effort or help design and run these 'experiments'? How can we use scientific advisors without compromising the secrecy of our project?

"Will his experience as Governor of Jakarta and later as a senior government official during the ruinous Jakarta floods of February 2015 be enough? If we explain the consequences of global warming for Indonesia, will that persuade him? What else might he want from us? I suppose we can promise not ever to do or say anything to connect him or Indonesia to the project. What else do we have to offer, aside from the preservation of humanity? What exactly are we asking him to do?"

This list was daunting. They soon found themselves disagreeing about which subjects should be addressed first and by whom. Doyal, who now felt responsible for the project and the meeting, was opinionated and adamant. He was determined that their presentations look professional, whatever the outcome.

"We first need to persuade Wijaya that Indonesia is suffering from the effects of global warming and the damage will grow dramatically in the coming decade, leading to economic decline, increased violence, and political instability. I can do that. Then Ibrahim should lay out the plan, the existence of the necessary funding, and the role Indonesia needs to play. Without a full explanation of this background, he might just say no immediately."

Panday strongly disagreed. "I don't think Wijaya will sit still for a lecture about the fact that Indonesia will suffer significantly from rising temperatures, changes in weather patterns, flooding, and rising seas. He knows the problem.

"He also knows that Indonesia's economy is heavily dependent on oil and logging. Unless he believes we have something new to offer, we won't keep his attention. We need to start by telling him our creative solution and stress that it can only work in complete secrecy. Then we can explain why it is in Indonesia's interest to support our project and answer his questions."

Doyal responded, "I understand your point, but I know Wijaya, and I believe he will want to start at the beginning before he gets any details. He's an orderly thinker."

Doyal and Panday turned to Ibrahim, silently asking, "What do you think?"

"It's a difficult call," he began, trapped between his two senior colleagues' opposing views. "I assume he's agreed to this extraordinary meeting in the expectation that we have something extraordinary to say. We don't know how knowledgeable he is about the impacts of global warming, but he was an agriculture student in school and inevitably continued some of that interest because of its effects on the apparel business. He probably understands the general outlines of the threat very well.

"He's a busy man and likely to be impatient. I think we need to give him a few sentences at the very beginning that justify the unusual character of the meeting, one or two short sentences about the Indonesia's exposure to climate change, followed by not more than three or four sentences describing our proposed project.

"I know we risk him cutting us short right there, but we don't know how much time he has allotted or whether some emergency will interrupt him anyway. He needs to know immediately the enormous significance of what we are hoping to do."

Doyal, taken aback, looked away in dismay. He tried a different tack.

"Then I should make that brief initial presentation. I got us the meeting and need to go first anyway. Then Panday can talk about the consequences of inaction for Indonesia. You, Ibrahim, can walk through the elements of the project in greater detail—funding, aircraft, chemicals, camouflage, secrecy, and deniability. And if we still have his attention, I will close the meeting with an urgent plea for his support."

After a pause, Panday raised another point. "I'm okay with that approach. Now, we know what we are asking for ultimately. But how do we want this meeting to end? We can't expect a 'yes' on the spot, and we don't want an immediate 'no'. I suggest we say we're not asking for a decision at this meeting.

"We should acknowledge at the outset that Indonesia's involvement is too important for a snap decision. We don't expect him to decide immediately, without thinking it over and perhaps consulting in some oblique way with advisors.

If he is favorably disposed, many crucial details still need to be resolved before we know if we have a viable project. We should offer to meet with him again at his convenience.

"If he declines on the spot, or later, we will just try to find another venue for the operations."

The other two signaled their agreement with silent nods. Ibrahim identified one more question.

"What do we say if any media spot us and wonder why we are in Jakarta? I don't think it's plausible to deny that we are here about climate concerns. It's what we've all been working on for years. I suggest we say something like this:

> We are visiting Indonesia to observe your nation's progress in implementing and expanding your Nationally Determined Contribution under the Paris Accords. We hope and believe that Indonesia is setting an example and exceeding its commitments, because it is a major emitter and needs to lead the way. We have complete confidence that President Kartawijaya understands that global warming presents a variety of serious threats to Indonesia's people, its economy, and its way of life.

If that's acceptable, I'll write it up."

Doyal offered one change. "Don't mention Kartawijaya at all. It may prompt someone to ask if we talked with him. Just say 'We have confidence that the people of Indonesia understand, etc.'" Ibrahim readily made the change.

Doyal rose from his chair. "We have done what we can together. All of us have traveled a long way. It's time to get some rest and spend the day tomorrow organizing and rehearsing our respective presentations. We can meet tomorrow at dinner, unless someone feels we need to meet sooner." The three shook hands all around, solemnly, as if going into battle. Panday and Ibrahim departed for their rooms.

All three spent Friday practicing the remarks they would present to each other on Saturday and hoped to present to the President on Sunday. Meanwhile, each envisioned various disaster scenarios:

- Getting too little time to explain, or for Wijaya to understand the project
- Getting bogged down in a disagreement over one small point or another
- Somehow destroying the confidentiality of the project, either intentionally or by accident
- Wijaya doubting that Indonesia itself has much to lose from climate change, or much to gain from the project even if it works, or fearing that the risk

of discovery would have unacceptable impacts on
Indonesia

- Indicating he leans toward yes, but eventually getting cold feet and saying no after weeks or months
  waiting for an answer
- Saying "thank you," departing, and never responding at all

The paths to defeat seemed more numerous and probable than the tenuous path to success.

After sunset, they met for dinner at Henshin. They
agreed they should discuss nothing of the immediate business. They took in the unparalleled view of the city and discussed their previous visits. "I first came here twenty-five
years ago," Doyal recalled. "The city has been transformed
since then, from an overgrown village into a thriving, cos-
mopolitan metropolis. It still lacks adequate public transportation, but with the ongoing expansion of the metro
and the introduction of self-driving electric cars, the city is
becoming far more livable."

Ibrahim offered a counterpoint. "It *is* a beautiful city.
But the reality is that Jakarta's geological subsidence, combined with rising sea levels and more intense typhoons and
flooding, is going to make the city increasingly unworkable
physically, perhaps even uninhabitable. At the same time,
the growing influx of dispossessed rural workers will strain
what little cushion of infrastructure and resources Jakarta

has. It won't be a pretty picture twenty years from now, I'm afraid."

Panday stopped them both. "We agreed not to discuss business at dinner." To fill the silence, he began elaborating the pleasant details of the upcoming family wedding and attendant celebrations for his daughter. A three-day event, including hundreds of personal and professional friends and many relatives, some quite remote. He invited Ibrahim and Doyal, but recognized how unlikely it would be that they could attend.

Because the bride was his youngest daughter, the ceremony was his last occasion to entertain on a truly grand scale. At this point in life he could afford it. The only frustrating part was planning the details. His wife claimed to want him involved, but she and their daughter knew exactly what they preferred. So they always requested his advice, but then frequently disregarded it. As a diplomat, he had learned long ago to accept such circumstances. And overall, he seemed quite happy with the plans.

Not wanting to monopolize the conversation, Panday turned to Ibrahim and asked, "What family news do you have to offer?" Ibrahim smiled. He finally did have news.

"Thank you for asking. I too have good news, although it's a little premature to tell the world. Adeela and I are expecting a third child, a boy this time, which will make the grandparents and all the relatives of that generation happy.

"Meanwhile, our elder daughter, now thirteen, is show-ing great promise as a student. She has learned English and Arabic and can recite extended passages of the Koran from memory. She has an amiable personality and makes friends easily.

"If society continues to open opportunities for women, I can see the makings of a talented diplomat. In a decade or so, I'll be calling on both of you to help me advance her career," he said, only half in jest.

Ibrahim's other preoccupation remained unspoken. He did not dare mention his fanciful desire for a second wife. These colleagues would disapprove of the practice, which was distained as increasingly anachronistic in the cosmo-politan world they inhabited. Worse, the only woman he could imagine as a new wife was Wang Shu. He still longed for her often, no matter how hard he worked to cast her out of his fantasies.

Ibrahim couldn't tell if either Ambassador had noticed the intensity of his interest in Wang, but talk of another wife would certainly heighten their awareness and suspi-cions. Talking about it, even in the abstract or facetiously, would create an unnecessary risk.

Ibrahim quickly turned the conversation to a different topic: his continuing dismay over the loss of Dr. Hartquist and her unresolved murder. It was difficult for them to imagine that anyone who knew her would seek her demise, for any reason. They speculated about various possible motives, but their theories all revolved around her passionate call for an immediate SRM veil to address climate change as the impetus for the murder. The true origin of the conspiracy remained a mystery.

Their shared personal experience with Dr. Hartquist continued to reinforce their bonds of friendship and their determination to succeed with what was, in some sense, her project, not theirs. At this point it was hard to see how that would be possible without persuading Indonesia to help.

Which brought their thoughts back again to Sunday's meeting. It was time to adjourn for the night and get back to work in the morning.

Chapter 12

MONTREAL

In the nondescript RCMP Headquarters on Dorchester Boulevard in downtown Montreal, Marie and Jon continued their research into what appeared to be their most promising lead: background information on the recipient of Mark Miller's last international phone conversation.

HQ was housed in an overcrowded office building, the result of a growing staff shoehorned into the old physical space. Marie had a small office to herself; Jon had only a cubicle with no privacy at all. They were not far from Montreal's world-famous McGill University, and the investigators regularly drew on the expertise of the McGill faculty when they ran into roadblocks in efforts to obtain or interpret their findings.

Marie worked with a McGill professor on communications law to map out the steps to acquire all stored information about the phone call. The primary obstacle was getting through the privacy law barriers in both Indonesia and Geneva. Jon undertook the chores of contacting relevant companies and government agencies, learning what permissions and forms were needed, and submitting them to the appropriate authorities. The work was tedious and boring. Eventually he obtained all the necessary approvals, and the recipient phone number and its owner were identified.

It was now 2021, more than six months after Dr. Hartquist's death. Not surprisingly, the phone number was no longer in service, having been canceled on Wednesday, June 25, 2020. It was registered to Stability, Inc., a Swiss corporation created in 2017, but no longer in business. A "Pierre de Fleurieu" had signed on its behalf for the phone service and given Stability's bank account number as security.

The Fleurieu name was apparently an alias. As might be expected, the Belgian passport he had used for identification turned out to be forged. The real passport with that number had been lost or stolen in Dubai in 2014. Neither the RCMP nor Interpol could find any other records of de Fleurieu's existence.

After another monotonous process, this time requiring a search warrant, Jon finally obtained the Stability bank records on March 8. Painstaking review of the transaction records identified several small transfers and a one-million-euro transfer on June 20, 2020, to an account on which Mark Miller and de Fleurieu were co-signatories.

Two days after Miller's death, de Fleurieu withdrew those funds. He also withdrew all the funds in the Stability account and closed it. The timing of these transactions persuaded Marie and Jon that Mark Miller had been funded to eliminate Dr. Hartquist, and de Fleurieu, whoever he was, was involved in arranging Hartquist's and Miller's deaths.

The source of Stability's funds was yet another Swiss bank account, this one with only a number. With further help from the Swiss police, Jon plodded through another round of privacy waivers and obtained a warrant to inspect the bank records connected with that account. A "Walton Anderson" with an American passport had opened it on April 11, 2017.

Investigation of that account revealed its use in connection with previous questionable activities, including arms sales, probably illegal, to various Middle Eastern organizations and governments. The RCMP had studied that name before. It was never able to connect it to a real person.

Marie, unwilling to rely on the thoroughness of earlier searches, initiated a new inquiry to the US Immigration and Customs Enforcement Service (ICE). To her surprise, ICE promptly reported that "Walton Anderson" was a real person with a current, valid US passport. His address was the Peaceful Valley Home, a community for Alzheimer's patients in Santa Fe, New Mexico.

At Marie's insistence, the FBI called the Home, which confirmed that Walton Anderson lived there and had not left the premises since he was admitted in March 2017. His condition made him incapable of any reliable factual conversation. A dead end.

In addition to the transfers to Stability, the numbered account's records showed three transfers to pay the credit card expenses of a "Robert McKenzie." The card had been used for several transactions in mid-June 2020. One was for a purchase from a chemical supply house in Jakarta. The company's records confirmed they were for small quantities of unusual toxic substances. Charges to the credit card also paid for a room at the Hotel Ciputra Jakarta on June 21–22 and a room in the Westin Jakarta June 15–24.

The card was still active and in good standing. Jon's investigation quickly revealed that the real Robert McKenzie had never stayed in those Jakarta hotels, purchased the chemicals, or even traveled outside of Australia. He did not have a passport. He was the owner of a small bookstore in Darwin, a town of 118,000 and the capital of Australia's Northern Territory.

McKenzie claimed never to have noticed either the charges or the deposits to pay for them. An aging leftist with looks to match his politics, he claimed he rarely used any credit card, and he never even looked at the credit card bills unless he knew he owed money. Further background investigation and more intense questioning satisfied Jon that McKenzie had no connection with the events in Jakarta.

After discovering the purchase of toxic chemicals with the credit card, RCMP forensics ran a further analysis on Mark Miller's cremated ashes. The results confirmed that he was poisoned by the same combination of chemicals that had been acquired with the credit card. How the chemicals were introduced into Miller's body was not apparent. But contrary to the coroner's report, his death was not accidental or health-related; it was definitely murder.

Marie and Jon surmised that the same individual or organization that hired Mark Miller to murder Dr. Hartquist was also responsible for his murder. The murders had all the earmarks of a carefully planned, professionally executed scheme to kill Dr. Hartquist and leave no traces of the identity of the responsible parties. Their plan had succeeded so far; this financial trail also led nowhere.

The card holder had fraudulently signed registration forms at the hotel. He also fraudulently signed forms asserting he was authorized to possess the chemicals, since they could be used for a variety of illicit purposes, including the manufacture of illegal synthetic drugs.

RCMP forensics suggested another approach. It had just acquired new handwriting-identification software that used technology analogous to the latest facial-recognition software. It connected to a vast database to compare these signatures with millions of other handwriting samples. The existence of several signatures would make the identification more reliable. A thorough study, which still took two days of computer time, confirmed that the signatures were written by the same person and pointed to three "author candidates."

One candidate was quickly eliminated, deceased in 2017. The other two were still alive: Walton Anderson and Alberto Corimondo. The FBI had already reported that Walton Anderson was an Alzheimer's patient who had not left the Home in Santa Fe, New Mexico, since 2017.

That left Corimondo, a convicted felon who had served time for international arms trafficking. He now worked for Harold Berkhoffer, a Silicon Valley venture capitalist with a net worth exceeding $12.4 billion, who contributed to an assortment of extreme political causes and alt-right media. Corimondo was Berkhoffer's bodyguard and all-around assistant.

The RCMP asked the FBI to investigate Corimondo's recent travel and connections to other individuals or organizations outside of his work for Berkhoffer, as well as Berkhoffer's own activities. The investigation was not a high priority for the FBI, which was swamped with ICE requests to assist in identifying and arresting deportable illegal immigrants. President Gonzalez had appointed a new FBI Director and Attorney General who could reverse those priorities, but the US Senate had just confirmed them. They had not yet looked at this question.

The FBI eventually reviewed Corimondo's international travel records, which showed he was outside of the US during June of 2020. They thoroughly questioned Corimondo. He acknowledged he had traveled abroad in June 2020, visiting his mother in Croatia. He had plane tickets, but no hotel or restaurant receipts from Dubrovnik, allegedly because he stayed in his family home.

Corimondo insisted he was never in Jakarta or Indonesia in his entire life. He knew nothing about Dr. Hartquist's death; he claimed he didn't even know who she was. The names Walton Anderson, Robert McKenzie, Mark Miller, and Mark O'Mara drew equally blank looks. He denied knowing any of them.

The FBI agents on the case were convinced Corimondo was stonewalling, but they could not find any further incriminating evidence to justify pursuing their investigation. Somehow the focus of the investigation leaked to the media. Sensational stories promptly appeared implying that Corimondo and Berkhoffer had arranged Dr. Hartquist's death, and then the death of Mark Miller. The FBI hoped someone with more information would step forward.

The internet was immediately flooded with reports that Harold Berkhoffer had invested heavily in natural gas companies. Bloggers speculated that he feared Dr. Hartquist's views could drive down the value of his stock.

Berkhoffer found it necessary to deny the "scandalous, nonsensical, unsubstantiated allegations" against him and his assistant. He promised to sue any media outlet that published these rumors without a full disclaimer stating that no evidence existed supporting them.

Nevertheless, the story continued to spread. It was reinforced when Dr. Hartquist's former secretary revealed that Berkhoffer had sought a meeting with Hartquist shortly after her 2018 editorial favoring an immediate SRM veil. Dr. Hartquist had refused to meet him. Now the blogger conspiracy narrative went that Berkhoffer was angry at being spurned by this climate science expert and media star; he wanted revenge.

Local authorities in Croatia interviewed Croatian friends of Corimondo and produced affidavits confirming that he had visited his mother in Dubrovnik in June 2020. None of them were very specific about when he arrived, when he departed, or if he had stayed there for the whole time. On April 17, 2021, the FBI submitted its full report to Marie and Jon. It only aggravated their frustration at their inability to find the prime mover behind the murders.

⸺◦◦⸺

In Langley, Virginia, CIA director Williamson found himself focusing again on Dr. Hartquist's murder. The rumors that Harold Berkhoffer, a right-wing American multibillionaire, had arranged her death threatened to undercut the new President's attempts to reassert leadership on global climate issues after America's four-year absence.

China and India were pushing back against new US efforts to shape the UN climate agenda. Activists and green political parties everywhere remained unconvinced that the US was really changing its policies. After four years of asserting that climate change was a Chinese plot, any US initiatives were tainted, despite the recent inauguration of a new President.

The wave of public sympathy for Dr. Hartquist, combined with the increasingly frequent adverse impacts of climate change, had strengthened domestic support for the SRM veil approach she had advocated. But there was strong opposition from both ends of the political spectrum. Any explicit US position on geoengineering would further complicate US foreign policy.

The President asked Director Williamson to prepare a full report on the circumstances of Dr. Hartquist's death and how the SRM issue would be perceived in the US and around the world.

Unfortunately, he wanted it in two weeks. Williamson knew that the CIA would barely have time for full internal review. That would leave no time to circulate it for comments or clearance by the Cabinet Departments.

The situation was a setup for attacks on the CIA's report by those who disliked its conclusions. Williamson hated these short-fuse projects. Worse, he hated being the bearer of bad tidings to the new President. But all too often that was his job.

Maybe I could persuade the President to extend the deadline by another week or two to allow input from the Cabinet Departments, he reflected, *but even a month wouldn't allow preparation of an accurate, thoughtful, coordinated document.*

Requesting anything longer would sound like the bureaucratic delay every new president hates. The President will just need to see for himself what happens when we aren't given time to prepare a balanced report with input from every agency.

Chapter 13

SANTA FE

In late February 2021, Marie and Jon had been diverted from the Hartquist case to investigate a series of recent terrorist attacks in Montreal. They spent a large part of the next two months conducting long, boring interviews with witnesses, then with the attackers and their families and friends. The process didn't have the intellectual challenge of trying to track down the person or organization behind the murders of Ilsa Hartquist and Mark Miller. And in the end, neither Marie nor Jon thought they had the same level of significance.

The FBI reports on the Corimondo investigation finally arrived in April. The terrorist attack interviews were done, but those reports still needed to be written. Then they could again devote their energies to the Hartquist case.

The FBI had found nothing. Despite the inevitable leaks, perhaps even quietly instigated by someone in the agency, and the resulting publicity, no further evidence emerged to link Corimondo or Berkhoffer to the deaths of Dr. Hartquist and Mark Miller.

The social media blogs have Berkhoffer and Corimondo tried and convicted, Marie thought, *with airtight evidence of means, motive, and opportunity. But their plausible-sounding theories won't hold up in court without concrete evidence beyond the handwriting similarity. And RCMP management is ready to close the investigation, leaving the case unsolved.*

Marie was still hoping for a breakthrough. She was intensely distressed and frustrated that she and Jon could not find the person or organization behind the two murders, despite the widespread publicity and the substantial reward offered by the Swedish government. She was determined to explore every possibility, if only to preserve the RCMP's reputation and their own.

She took the Hartquist file home on Friday and spent her weekend reading through it one more time, studying every document and investigative report. On the way into the office Monday morning, she prepared her arguments for continuing the investigation.

"I looked over the Hartquist file," she told Jon on Monday. "I see two loose ends. First, handwriting analysis had identified two suspects, Corimondo and Walton Anderson, who might have used the credit card that bought the chemicals and stayed in Jakarta at the time of Miller's death. We don't have a case against Corimondo.

"The FBI learned that Anderson was in a Home for Alzheimer's victims in Santa Fe, New Mexico, but never tried to interview him or the Home beyond a phone call. Suppose he's not really there, or suppose he doesn't have Alzheimer's, or suppose he was still healthy in June 2020 and paid the Home to cover for him? We don't have any of those answers in the file.

"Second, we traced the one international call Miller made from his cell phone, but suppose he made a local call on the hotel phone? We might be trying to find someone who was staying right in Jakarta or even the same hotel as Miller the night he died. Maybe they had a conversation that night on the hotel phone that could lead us to the murderer. I think we have some additional work to do before we give up on this one, if only to show our investigation is complete."

Jon wasn't persuaded. "Any local phone call from Miller the night he arrived in Jakarta is likely to go to a room registered in the name of 'Robert McKenzie,' which won't tell us anything new." Marie's face indicated she conceded the point.

"As for visiting the Alzheimer's Home, it's hard to believe you would learn anything the FBI didn't."

Making her arguments aloud, Marie realized she was grasping at straws. "I can't present this thin argument to the boss," she admitted, downcast. "I agree it's a long shot, but a trip to Santa Fe will close a gap in our final report. I'll be back in two days. I'll just use some sick leave."

"Okay," Jon muttered. "I can cover for you for two days, but don't forget we haven't actually finished writing up our reports on the Montreal attack interviews."

Jon paused and smiled mischievously. "Don't spend too much time enjoying Santa Fe."

Using sick leave was a bit irregular, but he didn't raise an objection. He was hoping for a promotion in the fall, and Marie would have the first, and probably the last, word on that.

"Of course not. I'll leave early Wednesday morning, and be back in the office Friday morning," Marie replied, a bit nettled by his suggestion this would be a pleasure trip.

<hr />

Marie took an early Wednesday-morning flight and arrived at the Pleasant Valley Home just after noon. She presented her credentials to Sharon Davis, the Home's Administrator, and asked to meet Walton Anderson. She was taken directly to his room. He was much younger than she expected, but he could not stand or walk. His unruly hands appeared incapable of signing, or even reliably holding, anything.

His mental grip was equally deformed. He looked at Marie with suspicion and repeatedly asked if she was coming to take away his house. He was completely unresponsive to questions about any subject, including his own past. She quickly realized he was beyond intelligent communication at this moment. She was done "interviewing" him in fifteen minutes.

The Home said Anderson had been there continuously since March 2017. Marie recognized it was completely implausible that he had traveled anywhere, transferred funds to or from a bank account in Geneva, or participated in a plot to commit murder in his present condition.

She was ready to abandon the Anderson lead and take the next flight back to Montreal. She found a 9:15 pm red-eye to Chicago, where she would transfer planes. She still had several hours on her hands. Under the circumstances, it would be unwise to spend them shopping or sightseeing in Santa Fe.

Partly to strengthen her justification for the trip, she asked Ms. Davis to bring her Walton Anderson's files. Then her report could include a "complete file search" in addition to the worthless personal interview.

Diffidently paging through the files, Marie suddenly stopped short. Walton Anderson's expenses from March 10, 2017, through June 2020 were paid out of a Geneva bank account in the name of Stability Inc., and the checks were signed by "W. Anderson." It didn't make any sense, but there was clearly some connection between Stability and this Mr. Anderson. After June 2020, the necessary funds came by wire transfer from the numbered Swiss account that had funded Stability.

The handwriting analysis had identified Walton Anderson's handwriting. But reading the medical reports in the file, it was impossible to believe that the person she interviewed was in Geneva or Jakarta in 2020. She was struck by the incongruities. *Is it possible I wasn't talking to Walton Anderson? If not, is the Home misleading me? Was the file doctored? Who is this man in the Home?*

She inspected the Home's Anderson files more carefully, all the way back to March 2017, when he was admitted. There were no visible signs of tampering with them. She returned to Ms. Davis's office.

"Are there any other files on Walton Anderson?"

"Only the application for admission. We keep those papers in a separate file system because we get so many more applicants than we can take in. That file is in the basement, but I can get it for you."

Ms. Davis returned with the admission file. The application file included a photo of Anderson from 2016. He looked surprisingly better at fifty-five, but there was a clear resemblance. The photo was a little loose, and Marie took the liberty of looking at the back. And there she found a faint scribble: "William Anderson." The last page of the file further aroused her suspicions: The application to admit "Walton Anderson" was signed by "W. Anderson."

Marie's creative mind quickly invented a number of possible theories: *The person whose handwriting matched the samples from Jakarta could not be the man in the Home, but was someone else, possibly a relative, if 'William' rather than 'Walton' Anderson was even his real name. Might 'William' Anderson be using the 'Walton' name for activities he wanted to hide?*

Switching identities would work better than using a false name, because the name and passport would lead investigators to a real person: this shell of a man living in the Home, who obviously could not have committed any crime and could not give any information. It sounded like a television crime script. But if it were true, the trick was working.

Marie texted Jon:

> The files here have opened a new trail. I need to work another half day here tomorrow. I'll fly back tomorrow evening. See you Friday afternoon.

He replied with a sad emoticon and brief reply:

> Don't come back with too many pairs of shoes!

He tried to lighten the snide tone with a smiley face. Marie tried unsuccessfully to find it amusing. She rescheduled her return flight to a new time: Thursday 5:35 p.m.

Marie immediately returned to Ms. Davis's office. She started her questions delicately. "I looked through the Anderson file yesterday, and I'm a little confused. As I was examining the photo of Walton Anderson on the 2017 application, it came loose.

"On the back there is a faint trace of the name 'William Anderson.' Who is the person who arranged to have Walton admitted and has been paying for his care ever since? Is it possible there is some confusion of identities here?"

Marie showed her the back of the photo.

Ms. Davis gave Marie a puzzled look. "I wasn't here when Walton was admitted, but I don't know any reason to doubt the records. The file seems to be completely in order. Isn't it more likely that the name on the reverse of the photo was incorrect, and that's why it was erased?"

Marie nodded her head, "That is certainly a plausible explanation. But I'd like to talk to Walton again tomorrow morning. Thank you for all your help." With that, Marie left Ms. Davis's office.

As Marie was getting her handbag and briefcase in the outer office, she overheard Ms. Davis on the phone.

"William? This is Sharon Davis at the Home. I've just been talking to an international investigator who came to see Walton. She's got the strange idea that there's some mix-up in his identity. She wants to talk to him again tomorrow morning.

"Walton could say anything or nothing. He's far beyond rational conversation. Should I ask her for a warrant? Do you think he needs a lawyer? I don't want the Home to violate his privacy or his legal rights. I don't know what she's getting at, but since you're his guardian, I thought you should know."

A brief silence. Then, "Okay, I'm sure it's just a routine inquiry. I'll let her go ahead and talk to him in the morning. If she wants anything more, I'll let you know."

Marie immediately departed, fearing she might be caught eavesdropping. She did not hear the rest of Ms. Davis's conversation: "Her name is Marie Veronique Roy. I'll spell it: M-A-R-I-E-V-E-R-O-N-I-Q-U-E-R-O-Y. The card doesn't have an office address, but it does have an email: M.Roy@RCMP.ca. I think she's staying at the Quality Court Hotel on Cerrillos Road."

Marie went directly to the Santa Fe Public Library to see if it had any information on either William or Walton Anderson. The FBI report noted that Walton was born and grew up in Santa Fe. She hoped the Library would have some record of the Anderson family.

The reference librarian, Lucinda Nuzzaco, was not as enthusiastic as Marie had hoped. "Anderson is a very common name, and I would guess that there were at least two dozen noteworthy Anderson families in Santa Fe thirty years ago, and probably three or four individuals named William. Walton is a less common name, so that might be more productive.

"Our old newspapers and official document records have all been digitized, so if there's anything there, we'll find it. But it will take me a few days to search through it all. And that's if I'm not especially busy helping our local customers. They pay for the Library, you know," Ms. Nuzzaco remarked in a rather curt tone.

Marie considered stressing the urgency of the matter but concluded that might be a mistake. Instead she simply replied, "I understand completely. Here is my card with my email address. Please send me anything you find. Your files could provide the key to resolving an important international criminal investigation."

Marie hoped that last information would speed the attention Ms. Nuzzaco gave the request. It immediately aroused Ms. Nuzzaco's sense of the importance of the search, and therefore her own importance as a participant in solving an international crime. That sort of request had never come to her before, and it would make excellent dinner conversation.

Chapter 14

SANTA FE

THe next morning Marie arrived at the Home promptly at 9:00 am, when visitors' hours began. She had read that Alzheimer's victims are more aware and alert early on sunny mornings, and she had some ideas for questions that might reveal the switch in names.

She was not allowed to see Anderson immediately. When she did see him, she wondered if he had been medicated. He seemed much more relaxed than he had the previous afternoon. He also seemed more alert.

She looked around the room to see if there were listening devices present and noted the television's red light was on. Was it too much to think that Ms. Davis or someone on her staff was listening to their conversation, or recording it? She dismissed that possibility as paranoid. Of course the Home maintained constant visual surveillance of its Alzheimer's patients. That didn't mean they were paying special attention to her conversation with Anderson.

She began the conversation carefully, with a brief, uninformative introduction.

"Good morning, Mr. Anderson. I'm doing some research on the Anderson family in Santa Fe. I don't know if you are related to the Andersons I am interested in. Could you tell me anything about your family? Who were your father, your mother, sisters and brothers?

Anderson looked up at the ceiling, then at the floor. "I don't remember much anymore because of this damned Alzheimer's disease. My father was always 'Mr. Anderson, sir,' so I never used his first name. My mother's name was Mary… No, that was my ex-wife. I guess I don't remember my mother's first name either.

I had two brothers. We all had names that began with W—my father thought that was stylish, though we hated it. We were all W. Anderson."

Barely able to contain herself, Marie asked, "What were their names?"

Anderson paused again and looked around the room. Marie could not determine whether he was thinking about the question or had lost the thread of the conversation entirely. Eventually he spoke. "Well, my brothers. We were William, Warren, and Walton. I think that's right. It's been a long time since I've seen them."

"Which one were you?"

Anderson stared at the floor for what seemed like an eternity. "I suppose I should know my own name. Everyone here calls me Walton, so they must be right. But I have a vague recollection of being called William when I was young. We were often confused together by our teachers. I can't honestly answer your question."

"Mr. Anderson, this question is very important to me. Please think hard. Maybe it will help you if you think about who was the oldest and who was the youngest. Or do you have any family photos we can look at?"

Confused at first by the multiple questions, Anderson was slow to reply. "I used to have a photo of the three of us from the *New Mexican* newspaper. Father thought our names were so cute he told a reporter about it, and the paper published a picture of us when I was about fifteen. I think I was the oldest, but that was a long time ago. Walton was just a kid. I remember when he was born."

Marie took a deep breath. If the man in front of her was lucid at this moment, as he seemed to be, her suspicion could now be a plausible theory. But the uncertain memories of a man with Alzheimer's disease, who is not always lucid, would hardly serve as persuasive, or perhaps even admissible, evidence in court.

"Thank you. That is very helpful information. I hope you have a good day."

Marie excused herself and left for the Library. She was hoping the reference librarian had found something but came away empty-handed. Ms. Nuzzaco had been too busy. Marie told her about the possibility of a photo in the *New Mexican* of the three brothers—William, Warren, and Walton—probably about forty years ago, when they were teenagers. She surmised this concrete starting point, which increased likelihood of finding something, would further incentivize her. But the results would not be available before Marie returned to Montreal. She reminded Ms. Nuzzaco of her email address and left. It was already mid-afternoon.

Marie returned to her hotel, recovered her small suitcase from the concierge, and headed for the Albuquerque airport to catch her 5:35 p.m. flight. Just as she was about to board the plane, two local police officers presented themselves, carrying a warrant for her arrest for impersonating a police official. They would not accept her credentials on the spot. After a trip to police headquarters, she again presented her credentials, which they verified through their data systems. They apologized and released her. But she had missed her return flight.

Another text to Jon, this time explaining that she had missed her flight and now would leave Friday morning and be in the office Monday. This time, his reply was a terse "Got it." She returned to her hotel, checked in again, and treated herself to a nice dinner at Margarita's Tex-Mex Restaurant across the street.

Ready to turn in for the night, Marie undressed for bed while mulling over the latest revelations of these two extraordinary days.

What could have caused my bizarre arrest on impersonation charges? Is it a coincidence it came only just before my flight? Is someone trying to keep me here another night? Why would they want to do that?

Suddenly, Marie felt a surge of panic. She arranged the pillows under the bed covers so they gave the impression of someone asleep, then dressed and packed, walked out of the Quality Court Hotel without telling the reception desk, and checked into the Quarto Hotel across the street.

She arranged for a room with a window facing her Quality Court Hotel room. Too excited to sleep, she tried reading more of the WWII history she had begun on the plane. Around 1 am, she heard what seemed to be four muffled gunshots. She ran to the window. At first, she saw nothing. The lights in her old room went on momentarily. Then darkness and silence.

It was time to get out. Abandoning her rental car in the hotel parking lot, she took Lyft to the Albuquerque airport and boarded the next flight east: 4:30 am, to Tulsa, Oklahoma. From there, a morning flight to Chicago. She eventually arrived in Montreal Saturday afternoon, frightened and exhausted.

◦

Jon arrived at his cubicle early Monday morning to finish the terrorist interview reports. His annoyance and discomfort had turned into a stream of unusually hostile feelings toward Marie.

Her trip is going to make us both look bad. I foolishly updated her record when she first left, saying she was taking two days of sick leave and would be back on Friday. She didn't show up Friday morning or afternoon, and now she's still not here on Monday. I'll be forced to revise it to Monday afternoon, or maybe even Tuesday. It's awkward to be correcting the entry, and the computer saves a record of the original anyway, if anyone looked.

Why didn't she just ask for vacation days if that's what she wanted? She has more than enough. This way it looks like she was AWOL and I was covering for her. What would others think if she recommended me for bonus—or even a promotion—now? I need that money for a down payment to replace the old gasoline-powered wreck Linda is driving.

Jon's annoyance evolved into anxiety as Marie uncharacteristically failed to arrive as the morning hours passed. He always feared for her safety when she traveled alone. Particularly this trip to Santa Fe, where she was flying blind. Probably she found nothing except new shoes, but what if she did find something? Maybe too much to handle alone?

His feelings ran deeper than he wished to acknowledge. Marie was attractive, smart, and charming. While they sometimes disagreed, and both had strong opinions, their discussions never became unpleasant. They spent many hours together in the office and at meals when they traveled together.

He couldn't detect any sign that she even found him attractive. But what would others insinuate if they thought he was manipulating the attendance records to cover up her absence?

Looking haggard, Marie arrived in the office just before noon. Jon's anxiety, now relieved, turned into a poorly concealed annoyance. "Well, welcome home—finally. You promised you'd be back Friday, then no word Saturday or Sunday, and now you come in late on Monday.

"While you were enjoying Santa Fe, I finished the reports on our terrorist interviews without your help. And amended your official absence report. You owe me for this one. So what's the story?" Jon tried to make this last comment sound like a tease, but without much success.

"You won't believe what happened," Marie began. She poured out the events that had transpired Thursday night. There was no need to dramatize her account. The bare facts spoke for themselves.

Jon stared at her in disbelief. "Do you expect anyone to believe that story?" He paused, realizing that of course everything she had just told him was true. "What could have prompted all that? Okay. Let's start from the beginning. We need to make a record of it."

Marie walked him through every detail of the week's events: the suspicious photo in the Anderson file at the Home, the Wednesday conversation with Ms. Davis and her call to "William" Anderson, the visit to the Public Library to get old newspapers, her conversation with "Walton" Anderson on Thursday morning and her unproductive return to the Library. Then the dubious arrest and release, her return to her hotel room, the sudden intuition that she was in danger, the move across the street, the gunshots, and her hasty departure.

Working to regain her professional composure, she concluded, "I'm hoping the Library will yield some confirming information. Right now, I have too many suppositions to make a viable case.

"More important, we still don't know where Anderson's money came from. Until we know more about him, I think we must assume that the large sums involved came from somewhere else. Didn't you learn that Anderson is just a small-time criminal, a lackey for others? We need to see where the trail leads."

Jon quickly concurred. "You're right. We need to pursue this. Do you think whoever was after you the other night got access to your files? They must have had some information about your flight so they could to arrange the arrest. If you think you are still in danger, we need to do something about it. And in any case, keep your eyes open!"

Marie grimaced. "When I went to work as a plainclothes investigator, I didn't expect to be shot at." She paused, absorbing the implications of Jon's comments. "I suppose I should requisition a pistol and practice using it. You should too. Meanwhile, I'll talk to the boss about giving us some leeway to extend the Hartquist investigation."

Jon nodded, reluctantly. He had never felt the need for a weapon before. He wondered how upset Linda would be knowing he was going to start carrying one. She would not be happy at the idea he was even potentially in danger.

Marie also requested a new computer, changed her email address and all her passwords. Unfortunately, it was probably too late. She knew she was up against at least one professional criminal. If he, or someone for him, had hacked her account as soon as he knew her email address, it would have told him everything he needed to know.

Reading just the previous few days' emails would have given him information on her flight reservations to Montreal and her Quality Court hotel reservations. A little more searching would reveal her bank account, her home address, her family photos.

He would also know from her email communications that Jon Wolfe was her colleague and fully familiar with the Hartquist investigation. Whoever it was had found her flight reservations, so she must assume he had found the rest.

I wonder if I should really change my life: new apartment, new bank accounts, new version of my name, new job? She considered it, then defiantly concluded, *It would certainly be a lot of trouble, and I'm not going to let some criminal drive me out of the RCMP.*

She had changed her entire life once before, when she left her first husband in 2005. Now that she was happily married with a supportive husband and a job she loved, she wasn't about to rejigger it all in response to the fear of a physical threat.

Over the next several days, the Walton Anderson identification fell into place. The Santa Fe Public Library supplied the photo of the three Anderson children. Santa Fe Hospital records showed that it was William, not Walton, who showed the first signs of Alzheimer's about seven years earlier, in 2014. It was definitely William, not Walton, in the Pleasant Valley Home. Whether anyone at the Home knew of the erroneous identity was unclear. Ms. Davis had referred to "William" on the phone and had never seen the application, so most likely she didn't know.

The RCMP and other police records confirmed that Anderson was not a kingpin, but an agent for hire. He regularly committed crimes, ranging from smuggling to drug trafficking to illicit arms sales for others. No suspected murders on record. But he had clearly arranged these murders, and he may have poisoned Mark Miller himself.

The identity theft of the "Robert McKenzie" credit card and creation of a physical copy, accompanied by a fake passport, would have allowed Anderson to stay in the Hotel Ciputra, where he could poison Miller, directly or indirectly. Indonesian immigration records showed "Robert McKenzie" was in the country in June 2020 and registered at the hotel the time of Miller's murder.

But the case was far from resolved. Anderson's transfer of funds to the Stability bank account from the numbered account begged the question of where the numbered account's funds came from. Jon reviewed the Stability records again, this time looking for deposits rather than disbursements. All the money had been deposited in Chinese renminbi, at one time. Probably by Anderson. About $2,000,000.

With the cooperation of the Swiss authorities, Jon checked several Anderson bank accounts, some under William Anderson, others under Walton Anderson. One of the William Anderson accounts revealed a deposit of $750,000 on June 23, 2020. The path to Anderson was quickly established, although the money came from yet another Swiss numbered account. Analysis of the relevant signatures confirmed Anderson's connection to all of them.

Marie and Jon thoroughly documented the trail, but it didn't reveal where the money came from in the first place.

Marie was ready to move. "I think we have reasonable cause to arrest Anderson at this point. In fact, aside from the murders, the transfers of those large sums, the use of fraudulent passports and credit cards, and the fraudulent certifications in connection with the purchase of the chemicals, all of which we can show, are crimes in themselves."

Jon grimaced and shook his head no. "I wish it were as easy as that. He has committed several crimes, and we have the evidence to prove it. But most of them were in Indonesia, and foreign governments don't generally prosecute for extraterritorial crimes. There are no extradition treaties between Indonesia and Canada, the US, or Sweden."

Marie pushed back. "The murder of Dr. Hartquist took place on a Canadian-flag vessel. So did his use of a forged passport. Our courts have jurisdiction over those crimes."

Jon was still not convinced. "I'm not sure we have enough evidence to prove the murder charge beyond a reasonable doubt. We don't think that waiter, Xavier, did it, but won't the defense use his story to raise doubts in the jury's mind? And by the way, further demean Dr. Hartquist? And will a prosecutor really bother with a forged passport case if that's all we have?

"Anyway, we don't even know where Anderson is right now. He may be in some other country that doesn't extradite anyone anywhere. Or for all we know, he might even be right here in Montreal."

Jon instantly realized that his last conjecture should never have been spoken. Marie turned white with fear. She caught her breath. "I've been trying not to think about that," she whispered. "I haven't moved or changed my name or bank accounts, and I'm still sitting at the same desk here in the office.

"Getting rid of me—of us—would be a worthwhile activity for Anderson right now. It would set back the investigation at least for months, probably permanently.

New agents might never pick up the trail without the facts we've just begun to document.

"At the least, it would give Anderson more than enough time to take on a completely new identity and move to a safe location. We are in danger right here."

After a moment of stunned silence, they went back to working on whatever was on the top of their Inboxes. Marie was still deeply disappointed at their failure to get to the heart of the matter: who funded Anderson to commit these crimes? Her most depressing thought was that Anderson would permanently escape their net. If so, the case might never be successfully resolved.

Chapter 15

JAKARTA

The National Museum of Indonesia, which was founded in 1898 and significantly expanded and improved in recent decades, is an elegant and impressive structure, with a vast collection of Indonesia's diverse archeological, historical, and ethnic artifacts, well worth a thorough guided tour. Its importance as an expression of national pride is evident from its location in the formal heart of Jakarta, across the street from Merdeka Square (the location of the National Monument) and only a few blocks from the Presidential Palace.

President Erwan Kartawijaya, universally known in Indonesia as Wijaya when not present, used the Museum's second conference room on rare occasions for private meetings that do not appear on his official schedule. Sunday, May 23, 2021, was one of those occasions.

Wijaya had no shortage of matters to worry about—political maneuverings by the opposition and some in his own party; unsatisfactory economic growth that was unlikely to change before the next election; conflicts with Singapore, The Philippines, and China over trade and continental shelf boundaries. A thorough briefing paper on his upcoming meeting with the President of The Philippines had been sitting on his desk for two days now, but he hadn't had time to read past the summary page.

He had agreed to this meeting with Doyal and his colleagues anyway. He was especially curious because he knew that the three diplomats work together on climate change, yet Doyal specifically insisted that no one else attend, including the Indonesian Delegate to UN climate change negotiations. If he did not owe Doyal a favor and know him well enough to trust him, he would never have agreed to a meeting on these terms.

Wijaya had always prided himself on being a curious person, eager to explore something new or examine an old problem from a different angle. Physically small, he had excelled as a child and risen in the political ranks through the creativity and objectivity of his thinking, his openness to new ideas, and his gracious, balanced personality. The Presidency demanded every one of those skills, but too many of Indonesia's problems seemed simply insoluble, even by the most talented president.

Doyal, Ibrahim, and Panday arrived promptly at 10:00 am and were shown into the hidden conference room. President Kartawijaya arrived at 10:15 am, always preferring to be the last to arrive. "Welcome to Jakarta and the National Museum of Indonesia. Do take a tour if you have some time. It's quite enlightening. I hope your travels here were comfortable and you are enjoying the view from the Westin. I'm still amazed by it myself."

Ambassador Doyal began as planned, after introducing his colleagues. "Thank you, Your Excellency, for allowing us to meet with you under these circumstances, which must seem quite mysterious. We are indeed enjoying the Westin and the beauty of Jakarta. I have not been here since our last meeting four years ago, and the progress of your capital city in that time is impressive. I'm sure your work as Governor of the Jakarta District had a lot to do with its development.

"We don't want to waste your valuable time in chit-chat. What we are about to ask is complex and sensitive, and if you choose to say no, we will understand. But what we must ask, even before we reveal our proposal, is that you keep this conversation completely secret, as we will. Is that acceptable?"

Wijaya nodded his consent. Clearly, this meeting would be as unusual as he had hoped. Doyal continued with his carefully prepared opening statement.

> We are here to ask your help in saving your country and ours, our species, and life as we know it on our planet. Rising sea levels, increasingly intense typhoons, disruption of time-tested agricultural practices, the death of coral reefs and col-

lapse of dependent fisheries, and massive human displacement will be increasingly destructive for Indonesia and many other countries. But for our three island homelands, the effects of climate change are a death sentence.

For all the efforts of the international community, our home islands, with a combined population of more than three million people, can foresee only disaster ahead—inundated coastal communities, famines, millions of international refugees.

There is good reason to believe these consequences might occur much sooner than the one-hundred-year linear models project. And substantial evidence suggests that self-reinforcing, potentially irreversible, changes are already underway.

We believe we must take affirmative action ourselves to induce a pause in the rise in global temperatures. Climate intervention in the form of solar radiation management, known as SRM or atmospheric geoengineering, is the only means anyone has conceived that could achieve that objective right now.

A small fleet of specially equipped planes spreading a veil of calcite particles in the troposphere could neutralize the atmosphere's growing heat absorption by increasing the earth's reflectivity and by the light-scattering effect of the particles.

Creating a tropospheric veil does not actually take significant physical resources, less than US$10 billion. We have secured the necessary funding, from sources that we cannot disclose, but which we know are reliable.

What it does take is political resolve. Resolve to bypass the current international institutions, to ignore the risk that other nations will object for their own narrow reasons, to disregard the qualms of overcautious scientists and skeptical or self-interested political and industrial leaders. Resolve to take the risks inherent in the success, or failure, of this secret effort to change the disastrous current course of human history.

We have come to you because you and Indonesia are in the best position to facilitate this project. Indonesian islands have many small airfields from which to conduct the missions, the geography to keep them hidden, and an overall level of economic activity that would camouflage the acquisition of the necessary equipment and materials as routine transactions.

Doyal paused to give the President a moment to assimilate this unanticipated concept. Wijaya's involuntary reaction was a look of skepticism and amazement. Those feelings were articulated in an appropriately politic manner.

"I understand that you are deeply concerned. Rising seas and changes in the weather and climate are threatening to both your countries and mine. I have been following climate change issues for some years, and I have a good understanding of them. My delegate to the Paris Accords and subsequent Conferences of Parties assures me that we and others are doing enough. Indonesia will survive. In addition, you may have overlooked how dependent our current economy is on exports by our oil, natural gas, and lumber industries.

"As I understand it, you are suggesting that we defy the international consensus on how to mitigate climate change, take unilateral action that will affect the climate of every nation on the planet, and disregard the lack of scientific consensus on the advisability of such a venture. Instead, you assume a much more radical threat that is unproven, and you proceed as if you know better than anyone else in the world what must be done. How can anyone justify doing that?"

Panday intervened, cautiously.

"Yes, Your Excellency, we are asking a lot, but our countries are literally drowning right now. Someone needs to throw us a life preserver, without first debating for years whether it is the best course of action or whether some other alternative approach would be more cost-effective.

"No government anywhere has stepped forward to offer even a portion of our three million people new homes. The illogical fear of foreign terrorists and thugs, incited by too many political leaders, makes the likelihood of open doors increasingly unlikely. I daresay that you and your people would have an even more negative response to a suggestion that you take in all our citizens as refugees.

"You are not the only leader who could help us, but you and your country are the best alternative, both for the reasons mentioned, and because your people, tens of millions of ordinary citizens, will also suffer greatly from the consequences of global warming.

"Your strategic economic and political interests are at stake as well. If Indonesia's marine boundaries are redrawn when a significant percentage of your minor outer islands have disappeared, your boundaries and resources will shrink dramatically. You are currently disputing these boundaries with at least one of your neighbors, Singapore, which is continually filling in its coastlines. Before long, you will have problems with all your neighbors. Given the offshore resources at stake, military confrontations are not only possible, but probable.

"Finally, we came to you first because we believe that you have the intelligence and imagination and courage to act. We hope you won't disappoint us."

Afraid to let the President answer immediately, Ibrahim began speaking even before the sound of Panday's words faded away.

"Let me add a few additional considerations.

"First, we believe you can protect yourself and your government from international repercussions by allowing us to work through Pertamina or one of Indonesia's other state-owned enterprises. Several of your SOEs have operations that require planes and materials of the kind we would need. This project can be easily disguised.

"Second, we do not expect or need an answer today. We know you will want to consult your environmental and foreign policy advisors before you decide. We only ask that you not tell them why you are inquiring.

"Third, I think you will be surprised at the deep pessimism that underlies the façade of optimism projected by the leaders of China, Europe, and Japan, and of course, your own diplomats. The world simply does not have this problem under control.

"We hope on reflection your answer will be favorable. We know that if you agree, many details will need to be addressed. We look forward to seeing you, or whoever you designate, when you are ready."

Wijaya had never imagined that this clandestine meeting would involve such radical ideas or result in such serious demands. He looked down for a moment, sighed, then stood.

"Thank you for coming. I recognize the seriousness of the problem, and I am flattered by your confidence in me and my country. I will think about your request and be back in touch with you when I have a definitive answer."

To the diplomats, Wijaya's noncommittal answer presaged a formal "no" after a decent interval.

———◦———

President Kartawijaya walked out of the National Museum into the sunlight of a beautiful May afternoon, heralding the beginning of dry weather and clear skies after months of rain. He decided to walk back to the Palace alone (aside from his security detail) and take advantage of the few moments to mull over the three diplomats' scheme.

He remained incredulous at what had just been proposed, given the scientific risks and inevitable political repercussions. *It sounds more like a desperate grasp for some Elixir of Eternal Life than a real-world plan. But the dangers of global warming to their countries, Indonesia, and the world are apparent, and nothing on the international horizon seems likely to change the current trajectory. They are right about that. I suppose I should at least give the matter deeper thought. This month is committed to budget decisions, political rallies, and media appearances to shore up support for my tax reform and budget proposals. Last July's re-election to the presidency gave me a clear victory, but I still need the support of the public and local business and political leaders to ensure the adoption and implementation of my legislation.*

First things first. Saving Indonesia will be hard enough. Saving the world will have to wait.

Chapter 16

JAKARTA

Three weeks later, President Kartawijaya returned from visits to the key provincial capitals, confident that he had built substantial, and hopefully sufficient, support for his budget and tax reform programs. Now more relaxed, he set aside some time to begin thinking seriously about the audacious scheme—it could hardly even be called a plan—that the three AOSIS ambassadors had put before him.

His travels had foreshadowed even more clearly the beginnings of climate catastrophes—eroding beaches and urban waterfronts; increased flood damage to villages and infrastructure; declining fishery and crop yields and resulting higher unemployment among fishermen and farmers; increases in property crimes and random sectarian violence.

Geological subsidence combined with sea-level rise was causing the inundation of many tiny islands—islands that were unimportant economically but serve as the baseline for Indonesia's exclusive economic and fisheries zone.

And the future of Jakarta itself was in grave doubt.

After a few more weeks of intermittent reading about the subject, Wijaya was eager for greater insight into the risks and prospects for success of an SRM veil. How could he obtain the views of his experts without raising any suspicions of Indonesian involvement, even among his most loyal staff?

He pondered various ruses to accomplish this result. After outlining a few options on his tablet and evaluating each one, he formulated an approach he hoped would generate balanced advice without revealing the possibility of Indonesia's actual involvement in any crazy scheme.

Wijaya scheduled a meeting with his key officials for Thursday afternoon, the end of the last full work day of the Muslim week. He entered the conference room a little late, as usual.

His subordinates were inured to waiting for him, but this time they were sitting uncomfortably around the table. *Whose meeting is this, and why haven't I even been informed of the subject?* each wondered silently.

Wijaya's opening statement began with a note of thanks.

> I realize it's the end of a long June, and you have no idea why I called you here. I appreciate your commitment and hard work. When you hear the purpose of this meeting, I know you will find the conversation stimulating, even though you must remember that this discussion never even took place.

I imagine you all know each other, but let me introduce you anyway. This is Ryamizir Pabamyo, Assistant Minister of Foreign Affairs for Environment and Science; Hidupu Linggankun, Deputy Minister of Defense for Policy Planning; and Preban Ryacidu, Deputy Minister of Environment for Climate Change. There is a lot of expertise and intellectual talent around this table. I need all of it.

I'm sure you all know about the tragic death of Dr. Ilsa Hartquist, a dedicated scientist and passionate advocate for immediate action to postpone at least some effects of global warming through a program of solar radiation management, creating a reflective veil by dispersing chemicals into the troposphere.

I have received intelligence that her death has spawned growing mainstream scientific discussion in various circles and in the media, encouraging the world's governments to initiate the experimental SRM veil she recommended. I've also heard that a few States may be prepared to proceed on their own, without waiting for approval from the various international agencies that would claim jurisdiction. They believe the world cannot afford the inevitable years of delay and uncertainty inherent in public global decision-making.

If a project went forward on that basis, I doubt that it could remain secret for long. There are too many leaks and too many reconnaissance satellites in the sky. The moment it became public, I believe it could easily become the most visible and controversial international issue of this decade.

At that point, we are likely to have allies and partners on both sides of the many contentious substantive and international governance questions associated with SRM. Like many others, Indonesia will be on the spot to take sides on both the process and the merits. We will certainly be pressured by various allies and partners to support their views or pay a price.

So in anticipation of something like that happening, I have three questions I want each of you to address briefly this evening

1. Purely as a matter of science and engineering, is there a reasonable

prospect that an SRM experimental project, as some would prefer to call it, will succeed?

2. Assuming it would accomplish the objective, will Indonesia benefit from the project, environmentally and economically?

3. What diplomatic, political, and military risks are entailed for the States that are involved in such a project without any prior global consensus or consultation?

Having laid out the issues, Wijaya added a brief postscript. "I need to make an urgent phone call, so I will step out of the room for a few moments. That will allow you time to organize your individual perspectives before anyone speaks.

"Please don't consult with each other in my absence. I am asking for your completely extemporaneous views. I don't want a consensus. I want your individual judgments.

"And despite your respective Departmental jurisdictions and individual backgrounds, I want each of you to address all three questions as if you know everything about everything—that is, as if you were President."

This last little quip was accompanied by a smile. The President rose, excused himself, and headed for the bathroom across the hall. He relieved himself and then called his wife to say he would be late again.

Five minutes later, he paused and drew a deep breath at the Conference Room door. *This could be one of the most interesting meetings I've conducted as president, even if I don't learn anything new,* he mused to himself. *We'll see just how clever these PhDs and politicians are when they are without staff to think things through for them and prepare talking points in advance.*

Reentering the conference room, the President surveyed the stressed faces around the table. He sat down and waited a moment, as they tapped their last notes onto their tablets.

"Who would like to go first?" he asked. After a few more moments of silence, he smiled mischievously. "Don't all volunteer at once!" Of course, everyone would prefer to go last, or at least not first. No one wanted to be openly challenged, or even subtly criticized, by later speakers as ignorant or illogical.

"No one? Then let's start with the Environment Ministry. It fits best in your pigeonhole, Preban, though the decision would affect every aspect of our government, not to mention our personal lives. What can you tell us?"

Preban Ryacidu, a former university professor and a climate scientist by training, was normally mild-mannered, deferential, and deliberate. He began speaking slowly at first, but soon he was talking so fast that the others could barely follow his train of thought, and he himself was short of breath.

He started by describing the crucial character of the climate problem for Indonesia and the world. Then he turned directly to the desirability of an SRM veil.

"Dr. Hartquist was absolutely right that great dangers threaten human civilization right now. Instead of going forward, Indonesia and most other nations are already beginning to slide backward toward poverty as climate change takes its toll. A tropospheric veil would hypothetically delay these disasters by putting a tropospheric 'translucent mirror' above some or all of the planet, reflecting and scattering into space some of the sunlight that now reaches earth's surface. If it works, it could avert or at least postpone the disaster that awaits us all.

"There are several crucial gaps in our knowledge about this idea, however. Releasing microscopic liquid or solid chemical bits into the troposphere is well within current technical capability. But the design of an SRM veil project would need to address a variety of unknowns: What chemicals should be used? In what quantities? With what side effects? How often? How long will the effects last once we stop? Can we ever stop once we start? The scientific and engineering communities barely know the right questions, let alone the right answers.

"If the project inadequately or too slowly increases the earth's albedo, disaster could strike while we are waiting for the experiment to show us the right levels of action. If it is too effective, we could conceivably find ourselves in another ice age that would be every bit as disastrous for humanity.

"Worse, if unforeseen consequences do not appear for a long time, we may only realize that we have overshot or undershot the mark when it is too late to restore the right balance. Either way, we may have done more harm than good.

"Even a perfectly functioning veil would have both physical limitations and political drawbacks. Physically, SRM doesn't stop the increase in carbon dioxide released into the atmosphere or oceans. Ocean acidification caused by carbon dioxide is already having measurable adverse consequences for our fisheries aside from the temperature increase. The many millions of our people who depend on fishing for their sustenance and livelihood will find themselves in need.

"Politically, SRM could give policymakers and the public an excuse to postpone painful actions to eliminate carbon dioxide emissions, which requires phasing out powerful carbon fuel industries. I don't need to tell you the impact on our economy of shutting down the Indonesian oil industry. There is every reason to fear that the benefits of SRM, even if it works perfectly, would be squandered, and merely postpone by a few decades some of the worst consequences. But at least it would provide the world a chance to get things right before we reach some unantici-pated point of irreversibility."

When Preban stopped for a moment to take a breath, Wijaya interrupted. "Thank you. That's very helpful infor-mation, even though it doesn't fully answer my three ques-tions. Before I ask anyone else to answer, does anyone around the table disagree with Preban's summation?"

After a few moments of silence, Assistant Foreign Affairs Minister Ryamizir Pabamyo raised her hand. A career foreign service officer, educated in Amsterdam and over the years posted to senior diplomatic posts in the world's major capitals—an articulate speaker, cunning in bureaucratic infighting. Seeing no objection, she pro-ceeded, softly but with intensity.

"Preban's summary ignores the international polit-ical ramifications of any unauthorized SRM project. Disregarding the established international institutions and procedures will be considered a breach of trust and a vio-lation of international law. What we like to call the 'world community' is far from homogeneous in its views on cli-mate change, and various interests and nations are likely to react strongly, both positively and negatively.

"In some quarters, this project could be interpreted as an act of aggression that threatens the livelihood and sur-vival of various nations, and certainly of various industries. The possibility of retaliatory economic or military action is quite real. Where that would leave even the most sophisticated scientific effort, which opponents will no doubt call a 'half-baked gamble with our lives and our planet,' is at best uncertain.

"What happens if the project is suddenly halted? What if the lives of some country's pilots or ground support personnel are lost in a hostile military attack? To me, this whole project looks reckless and dangerous in every respect."

At that point, Deputy Defense Minister Hidupu Linggankun, a gruff military officer for most of his career, though now technically a civilian, intervened.

"Excellency, I don't know where this idea came from, but I agree completely with Ryamizir. We shouldn't imagine for a moment that this project could be secret even in the earliest stages. One or more foreign governments and various NGOs would document the very first flight. Satellites are so cheap these days that anyone with modest resources can track any activity in any country. Greenpeace International has recently acquired its own space observation capabilities.

"How we vote in the UN or what positions we take in the diplomatic world are of no interest to the Defense Ministry. But physical participation in such a scheme by any country would be reckless and foolish, an open invitation to Singapore, Russia, China, or even the new President of the United States to take military action against not just the aircraft but also the bases from which they fly. The attackers would tell their domestic constituents that their country has won a national military victory of which they should be proud. Our limited budget doesn't give us the military resources to deter or prevent an attack. Any defensive response in kind on our part would be suicidal militarily, and failing to respond militarily would likely topple the government. I don't see why we are even discussing it."

Preban turned to face Ryamizir and Hidupu and began lecturing them like the professor he once was:

"No one has suggested that Indonesia participate in any SRM veil project. But as spokesmen for your departments and leaders committed to protect the welfare of our country, just how do you propose to defend Indonesia from the loss of land and offshore resources as hundreds of our islands drown in rising seas, from the destruction caused by increasingly frequent typhoons and floods, from the decline in agricultural production from unpredictable variability in the weather every year, and from the slow but inevitable stagnation of our economy, which together will lead to social chaos and political unrest? Climate change may not technically fall within your respective jurisdictions, but that doesn't mean you can ignore it. Diplomatically, the world isn't making anywhere near the necessary progress in eliminating carbon emissions, and the odds of a near-term disruptive catastrophe appear higher in each new climate study. Domestic economic interests are keeping Indonesia from even making a satisfactory contribution to the existing, global effort.

"Our military capability seems to be always too small for any practical action or reliable protection of our territory. The claimed weakness of our military has been a convenient argument for increasing the Defense Ministry's budget for over a decade, but somehow the military still can't protect us. So are we just going to sit back and let our people suffer as the world drowns and Indonesia's economy collapses?"

Preban's outburst was too much for the crusty Hidupu to accept in silence. "Next time you persuade the President to hold a meeting on a crazy idea like this one, at least don't blindside the rest of us. It would be common courtesy to let us know in advance what will be discussed."

At that point Wijaya, disturbed by the divisive tone and unproductive direction of the discussion, leaned forward and took control of the meeting, before Preban could begin the inevitable rejoinder.

"My friends, let's stop here. It's late and we are tired. I called this meeting without the urging of anyone here. Perhaps it was unrealistic of me to expect coherent, balanced recommendations without time for sufficient preparation. These issues are very complex. Their interrelationship calls for a broad perspective that doesn't naturally emerge from professionals trained to view the world and advocate policies that reflect the needs and perspectives of their departments.

"Let's reassemble next week, same time and place, and come prepared to consider this problem from a national and global perspective. Please, nothing at all on paper or in electronic formats, and no emails or other written communications. I hope that among this small group we can all remember that these meetings never occurred. Thank you for your loyal support."

The meeting adjourned. Those present departed in sullen silence. They quickly realized that from the President's perspective they had all failed. Hoping to do better next time, they spent many hours preparing for the next meeting. Their electronic research tools produced mountains of documents to support their analysis, organize their arguments, and defend their original positions.

Their conclusions, however, were unchanged in substance, only more subtly articulated and more cogently presented. Anyone reading the various papers would see how much easier it is to argue for one's preconceived position than it is to view the world from a more holistic perspective.

Over the next few days, Wijaya found himself preoccupied with the matter of an SRM veil, consciously and subconsciously. Suddenly, the choices became clear to him.

Another meeting and more discussion will never answer my questions or produce a consensus. It will just entrench everyone's explicit or implicit but already evident positions. Worse, the fact that the questions would have been discussed at a second meeting with me would increase the likelihood of a leak, sooner or later.

The next morning, Wijaya instructed his scheduler to call Preban, Ryamizir, and Hidupu. "Tell them I've canceled the meeting, and it will not be rescheduled. No subsequent meetings are planned. No papers on this subject should be prepared."

The recipients of the calls, already well into polishing their papers, filed them away for future use. The work was too valuable to be simply discarded.

Wijaya had reached some conclusions on his own. *First, I alone must make this decision, yes or no. That's what the people elect presidents to do.*

If I say no, that will be the end of it for Indonesia. If I say yes, my own path will be easy. I'll call my friend Ariki, ask him to set up a separate company to conduct the operation. I'll warn him that if questioned, I and my government will vigorously deny any knowledge of or involvement in the new company's activities.

But Wijaya was not yet ready to make the ultimate decision. That would take some further deliberation. Every day, he devoted an hour, or as much of an hour as he could afford, to reading or conscious contemplation of some aspect of the problem.

Two weeks later, on Saturday, July 17, Wijaya concluded, though not without serious doubts, that he should proceed. Using his personal phone, he called Ariki Martioto, the CEO of Indonesian Fuel Company (IFC).

Ariki was an old friend who had supported his election to the presidency and turned out to be an excellent manager. Wijaya had been happy to reward him with the position of Managing Director at IFC, then a state-owned Indonesian oil distribution company. Martioto had transformed IFC into a private company by buying out the government's interest with a combination of earnings and borrowed money. He was hoping to make an initial public offering soon to pay off the debt.

Wijaya began deferentially, thanking him again for his friendship and his support in past elections. He vaguely promised to include Martioto and his wife in a State Dinner with the new American President when he comes to Jakarta. Martioto, in return, thanked Wijaya again for appointing him to run IFC and reiterated their enduring friendship.

The true purpose of the call took only a few sentences.

"My dear friend Ambassador Anarood Doyal, a senior diplomat from Mauritius who has been very helpful to us, could use IFC's help on a small environmental project that will require several aircraft and support, along with various specialty chemicals. He has funding from unnamed outside sources to cover all the costs. Assuming you can work out a meaningful course of action, I suggest you set up a free-standing corporate entity to implement it.

"Please keep in mind that his project has no connection at all to the Indonesian government, which doesn't have any involvement or knowledge of it whatsoever. Except for me, that is true, and it is what we will insist to the media and anyone else who might ask. I'll have Ambassador Doyal call you. Please assist him in any way you can."

It was not the first call from Wijaya asking for a favor. Martioto knew not to ask for more information. Presumably it would come from the Ambassador.

Next, Wijaya called Doyal. "Good morning. I have a positive answer for you. Mr. Ariki Martioto, the CEO of Indonesian Fuel Company, is expecting your call. IFC is not Pertamina, but at this time it's privately owned, so its activities have much less public exposure.

"His personal phone number is +62 021-755-9107. It has been a pleasure to know you. Unfortunately, I don't expect to have the pleasure of your company ever again, at least on this matter. I wish you good luck."

Wijaya leaned back in his chair. *Well*, he mused, *I hope I made the right choice. Maybe I have just saved civilization. And if it fails, it is unlikely to produce an outcome worse than our present trajectory. Civilization will probably continue on the path to its own destruction, despite my efforts. At least I will have helped demonstrate one way that doesn't work.*

He smiled and took a sip of his best coffee. A real celebration would come much later, if at all. *Now it's time to get back to my day job, saving Indonesia.*

Chapter 17

YANGON

Doyal could barely believe his ears. He had received no communication whatever from Wijaya or anyone else in Indonesia for more than a month. He had slowly given up hope for a "yes," and had happily shed the anxiety that went with entanglement in this unlikely scheme. The anxiety immediately returned, as the uncomfortable potential for personal and political disaster suddenly appeared more imminent.

Ibrahim and Panday had counseled patience. In truth, they had little choice. They saw few other candidate States for the operational side of the project, and none of the diplomats had sufficient connections with them to obtain the intimate audience that Wijaya had given them.

Now they had a favorable answer, or at least the beginnings of one. Remembering the differences of opinion about how to present their case to Wijaya, Doyal decided to call Martioto, not just to set up a meeting, but to firmly establish himself as the primary point of contact in the process, and implicitly the person with authority to shut the project down if necessary.

Martioto hardly spent any longer on the phone than Wijaya had. Doyal barely got past his name before Martioto took over the conversation. He did not ask any questions.

"I understand you expected to meet with IFC. The meeting you want will not be with IFC, but with representatives of a new corporation, Sky Enterprises Sdn. Bhd. (SE) It will take place in Yangon. SE's leader will bring a few colleagues, and probably his wife. The SE representatives can arrive on a Thursday evening, either August 12 or 19, and stay through the weekend. I trust one of these dates will work for you. Ask for Mohamed Abdul Nazri, from Malaysia, at the ParkRoyal Yangon, on the Executive Level. If the weather is good, you can walk around the Shwedagon Pagoda. I'm told it's extraordinary, though I've never seen it. Please send a text message to this number identifying the more convenient meeting date."

Doyal hardly knew what to say. He had worked for the last two hours planning how to explain the project as succinctly as possible, but Martioto clearly didn't want to hear anything about it.

He quickly recovered his diplomatic poise. "Excellent. I'll talk to my two colleagues, both also from small island States, and text you one of the two dates you identified. Thank you. We look forward to getting to know the Sky Enterprises team." The call ended.

In a moment Doyal was on the phone to Ibrahim. "We will meet again, this time at the Thamada Hotel, Yangon, not far from the ParkRoyal Yangon, where our newest friends will be staying. Can you arrive on a Tuesday, either August 10 or 17, and stay for a long weekend? We'll need more time to prepare for this one."

Ibrahim was thrilled. "You heard from our exalted best friend? What does he want to know now? Will he really meet us in Yangon?"

"Yes and no. I heard from him, but he never wants to see us himself. We'll be meeting with Mohamed Abdul Nazri, an executive of a company called Sky Enterprises Sdn. Bhd. As soon as we establish the date, I'll get hotel rooms for us. Come prepared. We must be able to lay out a credible project plan—timeline, equipment, materials, and personnel needs, everything. I'll be trying to do the same. We'll only have a few days to reconcile our information and presentations."

Ibrahim was still absorbing the news. "Miraculous! Yes, we do have a lot of work to do. We'll need to identify a real project director. And who can provide us the scientific advice we need? We could really use Dr. Hartquist right now. She would have been excited to help. Maybe we can persuade Professor Feith to provide scientific support."

Ibrahim paused to consult his calendar. "My calendar says either week is OK for me."

Doyal seized the opening to slow him down. "Yes, we have many more questions than answers, and we will need help to sort through them. Unfortunately, the loss of Dr. Hartquist can't be fixed.

"As you well know, this whole project needs utmost secrecy. One word to the wrong person and we could all be on the gallows for trying to save the world. At this point we must not confide in anyone, so be very careful how you get help. I'll talk to Panday and get back to you with the date and exact places."

Doyal's next call was to Panday. He delivered the same news. Panday was as dumbfounded as Doyal and as excited as Ibrahim. They agreed on August 13, 2021. "Sooner is better," Panday remarked. "The uncertainty is a serious distraction. We need to know where we stand."

———◦◦◦———

Traveling on their personal passports and feeling like rogue undercover agents, the diplomats met for dinner the evening of their arrival on Tuesday. The less pretentious Thamada Hotel restaurant was almost empty, and they chose a table unlikely to have patrons nearby. They refrained from discussing the problematic questions they were facing.

Wednesday was an intense work day, trying to sketch out the basic elements of the project. Their lack of technical expertise reinforced the tension of the situation. Their differing views on tactics emerged forcefully over lunch.

Doyal, who had never expected their project to get even this far, was most distressed. The idea of pulling the plug on the whole effort seemed increasingly appealing.

"The truth is we have no idea what we are asking Sky Enterprises to do. They don't need to worry about costs, if they accept that we have money. But how many planes, for how long, using what materials, with what oversight? We're diplomats, not atmospheric chemists or aircraft engineers. Why should they trust our judgment about what must be done?"

Ibrahim, now more excited than ever about their prospects for getting action, countered those arguments with his characteristic enthusiasm. "We don't really need to know. We do know we will need to start small, a handful of planes and small quantities of materials. We must tell them that this is an experimental, iterative project, that we will be feeling our way forward, and we will cut back or stop if we see the slightest sign that the results are veering off in an undesirable direction, not as predicted."

Panday was also agitated.

"We can't afford to be seen as bumbling diplomats with a vague 'big idea' and no sense of how to carry it out. Ibrahim's approach is of course the only sensible way to proceed. We can say that we could not work out the details in the abstract. We don't know such basic facts as where we would be flying from and what physical facilities and resources will be needed or available to us.

"We need to get them to do some talking about their facilities and operational capabilities for implementing this project. Once we have some information about the practical limits of the applicable parameters, we and they can begin thinking constructively about how to calibrate the scope and timing of our experiment—how many flights, what quantity of materials, what control systems, what techniques for evaluating the impact. They can't expect us to have those answers before we even know the scope of their capacity or commitment."

At that point, Doyal put his face in his hands, then began whispering:

"Let's admit it, my friends. We are far out on a limb that cannot bear the weight. If our efforts come to light before we can get the project off the ground and show some results, we are all doomed. Worse, starting small is not viable for long. Either we do enough to get some tangible changes in conditions or our effort is worse than nothing. We'll just discredit ourselves and the whole rationale behind the project.

"The likelihood of being able to keep all this activity secret is slim. We already know we'll be watched by Wang Shu, and do we believe she won't be reporting back to her superiors? And don't forget the eyes in the sky. Won't they see our planes and wonder what they are doing?

"What if some trigger-happy general decides to shoot one down? The Korean Air 007 disaster of 1983 took place when you were a child, Ibrahim, but a Russian air force commander mistakenly authorized the destruction of a civilian Boeing 747 flying in Russian airspace, fearing it was a military flight. He killed 269 innocent people. He was disciplined, but that didn't bring anyone back to life.

"And what if our first little experiments are too successful? Instead of drowning, we could cause a brief ice age that destroys all agricultural production for a few years, killing literally billions of people. We're completely unprepared for this meeting. Maybe it's not too late to stop. Let's just postpone it until we can put together at least the rudiments of a sensible roadmap."

Ibrahim was about to begin a vigorous counterattack, but Panday, sensing that would be a disaster, spoke first.

"You're right, Doyal, that we are not adequately prepared, nor do we even have the necessary knowledge to prepare properly. But this is a one-time opportunity. Our newest friend went out of his way to set up this meeting at our request. We can't let him down or embarrass him by walking away. We claimed this matter is urgent and practical, and the damage being done is irreversible. We can't now say we need several weeks or months to figure out what we were talking about doing. Anyway, we don't even know who we are meeting with, what questions will be asked, or what answers will be demanded. At worst, we can say we are pleased with their interest and eager to know their capabilities. And then we will get back to them with more specific program plans."

A server interrupted the discussion with a request for their lunch orders. Relieved, they quietly took turns ordering. They ate in silence.

After this respite, they agreed that Doyal would open the conversation. Then Ibrahim would outline the technical aspects of the project as far as possible. Panday would serve as the closer, getting whatever commitments were possible and outlining the next steps. They again promised not to contradict each other unless it was absolutely necessary. If they couldn't agree among themselves on what must be done, why would anyone else take risks on their advice?

Thursday afternoon they came together in what was in effect a joint rehearsal, with each one speaking in turn and the others not interrupting, and only at the end offering practical stylistic and organizational suggestions. Each was responsible for his own substance, and they agreed once more that unity was more important than precision.

That afternoon Doyal left a message at the ParkRoyal Hotel desk for Mohamed Abdul Nazri. He gave his cell phone number, but not his hotel or room number. Around 7 pm, Doyal received the call they had been waiting for. He happily accepted the proposed schedule for two meetings:

"Let's get together tomorrow afternoon and meet again on Saturday morning at 10. We can't do real business on Friday, of course. But a walk around the Shwedagon Pagoda around 1:30 Friday would be a pleasant way to make one another's acquaintance. I'll be at the north entrance to the Pagoda in the lobby at the top of the elevators with my wife, who will have a red tote bag. A few hours wandering around should be sufficient." The Friday gathering came together as planned. The day was sunny and warm, and the golden pagoda sparkled.

Spotting the red tote bag, Doyal initiated the contact. "Good afternoon. I'm Anarood Doyal. We are here in accordance with the exchange of messages yesterday. I suggest we proceed with a leisurely walk around this spectacular shrine. It's well over two thousand years old and is said to contain hairs from the head of the Buddha himself. If it's agreeable, you and I can chat for about thirty minutes, then Ibrahim here will walk with you for a while, then Panday.

"I imagine your wife will be happiest exploring the shrine alone, but one of us will accompany her if you prefer. In any case one of us will always be within sight of her. We can carry her tote bag if you like. I hope these suggestions are acceptable."

After consulting his wife in a language Doyal did not recognize, he replied, "That's a well-conceived approach. I think it will work efficiently. My wife is happy to walk alone, knowing that she has protection nearby. She'll carry her own bag. Shall we go?"

The two hours passed quickly. The three diplomats hewed to the schedule, which allowed about forty-five minutes each, as they had planned. The two groups parted with friendly, ingratiating words on both sides.

When the diplomats shared their experiences over dinner, they were satisfied that the conversations had gone well. No hostile questions were asked. No skeptical comments filled the pauses. Before parting, they had reiterated the plan to meet in the Bangkok Room at the ParkRoyal Hotel, beginning at 10 the next morning.

Nevertheless, they were concerned that their combined conversations hadn't taught them very much about SE's ideas on the practicality or merits of the project or the resource constraints they would face. The diplomats looked forward to the next day's meeting with great anxiety. It could make or break the whole project.

The next morning, they went immediately to the ParkRoyal Yangon and ate a substantial breakfast at the elegant and bountiful buffet, internally rehearsing their answers to the tough questions they anticipated.

At 10, they made their way to the Bangkok Room, a small conference room well stocked with beverages and snacks to last for the day. As they looked around the room, their reaction was astonishment and disbelief.

Sitting in the room were two South Asian men and a Chinese woman, none of whom were the man they had talked with for two hours yesterday at the Shwedagon

Pagoda. Doyal was momentarily speechless, thinking to himself, *Who are these people? What do they know of yesterday's conversation? Did we waste our time yesterday, or are we wasting our time today?*

Their disorientation was not relieved when the first man introduced himself. "Welcome. I'm Mohamed Abdul Nazri. I'm an engineer by training." The second man called himself Abdulla bin Ami, a project manager. The woman called herself Erkinay, an unlikely name for a person with her Chinese features. She described herself as a budget officer.

Doyal wanted to ask the obvious question, "Who were we talking to yesterday?" But he knew better. He stared down his colleagues, who of course itched to learn the same thing, thinking, *If they want us to know, they will tell us, if not, there is no point in asking.*

Today the questions for the diplomats were numerous and thorough:

- Where is the money coming from? How much is available?
- How many aircraft will you need? What kind of modification do they need to serve your purposes? How do you plan to disguise them? Who will be your pilots?
- Who are your scientific advisors? What is the experiment protocol? How will you measure results? What constitutes success?

- What is your schedule? How quickly do you need to begin? Who will be your full-time point of contact?

- Do you expect to run this project, or just provide support when we request it?

The three did their best to present their prepared answers, without revealing the source or precise amount of the money or their complete lack of a technical support team or equipment. Ibrahim took the lead in responding, relying on his prepared statement:

> We can't reveal anything about the money except that I have a more than US$10 billion line of credit from a small Taipei bank backed by an anonymous donor with essentially unlimited funds.

> We hope to start as soon as possible. The aircraft will of course need modification, but since we don't know the specifications of the planes, we can't give you a more detailed answer. They must be able to fly to the Arctic and return, and identify and stay within the troposphere, a narrow layer of the atmosphere at around twenty-two kilometers.

Within that thin layer, the temperature and gravitational balance is stable, so the dispersed materials will not quickly scatter upward into outer space or downward toward the earth by gravity and natural convection currents. The troposphere's altitude and thickness are not uniform, so the aircraft will need special sensors and automatic controls to ensure that they adjust their altitude as necessary.

As for the materials, there is substantial scientific literature evaluating the possibilities. Stanford Professors Feith and Keach propose calcite, a constituent of limestone, which could counter ozone loss by neutralizing emissions-borne acids in the atmosphere, while also reflecting light and cooling the planet. You may have read that Professor Feith had proposed sulfate particles or nonreactive diamond dust as the best material, but by 2019, he had changed his mind and was recommending chemically active calcite to avoid damaging the ozone layer.

Our intention is to proceed based on the most mainstream scientific approach to the project. We're interested in minimizing the number of uncertainties as we know them. We believe the primary obstacles to global action on this matter are political and institutional, not scientific. We expect you will wish to provide the onsite project manager, and that will be acceptable to us. We assume you will want to use your own pilots and support staff, but they must be completely reliable in preserving the secrecy of the project, as they will soon realize what the project is doing.

It would be better to use drones if you feel confident they will be able to carry out the task. That would aid in preserving secrecy and eliminate the risk of injury or death in case of accident or outside interference. These will be very long flights, and the stress on a live pilot or observer would be great. We expect that at some point after our experiment is working, that fact will be evident to the world in weather data and observable effects. But we will need complete data to be able to explain exactly what we did and what effects we observed from our flights.

Doyal will be the sole point of contact
for you. No one else is to even know there
is a project or experiment. The fewer people who know anything at all the better.

The meeting continued for over four hours without any break. When it became obvious that the diplomats had elaborated their concept to the level of detail of which they were capable, Nazri closed the meeting.

"We appreciate that you have come a long way to meet with us. We also realize that this project is a meaningful concept, and its impact will be global, whether it works as planned or not. We will make our decisions with that thought in mind. Thank you for your time and effort."

He did not provide any guidance about whether, when, or how they would proceed.

The three diplomats staggered out of the meeting room. Exhausted, anxious, and feeling hungry, since none of them had relaxed enough to touch the ample food available in the conference room. After a brief respite in their hotel rooms, they returned to the restaurant for dinner, then adjourned to Doyal's room to evaluate the afternoon's conversations and the prospects for the project.

They reviewed every question asked and discussed whether their answers were even plausible, let alone persuasive. Despite their pessimism, they began to lay out a path forward on the assumption that whoever they had met with would accept the project.

Other questions continued to haunt them. Who was the man they talked to on Friday? Was it possible that they had been talking to Martioto himself? Yesterday or today? Who is really "Nazri," if anyone by that name even exists? What is "Nazri's" role? Attempts to find a good photograph of Martioto or anyone named Nazri on the internet were unproductive. Neither of the two men could be plausibly matched to the photos they found.

Doyal had a more critical set of questions: "Whoever Nazri is, can he give the go-ahead, or does the project need as much bureaucratic review in their enterprise as projects generated within our own governments? Did Wijaya's call to Martioto make a positive outcome a foregone conclusion, or was it just a pro forma introduction, a diplomatic 'thank you' for earlier favors?"

This time, it was Panday who felt most pessimistic. "We just aren't the people who know how to run this project. We don't know the science. We don't know the engineering. We don't know the logistics. We don't know the economic or political risks for IFC or Wijaya or Indonesia.

"I certainly hope they figure that out because if they come to us for answers, we don't have them, and we dare not ask anyone. I pray God takes charge of this project because I don't see any other way it will come out right. I expect whoever these people are, they will see through us and walk away shaking their heads."

Ibrahim's view was more optimistic. "It must have been perfectly obvious to them that we're diplomats who don't know how to execute this project. They surely have far more expertise and administrative capacity than we do. If they say yes, they can't really be expecting much technical or logistic guidance or support from us.

"I also noted that they didn't ask any fundamental questions about whether the project is a good idea for the planet or for Indonesia or for their business. They were only there to gain an understanding of the task at hand and a sense of what our underlying concept and goals are. I don't think they are worried about their ability to handle the logistics."

Doyal had a more cynical perspective. "I agree with Ibrahim. They couldn't possibly avoid concluding that we don't know the practicalities of implementing our concept. But very likely they can't afford to disappoint Wijaya, no matter what they think of our idea.

"My fear is that they will say yes, proceed very slowly, and hope the whole effort falls apart one way or another, without tarnishing their reputation or exposing Indonesia to international condemnation. They might be hoping for inadequate funding, technical difficulties in adapting the planes or drones, or unwelcome publicity that forces a halt. That approach would be a plausible, smart thing for them to do. I still think it will be a miracle if the first plane ever reaches the troposphere—or even leaves the ground."

What Doyal bemoaned aloud as his fear was in some ways his hope. His real fear was still that the project would proceed and eventually destroy all their careers.

He comforted himself with the notion that he could simply tell Martioto to terminate the project whenever he wanted. *Doing so without consulting Ibrahim or Panday would be duplicitous, of course, and if the truth ever emerged, they might seek revenge by exposing me. In that case, I will have been the architect of my own destruction.*

The time to make that extreme choice will come later, if the project is exposed and I see that we would all be exposed and vilified. But would I know soon enough to avoid that fate, assuming it is not already too late?

The three diplomats talked for another hour, but there was really nothing more to discuss. In any case, they would know more eventually.

Chapter 18

SETITOR

Ariki Martioto was annoyed. He and his wife had enjoyed seeing the Shwedagon Pagoda, which had long held a place on his personal bucket list. This secret geoengineered veil scheme was a little crazy, but he and IFC would just get SE organized and disown any connection to it. Nevertheless, the enormous risks of being involved in this project echoed relentlessly in his head.

Those soft-headed diplomats have no idea what they are talking about, no appreciation for the technical or logistic complexities of their proposed project, no understanding of the economic or political ramifications for IFC. Neither does Wijaya, our dear President.

We're not a big State-Owned Enterprise like Pertamina that doesn't need to worry about the views of shareholders or the impact of public demonstrations. We're legally a private company right now.

But I'd planned to take IFC public with an IPO next year. It would be suicidal to hire an independent accounting firm to conduct a due diligence review of our operations, or allow the US Securities & Exchange Commission to review their report, while we are entangled in this mess. I shouldn't touch this project with a ten-foot pole, as the Americans would say.

But Martioto knew Wijaya had already made the decision for him. His position at the helm of IFC was entirely the result of Wijaya's intervention with the IFC Board of Directors, not to mention earlier career advancements that Wijaya had facilitated. *I can no more say no to Wijaya than jump off a bridge—actually there wouldn't be much difference. I would be equally dead either way.*

They had met in college and became fast friends. They both studied science. Both were intent on going into business—Martioto aiming to succeed in the energy industry, while Wijaya returned to his father's apparel business. Over the years, Martioto had been able to help Wijaya make some quick money in energy investments, and he had raised funds for Wijaya's political campaigns. But none of that help even began to match what Wijaya had done for him.

The only question was how to handle Wijaya's "request." He briefly considered the idea of just muddling around for a few years, making a few test flights, and declaring the whole project a failure. The risk that Wijaya would learn of this political insubordination was real, and it carried potentially destructive personal consequences. Moreover, he had deep moral qualms about disregarding this request from a friend who had never forgotten him throughout their lives.

His personal obligation to Wijaya was reinforced by his keen sense of professional ethics. He believed in the

value of engineering. He reminded himself of the con-
comitant responsibilities of his profession.

*An SRM veil and other geoengineering concepts are logical
extensions of everything our species has been doing for the last three
hundred years. The extraction and use of fossil fuels has already
re-engineered our cities and the global climate, just as the development
of synthetic nitrogen for fertilizer has already revolutionized agriculture, making it possible to feed the earth's seven billion people.*

*We scientists and engineers who understand the unanticipated
consequences of the global re-engineering technologies we developed
are obliged to engage in the effort to save humanity from their adverse
consequences. Unlike those ignorant diplomats, activists, and lawyers,
who pretend to know everything, real experts must intervene and take
charge.*

*We cannot simply wash our hands of responsibility for the exter-
nalities and unanticipated adverse effects of our collective efforts to
improve the human condition, however innocently those consequences
arose.*

Martioto concluded he must go forward as honestly
as possible, making every effort to see the project succeed.

The next day he talked to his young widowed cousin,
Anna Muhamir Smithson, in London. He offered her
an opportunity for employment and adventure in rural
Sulawesi as administrator of a secret project to be managed by a new company called Sky Enterprises, or SE. He
knew she would jump at the chance, and she did. He gave
her specific instructions.

"Let no one know your maiden name or your personal connection to me, but keep me fully informed of everything you observe. You will be well compensated for your work, which is an important part of a controversial secret effort to help the environment. I know you want to know more, but the less you know about SE's activities at this point the better. That way you can't tell anyone what you are doing.

"You need to leave for the village of Setitor in Sulawesi, Indonesia as soon as possible. Find office space and living quarters for yourself and the three senior managers, Mohamed Abdul, Guo Xingwen, and Ami bin Memed, next to the small airfield there. They will arrive shortly after September 15. The staff will grow rapidly, but you should house the others elsewhere. You should all plan to be there for at least a year, probably two or more.

"Abdul will be the CEO of SE. I expect Guo will handle financial and logistical planning, and Memed will oversee the execution of the project, but their precise responsibilities are up to Abdul. I expect you to coordinate with Abdul and give him what he needs, but you will have control of the disbursements and personnel matters in the office. One of your jobs is to ensure that there is no corruption of any sort. I hope you enjoy the rainforest and the adventure."

"Thank you for this opportunity to re-enter the world of the living and do something useful!" she responded. It was exactly the kind of challenge she craved.

Then Martioto sat down with Abdul (who had used the name Nazri in the Saturday meeting with the diplomats), Guo (Erkinay), and Memed (Abdulla bin Ami). His formal instructions to them were straightforward:

I hope you enjoyed your visit to Yangon and were enlightened by what you heard. As you know, as of next month, you will no longer work for IFC. You will be the top management of SE, with Abdul as the CEO. I have added an office manager named Anna Smithson to your team to handle administrative support, including personnel and financial elements of the operation.

You will receive an email from Anna telling you to report for work on September 15 at an office and housing next to a small airstrip in the mountains near Setitor in South Sulawesi. You can get there by flying to Sultan Hasanuddin Airport in Sulawesi and chartering a plane to the airfield.

The funds will be more than adequate to execute the SE mission and compensate you appropriately as top management. I will know where every penny goes, and so will the sources of the funding. Eventually the entire world may be able to scrutinize SE's books and records. You must handle this money as if every penny were coming out of your mother's pension. I trust you and Ms. Smithson to manage SE by the same rules that IFC follows—no kickbacks, no bribes, no creative corruption.

You know at least as much about the objectives of SE as I do. The folks you talked to are diplomats, not engineers, chemists, or atmospheric scientists. It will be up to you to make the hard technical and scientific choices, design and execute a program that is most likely to meet their goals, and set up systems to record and evaluate the results. Eventually others will weigh the beneficial and adverse physical and environmental consequences and determine the project's long-term significance.

Finally, whatever you know is entirely confidential and must not be discussed with anyone without an urgent need to know, including Anna Smithson, and then to be revealed only as narrowly as possible. Do your best to forget everything that happened before August 15, including the fact of your former employment with IFC.

Make sure no one else knows anywhere near as much as you already do about what you are doing. SE employees, to the extent possible, should not be briefed on the company's mission. You are welcome to develop an appropriate cover story.

Whoever is funding this operation is likely to assign someone to observe your activities. If you discover who it is, please keep that information secret. You can be sure that others will eventually also be curious. It is likely that someone of importance will eventually discover what you are doing. At that point, you may lose control of the effort, and maybe your jobs. So you will want to put that off as long as possible. And please let me know immediately if you have any indication that someone else is seriously interested in your project.

If all goes well, IFC will offer to hire you back when the project ends. If things go badly, IFC will claim it never knew anything about what you have been doing since August 15. IFC cannot afford to see its reputation adversely affected by this project. In any case, I will personally do what I can for you if you need help, assuming I'm in a position to do so. In the meantime, we are strangers, and if you must acknowledge a connection to me, it is only as a former employer.

You have a very difficult but exciting challenge ahead. No one has ever done, or even tried to do, what you are about to do. I need you to succeed. IFC needs you to succeed. Indonesia needs you to succeed. Humanity needs you to succeed.

Good luck.

With that, Martioto rose, shook hands with each of them, and left the room. He did not take questions.

--------<>--------

For the first six weeks, Abdul, Guo, and Memed simply immersed themselves in the literature on climate change, an SRM veil, geoengineering generally, and atmospheric chemistry. They studied the research of David Feith and his colleagues at Stanford University's Solar Radiation

Management Research Program, and others who had already deeply analyzed the organization and atmospheric chemistry of such an effort.

They were encouraged and inspired by the advocacy in Oliver Morton's 2015 book, *The Planet Remade: How Geoengineering Could Change the World,* as well as numerous shorter essays published around the time the International Commission on Stratigraphy declared the end of the Holocene epoch and the beginning of the Anthropocene epoch. To understand the international legal concepts bearing on their project, they studied *Climate Change Law* by Dan Farber and Cinnamon Carlarne and the sources it cites. By early November they all knew almost everything that could be learned from the relevant literature.

By this time, they were well settled into their mountain retreat near Rampi in Sulawesi. Anna Smithson had efficiently acquired residential and office facilities, provided reliable internet access, and set up the more mundane systems for purchasing supplies and paying salaries. None of them knew where she came from, but she clearly had complete veto power over every financial and personnel decision. They wondered who she really reported to besides Abdul.

The intellectual demands of developing a plan for executing the project were stretching their abilities and energies. They were far outside the comfort zone of their comparatively routine work at IFC. The social and intellectual isolation was helpful in some respects, but Abdul feared it would take a psychological toll in the longer run.

All three were in their mid-thirties; Martioto had selected each of them in part because they had no spouses or children who would suffer from their absence. Physically, they might as well be on the International Space Station, except that their professional and personal contact with the outside world was even more limited.

In November, Abdul began to differentiate the team members' responsibilities. He gave each enough funding to employ a few assistants to help their respective efforts. He reserved to himself the logistical questions, such as when to purchase commercially available aircraft that could be modified to meet their needs, where they could inconspicuously obtain the materials, fuel, and additional staff they needed, whether they would use pilots or drones, and when flights could reasonably begin. He had studied project management as an engineering student and performed similar tasks at IFC.

He assigned Memed to evaluate the current publicly available climate experiment protocols, choose a few to use as models for their own efforts, and develop a precise, disciplined protocol for collecting and evaluating the results of their geoengineering project. Memed was the true scientist of the three, having studied and conducted research experiments in atmospheric chemistry in college. His duties at IFC had addressed air pollution issues created by their facilities in order to correct undesirable emissions problems and defend IFC against spurious charges of environmental damage.

Guo was assigned to conduct an in-depth study of the atmospheric geoengineering literature to identify the snares and pitfalls that could invalidate the value of the results of their project. It was unlike anything she had done before. She had been a brilliant finance student in school and was considered the most imaginative, far-sighted person in IFC's long-term planning office. Abdul was confident she could quickly learn any relevant subject.

Abdul briefed the team thoroughly on their task. "The team must be prepared to answer the attacks and criticisms that might ultimately be leveled against our activities. More practically, we want to structure our work to ensure we anticipate both the false and the legitimate criticisms that could arise.

"We must maintain comprehensive contemporary documentation of our activities, create a robust monitoring system that will allow proper evaluation of results, and develop a full, clear statement of our objectives and methods, which may change from time to time. You should assume that we will eventually share all this information with the public. We cannot afford to commit errors that will vitiate the scientific value of our project, which is really a grand science experiment.

As for your personal lives, that is none of SE's business, but it must not be allowed to affect the quality of your work or the integrity of your scientific judgments.

Beginning November 15, Abdul, Guo, and Memed came together weekly for organized, disciplined discussion of decisions on how to proceed. Development of a coherent, step-by-step overall plan was the most challenging and essential process. Abdul began the discussion by declaring that every opinion within the group must be heard. He warned that bureaucratic deference to each other's opinions or areas of research responsibility could be fatal to the project, and signs of such deference would be treated as insubordination.

The conversations that followed ranged across the entire spectrum of experimental and operational issues.

- What exactly is our objective—generating good scientific data, or actually changing the climate right now? Is there a practical difference?
- Who will decide when to move from experimental projects to efforts primarily aimed at slowing global warming?
- What equipment and materials do we need to conduct this effort? Do we have sufficient time and resources to try various chemicals and various locations and frequencies for release of the chemicals?

- How will we measure the effects of our activity and distinguish them from natural variations in the weather and climate?
- Assuming our benefactors don't cut off our funding, at what point should we terminate the project, end the flights, and make our data public? What constitutes enough data to validate our results?

The most elementary matters immediately became controversial. Straightforward questions, like how many aircraft to acquire or what materials to disperse in the troposphere, raised larger questions about the timing and aggressiveness of their program.

Abdul, more experienced in project management, wanted to proceed cautiously, testing the planes and monitoring equipment carefully with very localized, low-atmosphere practice runs. Guo insisted the project could be discovered or perhaps lose its funding at any point, so she urged a rapid, bold effort.

The question whether to use drones or pilots was similarly complex. Drones would avoid the problems of recruiting pilots and the risk of enlightening more people about the real purpose of the project. Unmanned planes would also avoid the danger that a catastrophic aircraft failure would involve the loss of life.

On the other hand, the early efforts of the American space program had demonstrated on several occasions that a live pilot or even an onboard observer could identify and address unanticipated problems, with a range of responses that far exceed those of a built-in autopilot.

Significant doubts arose about whether drones could be adequately programmed to disburse the chemicals precisely within the thin, variable tropospheric border between the stratosphere and outer space. But live pilots or observers might be far less reliable over the boring 30-hour flights required by the program.

The safety record of driverless trucks in the United States and Europe, where "accidents" had declined dramatically when computer-driven vehicles replaced drivers, pointed toward drones. Adding a pilot—really an observer—to evaluate the physical operations and handle the unexpected would impose substantial additional design requirements. Abdul concluded that only a few aircraft should be outfitted for occasional manned flights.

Integrating all the pieces of the project into an efficient schedule was less controversial, but more challenging. Refitting—virtually rebuilding—each aircraft for the purpose would take time. They would need numerous alterations:

- custom-designed wing and flap configurations to fly efficiently and accurately in the extraordinarily thin, frigid air at over 70,000 feet

- complex sensing equipment to detect and maintain position within the contours of the thin tropospheric zone
- computer-actuated controls to release the chemicals at the precise rate desired
- reconstruction of the cargo area into tanks for the chemicals and added fuel to sustain flights of up to 36 hours

Maintaining the aircraft would require a technically-trained staff who would inevitably become intimately familiar with the equipment and intended flight paths. That raised security issues, such as employees learning too much about the flight plans to keep the real objective secret.

Establishing a "pipeline" of materials and fuels to support the overlapping 30-hour flights would be another considerable task. Large storage facilities did not exist at the local airstrip, and building them would certainly alert many locals that something new and substantial was underway.

All these factors escalated the costs of the project far beyond the original naïve estimates, closer to US$15 billion. Abdul was pleased to see that the money kept coming as he expanded the staff, ordered the construction of new facilities, and began modification of the commercial aircraft SE had acquired from Taiwan.

Faced with the intense need for secrecy, Abdul began thinking about a plausible and coherent cover story. The obvious questions from their neighbors, service providers, and contractors required coherent answers about their mission and its implementation. Suspicions and conspiracy theories about SE had already emerged in the local community:

- An oil company program that will pollute and tear up the entire area once its search for oil and gas or other minerals is successful
- A logging or agricultural project that would leave the mountains defoliated and destroy the farm crops on which the locals relied
- A secret Indonesian military base to develop aircraft capable of delivering nuclear weapons to deter Chinese, North Korean, or Philippine attacks
- The headquarters of a secessionist movement that will free Sulawesi from the rest of Indonesia and establish a rich, Brunei-like Sultanate

Undergirding all of them was the presumption that powerful figures in Jakarta or somewhere would be somehow enriching themselves at the expense of the local people.

Abdul assigned Memed to prepare a draft press release with Q&As that the team members would review, refine, and adopt. Once approved by Abdul, these materials would be the framework for all conversations with outsiders, including Anna Smithson, who had so far indicated she knew nothing about SE's real mission.

The cover story summary read as follows:

> Sky Enterprises is pursuing a Sulawesi Water Discovery Project whose purpose is to map and measure groundwater and surface water supplies more precisely, using both traditional aerial photography and the latest infrared and ultraviolet radiation analysis. It may include the scattering of harmless calcite to make surface and near-surface waters appear more brightly in these tests.

> This effort is part of a much larger series of studies of water supplies and water needs of the entire island of Sulawesi. Its goal is to ensure that the entire island and the people of Sulawesi have sufficient water supplies to endure the longer drought periods that are occurring because of accelerating global warming.

Abdul hoped this approach would provide cover long enough to make at least several flights before any noticeable discrepancies brought the story into question. At the same time, he was concerned about the social and political impact of creating false expectations among the local people about the project's purpose and then disappointing those expectations. It was an unhappy deceit.

The cover story materials were not released; they were simply on hand in case supplier or public inquiries ever required a response.

Anna Smithson reported the text of the draft press release and Q&As to Martioto. He had not told her the real purpose of the project. But working every day with the staff, she had already learned enough to know it was a cover story when she read it.

For Abdul, Guo, and Memed, the cover story exercise was a salutary reminder that even if the available funds were as large and reliable as they seemed, it was urgent to do as much as possible as quickly as possible. The whole arrangement could collapse at any moment if the world learned the SE's project real purpose.

By the end of the year, the team had methodically overcome the logistic hurdles. They hired recently discharged Indonesian Air Force aircraft engineers, mechanics, and construction managers. Aircraft hangers, space for new employees, and fuel and chemical storage facilities were constructed.

The first two of six planes arrived, and the engineers went to work on physical modifications to enlarge the wings and fuel capacity and add tanks to hold the calcite and add equipment to release it into the troposphere.

They outfitted the aircraft with sophisticated computer hardware and software to allow them to operate as unmanned drones. The software suppliers offered a sworn commitment that the aircraft would be able to operate as self-contained, autonomous drones, needing only the most general instructions to accomplish their mission.

Two subsequent aircraft were modified to allow the occasional presence of a live observer, who might learn more about the actual operation of the drones and the effect of the calcite in the troposphere. The observer might also be able to respond more quickly and effectively to any surprises, without waiting for a command from the ground.

The new aviation staff called for improvements to the airstrip to ensure that the planes could fly safely and efficiently on a daily basis.

They also recommended an elaborate control room to provide real-time observation of the airspace around the plane, monitor the actual release of chemicals, and measure the atmospheric and light conditions.

The chosen chemical for the first tests arrived, calcite powder so fine it flowed like a liquid. The team had concluded that using inert diamond dust would be simpler to study. But the most recent research suggested that calcite, which is reactive, would better preserve the ozone layer in the troposphere. Given the secret character of this program, both tropospheric and lower-level atmospheric operations demanded use of the material that was least likely to do any environmental harm.

Since calcite is a common material on the earth's surface, SE would also have a more defensible answer to media claims that they were poisoning their neighbors or experimenting recklessly with unknown chemicals.

Using calcite did create an additional layer of scientific complexity. In a matter of weeks, it is transformed into other chemicals whose consequences would also need careful evaluation. But it still appeared to be the conservative course of action.

Meanwhile, Memed had designed and constructed a system of real-time monitoring, using sophisticated software that combined and analyzed data from four disparate sources:

- direct, live satellite observations of reflectivity from various national government programs
- creation of a weather benchmark based on predicted and historical conditions, including cloud cover, temperatures, and precipitation, which would be used for comparison with actual conditions resulting after the veil was operational
- available ground-level data measuring the intensity of the sunlight reaching the earth

- air samples taken by the drones in previously sprayed areas to calibrate the precise rate of decay of the calcite, and changes caused by the new chemicals created by the combination of the calcite with other chemicals

The ultimate success of the project depended on being able to demonstrate the effects of its activities on the earth's albedo in the areas where they operated. Thus, success required the ability to document the physical and chemical consequences of their activities, whatever the impact on the course of global warming. Abdul hoped they had all the pieces together. They would begin finding out soon.

Chapter 19

MONTREAL

Marie had taken a variety of steps to protect herself and her husband in their condominium. She believed their 10th-floor unit was secure, protected behind a twenty-four-hour concierge and a security guard. But as she approached her door after a long day at the office, her eye caught the glow of a faint light coming from inside.

It could not be her husband, the only other person with a key. She had talked to him in Vancouver an hour ago.

Could she have accidentally left a light on? Unlikely. She never left without turning off the lights. She stopped and listened intently. No sound. Robbers would make noise.

Quietly making her way back to the elevator, she returned to the lobby and talked to the concierge on duty.

"Did anyone come for a key to my apartment?" she inquired of the woman at the desk.

"Only the art appraiser you asked to come by," she answered.

"How do you know I asked him to come?" Marie asked, trying to hide her sense of alarm.

"He showed me your email, telling him you wouldn't be able to get here to meet him, but that he should come anyway. The email said he should show it to me, and I would give him the key. I know you travel a lot, so it seemed reasonable. I hope that was okay."

"No, it wasn't," Marie replied anxiously. "The email must have been forged. I would have called you to confirm, and in any case, you should have called me before giving out my key, or any resident's key."

"I'm sorry," she said.

It was hard to tell if the woman was taking the matter seriously. Marie scowled, but it was too late to do anything about it now. She immediately called the Montreal police. As they arrived with sirens blaring, she realized that she had made a mistake not to ask for a silent arrival. The sirens would likely tip off anyone who was in her unit.

At that moment a man hurriedly stepped out of the elevator. Marie confronted him with the gun she had been carrying for months now but never imagined using.

"Stop! You are under arrest for unlawfully entering apartment 1005. If you have a weapon, drop it on the floor."

The man gave her a quizzical look. "What? What are you talking about? I was just visiting a friend in 208, and now I'm late for dinner at home. Please put that gun away. Who are you anyway?"

Feeling a little foolish, Marie relaxed, but she kept the gun in her hand. Her mind raced. *The police are here, but how can I prove this man was in my apartment?* The two uniformed officers entered the lobby. One of the officers drew his gun and asked Marie to put hers away.

"I believe this man illegally entered my apartment using a forged email," she explained. "I think if you search him you will find the forged email and a key to apartment 1005 in his pocket."

The other officer asked them both for identification. Happy to turn the situation over to the police, Marie dropped her gun into her purse and flashed her RCMP plainclothes agent ID. The man offered no ID, but repeated his story and asked to be allowed to leave. Seeing no indication that permission would be granted, he reached into his jacket pocket and pulled out a Beretta 9mm semiautomatic.

"Nobody move. Drop your gun. I could kill you all in an instant. I'm going to walk out of here and disappear in the street. Don't try to follow me." The officer didn't shoot; the risk of death for one or all of them was too great.

The gunman quickly retreated out the door. He rounded the first corner, hid in a driveway alley for half an hour, then carefully emerged and hailed a taxi for Montreal Central Station. His original plan had been to take a night train to Toronto. It still seemed like the best escape. He wouldn't need to show a passport, and there's nothing unusual about a man traveling from Montreal to Toronto without a suitcase.

At the Station, he bought a briefcase from the luggage store with cash. Bought a ticket to Toronto from the automated kiosk with the forged Australian credit card bearing the name of Robert McKenzie. Went to a quiet corner of the station and wrapped his gun in the bag that came with the briefcase. Ordered a meal at the McDonald's and dropped the remains of the meal in the trash, along with the bag holding the gun.

Once aboard the train, he could feel himself relax. Nothing incriminating about his appearance, no illegal weapon—just another businessman returning home from a day in Montreal. He would arrive around midnight.

From the apartment lobby, the police officers immediately called in an All-Points Bulletin. They included a video image of the suspect from their body cameras. The police headquarters experts called on all the tools at their command. Surveillance cameras in Montreal Central Station, employing the latest facial recognition technology, picked out his image and recorded him buying a train ticket.

Other cameras showed him boarding the train to Toronto. They were not able to catch him in Montreal, but five hours later, the Toronto police arrested him when he arrived.

A canvas of the security cameras of the vendors in Central Station showed him entering the McDonald's. The video showed him eating there, then throwing what appeared to be the wrappings of his meal and another package into the trash. The station police were able to recover the gun.

⸺◦⸺

After fully briefing the police, Marie ventured up to her apartment, exhausted, anxiously wondering what she would find. She assumed the man with the gun was Anderson, but in fact she had no evidence whatever to support that supposition.

Someone had definitely entered her apartment, but everything inside was just as she left it in the morning. This wasn't an attempted robbery. He was quietly waiting for her to arrive. The most likely objective was murder.

She tried calling Jon to tell him what had happened and calm her nerves. No answer; probably eating dinner with his family or putting the children to sleep. She shut off her own phone, went to bed, and slept fitfully—her nerves still bathed in adrenalin.

In the morning she noticed a phone message from the night before, but decided to leave it until she got to the office. She needed the drive time to pull herself together.

When she arrived, she was stunned to learn the night's genuine disaster: Jon had been shot and left for dead in his apartment building garage when he returned from work. The security guard heard the shots and called the police and an ambulance. Jon was in the hospital in critical condition. His chances of survival were uncertain.

Marie was overcome. Distraught about Jon and his family. Feeling guilty that she was unscathed, at least so far. Her mind a cacophony of unanswerable questions. *What can I do for Jon? What should I do to protect myself? Do I still need protection? Was this gunman actually Anderson, acting on his own? Or maybe he hired a professional murderer for this job too?*

Driving to the hospital to see Jon, she was also beset with practical concerns. *Can I proceed effectively on the Hartquist investigation without Jon? Will I be allowed to, or will the boss transfer the whole matter to the uniformed police division? Maybe that would be the best solution anyway.*

Four days later, Marie was given a new assistant, Sally Watkins. The boss allowed Marie to continue to investigate the source of the funding for Hartquist's murder if she wished to do so. She was still traumatized by the week's events, but felt she could not leave the case after what had happened to Jon.

At Marie's suggestion, the police obtained a handwriting sample of the man arrested in the Toronto train station. The computer database quickly revealed that he was Walton Anderson, and he had used the aliases Robert McKenzie in Jakarta and Pierre de Fleurieu in Switzerland.

Marie, the police officers, and their body camera videos all identified him as the man in Marie's apartment building. The Beretta 9mm was purchased in Virginia by an "Allen Richardson" and somehow found its way to Anderson. Ballistic testing proved it was the same gun that severely wounded Jon.

The Canadian police filed charges of attempted murder, threatening a police officer, and illegal possession of an unlicensed handgun. Those crimes would be easy to prove and enough to put Anderson in prison for decades, probably the rest of his life. The identification of Anderson with McKenzie and de Fleurieu tied him to the Hartquist and Miller murders but did not advance the effort to identify the source of the $2 million.

At first, Anderson was adamant that the police had arrested the wrong man. He denied everything, claiming complete ignorance about the deaths of Dr. Hartquist and Mark Miller, and the false identities. He hired Laurence Wilson, an experienced defense attorney in Toronto who specialized in representing white-collar crime suspects.

The evidence of Anderson's guilt for the immediate crimes was overwhelming, and Wilson advised Anderson he would likely be convicted of serious crimes, with sentences that could vary from several years to life imprisonment without parole.

Nevertheless, Anderson continued to insist he knew nothing about the Hartquist murders, which were the most important matter to the public and the RCMP, and therefore the prosecutors. They refused to support any plea bargain until those questions were answered fully.

Peter Westfield, the lead prosecutor, stressed that even if he could not conclusively prove that Anderson had arranged the murder of Dr. Hartquist aboard the Canadian-flag ship and then poisoned Mark Miller, he had sufficient circumstantial evidence to put those charges before the judge and jury. He might lose on those counts if the jury concluded there was reasonable doubt, but the result would likely be more severe sentences for the crimes for which the court did find Anderson guilty.

Westfield then explained to Anderson he had only one viable bargaining chip. He must provide a concrete identification of the real source of the funds to pay Mark Miller to murder Dr. Hartquist, and someone to murder Miller. In that case, Westfield would recommend a reduced sentence in light of his cooperation.

Westfield sometimes threatened to recommend life in prison; at other times he sought to pry Anderson loose from his loyalty to those who funded the murders. "Why should you go to a maximum-security prison, where your physical well-being could be in danger, while those who masterminded those crimes remain free?" he asked.

To emphasize the point, Westfield took Anderson and Wilson for a tour of a maximum-security prison and a "country-club" minimum-security prison for white-collar criminals. The differences in the facilities and their occupants were plain to see. When that didn't change his mind, they assigned him to a maximum-security prison for a week, where he would get to know what it would be like to live there.

Anderson had lived most of his life in upper-middle-class comfort and security while pulling the strings to arrange white-collar crimes. He was shattered by what he saw. He allowed his lawyer to begin negotiations with Westfield.

Two crucial issues inevitably arose. First, what information would be "enough?" Second, what would the prosecutors recommend as a sentence if they obtained "enough" information? The uncertainties were crucial, and the negotiations were intense.

Both Wilson and Westfield worried about the possibility that Anderson didn't know enough to provide a definitive, or even useful, identification. Would he need to identify live individuals by name? Would more corporate or individual intermediaries beyond Stability be sufficient if that were all Anderson knew? How could Anderson demonstrate he was revealing everything he knew, when doing so might put his own life in danger?

Second, there were the external uncertainties: How could Westfield be sure the judge would accept his recommendation? If Westfield recommended an unusually lenient sentence, wouldn't the judge want to evaluate the justice of the result for himself?

After two months of haggling, Wilson and Westfield reached an agreement that was a gamble for both sides, but nevertheless seemed to be the best they could do. The hard reality was that no one could ensure that Anderson's information would enable the identification of the instigator of the murders. And no one could ensure that the judge would accept the sentence promised to Anderson and advocated by the prosecution.

From the RCMP's point of view, the decision of the court on the criminal indictment was not the primary matter of interest, despite that fact that its own officers were physically attacked and one of them was still in critical condition. The media were still pressing for answers about the death of Dr. Hartquist. The sooner the RCMP got whatever Anderson could provide, the sooner they could track down the criminals who had ordered the murders.

Wilson scheduled a rehearsal with Anderson before he gave his "tell-all" deposition. The lawyer began with an admonition.

"You must tell them everything you possibly can about the source of the money and instructions that led to Dr. Hartquist's murder. If you are concealing anything, even inadvertently, and they find out, they'll throw the book at you."

Anderson's face contorted into a pained expression. "But what if my sources are as ruthless toward me as they were toward Mark Miller? They had him killed because he might reveal something to the police under duress. Won't they find a way to do the same to me once they find out I've agreed to a plea bargain? They're not naïve. They'll assume I've agreed to give information to the prosecutor to get a sweet sentence."

Wilson's reply was devastating. "That's a risk you face whether you talk or not. You're a danger to them for the same reasons Miller was, and you know more than he did. Your sponsors could be planning to eliminate that risk as soon as possible, regardless of what happens in court.

"The odds that they can find someone to do that work for them in a maximum-security prison are much greater than in a white-collar prison. Your best bet is to help the RCMP catch the villains and put them in jail.

"Maybe I can get the prosecution to agree to a sort of 'witness protection' arrangement. Change your name on the prison records and send you to a prison where your sponsors are less likely to find you.

"I'll press for it. There are no sure things in this business. I reiterate: for now, your only hope of a sentence you can survive is complete honesty and openness."

Anderson looked glum; his insides writhed at the vision of his future life. Even the best of outcomes was dismal, and the idea that a professional killer might be hunting him down was terrifying.

"I get the picture. I'll do the best I can."

Wilson sat back in his chair. "Okay. Now, tell me what you intend to tell them. Rehearsing will help you sound more sincere and feel more secure when you're answering questions under oath."

The next day, Peter Westfield opened the Anderson deposition with a statement identifying himself, Marie Veronique Roy, Larry Wilson, and Walton Anderson for the record. He continued,

"Today is Friday, October 15, 2021. Walton Anderson, after conferring with his counsel, is changing his plea to guilty on the charges of attempted murder of Jon Wolfe, threatening a police officer, and possession of an illegal handgun. At this time, the prosecution no longer intends to pursue any further charges against Anderson.

"Anderson has agreed to disclose everything he knows about the murder of Dr. Ilsa Hartquist and in particular, who sought her death and provided the funds to hire Mark Miller for this purpose and then pay for Mark Miller's murder. This deposition is for the purpose of confirming that understanding and for obtaining and recording the information Anderson is disclosing."

Westfield's first question asked Anderson whether he agreed with everything in Westfield's opening statement. Anderson whispered, "Yes."

The questioning continued for several hours. First, Anderson was prompted to describe the crimes for which he was pleading guilty, followed by questions from Westfield as necessary to establish every legally required element of each of those crimes.

Then Westfield directed Anderson to reveal everything he knew about the murder of Dr. Ilsa Hartquist. Anderson verified a lot of information that Marie and Jon had already collected—the creation of the Stability account with funds from the numbered Swiss account, the selection of Mark Miller for the murder, the transfer of funds to Miller's account and then the reversal of that transfer, the bribe to the Hotel Ciputra busboy to place the "sleeping powder" of poisonous chemicals in Miller's vodka and tonic, and the cremation of Miller's remains.

Then Anderson came to the matter of greatest interest: the identity of the source of funds. "The sponsor of Dr. Hartquist's murder gave her name as Sylvia Jacobsen. She gave me no explanation of the motives behind the murder or how she had identified me as the person to arrange it.

"I gathered from some of her comments that she might be aiming to protect the fossil fuel industry, but she never said so explicitly. I have no concrete evidence to support my assumption. For all I know, she may have had some personal grudge against Dr. Hartquist.

"She deposited the funds in my numbered account at my request. She did not insist on any protection against my simply absconding with the $2,000,000.

"The funds came from a Chase Bank account in the United Kingdom. I suspected the transfer was a violation of the applicable banking laws, but I trusted that the funds would not be confiscated or reported to the authorities by my bank, Express Chartered. I chose that bank years ago because it was known not to be too concerned about compliance with those reporting procedures.

"I never communicated with Jacobsen after the funds arrived. I counted on the media to inform her that the project had succeeded. There was no request to return any remaining funds. I kept them."

"Where is the money now?"

"I used most of it to pay off my debts. A small amount remains in the numbered account in Switzerland."

Westfield paused and looked over his notes. He seemed to be about to end the deposition. Marie asked for a break.

"Peter, I think we can learn more about this Sylvia Jacobsen person. Can you ask about her language, her accent, her colleagues' accents if she spoke to anyone else or overheard anyone else in the background? And did she have an email address?"

"Certainly," Westfield replied, "Good point. Maybe he can tell us more than he realizes."

They returned to the room. Westfield began immediately. "We have a few more questions. Do you have an email address for this Sylvia Jacobsen?"

"Yes. I have it in my phone." After a few moments manipulating his cell phone, he came up with it. "It's SJacobs@cable.ca. I kept it in case I needed it."

"Have you communicated with her since you were arrested?"

"No, my lawyer pointed out that I might be putting myself in danger, the same as Mark Miller."

"How many times did you talk in person to Ms. Jacobsen?"

"I think we spoke three times altogether."

"Those conversations, were they in English or some other language?"

"English. I don't speak any other language well enough to carry on a phone conversation."

"Do you know what number the calls came from?"

"I suppose it was in the cell phone I was using, but I threw it out in June 2020, after Mark Miller died and was cremated. I don't have her phone number anymore."

Westfield grimaced at the answer. He had hoped for a useful clue. He dug deeper.

"Focus on the conversations with Jacobsen. Where do you think she is from? Did she have any accent? Were any people talking in the background? Did you hear, or did she say anything that might indicate anything about her?"

"Well, I knew she called from Canada because my cell phone showed a Canadian number. I remember being surprised once that she was calling from a strange country code. I think it was the Czech Republic. Maybe she was on vacation.

"She did have an accent, but it was nothing I would associate with Prague. She sounded more British than Czech. There was never any background noise. I guess I assumed she was always alone when she phoned me.

"Now that I think of it, I missed the call from Prague initially. A hotel operator answered my return call. She might have said, 'The Prague Hilton,' but I'm not sure. I guess that's why I noticed her accent."

Westfield pressed Anderson for more details. "Do you really mean British? Not Irish? Or Scottish?"

"No. I know my brogues. I lived in Britain for three years in the 1970s, when Scotch, Welsh, and Irish accents were still distinct."

"How old would you say Ms. Jacobsen was?"

"My guess is that she wasn't young. Probably over sixty, maybe in her seventies."

"Is there anything else you can tell us about her—her voice, her choice of words, her manner of speaking?"

"She did have a bit of a lisp. Not a real speech defect, but you could hear that her *s*'s were not quite ordinary. It made me wonder if her British accent was an affectation."

Westfield paused and looked over at Marie. She leaned over and whispered in his ear, "Why is the email address SJacobs, not SJacobsen? Was she disguising her name?"

Peter nodded and turned to Anderson. "Tell me, Mr. Anderson, do you know, or why you think, Sylvia's name was Jacobsen when this email address is Jacobs? Was she using a false name, or are you hiding something?"

"I honestly don't know the reason for the difference. She never mentioned it, and I never asked. Sometimes people use shortened versions of their names for email purposes. Easier for others to remember and spell."

Westfield stared at Anderson in silence. "Do you expect us to believe that? She promised you $2,000,000 to arrange two murders, and you weren't worried that she would double-cross you the way you double-crossed Mark Miller? Are you sure you don't want to add anything more? We need to have a believable story before we go to the judge asking for leniency."

"I honestly didn't want to know anything about her that I didn't need to know. I didn't expect to have any contact with her after the money arrived."

Westfield paused, looked at Marie for a signal, and then back at Anderson.

"OK. That will be all for today. We will give you a copy of this deposition to review and correct as necessary. Keep thinking about Jacobsen. If something more comes to mind that you haven't told us, please let us know. We may have further questions after we evaluate the information you have given us."

Outside in the hall, Anderson breathed a sigh of relief. Wilson had a few more words with him. "Think very carefully about everything you have just told them and review the deposition very carefully. Remember, if they find a single lie, the whole deal will be off. If Westfield or the judge finds your story suspicious or unbelievable, the deal could fall apart even if they can't find a specific lie.

"If you can think of anything new, please speak up, even if you think it's unimportant. The appearance will be good, and you never know what facts they might find useful. If the RCMP succeeds in capturing your sponsor, that may even make you safer than you are now."

Anderson listened, but he had already come to a different conclusion. *If the RCMP captures my sponsor, whoever she was, my life might be in greater danger*, he surmised. *I can't believe she was really acting on her own.*

But he was already committed to cooperating with the prosecutor to minimize the risk of ending up in a maximum-security prison for life. He tried coming up with additional information but could not think of anything even marginally useful. Marie and Westfield were disappointed, but they had no reason to believe he knew more than he revealed.

The deposition ended at 4:30 pm. Marie was eager to get to the office and begin pursuing these new leads. She was far too energized to sleep. No doubt it would take time to find Jacobsen, if that was her name, and the truth about who ordered the murder. The follow-up work would be slow, but Marie was more committed than ever to finding the answers. Jon deserved no less than a maximum effort to find the ultimate cause of his grievous injuries.

Jon was still alive but struggling in rehabilitation. Marie refused to think that Anderson might have succeeded in murdering Jon. The possibility brought tears to her eyes.

Chapter 20

SETITOR

On December 2, 2021, Singapore's embassy in Jakarta welcomed a new "environmental staff officer," a former foreign service officer by the name of Wang Shu. In a brief meeting with the Ambassador, she explained that the Prime Minister had personally asked her to keep her eye on a project underway in a remote area of Sulawesi. She told him nothing about the project, and he decided not to ask.

Three days later, Wang arrived in Rampi. Having studied a topographic map available on the internet, she had identified Setitor, a tiny village on a nearby mountain where the SE operations were underway. Luckily, she found an existing house with a perfect location for observing the offices and the airport.

Wang offered to buy the house, generously advancing enough funds to allow the owners to build a new house for themselves nearby. She was able to move into a spare room of their old home immediately, even before the owners moved out. They constructed their simple new home, lacking public water or sewer facilities, in sixty days.

Although Wang knew Bahasa, her landlord and neighbors mostly spoke a local language, one of over 240 in Indonesia. She quickly absorbed it well enough to buy food, furniture, and other supplies in the Rampi markets and shops, where proprietors worked patiently to win over this new, free-spending consumer. Occasionally she casually asked neighbors and shopkeepers what they knew about the activities at the airfield. No one seemed to know more than what she already knew—some company called Sky Enterprises had come to town. Perhaps it had something to do with ensuring adequate water for Sulawesi, though rumors proliferated they were up to something much more sinister.

Apparently, every SE employee lived and worked in the SE offices and housing. Someone from SE regularly came into Rampi to buy fresh local produce or supplies. Only on rare occasions did any other employees come to Rampi, and they only chatted about the weather, which always seemed to be unsettled.

When the sellers moved out of her house into their new home, Wang was able to set up her satellite-based phone, computer, and observational gear. She was once again fully in touch with the outside world. But without colleagues, an office, or meetings, it was a solitary existence, a new experience for a Chinese woman who had been surrounded by others her entire life. Most of the time she found herself enjoying the peaceful solitude.

She was pleased to see that new offices, storage facilities, and upgraded runways and control tower had already been completed. Soon after, a set of aircraft arrived. Each plane disappeared into a hanger for about four weeks after its arrival and emerged with subtle differences. Although substantial quantities of Singapore's money had been spent with no flights as yet, at least she could say it was not simply being siphoned off into Swiss bank accounts.

Wang sent a single text message to Prime Minister Li shortly after her arrival to reassure him she was in place and real work was underway at SE. A second text in April apprised him that regular flights had begun. The flights were relatively short, so Wang surmised they were tests.

—○—

On April 2, 2022, eight months after Martioto's final meeting with Abdul, Guo, and Memed, the first low-level flights began. Their primary purposes were to test the flight equipment, calibrate the amount of calcite sprayed by the planes, and check out the monitoring hardware and software.

The entire SE staff gathered at the airstrip to observe the first flight by one of the modified, computer-controlled drone aircraft. The employees watched in anticipation. Even though they had never been told the ultimate mission, most suspected it had more to do with climate change than Sulawesi water supplies. Whatever SE's purpose, this flight would test the success of the team's efforts to modify the aircraft to the new specifications.

The drone took off smoothly and returned twelve hours later. Real-time data feedback showed it had succeeded in reaching the desired altitude and releasing a nominal amount of calcite powder over a targeted area. The remote controls functioned as designed. Equally important, the computer software for evaluation of the results had functioned as planned. From an engineering standpoint, the performance was an unqualified success.

Two weeks of additional testing of each drone identified the desirability of several minor adjustments to the flight control systems, the calcite spray nozzles, and the monitoring hardware and software on various drones. Each of the aircraft flew several times to ensure they all worked equally well.

Without telling anyone except Anna, who needed to approve the expenditures, Abdul arranged a surprise. He flew in a real Jakarta banquet meal, and the whole team, from the maintenance men to the flight professionals to the software engineers, celebrated their success. Abdul's speech to the assembled group was congratulatory but necessarily vague.

I want to take this occasion to thank
every member of this team for your hard

work and extraordinary performance in making these first flights a complete success. Achieving this milestone in such a brief time frankly exceeded my expectations. You agreed to come here to provide your specialized expertise without any explanation of the larger purpose of this effort. Even without that knowledge, you performed with a diligence and skill that was more than I could have hoped for. Almost all of you will complete your work after the next few weeks of additional testing and training your replacements. Then you will return to your homes as scheduled.

The speed of your impressive success has saved this project both time and money, enough for me to give each of you a performance bonus. I hope it is sufficient to reflect our appreciation for your outstanding efforts. As you know, the larger objectives of this project, which will contribute to the sustainability of life here on Sulawesi, are still secret for a variety of reasons, not the least of which is the high likelihood that most of its benefits, if any, will only accrue to the children of those living here now. We hope to delay any public discussion of this effort until we can demonstrate our results in a scientifically sound, professional manner.

Accordingly, I remind each of you to keep everything you have seen and heard confidential, as your contract requires. And now it is time to eat well and enjoy our triumph.

One week later, a new professional team arrived, most of them also recently discharged from the Indonesian Air Force. In two more weeks, SE sent the original engineering and flight maintenance staff home, as they had been expecting, with generous bonuses. Some time was lost in the transition as the new arrivals came up to speed, but Abdul concluded that changing teams was safer than having the same professionals stay around any longer.

The first tropospheric-level environmental tests began over an area in Indonesia suffering from drought. Daily flights for thirty days over the same area released a precisely measured quantity of calcite powder. Memed calculated that the calcite raised the earth's albedo in the affected area by about 10 percent. These calculations were inevitably crude estimates, as no reliable data existed on how much light the calcite would scatter into other parts of the atmosphere. Neither was there accurate data on the extent to which the powder or its decay compounds would themselves trap heat radiated from earth, causing the same kind of impact as increased carbon dioxide and neutralizing some of the benefits of the lowered albedo.

The weather monitoring results were also promising, though statistically insignificant. The data and modeling showed small discrepancies between the predicted weather and the actual weather, with lower temperatures appearing most of the time. Satellite measurements also showed a dimming of the sunlight reaching the affected area of Sulawesi, as the powder did what it was predicted to do: scatter more sunlight directly back into space and off to the side.

Determining the effects of the chemically active calcite powder on the atmosphere itself necessitated careful measurement of atmospheric composition and the rate at which the powder slowly sank into the lower atmosphere, floated upward into space, or reacted with other atmospheric chemicals. Based on the changes over the thirty days, it appeared the powder would remain at measurable levels in the troposphere for about forty-five days after its initial release.

The satellite images clearly revealed the presence of the calcite powder above the affected area—too clearly for Abdul's comfort. "If anyone else looks carefully at these images, they will know what our aircraft are doing. That would immediately trigger questions about the origin and character of our operation. We can only hope no one pays close attention."

In late May, Abdul authorized another four rounds of high-altitude tests over a different area of Sulawesi and nearby ocean waters, which provided additional data while allowing continuing measurements of the effects of the previous sprays over time. A single round of tests using sulfate particles also showed favorable but imprecise results.

After thorough evaluation and analysis, the data looked good, but the statistical margin of error from these few tests was so great that no conclusions would be defensible for publication in a scientific journal.

The question whether to go forward with the real objective, constructing an SRM veil over the Arctic, was as controversial within the team as it would have been in the world at large.

Abdul convened Guo and Memed for a discussion of the crucial choice that lay ahead. He introduced the discussion carefully, hoping to have an open dialogue unimpeded by considerations of hierarchy.

"I'm the project leader, but I won't make this decision by fiat. We have all worked together as equals, as a team, and I deeply respect both of your insights and abilities, and the soundness of your professional judgment. I know we have all been thinking about this question since the day we agreed to take on this SRM project. Memed, what are your views?"

Memed was clearly the most skeptical and the most agitated. He suspected that the other two would want to proceed, but he made his strongest arguments.

"This data is promising, but it would take another year of testing and experimentation just to find out if we are really getting it right over a small patch of Indonesia, let alone whether we have the right operating plan for veiling the Arctic. There so many confounding factors that our results are subject to wide statistical error.

"Going to the Arctic, where we think that the impact of global warming is already much greater, but don't really know why, is worse than a roll of the dice. At least with dice we can calculate odds. We don't even know whether cooling the Arctic will significantly improve the climate of the rest of the planet. I believe we need to do more testing before we attempt to influence the Arctic."

He stopped there, realizing he was on the verge of a repetitious lecture about concerns they all already shared.

Abdul responded with his own opinion.

"Here are my personal views. I understand the risks, but I don't believe that this step is just another experiment with dangerously unpredictable results taken to satisfy scientific curiosity. It's true there is no way to conduct a controlled experiment without effects on this planet, and there is no Planet B. But that's precisely the point. We know that right now our species is on the path to destruction. The question in this context is what risks are appropriate. The answer to that question is inevitably based on value judgments.

"I think the risks are worth taking. Even the first steps in this project have taught us a great deal, and going forward will teach us more. We can quickly readjust our efforts as necessary once we see results. Start with a month of Arctic flights. Use calcite powder. Perhaps slowly experiment further by introducing some alternative materials if we are not happy with the calcite. Make full use of our real-time monitoring to evaluate the results as we go.

"In a few months we will have far more useful and relevant data than anyone in the world has now. If the data indicate we should stop, we will. Then we'll explain to the world what we did and share the data, along with our conclusion that our results were not what we hoped they would be. We were sent here with a mission. We've spent billions of rupiahs of someone's money to explore the viability of saving the planet with an SRM veil. We need to proceed far enough to have something meaningful to show for that expenditure and our effort."

Having completed his argument, Abdul turned toward Guo, eager to hear her views. After an uncomfortably long silence, prompted in part by her close personal relationship with Memed, she began very quietly. She recognized that her opinion would probably decide their future. "All three of us are technically trained. We have all studied the views of scientists and nonscientists on this topic, and we've all been thinking about this question from the beginning. For better or worse, neither of your views are new or surprising. Probably mine aren't either.

"Memed, I recognize the gross weaknesses of the data we have. We would need much more and much better data to approach the level of statistical confidence required before any government would approve giving a new medicine, vaccination, or some other medical treatment to a generally healthy child. But we are not dealing with a healthy child. We are dealing with something like an incipient epidemic for which we have no accepted cure. Our cure could protect the millions of children whose futures are dangerously at risk from the world's present course.

"If I felt confident that the world's governments would take prompt, responsible action, or were even seriously focused on prompt, responsible action, I would not even be here. But that is obviously not the case. I believe this decision is ultimately a moral and philosophical one. Science has no tools to weigh the risks and benefits underlying such a complex problem and tell us how to proceed.

I share the perspective Dr. Hartquist offered in her 2018 *New York Times* column. Let me remind you of what she said:

> When a person is drowning in an icy
> ocean, you don't debate whether the life
> preserver or the rope will be most effec-

tive to save him. And you don't try just one to see if it works before trying the other. You throw both, fully aware that he might not catch either one, or he might catch one and still freeze before he is rescued, or he might even get tangled in the lines and drown more quickly. Because action is the only hope.

"I think we must proceed until we have reason to believe we have learned, not to a scientific certainty, but in our best human judgment, that this SRM geoengineering technique is or is not a viable tool that can contribute to saving our species on earth. If our results are unfavorable, our species will need to search for some other solutions.

"So long as the results are favorable, we should continue with our flights. The world will no doubt discover what we are doing at some point, and someone may intervene to alter or stop our efforts. Favorable results might have the power to overcome the weight of inertia and change the global consensus from a status quo of inaction to a generally-accepted baseline that immediate action is essential.

"In a larger sense, if our actions are successful, we will be preserving the environmental status quo while the world develops a real program to respond to the fatal threat from continued carbon emissions."

After taking a few moments to absorb Guo's words, Abdul quietly announced his conclusion.

"I believe we have our decision. We will proceed carefully, work hard, and hope for the best. Thank you both for your professionalism and your thoughtful judgment. I hope one day we will all be happy with this decision."

By early June, SE completed final preparations for a one-month series of daily, overlapping thirty-hour flights, releasing calcite powder into the Arctic troposphere. Reflecting on Memed's concerns, Abdul concluded it was advisable to get as much data as possible on the impact of calcite dust, rather than take the theoretically more useful step of testing possible chemical alternatives. And they would formally review the data again every month before proceeding.

Abdul was reluctant to put pilots or observers on the few aircraft designed to hold them. The costs and risks inherent in adding a human aboard the aircraft were large. He considered it still an open question whether any flights should include them. For the time being, only about one out of five flights of planes capable of carrying an observer would be manned.

On the fourteenth flight, a drone unexpectedly lost its balance and plunged four kilometers before it could be brought back under control by the automatic systems on board, with the help of commands from the ground. Fortunately, that altitude was still well above any commercial airline flights, but it might have been observed by military pilots on their missions.

The scare reminded everyone of the necessity to ensure that the automatic control systems were completely reliable. Further adjustments were made to the controller software to facilitate more precise automatic adjustments and allow the ground controller to override onboard computer decisions if necessary. Further modifications to the drone wings would provide even more protection against a repetition of such an event, but Abdul decided against delaying the project to make them.

This incident also prompted further discussion of whether to include more observers on the flights. The first few test flights with an observer aboard had yielded useful insights and fabulous photographs in both visible and non-visible spectra, adding to the project's comprehension of what was happening to the calcite and the sunlight.

In theory, a live observer might also respond instantly and more effectively to any surprises, without waiting through the delay in obtaining a command from the ground control center. But the physical demands of a thirty-hour flight were punishing, aside from the inherent risks of a fatal pilot error or computer system failure. Abdul did not change the observer schedule.

If the flights continued to generate useful data and favorable results, and nothing else flashed a red light, Abdul intended to continue the flights at least until a reliable, statistically significant set of data was accumulated. *It's a trade-off of the risk of losing a drone against the risk of discovery or other termination of our project,* he concluded. *I think we need to go forward as quickly as possible.*

Wang spoke to Ibrahim weekly, updating him on what she observed happening at the airstrip, and getting his insights and advice. He was able to explain some of what she saw and didn't understand, based on his intuition and understanding about what must be accomplished for the project to work.

She was also happy to listen to him talk about his diplomatic activities at the various UN organizations where he represented his government. Important international disputes and global commons issues were at least being debated, if not resolved. She occasionally offered her own views, if only to exercise her mind on matters larger than food shopping and recording the activity at SE.

Aside from the pleasure of hearing Ibrahim's voice, their conversations subconsciously reassured her that he reciprocated her feelings. She wanted to believe that his questions reflected more than a general concern for her well-being reinforced by his responsibility for her lonely life in this isolated place. But she worked to keep these emotions under control.

He just depends on our conversations as the one thread that connects the three diplomats to the Sky Enterprises project. This is strictly and deeply a business relationship. She took care not to call him too often or direct too much of their conversations to personal matters. And she never said anything about her future.

Chapter 21

RAMPI

On Wang's regular biweekly trip to the Rampi market in late April, the butcher excitedly told her the big news. "SE brought over two dozen new employees to its base, and fourteen days later the old group of employees were sent home. No one knows why. It looks like a big change, though the new people appear to be a lot like the ones who left. I hope the project isn't in trouble. Their meat orders have been a big addition to my business."

"I don't know much about SE," Wang responded. "But I can see the airstrip from my home. I don't see any reduction in SE's activities. I think you'll be OK. The new people will also need to eat."

Wang had already concluded that SE must have replaced its staff, as old faces disappeared from the airfield and new ones took their place. Now she had outside confirmation.

From the greengrocer, she learned that two former employees had decided to stay in the Rampi area for a while. "They said they want to spend a few months relaxing here in the quiet rainforest before taking jobs in Jakarta."

Wang decided on impulse to stop by their new home after finishing her shopping. Anything she could learn about the inner workings of SE would be valuable. She could just say hello, offer them some tips on how to bargain with the local merchants, who they could trust, what local foods were good. It seemed a bit bold, perhaps even risky, for a Chinese woman to approach Muslim strangers this way, but she was sure she could handle it.

She knocked on the door. "Hello. My name is Wang Shu. I'm living in the nearby village of Setitor, where I am working for the Singaporean Embassy to study the effectiveness of local government programs for wildlife protection. I heard in the market that some new people had moved into Rampi, so I came by to welcome you."

The men who greeted her at the door happily invited her in. They were both young, well-built, trim military types. No doubt legally Muslim, but without prayer rugs or other religious trappings in the house. Mahmood was the shorter and more handsome of the two. They spoke English, which was rare in Rampi.

"I'm Mahmood and this is Ahmed. We were working for SE as aircraft technicians for the last four months. We were in the Indonesian Air Force before that. We'll eventually look for work with an airline in Jakarta, but we thought a few months of relaxation here in Rampi would be a nice break. Working for SE was pretty intense."

Mahmood had traveled in Europe and studied at Humboldt University in Berlin. Humboldt insists on a comprehensive liberal arts and sciences education for every student, in keeping with the views of its founders, Alexander and Wilhelm von Humboldt. His broad exposure to intellectual and cultural history made him far more enlightened and refined than his colleague, Ahmed, who was a more typical air force flight mechanic with only technical training.

After an hour of relaxed conversation, Wang volunteered to cook dinner with whatever food they had and the ingredients she had just bought in the market. *I can't bring them to my place*, she reminded herself. *My sophisticated communications equipment would raise questions. Dinner here serves my purposes just as well.*

She promised the meal would be a genuine Chinese dinner. She found a bottle of Australian wine in the kitchen, somewhat to her surprise. Turning to Mahmood, she asked, "Should I open it for dinner?"

"We were saving that for a special occasion," Mahmood replied. "You are our first guest, so this dinner certainly qualifies."

The dinner conversation was lively. When Wang asked why they left SE, they said their part of the work was completed. They were vague about their work, remembering their confidentiality commitments. Unnecessarily, they thought. They saw Wang as a charming female wildlife scientist. They could not imagine she would constitute a danger to SE or anyone.

Wang didn't ask more work-related questions. Too much curiosity might jeopardize the prospects for getting real answers later. *Get to know them better and the information will leak out,* she speculated. *Besides, it will be nice to have some reasonably educated, English-speaking friends here.* The six months essentially alone, combined with the underlying emotional tension of her regular conversations with Ibrahim, was wearing her down.

Shortly after dinner, she announced that she must return home. "I still have work to do. I need to write up my second quarterly report on my wildlife observations. Neither of you will be in it," she teased, though in fact everything they shared about their work would be reported to Ibrahim.

By now it was completely dark. Mahmood volunteered to walk Wang home, and she welcomed the offer. She still had some groceries to carry. The gravel path from Rampi to Setitor had no streetlights or sidewalks. It was uneven and rutted by oxcarts. Medical services were distant. Even a minor mishap like a twisted ankle could be a life-threatening problem if she were alone at night and could not walk.

As they walked in silence, Wang realized how pleasant it was simply to have company. When they arrived at her modest house, Mahmood handed her the groceries and whispered, "Thank you for a wonderful dinner. I hope we'll see you again soon."

"And thank you for your help," she responded. "Perhaps some time when I come to Rampi again for shopping." She was not more specific.

Her next report to Ibrahim described her new source of information, skipping over the social details of dinner. "I haven't learned anything very new yet, but I hope to learn more as I get to know them. I think they can give me a better sense of whether the project is really being pursued."

"Be careful," Ibrahim warned. "These men have been alone a long time, and they probably have no idea how to relate to a woman except as a wife or a sex worker. It may get ugly when you say no to them."

Annoyed by his paternalistic tone and indifference to the fact that she had been alone for a long time, Wang simply said, "I'm a career diplomat. I've dealt with predatory men at conferences all around the world. It comes with the territory. I can handle it."

"I'm just trying to look out for your well-being," Ibrahim said defensively.

"I appreciate your concern," she rejoined. "Thank you." She wondered if Ibrahim recognized that his characterization of her new friends arguably could apply equally well to himself.

Reflecting on the conversation, Wang was pleased to think she heard a slight hint of jealousy in Ibrahim's voice. Perhaps it was a sign he still cared about her more than professionally? She immediately chastised herself for grasping for that fantasy. *It just makes me miserable. I need to give it up*, she told herself.

On her next trip to the market, Wang did not stop to visit her new friends. *Too soon. I need to continue to be a special occasion, with wine.* Two weeks later, she ran into Ahmed at the market, also shopping. After exchanging pleasantries, she plunged ahead. "I was actually thinking I would knock on your door this afternoon. If you and Mahmood are free, you and I could shop for a proper dinner now, and I won't need to improvise."

After another conversation over dinner with wine, Wang ventured to draw them out about SE. "I'm concerned that whatever they're doing could damage the wildlife habitat," she began. "My Embassy wants to know more. We can't find anything about SE anywhere—no website, nothing on Google or Wikipedia. Can you tell me anything about their mission?"

Ahmed answered quickly, "We are bound by our confidentiality agreements not to reveal anything, and anyway, they didn't tell us anything. But I did see a draft of a press release, which described their project as aimed at monitoring and measuring ground water and surface water supplies in Sulawesi. Part of their project includes scattering chemicals into the atmosphere to enhance aerial surveillance. If it's in a press release, I guess it's not really confidential."

Wang's curiosity and the wine overcame her better judgment. Showing a bit too much interest and knowledge, she responded, "That's interesting. I haven't seen any press releases or news stories. This is a strange place for an entity named Sky Enterprises to set up its operations, hundreds of kilometers from anywhere. I wonder if something else is really going on."

Mahmood glared at Ahmed, who turned his gaze to the floor. Mahmood immediately changed the direction of the conversation. "Tell me, what have you seen since we left SE? Are they continuing with their flights? Is there any difference in the schedule?"

Wang quickly retreated. "I don't watch that closely. I'm just curious about what they're doing. If it's not about logging the rainforest or drilling for oil, it's of no concern. If you are barred from talking about SE, I certainly don't want to get either of you in trouble." After an awkward silence, Wang looked out the window at fading evening twilight. "Oh, it's later than I realized," she said. "I need to get back home."

Mahmood again offered to walk her home, and she accepted. When they arrived at her door, he put his hand on her arm and whispered, "We know a lot more than we told you this evening. If it's important for you to know, perhaps I could help you out. Why don't you invite me in for a while?"

Wang's heart pounded. She had little doubt what he wanted in return. "What do you have in mind?"

"I'll be honest. You are a beautiful and intelligent woman, and I haven't been near a woman in over two years. I've been thinking of you and dreaming of you since the last time I walked you home. I'm not violent or aggressive. I would just like some attention. I would pursue you more directly, but you are not that kind of woman. I'm afraid you would slap my face and never talk to me or Ahmed again. So I'm asking your permission. You seem very interested in SE, and I could tell you a lot. If I can help you in any way, I'm happy to."

Wang's head whirled. She instantly reviewed the many risks crowding her mind: *At least he's honest about his motives. But can I trust him? Who is he anyway? Is he working for someone else now? A spy? Am I potentially in physical danger? If I let him in the door, can I really control the situation?*

To Mahmood she said, "I won't give you what I imagine you want, but I am eager to learn whatever you can tell me about SE."

"I'll take whatever you are willing to give. Even just your company for another hour," he responded. It was a lie, and they both knew it. But she opened the door.

They put her groceries in the kitchen and sat down in the two chairs in her living room.

"So what can you tell me about SE?"

Mahmood was surprised and a little frightened by the blunt question. It was not at all where he hoped the conversation would go.

"Can I trust you? You know Ahmed has already violated our confidentiality agreement in a very minimal way, and you are asking me to tell you everything. I'm entirely at risk if I say anything. For all I know, you actually work for SE."

Wang smiled and replied firmly, "I just trusted you by letting you in my door. I'm trusting right now that you won't force yourself upon me or physically harm me if you don't get what you want from me. It's your turn.

"Or you can just say goodnight, and I'll see you another time."

Mahmood saw the possibility of ever having a closer relationship with Wang was at stake. *If she is ever to welcome me again, I need to tell her something, as I promised*, he thought. His desire for her overrode all caution.

"Here's what I know. SE never told us what they were trying to do. The press release Ahmed saw was just a draft, never released. That's why it wasn't reported anywhere. I think it is a cover story, in case they need to say something to tell the public.

"The tech group had lots of theories, most revolving around climate change and global warming. Some thought it was a top-secret UN project. Others speculated that it was private, funded by Bill Gates or some other billionaires who do not trust the world's governments to handle the problem. A few thought the Indonesian government was using the water shortage concern as a cover story for its search for oil and minerals."

"I'm aware of those theories. I even hear them in the marketplace. So am I right that you don't know which one is the truth?"

"Not for sure. I'm convinced it's a global atmospheric research project that's being kept secret to avoid a backlash of some kind—you know, demonstrations, government inquiries, media coverage."

Wang pressed for more. "Okay. So tell me your evaluation of the operations you observed. Is the management professional about its work? Is the money being spent honestly, or is this another self-enrichment scheme for someone? Are they succeeding? Making real progress?"

Mahmood answered openly; he knew he was already over the brink. "Everything they are setting up seems to work, but I don't know if that constitutes meeting their objectives, since I don't know exactly what they are. I suspect we were replaced so no one except the inner core of managers would know enough to say what the mission really is. They will probably replace the next group as well in another four months."

After another half hour of more probing questions and answers, Wang stood up. "Thank you. You have been very open with me, and I appreciate it. I'm sorry, but I'm exhausted tonight. I need to go to sleep. Perhaps we can continue our conversation another time."

Mahmood stood and took her in his arms. The warmth of his body felt good to Wang after months alone. After a moment, she softly pushed him away. "Good night."

He did not resist. "Please see me again," he begged. "I gave you what you asked. Now, you have me in your control. I'm desperately lonely. I hope you will see me again."

Suddenly his pleading look turned to fear. "You promise you don't work for SE? Are you going to turn me in for violating the confidentiality agreement? That would ruin my career!"

"No, I don't, I'm not, and I won't. But please go home now. You have behaved honorably toward me. I won't forget it. We'll talk again."

She walked Mahmood to the door and closed it after him.

Once alone, Wang took a deep breath of relief. She had learned what she wanted to know at a minimal cost. As she prepared for bed, she felt a sense of triumph, along with a mildly erotic urge that had been absent for a very long time.

She liked him. She would see him again. Next time, maybe they would do more than talk. After all, she was here on a temporary assignment, and any relationship here would end when she left.

Why be alone for another year or more? What difference would it make to anyone? she thought. With that frivolous idea in mind, she drifted off to sleep.

Wang reported what she had learned about the project to Ibrahim the next day. "According to one of the former engineers I met, the management at SE is pursuing its work very professionally, and its efforts seem to be going well."

Ibrahim was delighted by the news, which he passed along to Panday and Doyal. Panday was pleased; Doyal continued to have secret forebodings of disaster ahead.

Ten days later, Wang invited Mahmood to her home for dinner. This time there was little pretense about the nature of the evening. After her lonely months in this isolated village, Wang was almost as eager for human contact as Mahmood.

Their first evening together was a satisfying experience. They were pleasantly surprised at their emotional compatibility, considering their radically divergent backgrounds and education. Over subsequent dinners together, their relationship grew stronger emotionally and more intimate physically. Mahmood talked more about the details of his work at SE and his speculations about its true mission. Eventually he asked directly about Wang's work, pointing out that her house contained a surprising array of electronic equipment.

Wang answered crisply, "I cannot discuss those matters, and I am depending on you not to share your knowledge or speculations about me with anyone, including Ahmed. My relationship with you is already out of bounds, and telling you anything more would be suicidal. You are better off not knowing. That way I'll not be suspicious of you if my mission becomes public."

She reassured him, however, that his inquiry did not jeopardize their personal relationship. Mahmood was relieved that Wang's attachment to him was strong enough to survive his inquisitiveness, but he knew where the line was drawn. He would not test that boundary again.

In June, Wang observed that the flights became a continuing relay and lasted much longer. Making some rough calculations, Wang and Mahmood inferred that the pattern would allow for a drone to be over the Arctic at least four hours out of every eight.

Apparently, the real veil-creating operations had commenced. Over the next two months, Mahmood became a useful aid, helping her keep track of the flights, identifying the subtle differences in the individual planes, and explaining the mechanical and software elements that made them function.

Wang didn't reveal anything to Mahmood about her real mission, limiting his work to the technical details that were his strong suit. Nevertheless, he quickly recognized the general nature of the SE activities and her role as an observer.

It was apparent to him that Wang's work in Setitor had nothing to do with wildlife. It was about watching SE. Whatever his curiosity about the SE project's goals and Wang's mission, he discreetly avoided asking.

After two more months, Wang was confident enough about Mahmood to legitimize her regular contact with him. She told the Singaporean Ambassador she needed some additional funds for an assistant to help her carry out her assignment.

By Singapore or even Jakarta standards the salary was quite small. The Ambassador knew only that she was in Indonesia at the express direction of the Prime Minister, so he gave her the financial support she requested.

Mahmood was delighted to become her assistant. He didn't really need or care about the money. He just enjoyed being with Wang day and night.

Wang continued to report regularly to Ibrahim, who then shared her news with Panday and Doyal. Doyal also occasionally heard directly from SE because the proposed expenditures were substantially exceeding the original monthly estimates. But he had no reason to believe the money was being misspent or skimmed.

In the fall, Mahmood persuaded Ahmed to get to know some of the newest IT technicians at SE and learn what he could about SE's internal workings and results. Ahmed's first tidbits indicated that the SE project was still running quite smoothly, though with the usual start-up difficulties and missteps. No signs of poor management or corruption.

Ahmed's big breakthrough was his acquisition, for a small fee, of a copy of an internal year-end Memorandum that summarized SE's data as of the end of 2022.

At that point SE had already accumulated six months of data, and plausible, if not scientifically rigorous, conclusions were emerging. The impact of the calcite powder on reflectivity and light scattering was evident from satellite imagery, and temperatures and ice-formation patterns were showing positive effects.

The analysis of the data also addressed the estimated residence times and horizontal distribution of the powder in the troposphere, as well as the increase in the chemicals known to be by-products of the interaction of calcite with ozone. This information would be useful in calibrating future calcite releases to form an appropriately dense atmospheric veil.

The Memorandum erased any doubt in Mahmood's mind about the purpose of the SE mission. When Mahmood gave it to Wang, she responded with a heartfelt "Thank you," and a caution. "Neither you nor Ahmed must ever reveal the existence or contents of this document to anyone."

Mahmood in turn pressed Ahmed to promise not to tell anyone anything about it. Recognizing the importance to Mahmood of his relationship with Wang, he agreed.

After reviewing the document, Wang sent another text directly to the Prime Minister. It read:

New information from an orchard
worker indicates that the trees are growing

nicely. A promising investment so far. No diseased fruit, no signs of rot, no unusual, unanticipated expenditures. Whether the result will be profitable depends on the weather, which you can follow in the media. This is a long-term investment, and months or years may be needed to assess its ultimate value.

———◦———

At a management meeting, Guo shared some gossip from the town that she picked up second hand.

"I just heard the other day that a foreigner moved into Setitor in late December, a woman who says she has come to study wildlife. She bought a home just up the hill from our airfield. She can see everything from up there. She has apparently befriended two of our former aircraft technicians who decided to hang around here for a few more months to enjoy the countryside.

"The woman says she's from Singapore. I wonder just what birds she's watching."

Abdul replied, "We should not be surprised that we are being watched. Ariki told us someone from the funding source would be keeping an eye on us. And Singapore would be a plausible place to recruit an observer.

"At least let's hope that's who she is. Otherwise, we may have an additional observer with unknown motives. Keep listening for more gossip. Are you pretty sure this rumor is accurate? I probably should report it to Ariki if we're confident about it."

Guo responded, "I think it's pretty reliable. Yes, report it. I'm sure he'll be interested."

That afternoon, Abdul sent a text to Martioto:

> A birdwatcher from Singapore has moved into our neighborhood and befriended two of our former employees. No contact with us.

Martioto did not answer the text. He debated whether to tell Wijaya, but decided not to disturb him with this unsurprising news that did not call for any change of course. Nevertheless, his sleep was more restless than before.

As the months passed, Wang found herself increasingly comfortable with the character of her world in Setitor and Rampi. What it lacked in intellectual challenge and sophistication, it made up for in stability, companionship, and a sense of control and predictability in her life.

Wang felt sincere affection for Mahmood and knew he was deeply attached to her. She also found herself happy with her position of power rather than supplication.

I'll never again allow myself to be the desperate other woman, pleading for more attention, dreaming about implausible futures, the way I was with Ibrahim, she insisted to herself.

Ibrahim had noticed Wang's calls were not quite as frequent as before. The character of their conversations had also changed. Wang was more businesslike, less stressed, more cheerful, no longer turning the conversation to personal matters, less interested in hearing about his disappointments and frustrations.

Ibrahim could not help wondering what was causing this transformation. He suppressed his jealousy at the idea someone else had become the focus of her attentions. *Who could she possibly find out there?* he thought. *Perhaps one of those aircraft maintenance technicians she met? A mere mechanic replacing me in her feelings? In her bed? Inconceivable!*

Chapter 22

TIMMINS

Anderson had been captured and was on the way to jail. But the murder of Dr. Hartquist was still unresolved after almost two years. Marie refused to abandon the search, whatever danger it might entail. She missed Jon every day. Her new assistant, Sally Watkins, was a novice who still needed constant guidance and supervision.

Rationally, Marie knew her investment in training Watkins would pay off for the RCMP. But she was impatient for results. And if Jon returned, as she hoped, Watkins would be reassigned, and the benefits of Marie's training efforts would flow elsewhere.

Marie tasked Watkins with the easy part of the follow-up: documenting the case against Anderson and connecting him to other criminal activities. Sally also combed through the records of his communications by phone, email, and the internet in the hope of finding more information about his communications with "Sylvia Jacobsen." Jacobsen's existence and identity were crucial. Finding her would determine whether the RCMP could identify the prime mover behind the murders.

Marie focused on tracking down background information on the "SJacobs" email address. Cable Canada's records showed that it was created early in 2020, and it had been active for only about four months. It was formally closed after ten months. Cable Canada was unwilling to reveal who had created the account without receiving a warrant.

Getting the warrant issued and delivered took another three weeks. Finally, Cable released the records. The account was set up in the name of "Sylvia Jacobsen." Anderson's story was accurate, but it didn't help as much as Marie had hoped.

The mailing address on the account was an abandoned warehouse in Timmins, Ontario. Timmins, a town of about fifty thousand, was founded in 1910 and still thrives on gold mining and, more recently, tourism. Researching "Sylvia Jacobsen" through the internet, including Facebook and social media, proved fruitless. No Sylvia Jacobsen could be found in any directory.

Marie next tried looking for anyone named Jacobs in Timmins. That search brought more interesting results. "Steven Jacobs" was a young lawyer in Timmins. His Facebook page revealed he was a recent graduate of Thompson Rivers Law School, a new public law school in Kamloops, British Columbia. He was not an outstanding student. He apparently considered himself blessed to be working at Clare & Markus, a well-established local law firm. He was eager to work on corporate matters for "the real world" of industry.

Marie arranged an appointment to interview Jacobs on May 17, 2022. She traveled to Timmins on the 16th and checked into the Moneta Hotel. Then she dropped in on the local police to alert them to her presence and ensure they would be around if she needed them.

The next morning, she walked the five blocks to Clare & Markus to meet Jacobs. She found a pleasant, unassuming young man, cordial and cooperative. He denied knowing anyone named "Sylvia Jacobsen," but he became visibly uncomfortable and flustered when asked about the SJacobs email address.

"I don't know anything about any SJacobs email address." He paused. "I mean I can't tell you anything about it. My—our client directed us to keep any information about it confidential."

Marie bore down. "Mr. Jacobs, I'm investigating a murder. Do I need to get a warrant and a subpoena for you and your firm's records to find out the truth? You're a lawyer. You know that in these circumstances I can get access to your files and put you under oath to reveal everything you know.

"Wouldn't you rather just provide the information without creating a public record and possible charges of obstruction of justice?"

Jacobs turned white. Adverse publicity in a town the size of Timmins would damage him and Clare & Markus, and probably end his legal career. He would be looking for a new job with no good explanation for his botched handling of this tangle with the RCMP. He slumped in his chair.

"I didn't do anything wrong. A senior partner in the firm brought the client to my office. He said the client wanted to set up a disguised email account—he said a 'Virtual Private Network'—to protect the client's identity, and neither he nor the client had any idea how to do it. They assumed I would.

"I didn't want to admit that I didn't know how to set up a VPN either. I assured him I would take care of it. I set up SJacobs@Cable.ca and gave the client the email address and password, which I told the client to change. The fees we charged the client included the Cable Company's monthly charges."

Jacobs paused and considered whether to continue.

"After several months, the client asked me to close the account, and I did. I never used the email or looked to see what was on it. Reading the client's email would have violated the client's confidentiality. I never got the new password, so I couldn't look at it even if I had wanted to. For all I knew the client was pursuing an affair or something. That's all there was to it."

Marie asked the obvious, but crucial, questions, "Who is the client? Who is 'Sylvia Jacobsen'? Is she a real person?"

Jacobs pleaded for time. "I can't answer that right now. I need to talk to the senior partner about our obligations before I answer. I really don't know what the rules are. I'm just a beginner at this sort of thing, and I don't want to make a mistake. Can you give me twenty-four hours?"

Marie considered her options. *Getting a warrant and subpoena would take time, and my boss would need to clear it. Issuing a warrant to a respected local law firm and one of its clients would not be popular in a small town like Timmins. The local prosecutor might not even be willing to handle the matter. He has his own future to think about.*

Marie leaned forward in her chair and looked Jacobs in the eye. "All right. I'll give you twenty-four hours. Meanwhile, you might consider the possibility that you are an accessory to a crime. If you can't answer my questions, please have your boss join us. I don't have time to wait any longer to talk to someone who understands his legal obligations and can make a decision. I'll see you tomorrow at 10 am."

Marie searched the Timmins website for sights to explore and found nothing except a tour of an abandoned gold mine. She decided to settle for writing up her results so far and then a leisurely dinner at the Pub & Grub Restaurant in the hotel. A "hidden gem," according to the website.

The steak was better than she anticipated, and she topped it off with a "Tin Roof" ice cream sundae. As she was finishing her tea, a stranger walked past her table, left an envelope, and walked away.

She did not open it at once, thinking she would look at it in the privacy of her room. Then, remembering her earlier experiences in Santa Fe and her own apartment, she took the envelope to the ladies' room to read before she went upstairs.

The note inside was typewritten and unsigned.

> If you want to leave Timmins unharmed, don't proceed any further in your investigation here. Take the morning flight out.

There was no signature, of course.

Marie immediately regretted having handled the envelope and the note without gloves. It reduced the likelihood that the author's fingerprints could be separated from hers or any others to a court's satisfaction.

Trying to avoid adding more fingerprints, she examined the note and the envelope carefully. The envelope was blank. The note itself was on a half sheet that had been cut from standard letterhead. Careful examination revealed a portion of a diagonal watermark: "Clare & M…"

She carefully copied the note in the hotel's business center, replaced the original in the envelope, and slid the copy into a small compartment in her purse. Returned to her hotel room. Checked the continued presence of the thread she had placed across the door and doorjamb. Then entered.

Once inside, she immediately called the local police. No one answered the phone at 8 p.m. The office was closed for the night, and calling 911 got a recording. Timmins' municipal budget was insufficient to fund a twenty-four-hour response. She left a message anyway, hoping someone might check for messages and call her back. She took her gun out of her purse and set it down beside her.

An hour later, she was still waiting. *Time for another approach*, she decided. She did not expect anyone to be in the RCMP Montreal Office at 9 p.m., but it was worth a try. She was surprised to hear Sally's voice.

"Hi. It's Marie. I need your help. Please call our office in Sudbury and tell them to send two uniformed officers to meet me at the Moneta Hotel, 331 Pine Street South in Timmins. I need—"

"Just a minute, let me write that down. Did you say 300 Pine Street?"

"No, 331 Pine Street South." Silence.

"Okay, got it. When do you want them?"

"As soon as humanly possible. Ask them to call me on my cell number, which you have, when they get into

Timmins. I need their protection tonight and their help tomorrow. They will need to be here at least two days. It's about three hundred kilometers, so they should arrive around 1 am if they leave right away."

"Okay. Hold on. Let me find your cell number. I'm sure I have it here somewhere." A long silence. "Here it is. I'll look up the Sudbury Office phone number and call them right now. I was about to leave for home when the phone rang, so I'm happy I got your call. I was just finishing up my—"

"Thank you. It's urgent. Talk to you later," Marie uttered in a tone of exasperation. She tried to remind herself she was lucky Sally was in the office at all. *Sally may be loquacious, but right now she is my lifeline.*

Partly to distract herself, Marie took out her iPad and began making notes on what she would say at the meeting in the morning. No luck. She heard every noise in the hall. Feared that her call had been intercepted. Wondered if Sally had reached anyone in Sudbury. If they would have anyone to send. What time they might arrive. How to explain the situation to the officers. Whether she would get any sleep.

She tried to stop thinking about the possibility they would not arrive at all, or until it was too late.

She managed to make a few notes for the morning meeting but dozed restlessly in the uncomfortable chair in her room. Awoke dreaming of the gun shots in Santa Fe. Her cell phone was ringing.

Sally was breathless. "I just got off the phone with Sudbury. I had a long talk with the officer on duty. He wanted—"

"Are they coming?"

"I finally explained who you are and what you—"

This time Marie practically shouted, "Are they coming?"

Sally was so excited about her success she wanted to share every detail.

"The Sudbury Office was reluctant to send two uniformed officers to Timmins immediately and commit to them staying for two days. They already had other assignments. And I had no details to explain the necessity or urgency. It took some wheedling and cajoling to persuade the desk officer to trust my word."

Suddenly Sally realized she had been talking too much. "Yes. They should leave about two hours from now. Based on what you told me about the distance, they will probably arrive around 5:30 am."

Marie took a breath. Six more hours! She restrained herself from screaming, *My life might be in danger! I need them* HERE NOW!

But she hadn't told Sally about the threatening note, and she didn't want to worry her at this point. It was impossible for the RCMP officers to get here much sooner than 5:30 am, whatever the circumstances. Marie took a long breath.

"Thank you," she mumbled. "That's excellent. I'll be waiting for them." It was all she could get out of her mouth at that moment.

"I hope everything works out. Do you want me to stay up?" Sally replied.

Marie regained some of her composure. She owed Sally more than a curt dismissal. "I'm sure everything will be fine. Please write a full report on your conversations with me and the Sudbury Office. I assume you will be in the office at the usual time? I'll call you there if I need anything.

"Thank you again for your prompt assistance. It is crucial to my plans for tomorrow. I hope you are calling from home. If not, please go. I'll call you on your cell if there is any emergency."

The RCMP officers arrived at 6 am. Marie greeted them with relief. She explained the situation in five minutes. Gave them the note for safekeeping. Apologized for the long night of driving and for making one of them stay awake on guard in the lobby until they all left for the Clare & Markus appointment.

Once they understood the situation, the officers were much friendlier. Marie went back to her room. She slept intermittently for about an hour. *Better than nothing.*

Chapter 23

TIMMINS

Marie was dressed and ready at 8 am. She reviewed the situation and her plans with the officers over breakfast. They proceeded to Clare & Markus at 9:45 am. Steve Jacobs greeted them at the door and escorted them to the conference room. He turned a bit pale at the sight of the two uniformed RCMPs.

"I'll get Mr. Clare immediately," he whispered as he left the room. Mr. Clare entered and immediately initiated the conversation.

"Welcome to Timmins! I'm Gary Clare, and I know you've met Steve Jacobs. Please call me Gary. This is a small town. We're not very formal here. How can we help you?"

"I'm Marie Roy. This is Officer McNamara, and Officer Martineau. We need to clear up a couple of matters with you in connection with our investigation of a murder on a cruise ship a few years ago. Our efforts led us to an email account in the name of SJacobs, which was set up by your associate and paid for by your firm.

"Mr. Jacobs told me yesterday that the address was set up at the request of a client. He never used the account himself, and he has no information about who did or for what purpose. We need to know the identity of the client to pursue our investigation. Steve was unsure whether he should give out that information, which might normally be protected by an attorney-client privilege. In these circumstances, however, we could easily subpoena your firm's files and find the answer, and who knows what else.

"I was hoping we could spare you and your client the public embarrassment of putting this matter on the court record here in Timmins, at least until we have a more concrete reason to do so."

Gary Clare seemed unfazed by Marie's description of the situation. "Ms. Roy, I understand your objective and appreciate your effort to understand our situation. However, Steve was correct in his decision not to share confidential files or other client information without a subpoena or a warrant based on probable cause.

"Our ethical obligation and legal right is to protect our client's privacy in the absence of a warrant or subpoena. If you are confident you can obtain one, please proceed. In the meantime, we must refuse to provide you any information. Is there anything else at this time?" he said, intending to close the meeting.

Marie paused to take in his answer and responded with equally calm self-assurance.

"Yes, there is one other matter. Last night someone walked by my dinner table at a local restaurant and left this note. It is certainly a threat against an RCMP officer, and since it was delivered less than twenty-four hours ago and I'm still in Timmins, it appears to constitute a continuing criminal act. Do either of you know anything about it?"

Clare glanced at the copy of the note, then looked at Steve Jacobs, who blanched. Then he looked more carefully at the note. After another pause, he spoke.

"Steve, do you have any idea what this is about? Threatening an RCMP officer! That's terrible!"

Before he could say anything more, Marie added an additional fact. "I should also tell you that the note appears to have been written on Clare & Markus watermarked stationery. It seems likely that someone in this firm wrote it. I'm sure the fingerprints will tell us."

Clare, apparently startled, stared at Jacobs. "Steve! Did you do this? How could you be so reckless? Don't you know it's a crime to threaten the police? What were you thinking?"

Steve's look of fear hardened into anger. "You know I did it, because you told me to do it! 'We can scare this girl off,' you said. 'Just deliver her a note that says get out of town. She'll run.' And I believed you!"

At that point, Marie interrupted. "Officers, I think we've heard enough to put both men under arrest on suspicion of threatening an RCMP officer. I'd like one of you to take them to the police station for booking, while the other one guards the files here to ensure they are not tampered with.

"Mr. Clare, perhaps now you would like to tell me who your client is, so I don't need to search all your files."

Clare said nothing in response. Instead he asked to be allowed to call his lawyer. "That can wait until we book you at the station," Officer McNamara replied. He locked his handcuffs on Clare's right arm and Jacobs' left arm, and walked them out the door. They were booked at the local police station and released on their own recognizance.

Meanwhile, Marie and Officer Martineau rounded up all the firm's staff. Marie told them the news.

"Mr. Clare and Mr. Jacobs have been arrested on suspicion of threatening an RCMP investigator. Until this matter is fully resolved, no documents or records of any kind, electronic, paper, legal, financial, or personal, are to be moved or destroyed. We will be reviewing them, starting with Mr. Jacobs' files, accounts, and records, today. I hope we can count on your cooperation. Except for Mr. Clare's assistant, the best thing I can advise you to do is leave for home right now."

Eager to be far from this situation, they all left immediately. Mr. Clare's secretary stayed to ensure that none of the firm's files were damaged or destroyed in the search.

It didn't take long to identify the client. She was Margaret Schakowsky Taylor, the sole child of Adrian Schakowsky, an immigrant dairy farmer who moved to Timmins from rural Lithuania in 1947. He unexpectedly became wealthy in 1957, when Chevron discovered and developed oil and natural gas on his land.

Ms. Taylor, now eighty-three, was brought to the police station for questioning. She was accompanied by a lawyer, but paid no attention to his advice. Confronted with evidence from the Clare & Markus files, Taylor acknowledged that she had contacted Anderson, using the name Jacobsen, to arrange for the demise of Dr. Hartquist. Her motivations were clearly stated in her formal confession to the prosecutor.

> Dr. Hartquist was a danger to civilization. Her rabble-rousing in the media about climate change and global warming, all malicious nonsense, was intended to end the use of oil and natural gas for any purpose. The progress of civilization, which has brought so much good to so many people of all races, was built upon those energy resources. Without them, most of Canada, and Dr. Hartquist's native Sweden, would still be a frozen wasteland.
>
> My family, my children, grandchildren, and great-grandchildren, all depend on oil and gas to heat their homes, provide their electricity, and run their cars.

All this talk about solar and wind power taking its place is fantasy.

Our planet cannot possibly support more than a small fraction of its seven billion people without the use of oil and gas. The result of barring its use would be famines, disease, political and social upheaval, civil and international wars, and massive numbers of deaths as the population shrinks year after year. Even the wealthiest elements of society will suffer, and our culture and institutions and traditions will be lost in the deluge.

I couldn't allow that to happen to my children and grandchildren because of some misguided concern for polar bears. It had to be stopped.

Inquiries into Margaret Taylor's political activities confirmed her opposition to all regulations, research, and references to climate change, global warming, and related topics. She had bankrolled political candidates who espoused her views and hired lobbyists to oppose climate-related laws. She was appalled when the Democrats swept the US House in the 2018 national elections.

Taylor had developed the physical and mental disabilities that go with old age and infirmity. She walked with difficulty, ate and slept erratically, and seemed to be in constant pain. Inquiries into her mental condition indicated some level of dementia, accompanied by a growing paranoia and an obsession with preserving her family's wealth against all threats. Increasingly isolated, she talked only to those who reinforced her views.

Taylor had occasionally threatened to disown any family member who disagreed with her on climate change or other political issues. *They have no idea what life would be like without the benefit of oil and gas*, she sometimes muttered. Naturally, her children and grandchildren humored her, whether to be kind or to protect their own financial prospects. No one considered her a practical danger to anyone.

When questioned about whether her disapproval of Dr. Hartquist's views justified murder, she became defensive and uncomfortable. But she professed complete confidence that she was doing God's work by expunging this great evil from the planet. She had seen Dr. Hartquist many times on television and was convinced that Hartquist alone was the key threat to the continued use of oil and natural gas. "Without her, the whole charade will collapse, as people look past her beguiling appearance and politically-motivated distortions to consider the real facts of the situation."

Taylor insisted she knew nothing of the details of the Hartquist murder, the subsequent murder of Miller, or the threats and attacks on Marie and Jon. She left it all to

Anderson and had no interest in anything he did once she knew Dr. Hartquist was dead.

Faced with their client's explicit admissions, Taylor's lawyers asserted she was not guilty by reason of insanity— her failing mind, isolation, and paranoia had led her to hire Anderson. Given her age and condition, the prosecution finally agreed to the plea on the conditions that (a) Taylor be confined to her estate and her communications monitored, and (b) her finances be placed in the hands of a guardian who would be barred from devoting funds to political or related activities regardless of the beneficiary's stated wishes. Taylor was released to the physical custody of her children under the supervision of the parole system.

Clare and Jacobs pleaded guilty to the charge of threatening an RCMP officer but sought leniency on the ground of lack of premeditation. Their argument was specifically rejected by the court, but they were given only one-year jail terms at a minimum-security prison. Both were permanently disbarred from the practice of law.

———◦———

Marie's reward was two weeks of paid leave. She was glad to have the break. The only thing she wanted to do, besides sleep, was spend time with her husband. Chris took time off, and they vacationed together for ten days in

Hawaii, enjoying the beach, the food, the tropical environment, and the absence of responsibilities.

She was still distressed about Jon. While no longer in critical condition, he was seriously incapacitated, living at home, and undertaking an extensive program of physical therapy.

Marie had visited the house to tell Jon and Linda that Anderson had been found guilty and put in jail. She visited again to tell them that the Hartquist case had been successfully resolved and that Taylor and her lawyers were suitably punished.

Jon evidently understood her words, though he could not speak. It was all Marie could do to maintain her composure on seeing Jon so disabled.

The doctors were optimistic that some speech capability would return, but they could not say whether Jon would ever be capable of carrying on a complex conversation. His most likely future was retirement on the generous pension provided to RCMP officers wounded in the line of duty. He might eventually be able to handle a quiet new job, far from the investigative work that had put him literally in the line of fire, if his speech recovered sufficiently. The doctors strongly recommended against his ever trying to cope with the stress of investigative work at the RCMP.

Marie returned to work after her vacation, resigned to the reality that Sally would be her assistant for the indefinite future. Looking at the stack of pending cases on her desk, she realized that none of them would be as challenging as the Hartquist case.

She seriously considered the idea of retiring. When she mentioned it to Chris, he replied there was no reason for her to work if she was not enjoying it. He would be happy having a wife who met him at the door with a martini and helped him relax after his day's work. Weighing her choices, Marie promised to decide within a year.

At first, she wasn't certain that she could stand to live without working. But after taking a longer leave of absence, she realized that a full life awaited her in retirement. She left the RCMP six months later.

⁂

The media headlined the news that the RCMP had captured the person who initiated and financed the murder of Dr. Ilsa Hartquist. They variously described Margaret Taylor as an evil capitalist seeking to protect her own wealth, or as a dupe or front for oil and gas industry propagandists and unscrupulous politicians eager to use her money for their own advancement. Some commentators on the left and on the right preferred to characterize her as merely a deranged and demented old woman whose paranoia and anxiety led her astray.

The news about Taylor prompted massive street demonstrations around the world. Speakers protested against fossil fuels and those who own, operate, and use oil and gas at every level of industrial activity, from drilling wells, to building gasoline-powered autos, to generating electricity.

In many countries, including parts of the US, the demonstrations and rhetoric took on a decidedly anti-American tone, focusing on the fact that Taylor was an "oil tycoon" who acknowledged that her motivation was to protect the privileged financial position of her family.

Proponents of radical action to forestall destructive climate change argued that the murder showed what industry owners and managers were willing to do to misinform the public, skew the legislative process, and destroy their opponents.

Demonstration leaders who advocated an SRM veil exhorted the public to watch the online videos of Dr. Hartquist's interviews and her speech to AOSIS, and millions of people did so. Activists opposed to "planetary manipulation" advocated policies designed to protect natural ecosystems and a return to local, self-sustaining lifestyles instead.

The European Union announced it had already begun an intensive laboratory research program on the feasibility of an SRM tropospheric veil to slow climate change in 2019, despite the refusal of the US to participate. But it stressed that it had not yet concluded that an SRM veil was sufficiently safe to warrant its use.

President Gonzalez convened his National Security Council (NSC) to discuss the idea of adopting a more aggressive climate policy, including work on a tropospheric veil. Harold Williamson, still serving as CIA Director in the Gonzalez Administration, found himself in the awkward position of advocating strong action, quite contrary to the Trump Administration policies he had participated in shaping.

Williamson's position on climate issues during the Trump Administration had always been somewhat ambiguous. Trained as a systems analyst, he could never be comfortable with the climate science deniers. He had often mentioned the adverse impact on the US leadership position internationally, particularly as China and India extended their dominant influence in the climate change field.

It was hard to know how vigorously Williamson had tried to educate President Trump on the issue. If he had seriously tried, he had obviously failed. Several other members of the NSC were convinced he was now working to ingratiate himself with the new President, whose campaign and subsequent actions strongly favored an aggressive carbon emissions mitigation program.

After listening to the NSC discussion, which by now sounded familiar, the President concluded he was unwilling to get ahead of the EU without a stronger international consensus. Instead, he proposed doubling the US budget for geoengineering research. His official Fiscal 2023 Budget

Request to Congress included the following statement in support of increased climate research:

Whatever one thinks of the wisdom of Solar Radiation Management (SRM) or other forms of geoengineering, the gap between the theoretical concept and its practical implementation remains much too large. Our best scientists and engineers have not reached consensus on whether any kind of SRM veil would be effective, how to calibrate the frequency and quantities of chemicals to accomplish the mission with the least adverse side effects, or even whether an SRM tropospheric veil is the most desirable geoengineering alternative....

At the same time, our scientists are increasingly concerned about a variety of near-term risks that are nonlinear and potentially disruptive in character. Unfortunately, any climate intervention could also create some risk of nonlinear, disruptive consequences, either immediately or over the long term.

While we cannot be complacent or timid, it would equally be a mistake just to try anything and everything without adequate knowledge of the consequences of such actions. "First, do no harm" must be a crucial consideration in our decision process.

The enlarged research program I am asking Congress to fund will accelerate our efforts to get reliable answers to the central unresolved questions.

The more cautious members of the scientific community believed the President was taking the right path. To many people in the United States and elsewhere in the world, however, this step was too little too late.

More skeptical observers and various anti-American organizations attacked the President's plan as just a delaying tactic to protect the fossil fuel industry in his home state of Texas, at a time when the world's life-sustaining natural systems were beginning to come apart at the seams.

Chapter 24

MOSCOW

The winter and spring of 2022–23 brought a modest, but tangible, improvement in weather patterns around the world. The September 2022 Arctic ice low-coverage point was measurably higher than the previous year, reversing a consistent trend of disappearing ice for the first time in almost a decade. The SE staff celebrated a successful year of active intervention, apparently with positive results.

The Arctic ice change appeared to produce a reversion to a milder winter, less forceful hurricanes and monsoons, more rapidly moving storms, and a more even distribution of precipitation. Farmers praised their gods. Coastal residents enjoyed less erosion and storm damage. The world's weather patterns and climate systems seemed to be regaining their balance.

People in Eastern Europe and Siberia were especially pleased with the winter's weather. The last several winters had been extremely bitter, as the increasingly ice-free Arctic Ocean had generated more severe, slow-moving winter storms and longer-lasting cloud cover. Moreover, the warmer summers had been disrupting agriculture and melting the permafrost that physically supported much of the Siberian Arctic's infrastructure.

The sunnier, milder winter in Moscow made most of its residents happy, but not President Putin and his bureaucrats in the Ministry of Transportation. The expanding Arctic ice threatened to undermine achievement of their goals. At Putin's direction, they were busily designing and preparing to build the facilities necessary for year-round maritime commerce in the Arctic region.

Year-round ice-free Arctic navigation for commercial vessels, including cruise ships, would justify a building boom all along the Russian Arctic coast. Putin was planning for the end of his fourth term, and these projects would allow him to finish his presidency with a flurry of ribbon-cuttings and improved economic performance numbers.

Putin's current term would end in May 2024, after the March–April election process. He was not eligible to serve another consecutive term after his second set of two consecutive terms, unless he could arrange an amendment to the Federation Constitution, as Chinese President Xi had done.

Putin hoped his Arctic infrastructure program would spark an outpouring of support for allowing him to run for another term as President. The projects would also provide one more opportunity for his friends in the "quasi-private" construction and maritime sectors to add to their wealth.

So he was not just idly curious about this winter's surprising weather. *Is this reversal an anomaly or part of a new trend?* he wondered. *Should I give up on the Arctic project and look for another way to go out with a flourish?*

He called in his Minister of Environment, Dimitri Romanov. "Dimitri, my friend, if this year's weather continues, it will threaten the timing of my Open Arctic project. Is this a onetime occurrence, or is climate change surprising us again? You know how I feel about surprises."

"I do, Mr. President. My climate experts and modelers in the Meteorological Bureau have been studying this matter carefully. We don't have an answer just yet, but I can tell the Director to put more resources to work on the project and try to get you an answer more quickly."

Putin responded with annoyance. "In other words, you don't know what's happening either. I was afraid of that. I need an answer in two weeks. I don't want to make any more speeches extolling the glories of my new Open Arctic projects if the ships will be blocked every winter for some years. My program must be seen and understood as a triumph, not a 'bridge to nowhere,' as the Americans used to say."

"I understand completely, Mr. President. We have no doubt about the long-term trend. Explaining a single year's weather is always more difficult."

"Dimitri, the great British economist John Maynard Keynes pointed out almost one hundred years ago that 'in the long run we are all dead.' And our run is getting shorter every day. We can't afford a miscalculation. I will not be the only one held accountable."

Dimitri tried to smile, without success. Putin rose and ushered Dimitri out of his office.

Thirty minutes later, Dimitri was in the office of Valery Ignatov, the Director of the Meteorological Bureau. "The President is very worried that this year's weather will undermine or at least delay his Open Arctic project. You assured me we were taking positive steps to ensure the ice would melt rapidly. What's happening?"

"Sir, we have been studying this weather situation day and night. We do know that if next year follows this year's trend, the Open Arctic will be delayed by at most a few years. It's just a small glitch. The larger trends are irreversible at this point."

"Valery, you obviously don't understand. The President wants this to happen during his term of office, which ends next May. The 'long run' for him, and therefore for us, is a year from now. The Arctic must be sufficiently ice-free next winter to justify his pronouncements later this spring. He plans to announce that Russia is beginning a massive Arctic coastal construction program to take advantage of the new ice-free conditions. It would be embarrassing to have the Arctic refreeze. I need a better answer than the long-term trend. By the end of this week."

"Yes, sir. I'll give it my full attention."

As Dimitri returned to his office he saw a stranger sitting in the waiting room. He sat down at his desk and buzzed his assistant.

"Who's the guy sitting out there? I don't have anything on my calendar, but I don't have time to waste on petty problems."

"He's an employee in the Meteorological Bureau. He claims he has some news you personally need to know."

"That's what they all say. OK, show him in, but come get him in five minutes, not more."

"Yes, sir."

He ushered the young man into the office. Dimitri did not invite him to sit down. "What's so important, young man?" Dimitri made a point of displaying his impatience.

"Thank you for seeing me, sir. My name is Aaron Osofsky. I have a friend who works in the Defense Aerial Surveillance Office (DASO)—"

"If this is about getting someone a job, please leave now, and I'll pretend this interruption never occurred."

"No, sir. I'll come to the point. He told me that his office has found data showing unidentified planes flying over our territory at tropospheric altitude for several months. He wondered if we were doing any climate modification experiments that would explain the flights. DASO is always nervous about unidentified aircraft, but his senior management assumed it was one of ours. He gave me the times and locations. I checked our scheduled flights. They are not our flights, and the altitude is higher than anything our program calls for. I'm afraid to tell him that because he says if they are foreign, Defense will probably shoot down the next flight. But don't we need to know who it belongs to and what they are doing, first?"

Dimitri stared at the man for a long moment, trying to understand what he was implying.

"Are you telling me that unidentified flights are cruising the Arctic troposphere, and they are not part of our weather modification programs in the Arctic? Does he know where these flights are coming from?"

"These flights are certainly foreign, sir. The flight path doesn't reveal where they're coming from, except that it's somewhere well south of here. Without knowing the flight duration or trajectory, it's difficult to reconstruct the origin."

Dimitri needed time to think, and to be sure he was getting the full story. "Sit down, please. What's your name again?"

"Osofsky, sir."

Dimitri sat down in the chair directly opposite him. At that moment Dimitri's assistant walked in. "Your next appointment is here, sir. Shall I show this gentleman out?"

"No, we aren't quite finished. Please don't interrupt us again. Thank you." Bewildered, his assistant retreated to the outer office.

Dimitri turned again to Osofsky. "Let's go over this all again. This time, tell me first, is this an authorized inquiry from DASO, or just some bureaucrat's curious chatter?

First-hand, reliable data, or just a rumor? Has he brought these matters to the attention of his superiors? What did they tell him? And what have you already told him?"

Shaken by the intensity of the rapid-fire questions, Osofsky gathered his wits to answer in full. "Yes sir. As far as I know, this is not an official inquiry, and none is to be expected. My friend reviewed the surveillance data himself. He didn't have any doubts about its accuracy.

"He told his superiors, but they brushed it off and told him not to worry about what are clearly unarmed planes. He figured maybe the flight was part of a secret intelligence operation that he wasn't cleared to know about. But he also wondered whether someone is conducting secret climate experiments that no one at DASO knows about. He asked me what I knew. I told him I was completely in the dark. I didn't tell him what little I know about our "positive steps" program, or even that it exists.

"Is there anything more I can tell you? I'm not expecting you to tell me anything. I just wanted you to know about this unusual situation." Osofsky lapsed into silence, regretting that he had ever raised the matter.

Dimitri sat back in his chair. "No, you did the right thing to bring this subject directly to my attention. Please don't tell your friend anything more for now. What's his name, by the way?"

Osofsky hadn't anticipated that request. He felt trapped. If he refused to say, he would certainly be punished, probably sooner than later. If he gave his friend's true name, there was a real risk his friend would be punished. He took a breath and quickly analyzed the moral and practical implications of his choice.

Gennady put himself at risk, Osofsky reasoned. *I shouldn't pay for his breaches of DASO or Ministry of Defense rules, if there are any.* He concluded he had no obligation to protect his friend.

"His name is Gennady Morizov. He's an honest and dedicated worker. He is just trying to do his job."

"I'm sure that's the case. Thank you." Dimitri stood up and walked Osofsky to the door. "Don't do or say anything to anyone about this. I'll take care of the matter from here. Leave your email and phone number with my assistant."

Dimitri returned to his desk, his mind digesting this new information. An experienced bureaucrat, he had risen to the top of his Ministry by stopping to think ahead when others acted on impulse. Thirty minutes of careful thought with paper and pen identified many pitfalls ahead and the course of action most likely to ensure his survival as a powerful and effective bureaucrat, whoever was President:

- I need to know about the potential impact of these planes over the Arctic. Valery should be able to tell me if these small-scale flights could possibly change the Arctic climate. Maybe the whole issue of foreign flights is irrelevant.

- We just presented Putin a proposal to test an SRM veil. He would not hear of it. "We need to open the Arctic to year-round commercial shipping," was his response. "Saving the planet can be the next president's job."

- Could someone in my own Department be conducting some unauthorized experiments? No point in raising a finger if it points at me.

- Maybe some flunky at Defense or in the Air Force has decided to be a planetary hero? The military always claims it is only carrying out its mission, but its mandate to "defend the Motherland" is quite broad. They have interpreted it many ways.

- I should talk to Gennady or his boss at DASO to see if they can locate the origin of the flights.

- Assuming my Ministry's skirts are clean, I should alert the Foreign Office of the potential for a diplomatic, or even military, crisis.

- Then I will arrange a meeting with the President about this development. Unfortunately, Putin's most likely response will be less thoughtful than Osofsky's: "Just shoot them down. We'll find out very quickly who is intent on undermining Russia's Arctic future." I should bring Defense and Foreign Affairs to the meeting, to slow him down.

The prospect of an immediate military response deeply dismayed Dimitri. *Russia has had enough of impulsive actions by our chess-playing President, who unfortunately only thinks about two moves ahead,* he muttered to himself.

Did we really win anything in Crimea and Ukraine? In Syria? They are just sinkholes for valuable political chits and scarce economic and military resources. How long will we continue to pay the diplomatic and economic price for those macho ventures?

If we shoot down one of these planes, we might be attacking peaceful scientific research being conducted by an ally, or a consortium of European powers, or even by some US organization. No one could take kindly to a military attack on its research planes. It could end up being another justification for maintaining economic sanctions on Russia, or even on Putin himself.

Over the next two days, Dimitri worked systematically through his action list. He talked directly to Gennady Morizov, then with a high-ranking friend in DASO to ensure that the information was accurate and complete. He quickly got the military's answers: They have no other explanation; no Defense Ministry projects are involved. DASO's antiquated radar tracking systems are incapable of determining the precise origin of the flights. "Yes, of course we could shoot down a plane over our airspace, even at tropospheric altitude," his friend added, "but why would we shoot down an unarmed civilian aircraft?"

Valery confirmed that the Environment Ministry's only climate-related operations and experiments were aimed at melting the Arctic ice, and that none of these unknown flights were connected with those efforts. "Look," Valery explained defensively, "we're as committed to an ice-free Arctic as Putin is. We have no good explanation for this year's weather, which is probably just a one-off aberration."

Dimitri tried out a different explanation: "Is it possible there is a rogue operation in your bureau or someone subverting the official program to reverse its effect?"

Valery, shocked by the question, answered heatedly, "It's a very small group of scientists and technicians. I know them all personally. I can't imagine that. But I'll work on confirming that everyone in the program is on the same page."

"Okay. Let me know," Dimitri responded, ending the conversation.

Valery called back two days later. "I've gone over the individual files and talked in person with every team member. Some are militantly patriotic and agree with Putin entirely. Others are lukewarm on the current program.

"I picked the least enthusiastic one and transferred her to a different office. Now she's working on automating retrospective daily weather data, where she has no access to our current climate program. I have no evidence whatsoever that she's done anything wrong, and I doubt that this one person could have done any damage even if she had tried. But I think the rest of the staff has the message."

Dimitri sighed, dismayed by Valery's arbitrary action. *It's only a minor injustice*, he reflected, *and already done. I didn't ask him to do it. I wonder if Valery also has other reasons for the reassignment. I'm in charge, but I'm not the Human Resources Office in this Ministry. If she has a complaint, she should talk to them.*

To Valery he said, "That's good news. Thank you."

Reluctantly, Dimitri requested a meeting with Putin for himself, Defense Minister Boris Ivanov, and Foreign Affairs Minister Nicholas Tretyakov. He spoke briefly with the other two Ministers to alert them about the subject of the meeting he had requested. His fears about the outcome intensified when Putin scheduled the meeting immediately.

Dimitri began calmly, but he had difficulty maintaining that pose. "Mr. President, I have learned, initially through informal channels whose data I have verified, that DASO radar has detected a steady stream of small aircraft, possibly drones, flying over Russia at tropospheric levels, en route to the Arctic.

"We know nothing about their mission, but it could well be a secret attempt to cool the Arctic, and thereby delay global warming by a type of solar radiation management, namely, placing a chemical veil over the region to reflect more sunlight out into space. Of course, the public in northern Siberia would welcome any action that refreezes their permafrost and increases the frequency of sunny, if cold, winter weather.

"But we all know you have more important things in mind. My understanding is that DASO has not been able to gather definitive information about the origin or function of the flights.

"Without putting anything in writing, I have done what I could to verify this information and confirm that this operation is not internal to our government or a private Russian operation. If it is what I suspect, and it is succeeding in refreezing the Arctic, that would have a global environmental impact. We would face some agonizing questions."

At that, Putin's face turned red. "You're damn right you would. Year-round ice-free Arctic navigation is my number one priority."

He turned to Boris. "Why hasn't our air force just shot them down? They're trespassing Russian airspace without authorization. If attacked they will have no choice but to discontinue the operation. How quickly could you stop these flights?"

Before Boris could answer, Nicholas intervened. "I understand your concerns, Mr. President, but we should not move to military action yet. We don't know whose aircraft these are, what their long-term mission is, whether they belong to friendly or hostile nations, or even whether they are manned or unmanned. The diplomatic ramifications could be very negative."

Seeking to slow Putin's rush to a decision, Nicholas turned in his chair to face Boris. "Boris, isn't there some way to determine their origin quickly? Shouldn't we at least make some inquiries through the UN to find out who is behind these flights? Maybe the US would even help us. These aircraft may be flying over Alaska or Canada as well. They can't be very happy about unauthorized flights either. And these flights may be changing the climate of the entire northern hemisphere."

Boris glared at Nicholas. He felt too old to be spending time in meetings on such nonsense. He would have already retired if Putin had let him.

"No, Nick, we can't determine either their origin or their flight path over other Arctic countries without knowing the duration of the flights." He turned to face Putin. "Mr. President, we still have not been given funds for equipment to match the sophisticated American global systems.

"Our best equipment is devoted to defense against missiles from the US, China, North Korea, Europe, or Israel, among others. As much as I share your concerns, I suggest that you ask the Foreign Intelligence Service (FIS) to collect some information on who we would be attacking and give us an estimate of whether they can or will counterattack.

"Shooting down foreign planes could provoke an immediate military response from the owner. These flights might even have military protection of which we are not yet aware, putting our own pilots at risk. The continued operation of the aircraft for a few weeks won't change the world. We don't want to put Russian lives at risk."

Faced with these additional considerations and the evident opposition of his key Ministers, Putin retreated. "All right, let's see what FIS can deliver. I'll give them two weeks." He rose impatiently, signaling to the Ministers the meeting was over.

When the three Ministers reached the hallway, Boris railed at Nicholas, "There was no reason to embarrass the Defense Ministry like that. You knew we don't know the origin or character of the flights. Now I'll probably need to send up some pilots to inspect these aircraft, photograph their markings, and see if they have pilots or escorts. It's one thing to shoot down a drone, but quite another to kill a foreign military pilot."

Nicholas suppressed a smile and replied somberly, "I understand your feelings. I just couldn't take a chance that our macho President would get a favorable response from you. Dimitri's position was obvious. He brought us in to slow Putin down. But I was afraid you might not see it that way."

Boris responded angrily. "You won't get very far by underestimating my intelligence or trying to manipulate me at meetings with the President. You'll be sorry in the long run." He walked away abruptly.

"Sometimes these matters can't be left to chance," Nicholas whispered to Dimitri, seeking his confirmation.

Dimitri changed the subject. "I guess we've got two weeks to solve this riddle. Can you get any help from the US or China without making the whole story public?"

Nicholas responded with a mildly condescending smile, "Not the way Washington works these days. We might just as well tell the *Washington Post* outright as try to keep something like this secret. That would just make it a bigger story. But maybe FIS can get a simple confirmation from the CIA that the US has no knowledge of or interest in protecting these flights. Let's see what Grigori can do."

Two weeks later the three Ministers were back in President Putin's office, along with Grigori Mordichov, the FIS Director. Putin was impatient, as usual. "Well, my dear Grigori, what do we know about these aircraft?"

Putin's tone was not calculated to make Grigori comfortable. Putin had been unhappy with him and FIS since they failed to warn him that President Gonzalez was likely to impose economic sanctions aimed specifically at Putin's own financial interests. Putin lost access to several of his personal foreign bank accounts, including substantial sums in Switzerland and the Comoros Islands.

Ignoring the President's hostile tone, Grigori proceeded with as calm a demeanor as he could muster. "Very little, sir. The planes are commercial cargo jets readily available on the open market. They might be drones, based on the nature and infrequency of their communications, but that does not mean they are truly unmanned. They could be just running on autopilot while a live pilot or observer is sleeping on these long flights. The Air Force interceptor pilots that tracked the most recent flights could not determine whether a live person was aboard. No State has sought approval for the overflights, but it could be argued that they are so high that no approval is necessary, like spacecraft.

"The planes seem to have been modified in several ways to facilitate operations in the troposphere. We don't have specific evidence of the release of chemicals over Russia or the Arctic, but that would seem to be their purpose. We've tried to determine their origin, but without success. We know they're coming from the south over China, but we cannot trace their specific takeoff or landing sites without stationing intelligence vessels in the South China Sea. Right now, with all the controversy there, that seems to be an unwarranted risk."

Putin stopped him right there. "You are saying we don't know if the planes have pilots or where they are coming from, yet you think it would be an unwarranted risk to send a few intelligence vessels into the disputed

Chinese waters to find their origin? Do the Chinese or the Americans know anything more? Would they object?"

"Sir, the Chinese surveillance equipment is so poor that it can't detect anything at that altitude, and they say they know nothing. They sometimes track commercial flights around their region, but they don't seem to have detected these. They might be suspicious of our story that we are sending surveillance ships into their waters only to track unidentified foreign flights.

"The Americans probably know at least as much as we do. I didn't ask for any help from them. They might also be suspicious of our motives. Their continuing Korean peninsula maneuvers and our countermeasures are a delicate topic right now."

Putin stared into space, obviously frustrated. "So if no one knows anything about these flights, and they're over our airspace and probably aimed at undoing our Arctic program, why don't we just shoot one down and see who complains?"

Boris Ivanov sat up in his chair. "Mr. President, we don't shoot down commercial flights or kill innocent people, or even military pilots, on mere supposition. Remember Korean Air 007? Let's not repeat that mistake.

"I've given this matter some thought. I think we can put an end to these flights just by having our fighters fly close alongside, make radio contact, and order the planes out of our airspace. I suggest we start there."

Putin's face twisted in anger. "That's a pretty minimal response to repeated, unauthorized overflights. For all we know, these planes are carrying nuclear bombs. Or the US, or the Chinese, or who knows who, might be spooking our air defense system to see how we respond. Just because we assume these flights are not an immediate threat doesn't mean we shouldn't demonstrate our capability to respond immediately to a potential threat to our homeland!"

Faced with the President's wrath, Boris hardened his approach. "If we don't get a satisfactory response, we can destroy the intruder at a point where the remains will land on our territory. That way, we could find out who is really behind this and what the mission is. We don't need to trust or believe anyone.

"But let's learn from the Gary Powers U-2 incident in 1960. Shooting down that intelligence flight appeared to be a clever idea, and we played the innocent victim in the media. But Chairman Khrushchev lost a wonderful opportunity to improve relations with the US at a time when they were vastly outspending the Soviet Union on military hardware. A new disarmament deal at the impending summit with Eisenhower might have saved the USSR.

"The downing of the U-2 destroyed that option. These days, the US is already looking for reasons to impose additional sanctions because of our activities in Ukraine and elsewhere around the periphery. We don't need to hand them another one."

Putin meanwhile relaxed in his chair. He had made up his mind. Disregarding Boris's cautionary words, he focused on the need to demonstrate Russia's ability to take prompt action against any intruder. "All right. Do as you say. I trust you will have resolved this matter one way or another very soon."

Turning to Dimitri, he added, "In the meantime, my dear Environment Minister, please make sure that our own efforts have the desired effects. If that means adding flights to ensure that we continue to make progress toward an ice-free Arctic by next year, do it. If you need more planes or other resources, let me know.

"And Nick, be prepared to take this matter to the UN Security Council the moment we down the intruder. We aren't going to let some nonentity invade our sovereign rights in the Arctic."

Putin stood up. *Now we're getting somewhere*, he thought to himself, with some satisfaction. The meeting was over.

Chapter 25

BEIJING

In China's Xinjiang, Qinghai, and Gansu provinces, March 2023 brought gentle spring rain for the first time in several years, ending debilitating droughts and promising a return to greater agricultural production. In Beijing, the conditions were also a bit better, with more clear days, less smog, and more moderate temperatures.

In mid-June, President Xi called in Yu Wenzhou, his Environment Minister, for an explanation of the unexpected weather patterns. "Is this weather an anomaly or the beginning of a new ice age? Is global warming actually an American hoax to undermine Chinese economic development?"

He proffered this last question with a smile, lampooning former President Trump's repeated assertions that climate change was a Chinese hoax. Although somewhat paranoid like many Great Power leaders, Xi was far too smart to disregard scientific realities and too Chinese in perspective to ignore long run consequences.

Yu replied in her usual confident, professional manner, "I cannot explain this year's weather, but it seems impossible that it reflects a reversal in the process of global warming. It's simply basic science that annual average temperatures will rise because of past and current carbon emissions. We don't see any natural phenomena that suggest that this development is a new trend, rather than an anomalous natural variation.

"Of course, it's theoretically possible that someone is actively altering the earth's climate in some way, but I haven't seen any evidence of that. So I expect that next year is likely to be more like 2021–22 than like this year."

"Have you actually explored the possibility that someone *is* altering the climate?" Xi asked. "We need to know if someone is playing games with our future. Please check with 3PLA (the People's Liberation Army (PLA) Strategic Support Force) and MSS (the Ministry of State Security) to see if either of them can shed any light on this question. I need to know if we're wasting resources unnecessarily converting from coal to solar and wind."

"Yes, sir. I'll do it immediately. But as you know, there are many other good reasons to convert from coal to solar and wind besides the long-term threat of climate change.

"The sooner we can shed the image of Beijing and other Chinese cities as places with dirty air and undrinkable water, the sooner we can join the ranks of truly developed nations in the world's view, attract more tourists and major investors, keep our best and brightest here in China instead of Silicon Valley, and protect our urban citizens from the adverse health effects of air pollution that make them so angry."

Xi didn't feel the need for another lecture on the dangers of pollution. "Of course, but the remedies for those problems could be locally focused and adopted at a more leisurely pace if we weren't worried about climate change. We haven't got the resources to pursue unnecessary projects."

"Agreed." Yu stood up to leave. She realized that nothing would be gained by arguing about the appropriate policies in this hypothetical alternate reality. No matter how much the President wished he could forget about investing to minimize and adapt to climate change, that could never happen.

Dutifully following Xi's instructions, Yu called 3PLA to see if its satellites had observed anything that might provide clues about any sort of atmospheric geoengineering project. The staff at 3PLA brushed off her inquiry as a nuisance. They were intent on tracking the repeated US military incursions into Chinese air and sea zones in the South China Sea. Trump was gone, but it was still not clear how the new Latino president from Texas would reshape long-term US military policy in Asia.

After repeated calls, a junior staff person in 3PLA responded with a curt email. "The high-altitude foreign commercial flights over China and Russia were noted in 3PLA's last monthly Air Defense Report to President Xi. It's right there on page 49."

Two sentences. The 3PLA Monthly Report did not include the flights in the Executive Summary. Apparently 3PLA felt they did not constitute a threat to China.

Yu requested all the data in 3PLA's computers on these flights. 3PLA provided the data, but only after Yu called the Defense Minister and explained the reasons for her interest. He'd been a friend since they attended college together at Beijing Foreign Studies University, and he was happy to oblige—surely this favor could be called in for repayment some time.

Yu promised to hold the data close in the interest of protecting the security of 3PLA's sources. The source could only be surmised by examining the data itself, but its formatting looked suspiciously similar to output from NORAD (the US North American Aerospace Defense Command) and NASA Landsat imagery. There was nothing to hide, except the possibility that China had surreptitious access to the entire NORAD database.

The quantity of undigested data was enormous. Yu asked Bao Mengzhen, her special advisor on climate, to study the data and report to her by the end of June.

⊸◦⊶

Later that same week, CIA Director Williamson also requested a briefing on the causes of what appeared to be a reversal of the long-term global weather trends. From his years of experience, he anticipated that the President would want a report eventually.

Williamson expected to learn that 2022–23 was probably just a natural variation in weather patterns, not a real change in the inexorable increase in average annual temperatures, with their correlative increases in damaging weather events. But he would go through the process so he could say he was ahead of the curve when the President called.

A week later, two young analysts came to his office—James Porter Jr., who introduced himself as Junior, and Wallace Thurber. They were new to intelligence, but they had the requisite background in climate science and analysis of big data that was required for this kind of work.

To Williamson's surprise, they had considered the matter systematically and had several theories to offer. Their presentation was more formal and complete than he had anticipated. Junior presented their report, complete with PowerPoint slides:

> This analysis is based on our own thinking and on consultations with two experts at DNR - the Director for Air, Noise & Radiation at EPA, and the senior climate modeler for NOAA in Boulder. We think that together we've identified all the possibilities.

> 1. The default explanation is that 2022–23 is just an example of the natural

variation that sets records one year, usually followed by reversion to mean values or opposite extremes in subsequent years. To disprove this explanation requires evidence to the contrary.

2. A second possibility is that someone was intervening in the natural weather processes to accelerate climate change, but then stopped doing so last year. That would explain the surprising shrinkage of the Arctic ice cap over the last half decade and this year's reversal.

    One or more Arctic coastal states, especially Russia, have an economic interest in hastening the retreat of the Arctic ice cap. President Putin is promoting ice-free year-round shipping through the Arctic Ocean to create an economic boom in Russia.

    NASA Landsat and classified NORAD satellite images show some years of recurrent, relatively low-altitude flights based in Russia that could be dispersing ice-melting chemicals.

But these activities have not stopped. Their weather effect should be the opposite of what we have just experienced.

3. The third possibility is that someone else is intervening in the natural weather processes to slow recent climate changes by reversing the retreat of the Arctic ice cap.

In response to our inquiry, NORAD identified a continuing series of small commercial jet flights from Indonesia to the Arctic and back, beginning last summer. They posed no conventional or nuclear military threat to the US, so NORAD disregarded them. These flights proceed directly over China and Russia at very high altitude.

NASA Landsat imagery suggests that these flights are releasing a material that reflects sunlight, counteracting the warming effect caused by increased atmospheric carbon. This year's weather may mean that it is accomplishing that purpose.

4. A fourth possibility is that both the Russian and Indonesian activities are underway; that is, Russia is acting to accelerate the Arctic ice cap's retreat, while someone else is acting to delay it.

We believe the evidence supports the conclusion that this last explanation is the most likely one.

We have not put any of this analysis into a Memorandum, pending your direction.

Junior stopped speaking and waited. As the Director absorbed their analysis, his face showed the impact their report. His thoughts and emotions were mixed.

"I imagined I was ahead of the curve by requesting a report," he declared with pride. "And here you two have been investigating this subject for two months! And you have a great deal to show for it. I'm always happy to see that our organization is capable of really doing its job.

"But the idea that the Russians would affirmatively destroy the Arctic ice cap to promote their short-term economic interests is almost as unbelievable as the idea that some secret, unauthorized operation based in Indonesia is experimenting with a tropospheric veil to cool the Arctic region. Either possibility seems farfetched, and either would have immense political and diplomatic implications.

"On the merits," he continued, "how confident are you of these conclusions? Is the data good enough to be defended in a public forum like Congress or the UN?"

Junior and Wally looked at each other. They hadn't anticipated that question. Wally responded.

"I believe we can provide compelling documentation for our conclusions about the Indonesian flights. With respect to the Russian climate modification activity, I am personally equally confident. The data are subject to varied interpretations, but nothing else explains the dramatic shift in the current weather patterns as well."

Williamson needed no more. "Thank you for this thorough, creative, and enlightening analysis. Please start putting together a Top Secret Memorandum to the President. We may also need to present and defend your conclusions with unclassified information, so see if you can defend this analysis without classified information and prepare an unclassified version of your Memo as well.

"Oh, and please separate out the Russian activities and the Indonesian activities in freestanding classified and unclassified Memos. We may or may not use both or either publicly. I'll need to explain the connection between the Russian and the Indonesian activities orally, so give me some talking points."

"Yes, sir. We'll do our best, sir."

Junior and Wally left the room and high-fived. They were thrilled that their analysis, which began as a self-generated sideline to their assigned work, was a matter of interest to the Director. They were eager to make it their priority, even though documenting their conclusions properly would take much more careful work.

Williamson could envision his meeting with the President. After he presented Junior's Report, the President would raise the inevitable cascade of questions:

Two sets of planes? Russia trying to accelerate global warming? Are they really that crazy? Who do these other planes belong to and what precisely is their mission? Does the Indonesian government know about this? Are you sure these flights are all connected to the change in the weather?

And finally, the most important question: What should we do about all this?

Williamson called his Deputy. "Good afternoon, Art. James Porter and Wallace Thurber have just briefed me on some climate geoengineering activities originating in Indonesia. We need to know who is funding and managing that operation.

We also need to learn whatever we can about Russian weather modification activities in the Arctic. They appear to be designed to hasten the retreat of the Arctic polar ice cap, regardless of the national and global consequences.

I think the President will be very interested in both. Please keep these two inquiries separate. We don't know which information we will want to use, or when."

Williamson frowned as he mulled over the enormous implications of what he had just learned. *I'll be on the spot to produce reliable, defensible answers, probably using only unclassified data. I doubt we can satisfy that demand.*

If the matter becomes a public, international controversy, our analysis will be subject to thorough scrutiny and skepticism around the world. We can't afford another 'slam dunk' like the one that 'proved' the existence of WMD in Iraq. The CIA will never live that one down.

I wish it were as easy to answer the President's questions as to ask them. This novel, obscure, complex SRM veil stuff is a perfect opportunity for me to make a mistake that would tarnish my reputation.

Chapter 26

SETITOR

In the SE offices, Abdul was anxious about the imminent threat of a disaster after a year of successful flights. Three months earlier, in March, one of the drones had detected another aircraft, flying at a lower altitude and presumably Russian, that seemed to be on a similar mission to alter the Arctic ice cover. It was spreading some unidentifiable chemical material into the atmosphere. Subsequent drone flights, now looking for the Russian planes, found them regularly.

The existence of other unknown weather modification activities in the Arctic region unquestionably compromised the scientific validity of the SE work. Without knowing what the other project was doing, it would be impossible to calibrate the impact of SE's own efforts.

Abdul, Guo, and Memed began thinking about whether the SE flights should continue at all, and if so, how to modify their project to take account of this other project, whatever it was. This circumstance also renewed the discussion of whether a live observer should be aboard more often to watch for other aircraft and facilitate a response to the unexpected.

Meanwhile, the daily flights continued. Then last week, the cameras and sensors on a drone had recorded a Russian fighter jet alongside, requesting identification, which of course was not answered. At the next morning meeting, Abdul expressed his fears to Guo and Memed.

"If the Russian pilot gets no answer, he might shoot down our plane, and Russia would arguably be within its legal rights to do so, despite our high altitude. Losing a drone would be a major financial loss. If it happens to be a flight with a pilot or observer aboard, we would lose a human life."

After further discussion, Memed suggested a modification of the program. "It's not surprising that the Russians are unhappy about an unidentified aircraft traversing their airspace. We really should have thought more about that in the first place. They have a long history of responding forcefully to unauthorized overflights. They may or may not know that our planes are releasing chemicals or what the chemicals are. If they do know, I imagine they are even more unhappy with our presence.

"I think there's a technical solution, however, if we want to keep flying. We don't need to fly over Russia to get to the Arctic. If we fly northeast from here, we can fly entirely over the ocean without crossing Russia or China and enter and depart the Arctic region through the Bering Strait. It would only add about an hour each way to the flights. Even if the Russians or the Americans see us, they have no basis for attacking a commercial aircraft when no military or hostile activity is occurring."

Abdul was skeptical. "Do you really think the Russians are going to sit back and let us fly into the Arctic without knowing who we are or what we're doing? Forget the law. The easiest way for Russia to end this exercise would be to shoot down one of our planes, study the wreckage to determine its origin, and see who objects to their action.

Guo took a more comprehensive view. "We've been naïve in assuming this whole project would remain secret for very long. At this point, we have dozens of employees, ex-employees, suppliers, and probably some eyes in the sky recording our flights, in addition to the birdwatcher up on the hill. One or more national defense intelligence units will raise questions with their superiors about what is going on.

"We know that the diplomats who initiated this project anticipated that it would become public before long. I think they must expect it, and only hope our project will survive long enough to make the data scientifically credible. They want to change the political environment and reinforce the argument that a well-designed SRM veil is feasible and desirable.

"No one has told us to stop. Each week we're getting additional data about the impact of our flights on Arctic ice and global weather patterns that we cannot obtain any other way. So far it looks surprisingly successful. I believe we should continue to fly on the schedule that best serves our mission until we are told to stop. Maybe we should put pilot/observers on a few of our flights so we are ready to retreat immediately if Russian aircraft demand it."

Abdul looked at her uncomfortably. "And what happens when we do lose a plane?"

Memed jumped in. "Unless we stop flying, losing a drone is more than a risk. It's virtually a certainty. Starting now, we must also begin preparing for the day when we publicly announce what we've been doing and what we've demonstrated.

"We should also document Russia's secret geoengineering project. Forcing the Russian geoengineering project out into the open would be good for almost everyone. We or others can decide whether to reveal it when the time comes. We'll be welcomed as heroes in some parts of the world, and certainly castigated as villains in others, but we will have accomplished our mission."

Persuaded by this logic, Abdul agreed to continue the flights, redirecting them northeast on the oceanic route, until told to stop. Despite Guo's recommendation, he reduced the number of observers from one flight in five to one flight in eight, in light of the risk of hostile Russian action.

He also decided to put only one plane in the air at a time, to further minimize the risk of loss. The change would result in intermittent, rather than constant, release of calcite powder over the Arctic. The climate impact would presumably be less, which would further weaken the value of their data. In any case, it would take extraordinary scientific expertise to untangle the impact of the two apparently competing climate modification programs.

———◦———

Two weeks after receiving President Putin's order, Defense Minister Boris Ivanov requested an immediate private meeting with Putin. Annoyed at the interruption of his schedule, he nevertheless agreed. Such requests are far out of the ordinary, as everyone knows Putin prefers rigorous adherence to his daily schedule.

The meeting took place in the opulent conference room adjoining Putin's office, a small but lavishly decorated space originally designed for Tsars to conduct confidential conversations and erotic liaisons. Boris began reciting his prepared remarks.

> Mr. President, I have important news. Ten days ago, I sent a reconnaissance flight to observe one of these mysterious overflights at close range. It was clearly a drone and unarmed. It didn't answer any attempts to communicate. It had ordinary

commercial markings, which claimed a Taiwan registration.

And it was releasing something into the troposphere. We took air samples. It is almost certainly calcite powder, which has strong reflective properties. Scientists in my ministry say it could well be responsible for this year's change in the Arctic ice cover. They are seeking confirmation of that conclusion from the Meteorological Bureau.

In accordance with your directive, last week I gave the order to shoot down the next flight unless it reversed course and left Russian airspace. I sent instructions that the pilot should hit the target from a point and angle where the wreckage would land in a convenient location in Russia, so we could learn what exactly this is all about.

But drones never returned. At first, we believed we had scared them off. Then yesterday we discovered that they are still flying to the Arctic, but now over the Pacific Ocean and through the Bering Strait, avoiding Russian airspace.

They are still operating and still releasing calcite into the troposphere. The climate effect is the same. But we no longer have any legal basis for stopping the overflights because they are not entering our airspace.

Boris stopped short as he saw Putin's face turn red with anger. Inventing a new legal theory on the spot, Putin raged, "Boris, this isn't about overflights! It's about changing the Russian climate! It's about threatening our ability to begin year-round ice-free shipping in the Arctic! It's an act of aggression! We have the right of self-defense under the UN Charter. We need to stop this unauthorized alteration of our region's climate system.

"It doesn't matter if they aren't trespassing on our airspace. We've got other law on our side. We have the right to manage our natural resources as we think fit. And who is going to enforce any so-called law anyway? Just shoot down the next flight, and let's see who claims responsibility. That will get us to the truth very quickly."

Putin sighed and shook his head. "Maybe I should have let you resign when you asked." Without waiting for an answer, he stormed out of the room and back into his office, leaving Boris flustered and dismayed. Boris felt he had a compelling answer for Putin, but the opportunity to explain it was gone. It wouldn't fit in a Tweet, but it was airtight.

Boris returned to his office. He considered re-submitting his resignation and leaving this self-destructive move to his successor. Instead he put his argument into a brief Memo to President Putin.

> Russia is currently conducting "weather modification experiments" that are intentionally accelerating the shrinkage of the Arctic ice cap. We have never announced the existence or purpose of our program, on the theory that the flights do not enter any other nation's airspace. We have conveniently ignored the predicted and actual effects on the global climate.
>
> If the "self-defense against climate alteration" argument is sound, Russia's own flights are legally and physically vulnerable. Shooting down one of these unidentified foreign flights would set a precedent for action by others—the US or Norway, for example—to shoot down the Russian weather modification flights.

He gave a blind copy to Nicholas, but not Dimitri or Grigori. He feared Putin would feel embarrassed and angry if others saw the Memo; that might encourage him to double down on his position. Boris desperately hoped Putin would calm down and reconsider his decision.

Those hopes were not realized. President Putin returned the Memorandum to Boris with a brusque handwritten note at the end. "I have carefully reconsidered this matter in light of your comments. Please proceed as ordered."

In response, Boris again submitted his resignation, effective immediately. Putin again refused it and followed up with a phone call.

"Boris, I know you disagree with my decision, but I am the final arbiter of what is good for Russia. I can't let you leave your ministry until these unidentified tropospheric flights are stopped. It shouldn't take long, and I would need some time to identify a successor anyway. Please just be patient."

Boris issued the order, as directed. He concluded he had no choice. *Putin could revoke my pension for insubordination. Or perhaps the charge would be treason, with penalties for my family members as well.*

Eighteen hours later, at 0825 GMT, June 22, 2023, a Russian military jet approached an unidentified aircraft heading north through the Bering Strait. After initiating radio contact and getting no response, the pilot made a further announcement.

"Your aircraft is within the Russian Federation's Air Defense Identification Zone. We do not know your identity or your mission. I am under orders to shoot down any unidentified and unresponsive aircraft that does not immediately reverse course and leave the ADIZ. If you do not leave now and return to your point of entry into the ADIZ, I have orders to destroy your aircraft. I will wait five minutes for a response, either by radio or by a visible change of course."

At SE, Abdul received an urgent text message. The drone's flight controller had forwarded a recording of the Russian pilot's statement, so Abdul could hear it himself. The controller requested instructions, noting the time deadline. He also noted that in seven minutes the drone would be outside the Russian ADIZ and into the Arctic.

Abdul had about ninety seconds to decide what to do. He suddenly realized he did not know if this flight had a pilot/observer on board, perhaps asleep or otherwise unable to hear the Russian communication. He called the controller. "Is there a pilot or observer aboard this flight?"

The controller answered, "One moment, sir. I don't think so but let me confirm that." After a pause, he continued, "Our records show this flight does not have anyone aboard."

Relieved, Abdul replied to the controller, "Good. Turn back. No point in losing a valuable piece of equipment. If it succeeded in escaping into the Arctic beyond the ADIZ, it would still need to return through the Russian ADIZ over the Bering Strait. It would surely be tracked and shot down there."

The drone controller received the order to turn the drone around. He instantly transmitted it. But the "instantaneous" transmission was not truly instant. The computer time to encode and send the controller's message, the propagation time through the internet, and the drone computer's response to the message consumed more than a minute.

The Russian fighter pilot was already counting the seconds until he could use his years of training. Talking to himself, he reviewed his orders and evaluated the situation.

I can't let the drone escape the ADIZ into the Arctic before I act. If I wait even another half minute, this unidentified aircraft will get away. And my plane is low on fuel for a return to base. It will be a struggle to squeeze enough range from the remaining fuel.

The continued radio silence and failure to change course for almost five minutes are a sufficiently clear signal of the intruder's intention. No grace period is necessary.

He had armed his missiles and aligned his fighter to ensure that at least most of the debris would land on

Russian soil, as instructed. From that position, the pilot could not see the wing flaps on the drone begin to tilt gently into the beginning of a turn.

The fighter destroyed the drone at exactly 0830 GMT.

Abdul read the controller's report of the destruction with dismay. The loss of the drone was costly. After a moment to absorb the significance of the disaster, however, he felt a surge of relief.

The question whether Russia would respond to our program militarily has been answered. Russia will probably make a formal public announcement of its action soon, he calculated. *The downed drone's markings, equipment, computerized guidance system, and calcite powder will reveal enough to establish the probable point of origin and the nature of the project.*

It's time to close the operation and leave Setitor as quickly as possible. The adventure is over.

Arissetyanto Buana Counselors at Law, the firm that incorporated SE, had prepared a plan for quick dissolution at the same time they created SE. When Abdul informed them that SE should be shut down, they put the plan into effect immediately.

They dissolved the corporation, sold the planes to IFC at fair market value, transferred the aircraft technicians to a defense contractor that provides maintenance services for the Indonesian Air Force, and paid all outstanding accounts in full.

Abdul, Guo, and Memed joined the staff of the Climate Research Institute of the Department of Engineering at Universitas Tarumanagara in West Jakarta, taking copies of the crucial data with them. The termination of the Arctic flights highlighted questions that Abdul, Memed, and Guo had discussed, but could never untangle in a scientifically sound way: What are the likely weather and climate effects of suddenly ending the calcite releases over the Arctic? What was the effect of the Russian program on their project? What if it also ends? In their new academic positions, they could explore those questions in earnest.

All official SE corporate and financial information, and all original data, were placed in storage in the law firm's private vault with instructions to seal them for fifty years unless instructed otherwise by Ariki Martioto or Anna Smithson.

Wang and Mahmood realized within a few hours after the attack that SE's operations were changing radically. Today's drone did not return. All the remaining drones took off as quickly as the airfield runway allowed. Trucks arrived and began removing supplies, chemicals, and file cabinets from the base. The whole SE operation was being dismantled before their eyes.

Mahmood and Ahmed's informal sources soon confirmed that SE was closing down and moving out. It would be gone completely within forty-eight hours. Wang immediately sent a text to the Prime Minister, saying simply,

> A hurricane has destroyed the orchard. I will make sure to turn off the irrigation water.

No need to say anything more at this point, she realized. *I expect we will all find out what has happened in a few days.*

The cryptic message puzzled Prime Minister Li, but he was too engrossed in re-election campaign events to follow up immediately. The opposition parties had brought together social and environmental activists with long-time opponents of the Li family in a populist-style campaign that posed a threat to his continuation in office. *I'll find out what happened to the project sooner or later*, he assumed.

Wang sent the same obscure message to Ibrahim. She imagined he might already know what was happening through other channels. In any case, now was not the time for a substantive communication that might be intercepted.

Chapter 27

NEW YORK

The Russian Federation announced the destruction of the drone less than twenty-four hours after it occurred. It issued an extended statement at the UN that left no doubt about its view of the circumstances and called for an emergency meeting of the UN Security Council.

The Council President for June was the Russian UN Ambassador, Arcady Andropovich Myshkin, a hardheaded, seasoned career diplomat, capable of saying *nyet* in a myriad of ways. Not interested in the luxuries of decadent, capitalist New York that lead many diplomats astray, he devoted himself to protecting the interests of Mother Russia, even though the current Russian president often disregarded his recommendations for constructive steps toward peace.

To allow time for the Security Council Members to prepare, Chairman Myshkin scheduled a meeting for Saturday, June 24, 2023. He was delighted to be on the offense for a change, unlike the usual Russian situation. He began the Council meeting with a previously prepared written statement of the reasons for Russia's meeting request and a draft Security Council Decision:

> Two days ago, a drone of unknown origin entered the Russian Federation's Air Defense Identification Zone near the Bering Strait, headed for the Arctic Ocean. It did not respond to a demand for identification from a Russian Federation Air Force jet fighter pilot. The pilot gave an unequivocal warning and a five-minute grace period to reverse course and leave the Russian ADIZ. Hearing no radio response and seeing no change in course within the grace period, the pilot destroyed the drone. Most of the drone debris landed on Russian soil, and our Ministry of Transportation is recovering it.

> This flight was not the first over our territory. Similar drones had passed directly over Russia daily for several months en route to the Arctic. The first flights were observed and ignored as not constituting a military threat, but their repeated violation of Russian airspace could no longer be tolerated.

Our investigation of these flights is not complete, but certain facts are clear:

1. The drones were registered as commercial aircraft in Taiwan. They were apparently based at a remote location somewhere in Indonesia.

2. These aircraft were releasing calcite dust into the Arctic troposphere. The only plausible reason for doing so would be to increase the earth's albedo (reflectivity), creating a Solar Radiation Management (SRM) veil.

3. This project is unquestionably an act of aggression against the Russian Federation and all States bordering the Arctic Ocean. It affects our coasts, waterways, shipping, economy, and people, with no international authorization, transparency, consultation, or even notification.

4. This secret project violates the Russian Federation's sovereign right to manage and control our natural resources and our right to enjoy the benefits of the natural environment, both of which have been repeatedly

recognized by multiple organs of the United Nations.

We therefore ask the Security Council to adopt a formal Decision with the following operative provisions:

The United Nations Security Council

a) Formally declares that intentional, unauthorized extraterritorial atmospheric climate modification projects, by whatever name, are acts of aggression against every affected State;

b) Acknowledges that every affected State is entitled to take individual or collective action against such activities as an exercise of the inherent right of self-defense guaranteed by the Article 51 of the United Nations Charter;

c) Demands that the Government of Indonesia

    i. Give the Secretary-General any information it has or

can obtain about these drone flights;

ii. Ensure that no further operations of this kind originate from its territory;

iii. Find and appropriately punish any organization or individual involved in an operation of this kind.

d) Directs the Secretary-General to

i. Report on Indonesia's compliance with this Decision within thirty days;

ii. Prepare a report on the legal rules governing or that should govern the conduct of any atmospheric geoengineering or climate alteration research, demonstration, or other program that might reasonably be expected to alter the climate or related natural conditions in other States, including the necessity for advance consultation with all potentially affected States.

After reiterating these arguments and demands in numerous ways for another two hours, Myshkin finally concluded his remarks:

"We do not know whether our decisive act of self-defense has changed the plans of whoever is directly responsible for these flights. In any case, the State from which they originate bears full legal responsibility under international law for this aggression arising from its territory. We call on the Indonesian government to explain the flights and to terminate all such activities.

"To be clear, our view is that any intentional atmospheric geoengineering program is illegal under the UN Charter and international law unless first fully evaluated and authorized by a formal Decision of the Security Council, acting under Chapter 7 of the UN Charter and subject to a veto. Absent Security Council authorization, such activity is lawfully subject to a military response in accordance with the inherent right of self-defense guaranteed by Article 51 of the UN Charter."

As Chairman, Ambassador Myshkin then asked if any of the other twenty Members of the recently enlarged Security Council wished to speak. Seeing none, he adjourned the Council for the weekend.

On Monday, Indonesian UN Ambassador Jennifer Hendra presented her government's prepared statement:

> The Government of Indonesia categorically denies any knowledge of the flights alleged by the Russian Federation or any authorization of them. Neither our Ministry of Defense nor our Ministry of Environment has authorized them or even knew of their existence. We question whether such flights actually originated in Indonesia. A careful reading of Russia's statement shows that it has not positively established the origin of these flights. They could just as easily come from one of several neighboring countries—East Timor, Brunei, Malaysia, Papua New Guinea, Singapore, or the Solomon Islands, among others. They might even have come from a foreign military base or aircraft carrier. Russia has not provided Indonesia or this Council with any information supporting the alleged origin of the flights.
>
> It is possible that one or more flights originated in a remote Indonesian location among our 17,000 islands, of which about

1,000 are permanently inhabited. There is no national or international obligation for operators of small non-military aircraft to report their flights to the Indonesian national government.

Routine small aircraft flights in remote areas of other countries are also not reported. For example, Russian flights over the Arctic region apparently need not be reported to its national government, and no records of such activities are publicly available.

In any case, the drone that the Russian air force destroyed no longer poses a threat to anyone. There is no evidence of subsequent flights.

The Russian Federation did not first consult with, or even inform, this Council, the Indonesian Government or, as far as we are aware, any other government, before taking military action. This unilateral military action of the Russian Federation once again demonstrates its tendency to disregard the authority of the UN Security Council and the opinion of other affected Member States.

Accordingly, Indonesia believes the only immediate action by the Security Council should be a Decision calling on all parties to refrain from unilateral military action.

A Security Council Decision that adopts Russia's novel legal arguments should wait until the Secretariat thoroughly investigates the factual and legal circumstances surrounding this flight and reports back to the Council. At that point the Council will be able to engage in an enlightened discussion of the legal and policy implications of the Russian draft Decision.

The Russian Ambassador responded in blunt terms: "Unlike Indonesia, which may know more than the rest of us, we have no reason to believe the flights have ceased, and every reason to believe that the flights were specifically intended to change the climate in the Arctic region. The Council must take prompt action to make clear that such activities will not be tolerated without express prior Security Council authorization."

No other Member acknowledged any responsibility for planning, organizing, authorizing, or funding the flights.

Taking advantage of its new UN Observer status, the Special Representative of Taiwan addressed the Security Council for the first time, over the objection of the Ambassador of the People's Republic of China:

> The Republic of Taiwan acknowledges that many aircraft are registered in Taiwan, but we have no knowledge of their flights or their missions. Maritime and aircraft registry States like Panama, Liberia, and Taiwan have no legal obligation or practical mechanism to keep public records about the activities of aircraft or vessels flying their flag. The Republic of Taiwan will cooperate fully with the Secretariat's investigation of the drone flights.

No other Members of the Security Council spoke, but several requested that their names be placed on the agenda for the next meeting. The Council adjourned for the week to allow Members to consult and develop their respective positions on the Russian Federation's draft Decision.

News of Russia's announcement about the drone and its call for a UN Security Council meeting gave Singapore's President Li a full understanding of the meaning of Wang Shu's cryptic text. A few days after the Russian demarche, Singapore's UN Ambassador, Rachel Zhu Tan, called President Li from New York.

"Mr. President, someone said something to me yesterday that implied Singapore was involved in the Indonesian SRM project. Is that true? And what, if anything, do you want me to say about it here at the UN?"

After enlightening her about Singapore's clandestine financing of the drone flights, the Prime Minister asked, "Do you think this matter will attain high visibility? How concerned is Russia about these flights, which have ended anyway?"

"Russia is very concerned," she replied. "It seems that President Putin has great plans for year-round shipping in the Arctic. He has no intention of letting anyone interfere with them. His term ends in less than twelve months. This program is his swan song, though he may try to use it as an excuse to extend his presidency."

"I see. Well, I have my own election to deal with, and I can't do it the way he can. I am attending a campaign dinner right now. Let me think about this overnight, and I'll have some direction for you in the morning."

Mulling over the matter after the dinner, Li realized that Singapore's role would certainly be discovered, probably very soon. *Maybe there is a way to make some political use of this turn of events,* he calculated. *I'll show the world, and the voters, I'm more forward-looking and more of an environmentalist than my opponents ever imaged.*

Early the next morning (still evening the night before in New York), he called Ambassador Tan. "Good morning. I've thought it over. We should not be defensive about trying to save the planet and slow global warming. So what do you think of preempting the inevitable discovery of our role, and instead announcing it ourselves and defending it on the merits? Can you prepare the necessary presentation?"

"I can easily put together some legal and political arguments. I really don't know enough detail about the project to describe or defend it on scientific or policy grounds. The Russians will viciously attack us for having proceeded in secret. But I understand the merits of the decision to proceed as you did."

"Please begin working on it," Li replied. "I'll just have to risk Putin's wrath. Do you know a young Foreign Service Officer by the name of Wang Shu? I sent her to Indonesia to keep track of the project. Now that the project has ended, I can send her to New York to provide you technical and policy support."

"I do know her," Ambassador Tan responded. "She's very competent and a quick study. I'll be happy to have her here at my side to work on our presentation to the Security Council."

"Excellent, I'll arrange it. Don't say anything to anyone yet. Just prepare your presentation to the Security Council and reserve an opportunity to speak. We can talk again before we finally decide to proceed. And try not to let the story leak! I will want it to be a surprise for everyone. I'll talk to you again whenever you are ready."

Prime Minister Li's next call was to the Singaporean ambassador to Indonesia. "Good morning, Mr. Ambassador. I suppose you are hearing the news from the UN about Russia's downing of a drone allegedly based in Indonesia. I need two actions on your part. First, please inform Wang Shu, the environmental specialist I sent your way eighteen months ago, that she is to report to Ambassador Tan at our UN Mission in New York within forty-eight hours, or as soon thereafter as transportation and logistics will allow.

"Second, please speak to President Kartawijaya in person, and alone. Tell him I intend to reveal Singapore's financial support for the SRM veil project at the UN, but we will not say anything to anyone before then, and we will never mention Indonesia."

"Yes, sir, Mr. President. I'll inform Wang Shu and try to schedule a meeting with President Kartawijaya within the hour."

"Excellent. Thank you. Please keep me informed, and don't talk to anyone else about any of this."

———◇◇◇———

Wang received word from the Embassy that she was to leave immediately for New York to assist Ambassador Tan. She had read about Russia's downing of the drone and its call for a UN Security Council meeting on the subject. But she had not anticipated these instructions.

Her quiet life in Setitor was abruptly ending. In two days, she would be in the center of the UN diplomatic swirl, working continuously day and night until the SRM veil issues were resolved. Ibrahim was in New York, serving as the UN Ambassador for the Maldives, which was currently a rotating Member of the Security Council. She realized, with mixed feelings, that she would probably see a lot of him in meetings there.

Wang had occasionally mused about what she would do when her Indonesian assignment was over. It was a complex question, both professionally and emotionally, with contradictory elements that she could never comfortably resolve. Until now, her thinking was more like daydreaming than practical planning.

She had always felt confident that Prime Minister Li would protect her professionally. She was pleased to see he was doing so, at least at this initial point. If she wanted to continue her career in the Singapore Foreign Service, the door of opportunity appeared to be opening. Was that the future she really wanted?

The rewards were intellectual challenge, professional status and pride, a comfortable life in a variety of world capitals, and a sense of involvement in the great issues of the day. But for a woman her age, it probably meant a life without a husband, children, or roots in a stable community. The sacrifice seemed more severe to her now, after enjoying the pleasures of a quiet life in Setitor for over a year.

The more immediate and emotionally distressing question was Mahmood. He would certainly ask if or how he fit into her new assignment. She needed an answer. Assignment to the UN Delegation was a wonderful opportunity, but she could not bear to leave Mahmood behind.

With some trepidation, she sent a request to New York. Could she bring her project assistant with her for six months, or longer as necessary? "He's a flight engineering specialist and former employee of SE who has worked for me here, tracking SE operations. His technical knowledge and insights will be invaluable." Ambassador Tan granted her request. She would need all the help she could get.

So now Wang would have at least one friend in her new home besides Ibrahim. She suddenly realized she had never seen Mahmood at any social group larger than three. *Can he make small talk with diplomats? Present an appropriately professional, office worker image? Be effective in drafting diplomatically phrased documents describing the SE project? Find any other work or role in New York?*

He had received a good liberal education in Berlin, but he's been a flight engineer ever since. Maybe he doesn't even want the diplomatic life, wearing a suit and sitting in an office all day. We'll see what he's like in new, very urban and social surroundings. Fortunately, I can postpone any real decision about our future for at least six months.

Chapter 28

WASHINGTON

In Washington, the President assembled the NSC in the Oval Office, along with US UN Ambassador Alex McMillan, and Natural Resources Secretary Kristi Sheppard, formerly the Junior Senator from California. He outlined his objective to the group.

"We need to establish our position on the Russian draft Decision. To begin that process, Harold will give us a summary of the CIA's Memorandum, including what facts we know with sufficient confidence that we could present them to the UN Security Council.

"Most important, I want to know what's wrong with the Russian draft Decision. My first thought is that it sounds reasonable, but I'm here to listen to everyone's views."

Director Williamson first apologized to everyone for the CIA's failure to seek interagency clearance or even distribute the Memorandum before today. He summarized the facts that he had reported to the President, with a few confirming updates. Then he read the conclusions in the Memorandum:

In the CIA's view, the debate on the draft Decision is an opportunity to expose

Russia's own program, put it under UN Security Council supervision, and define America's "inherent right of self-defense" as including actions to stop SRM or similar geoengineering projects that adversely affect us, including the current Russian project.

The CIA has not yet sorted out exactly how the Decision should distinguish geoengineering activities that have global impacts from those that do not. Keep in mind our own current programs and our desire to preserve our future freedom of action. Drafting precise amendments to the Russian draft Decision is a task better performed by the State and Defense Departments and our UN Ambassador.

Our strategic view is that the current situation provides an opportunity to embarrass Putin, put Russia on the defensive domestically and internationally, and undercut any effort to extend his tenure as President.

Accordingly, we recommend that Ambassador McMillan reveal the Russian program's climate-changing consequences and challenge its legality in the

UN Security Council. We should support the Russian draft Decision only on the condition that the Russian program stop until it is reviewed and approved by the UN Security Council.

This approach will win widespread UN Member support and give us a veto over the Indonesian and the Russian activities. We believe that would be the most desirable outcome of this situation.

As Director Williamson stopped speaking, President Gonzalez exhaled audibly. "So you want to make this into a big deal. We would be attacking Putin's pet project at the same time we are essentially agreeing with most of the text of the Russian draft Decision. An interesting position. Where does that leave our friends in Indonesia? As my predecessor would have bellowed, 'Who knew this could be so complicated?'"

The President looked around the table. "Who else would like to comment? Robert?"

Robert Schwartz, Director of Policy and Planning in the Office of the Secretary of Defense, cleared his throat, organizing his thoughts.

Thank you, Mister President, for the opportunity to speak. First, let me convey the regrets of the Secretary of Defense. As you know, Secretary Radford and Secretary of State Carmell are currently in Geneva to attend the opening of discussions with the Taliban on a final settlement in Afghanistan. They concluded it would be unacceptable to tell our NATO allies that their presence in Washington for any reason is more important than ending the fighting in Afghanistan.

Thank you, Harold, for that summary of your very helpful Memorandum. Defense has been cooperating with your efforts for several weeks. Your Memorandum didn't mention that the Indonesian flights have stopped, and our latest satellite imagery indicates that the entire base of operations has been dismantled. That fact makes some aspects of this discussion somewhat hypothetical because Russia will have no need to take further action against the flights.

We agree that the pending draft Decision is acceptable to the US with some additional precision about what constitutes atmospheric geoengineering. We need to protect our ability to use weather-altering techniques in our surveillance and anti-drug activities.

Exposing the Russian program at the UN Security Council, while intriguing, could be costly. Year-round ice-free shipping through the Arctic, as already noted, is President Putin's personal project, and he is deeply committed to it. Challenging it is likely to upset our efforts to work with Russia on other pressing problems— settlements in Syria and the Middle East generally, and pressure on Iran and North Korea to permanently abandon their nuclear and missile programs.

Our Department suggests that we not discuss the Russian program in public. It might be powerful leverage for our proposed revisions to the draft decision, but that should be the result of private discussions with the Russia. We think they would accede to amendments very quickly in exchange for US support. Defense will be happy to participate in developing the appropriate text and negotiating strategy. Thank you.

"Thank you, Robert, for those insights. This problem becomes more complicated the more I learn. Stan, what is State's take on this subject?"

Stanley Marshall, Special Assistant to the Secretary of State for Global Issues, responded nervously. The youngest and newest in the group, he had never before been called upon to speak at an NSC meeting with the President, and he was eager to make a positive impression. His statement took the safe approach:

> Thank you, Mr. President. Secretary Carmell also sends his regards from the Geneva Summit. I will be brief. The State Department agrees with the Department of Defense. There is little to be gained by aggravating Putin, who will likely persist with his Arctic project despite any public embarrassment or diplomatic objections from the US. And Russia's Arctic program certainly doesn't warrant a US-Russian military confrontation.
>
> We have no reason to believe a Putin successor would be any more malleable. While often at swords' points with Russia according to the media, we have worked quietly with Russia to avoid direct conflicts and larger local wars in several recent

circumstances. Coping with the North Korean and Iranian military programs necessitates Russian cooperation far more urgently than climate change.

Marshall quickly silenced himself, visibly relieved that he had successfully delivered his department's message without mishap.

The path forward seemed clear, and the President was eager to close the meeting. As a formality, he asked, "Does anyone disagree with this position?"

He was disappointed to see DNR Secretary Kristi Sheppard raise her hand. She was not a regular NSC participant, but was present because the meeting was about climate change. She was also a close friend of the President and one of his most astute political advisors. Wearily, the President invited her to speak. She refused to be rushed.

Thank you, Mr. President. I appreciate that this meeting is getting long, but now that EPA and NOAA have been folded into DNR, we are the only agency truly responsible for our policies and programs on climate change and global warming.

I won't bore everyone with a general discussion of the global warming problem, which we all read about daily in the

Washington Post and *New York Times*. The specific data for 2022–23 show that the respite we experienced this year is very likely the result of the Indonesian SRM veil flights. Now that they have stopped, we expect temperatures to jump upward in their decade-long march to destructively high levels.

We agree with Defense and State that we will gain little by publicly confronting Russia about its globally destructive 'weather modification' program in the Arctic. But we must insist on its immediate termination, whether President Putin likes it or not. Our own citizens in Alaska are suffering dramatically from the melting coastal permafrost. Unpredictable weather conditions are impairing our farm yields. Many of our lakes and rivers are drying up from droughts. And our forests are burning at an unprecedented rate.

We also agree with Defense and State, and the Russian draft decision, that any intentional geoengineering program, including the Russian program, must be conducted transparently, rely on good science, and be subject to an appropriate level of international supervision. But with all due respect to my colleagues, the idea of supporting the current text of the Russian draft decision reflects 19th century thinking on a subject that needs 21st century thinking. The draft needs to be improved in three respects, none of which Russia will be eager to accept.

First, it must explicitly expand the coverage of the draft Decision, not narrow it, so weather modification programs that could have a significant effect on global climate, intentionally or not, are included. Russia will surely object to this amendment, whether we address its program publicly or privately.

Second, we cannot accept the Russian assertion that any state can act unilaterally under some antiquated concept of an 'inherent right of self-defense' if it concludes that someone else's geoengineering or weather modification project threatens its vital national interest. That concept is a recipe for international paralysis and disorder because any state could unilaterally destroy anyone else's SRM program, no matter how widely supported by the world community. Keep in mind that dozens of states now possess the military capability to create a tropospheric veil, and an even larger number have the capability to attack someone else's efforts to do so.

Third, we cannot agree that intentional atmospheric geoengineering programs should be subject to veto in the UN Security Council. As we look to the future, we need to preserve the global community's ability to act. The draft Decision would put the US and the world community at the mercy of the veto power of Russia, China, England, France, or now, in the enlarged Security Council, India. We cannot allow programs that address climate change to be held hostage by a veto threat, giving every Permanent Member of the UN Security Council unacceptable leverage over the world community.

The prospect of a US-backed international SRM program is not at all hypothetical. A consensus favoring SRM is rapidly emerging in the international climate science and policy community, prompted in part by the advocacy of the late Dr. Ilsa Hartquist. Her stress on the potential for a climate disaster in the near term is being verified and reinforced by scientists in many disciplines and accepted by the public around the world. DNR's climate experts fear that Russia's abrupt termination of the Indonesian SRM project increases the risk of even more volatile, unpredictable changes in weather and climate.

DNR has been exploring the feasibility of a tropospheric veil project. We aren't ready with a decision Memorandum yet, but we are aiming for an internal draft soon on whether to announce our support for such a program in 2024. The Russian draft Decision would make our project subject to UN Security Council approval and the veto. It would leave the UN and the US legally helpless to act without unanimous Great Power acquiescence.

The ability of our international institutions to act positively to slow climate change is just as important as our ability to prevent others from acting in destructive ways. I recognize that amending the Russian draft Decision in these three ways makes the diplomatic task more difficult.

But the action being proposed today is a setup for continued international paralysis and future claims that any US or alliance veil project violates this Security Council Decision that we supported. Then the US will be the one that is embarrassed and on the defensive.

I have every confidence that Ambassador McMillan and the State and Defense Departments can accomplish these objectives. I hope you will include these elements in your instructions to them. Thank you for your patience, Mr. President. I'm sorry to have taken so much of everyone's time, but this issue goes to the heart of DNR's climate change program.

The President looked around the room and noted the uncomfortable looks on the faces of Robert Schwartz and Stan Marshall. His response took that into account.

"You've made a pretty compelling case, Kristi. I recognize the value of adding your changes conditions to the Russian draft Decision. But I don't want to preempt other departments' responses to your approach. I'm late for my meeting with the EU Commissioners for Agriculture and Trade. If anyone strongly disagrees with Secretary

Sheppard's approach, we can convene again for further discussion. In the meantime, my tentative decision is as DNR has proposed. Stan, please work with Robert, Alex, and Kristi to map out our tactics. Thank you all for your time, intelligence, and diligence."

Within forty-eight hours, the President received urgent calls from Secretary of Defense Admiral Clarissa Radford and Secretary of State David Carmell, each expressing the same concern. "We can't afford to alienate Putin if we want to make progress on Syria, Iran, or Afghanistan. If we challenge his Arctic project, we are effectively challenging his dream of continuing as the Russian Federation's president for another six years or more. Russian cooperation on all other issues will end. Climate change and weather modification are important, but they are not urgent. We can take on those issues after 2024, in your second term."

The President's answer to each of them was essentially the same:

"First, climate change has become a 'now' issue politically, and my global leadership on the issue will be a crucial element in winning public support for our climate change program. President Obama imagined he could make progress on climate change in his second term, and it didn't work. We can't afford to make that same mistake. Second, if we don't get the UN Security Council Decision right, we will be legally barred from ever acting unilaterally or with the EU, without Russian, Indian, and Chinese acquiescence.

"Finally, I believe that overall, Putin or his successor will cooperate with us on Iran, Syria, Afghanistan, and other trouble spots exactly to the extent it's in Russia's interest to do so. We just need to offer the right carrots and sticks to incentivize him. I'm sorry to make your job more difficult, but DNR's recommendations are the right approach."

Chapter 29

NEW YORK

At the request of the ambassadors from the US and Russia, Lena Pavlik, the German UN Ambassador serving as Security Council President for the month of July, did not reconvene the Council on Monday, July 3rd. Instead, the two Ambassadors met alone.

McMillan explained the US concerns with the Russian draft Decision and presented three suggested US amendments, echoing the recommendations made by Secretary Sheppard. Then he calmly laid out what the US knew about the Russian "weather modification" program. He concluded with an olive branch:

"We would rather not demonize Russia or turn this matter into a public *cause célèbre*. We want to continue working cooperatively with you on this issue and many others. But Russia's Arctic program must stop immediately. It is creating havoc for agriculture around the world. It is also destroying infrastructure in the US and Canadian permafrost regions, and I assume in Iceland, Greenland, Norway, and Siberia as well.

"Your action in shooting down the drone as an act of self-defense sets a precedent that the US might feel compelled to follow if you continue with this reckless course. Actually, you are lucky that this mysterious SRM veil program existed. Otherwise, when your program was eventually discovered, the outcry could have been much stronger."

Ambassador Myshkin stared McMillan straight in the eye. If there was one thing he did not feel at this moment, it was "lucky." His demeanor hardened into a poker-face mask as he responded.

"First, it is inconceivable that any small-time weather modification experiments Russia might be conducting could have significant effects outside of Russian land and territorial waters. You may have photos of some flights. That is far from proof that any atmospheric experiment to accelerate Arctic melting is underway, let alone that it could be influencing the global climate. Indeed, this year's weather is ample evidence that we are not having any negative effects. Your last President and Administration repeatedly told the world that climate change was a Chinese hoax. Do you think anyone will believe that your sudden suspicions and anxiety about climate change are legitimate, not just an excuse to disparage Russia?

"Second, you should be under no illusions about President Putin's determination to initiate a major Arctic infrastructure development program on a scale never before seen in the Arctic region. He will announce a vast construction program within a few months, as the capstone of his last term. Planning for these projects is well underway. It is premised on the existence of year-round ice-free Arctic shipping. I can assure you he will not let anything stand in his way.

"Any effort to prevent President Putin's signature achievement will poison US-Russian relations for as long as Mr. Putin or his associates are in power in Russia. As President Medvedev's term in office illustrated, that may be a long time.

"Third, I and my diplomatic colleagues have been trying to improve cooperation between our two countries since the election of your new President. Is disagreement on this issue really worth undermining what progress we have made over the last two years?"

McMillan rolled his eyes theatrically and responded to the Russian's comments, which were mostly along the lines he anticipated.

"I'm sorry, but the answer must be yes, it is. Mr. Putin may be intransigent and unwilling to acknowledge the substantial and irreversible damage he is doing to Russia and the rest of world, but eventually it will become apparent to everyone.

"Right now, Putin has made Russia relatively popular in many countries as a stable, if autocratic, government with growing international influence. But that could change overnight. There is much to learn from Prime Minister Theresa May's surprise humiliation in the 2017 elections she so eagerly arranged. Prime Minister Merkel didn't do much better when she unexpectedly found herself entangled in the immigration issue.

"The US believes Putin and Russia will pay an enormous price if your Arctic weather modification program continues. Government leaders and their people around the world will recognize it as selfish and reckless. Millions of educated people around the world rightly believe global warming is destroying their homes and their lives. Neither Putin nor Russia can afford to be seen as the cause.

"We only have a short time to reach agreement on these changes to your draft Decision. If we reach agreement on revisions, we can deal with the cessation of your Arctic program quietly. Otherwise we will do whatever we must to defeat your draft Decision, by veto if necessary. And we may need to explain to the world why we are doing so. If the Russian program still continues, the US may also need to take steps comparable to those you just took against the Indonesian drone.

"We will of course make every effort to avoid any loss of life.

"I trust you will make every effort to bring some enlightenment to the Kremlin, and I hope you succeed."

After this "full and frank exchange of views," as contentious diplomatic meetings are often described, Ambassador McMillan stood, thanked Ambassador Myshkin for his time, and left. They did not shake hands. Soon the United States was educating other UN Ambassadors about the proposed US amendments to the draft Decision, without mentioning the Russian Arctic program.

Ten days later, McMillan was still waiting for a Russian response. He was thinking about calling Myshkin to see if there was any reason to wait longer, when an aide rushed into his office.

"Sir, we have just been informed that Singapore, though not currently a Member of the Security Council, has requested permission to address the Council on the subject of the Russian draft Decision. They haven't provided the Council Members any information about what they plan to say. The Security Council President has scheduled a meeting for Tuesday and invited Ambassador Tan to speak."

McMillan was simultaneously dismayed and outraged. "Singapore? What are they thinking? I hope they are not going to press for an immediate vote or propose a slew of amendments. Without US-Russian agreement, we'll end up with a train wreck, accomplishing no one's objectives.

"Please let Singapore know that we and the Russians are not that far apart. If Russia is just a little flexible, we might make some real headway on climate change and SRM. Ambassador Tan must know she is further complicating an already delicate negotiation. And please tell her I hope to hear something about her presentation—in advance."

McMillan waited for Ambassador Tan to explain Singapore's position and strategy, but no call came. His concerns increased.

⸺◦⸺

Ambassador Tan and Wang Shu were working at break-neck speed to prepare the text of the Ambassador's presentation and secretly round up approvals from the AOSIS Members. They had won Members' sympathetic support before seeing the text, but getting agreement on a precise text that voiced the position of all AOSIS Members was a formidable challenge.

Wang had the advantage of knowing about the prior involvement of Panday, Doyal, and Ibrahim. She kept that information secret, but she enlisted their help to get AOSIS Members to approve the text. She said they could tell them about the Russian program, but only on condition of secrecy.

The initial responses of the AOSIS Members on the Russian program varied widely. Some wanted the text to include all "weather modification" programs that could have global climate effects and identify the Russian program explicitly. Others feared that doing so would simply intensify Russian hostility to AOSIS and its Members. It might even engender US reluctance to support Singapore's Initiative.

In the end, Ambassador Tan, the other three Ambassadors, and Wang succeeded in negotiating a consensus speech text that did not explicitly reference the Russian program or say that every AOSIS Member endorsed its recommendations.

Ambassador Tan's formal Statement to the UN Security Council injected a dramatic new set of facts and a new perspective into the SRM veil discussion:

> Thank you, Mr. Chairman. The Government of Singapore wishes to apprise the Council of its relationship to the drone flights that prompted the Russian draft Decision.
>
> As you know, Singapore has been an active Member of the Alliance of Small Island States (AOSIS) since its founding in 1991. AOSIS Members were deeply impressed by the passionate intensity of the late Dr. Ilsa Hartquist's speech to our Annual Conference in 2020, warning the world of the growing danger of a near-term, nonlinear catastrophe. She often repeated those warnings in her public speeches and media appearances.
>
> Her analysis convinced Singapore, and many other governments, that imme-

diate initiation of an SRM program, particularly a tropospheric chemical veil, is essential to minimize the risk of catastrophic destruction in coming decades, not just a century from now.

In 2021, a small group of reliable and experienced diplomats approached our government seeking funding for an experimental, non-governmental SRM project. They insisted that the other participants and the details of the location and operations be kept secret. They saw secrecy as the only way to avoid the inevitable years of delay entailed in seeking governmental and international support, even if the approval were ultimately granted.

Singapore made the funds available on the express conditions that full records of the activities and results of the project would be maintained and shared with the international community once the project had gathered sufficient data to draw scientifically sound conclusions. The project began in the fall of 2021 and continued until the recent Russian military action.

Singapore does not yet have access to the project records, nor do we know who has them. We expect them to be made public soon, as promised. What we all know is that the world has experienced dramatically improved weather conditions over the last year. We believe the project succeeded, interrupting a trend of rapid Arctic warming over the last two decades.

Singapore and AOSIS members agree with the proposed requirement that all weather modification and atmospheric geoengineering programs must be public, transparent, based on the best available science, and subject to international supervision. We urge that all information about this project and all others currently underway be immediately given to the Secretary-General and the IPCC for analysis and evaluation.

Nevertheless, most AOSIS members will not support the draft decision as written. The world cannot afford to make SRM, whether by that name or as "local weather modification," subject to either a formal veto in the UN Security Council or a unilateral military veto on grounds of self-defense. We simply cannot let the community of nations be held hostage to every State with a veto or an air force.

Singapore has drafted General Assembly Resolution A/78/413, which we expect will win the overwhelming support of AOSIS Members and all UN members. It proposes establishment of a procedure for approval of atmospheric geoengineering projects by a two-thirds majority of the General Assembly and two-thirds majority of the Security Council, with no permanent member veto. It also rejects the theory that such projects are subject to unilateral self-defense under Article 51 of the UN Charter.

We are currently working with the Secretariat on technical improvements to our draft Resolution, which we will present to the General Assembly later this week. I requested permission to speak to bring this information to the attention of the Security Council and express the hope that you will adopt a binding Decision that incorporates the procedures set out in our General Assembly Resolution. Thank you.

The Chair thanked Ambassador Tan for her remarks.

Ambassador Myshkin asked to speak.

"So now we know the origin of this outrageous, secret, radical conspiracy to intentionally alter the planet's climate, without notification, without consultation, without the approval of any international institution. We now know Singapore was the enabler, providing the funds for this outrage, unless the funds actually came from another source and were merely funneled through Singapore.

"In these incredible circumstances, I must ask—no, I and this Council must demand—that Singapore reveal the names of the nefarious individuals, alleged to be diplomats, but more likely intelligence agents, who initiated this whole scandal. The world must know what other States and what individuals are behind this scheme, so we can impose appropriate punishment for their blatant disregard of international law, world opinion, and the global institutions designed to avoid such unilateral, potentially destructive, behavior.

"So I ask the distinguished Ambassador for Singapore, please tell us exactly who these 'diplomats' were and what countries they represented. If this question is not answered, Russia will assume that these 'diplomats' are fictitious. It seems highly likely that this is a cover story, since only a Great Power would have the resources and the scientific and logistic capability to carry out this operation.

I look forward to a full response from the distinguished Ambassador from Singapore."

Ambassador Tan, taken aback by the virulence of the Russian Ambassador's demand, nevertheless responded firmly, "I can assure the Russian Ambassador and the Council that every word of my statement is the truth. Singapore itself provided the funds. I do not know, and therefore cannot name, the States or diplomats who asked for the funds and initiated the project.

"But Singapore believes that far from being destructive, this project has made a positive contribution to scientific knowledge and at the same time gained for the world more time to act to avoid the climate catastrophe that awaits us. Again, I thank the Council for allowing me to speak today."

The Council adjourned for the day. No date was set to reconvene for further discussion of the Russian agenda item.

As they were leaving the Council chamber, Ambassador Myshkin dug his fingers into Ambassador McMillan's arm. "You arranged this whole charade, didn't you?" he snarled, spitting out his words in a very undiplomatic display of bitterness. "No doubt your CIA is behind this veil project. Don't think you can get away with hiding behind a handful of toothless island states."

McMillan, somewhat surprised at Myshkin's vehemence, tried to respond courteously but unequivocally.

"On the contrary, we were completely ignorant of the project until you shot down the drone. We had to review our own air surveillance data to find the flights after your announcement. Neither Singapore nor anyone else consulted with us about its activities.

"Moreover, we were never consulted about their draft General Assembly Resolution or today's presentation. In fact, at this time I have no guidance or authority to support or oppose the Singapore Initiative. I will immediately consult my government for instructions, and I suppose you will do the same.

"By the way, Singapore's allusion to data from other weather modification programs suggest that they, and perhaps other States, may know about your Arctic program. It may also show up in the data that comes to the Secretary-General as Singapore promised. You may want to alert President Putin that his pet project may soon become headline news."

Ambassador Myshkin turned pale. His worst nightmare was coming true. "Good day," he replied stiffly, and quickly walked away. After thinking through his alternatives, Myshkin went to the UN Secretary-General to discuss how the Secretariat would handle whatever information it might receive. He urged the Secretariat to take the time to verify the authenticity and value of such information before releasing it or drawing conclusions from it.

Immediately after the Security Council meeting, Ambassador Tan requested a meeting with Ambassador McMillan. She apologized profusely for disregarding his request for an advance copy of her presentation, but explained, "I was acting under explicit instructions from my Prime Minister not to tell anyone in advance about Singapore's funding of the veil project. I hope you can understand my Government's situation.

"We could not afford to have our action leaked piecemeal to anyone before we could unify at least the AOSIS Members and give a full explanation of our motives to the world. Unlike the US, we are a tiny, basically indefensible State that depends on the world's sympathy and confidence for our survival."

Ambassador McMillan accepted the apology, but not without a stern note of disapproval. "I understand your Prime Minister's motives, but I must tell you that the US-Russian negotiations on this subject are at a precarious stage. I am very concerned that your indirect reference to Russia's Arctic program may have destroyed any hope of getting agreement on proposed US amendments to the Russian draft Decision. They believe the veil project was a disguised CIA operation, as Myshkin asserted in his public remarks.

"Our negotiations may collapse acrimoniously, leaving the world deeply divided on governance of SRM projects. I cannot promise that either the US or Russia will support your Resolution or your notion that action on SRM in the Security Council should be non-vetoable. Please don't ever spring something on us like this again."

Two weeks later, Anna Muhamir Smithson contacted the UN Secretariat and offered to turn over copies of the SE project documents, on condition that everyone with any connection to the project be granted immunity from prosecution, to the extent possible. The Secretariat refused to agree to the condition, noting that the UN has no authority to prevent any country from prosecuting illegal acts.

Anna consulted with Ariki on how to proceed. "There's really no choice about supplying the data, but make sure all names are redacted. We don't need to make it easy for everyone to find us," he muttered.

⟶○⟶

At this point Panday was in a state of panic. He met Doyal and Ibrahim at Mauritius's UN Mission offices and came straight to the point.

"The bear is angry. Our little project learned too much. When Singapore delivers the SE records, it's likely our identities will be uncovered. What are we going to do? I don't see any place to hide. We and our countries will be punished for it. Look what happened to Dr. Hartquist! Look what Putin has done to his other enemies, even outside Russia! I will be looking over my shoulder for the rest of my life."

Ibrahim was not entirely sympathetic. "We did the right thing, whatever the consequences. If we aren't willing to take risks to save our people from catastrophe, we should all retire."

Doyal tried to reassure Panday. "We always knew we were taking a risk of exposure, but I expect the records will have been cleaned up so our identities are not actually revealed. As for global condemnation, I doubt the world's reaction will be disapproval. Everyone except Putin seems to be happy with the temporary reprieve our project has provided. If world opinion is strongly favorable, we may turn out to be heroes, not villains. It's just too early to tell. Please be calm." Panday was not persuaded. He remained fearful.

"We may be heroes to 95 percent of the world, but that will not include the government in Moscow. I think maybe it's time for me to retire gracefully before this matter explodes."

"I cannot advise you to do that," Doyal responded. "Once Russia knows who we are, retirement is unlikely to provide much protection. Remember Trotsky and those retired spies in London. You know I'll never implicate you or Ibrahim, and I trust you will do the same."

Panday gave them a fatalistic smile and stood to depart. "We did the world a favor, and as we know, no good deed goes unpunished. You know you can trust me. I wish us all well."

Behind his sanguine facade, Doyal was equally worried. Retirement was not a palatable option for him at this point. He was too young and ambitious. He hoped whoever had the SE documents had the good sense to redact all the incriminating information, and that world opinion would neutralize the threat of punishment. It was a slim reed on which to rely.

———◦———

In Singapore, Ambassador Tan's presentation to the Security Council was headline news in every media outlet. Prime Minister Li revealed the approximate amount of the financial support for the project. He asserted that national security concerns prevented him from releasing any information about the exact source of the funds or the channels through which it was delivered.

The Singapore Parliament and public were pleased to see that the amount of the expenditures was relatively small. Rumors that the funds came from some foreign aid program, not from domestic programs, further calmed public concerns.

Prime Minister Li claimed full credit for Singapore's pioneering role in fighting climate change. He brought Ambassador Tan and Wang Shu home to explain the project and the success of his daring gamble. Over two-thirds of Singapore's adult population proudly watched videos of Ambassador Tan's UN speech on the Singapore Initiative, including Wang's proud parents. So did hundreds of millions of Chinese everywhere.

Five days later, Ambassador Tan returned to work in New York, but Wang Shu stayed another week in Singapore for more public presentations and interviews with the media. Soon Wang was as well-known as a movie star and more respected than most local political personalities. Political insiders began discussing Wang Shu as a possible Member of Parliament, in one party or another.

The local media hailed the Prime Minister as a shrewd hero with a previously unrecognized degree of long-range, global vision. Commentators around the world echoed that favorable perspective. Most environmental leaders praised him and Singapore for this leadership and urged other nations to follow their example.

In Russia, the media condemned the project as a secret plot to infringe on Russian sovereignty and the sovereignty of all Arctic nations. Media and social network commentary in Belarus and a few of the "-stans" dutifully repeated those views. "Independent" bloggers asserted that the CIA was behind the whole SRM effort, hiding behind small States that were merely pawns in the capitalists' plans.

Opinion polls in Singapore reported Prime Minister Li's popularity rising dramatically. Its citizens were pleased that their country had taken such a forward-looking step. Li and his party looked forward to a landslide victory in the Singaporean elections on Saturday, November 4, 2023.

⸺◦⸺

Within the UN Secretariat, senior officials, most of whom are assigned to the UN from their national government agencies, heatedly debated how to handle the SE data. Seeking to avoid inflaming the already confrontational atmosphere, the Secretariat's First Report simply summarized the relevant data about the SE project and correlated the SE activities with available satellite and earth observations of the Arctic. It did confirm that the project had most likely succeeded in increasing the earth's albedo over the Arctic Ocean and reversing the long-term warming trend evident before 2022.

The Report did not speculate on whether the results demonstrated that a tropospheric veil would accomplish desirable results over the long term. It also did not include anything about other activities that might also be affecting Arctic or global conditions. The Secretariat asked the IPCC to study the SE materials for whatever additional lessons might be learned.

Once the data were made available, the IPCC's skilled, curious, and enthusiastic scientific network quickly discovered unmistakable evidence of the previously unannounced

Russian program. Recognizing the sensitive nature of their conclusions, the IPCC leadership insisted that they not be released to the public at this time.

Meanwhile, the Secretary-General privately urged Ambassador Myshkin to release data from Russia's program.

"Professional scientific evaluation of the SE data depends on knowing the baseline conditions against which it was operating. If other parallel projects were underway, as the data suggest, useful conclusions about the impact of the materials, quantities, flight patterns, and other elements of the project are much more difficult to determine with any accuracy."

Ambassador Myshkin's response was diplomatically bland and opaque. "Thank for your views, Mr. Secretary. I will bring them to the attention of the relevant offices in Moscow." The Secretary-General rightly took that to mean, "It's highly unlikely Russia will acknowledge any program or provide any data."

In Moscow, President Putin was furious. He called in Foreign Minister Tretyakov and FSI Director Grigori Mordichov. "Whoever sabotaged our project must be identified and suitably punished. We need to make an example of Singapore and those so-called 'diplomats,' so the world knows not to twist the bear's tail."

Both advisors counseled patience, at least until the conspirators were conclusively identified. But Putin was having none of it. "Tell Myshkin to find out who they are. And destroy them."

Tretyakov called Myshkin. "Putin insists we find out who are the plotters who betrayed us."

Myshkin replied guardedly. "Of course I'll try. I've already demanded this information from Singapore, but it has not been provided, and the documents were carefully redacted to hide their identities. I'll keep working on it." Myshkin was more worried about the unanimity of world reaction against the revelations about the Russian program. He feared that punishing the plotters as individuals, if they really were diplomats from small island States, would just make them heroes and martyrs.

———◦◦◦———

In October, the UN General Assembly began debate on Singapore's draft Resolution. Member sentiment was almost universally favorable, especially from the AOSIS Member States. The other Arctic coastal states—Canada, Iceland, Norway, and Denmark (speaking on behalf of Greenland, its self-governing but not yet independent territory)—strongly supported the Singapore Resolution and its proposed approach to Security Council decisions on SRM.

UN Ambassadors Ibrahim, Panday, and Doyal were particularly active in rounding up support for the Singapore

Resolution, along with Indonesia's UN Ambassador Hendra. Russia's UN staff suspected that those AOSIS Member Ambassadors may have been involved somehow in SE project, but they had no tangible evidence to support that hypothesis. Anyway, they could see no political advantage in antagonizing those States at this point.

Ambassador McMillan met again with Ambassador Tan and informed her, confidentially, of the elements of the American strategy to induce Russia to change course. He followed up with a strong "request."

"I suggest that our chances of success will increase if Singapore puts off a vote on its Resolution until the US can get a meaningful response from Russia. The US position is still in flux. It's likely we will want a change in your Resolution to allow for weather modification without advance approval in cases of 'extreme, urgent situations.' Such situations would cover, for example, the frequent massive forest fires in the Western US and similar fires in Indonesia, which directly affect Singapore. Let's talk about some language to harmonize our positions."

Ambassador Tan readily acceded to McMillan's request for delay, despite her reservations about the exception. On a worldwide basis, "extreme, urgent situations" seemed to be occurring all the time. But if Singapore could satisfy the US concerns and win its vote in the Security Council, the prospects for the success of its Initiative would rise dramatically.

In Washington, President Gonzalez asked for an update from CIA Director Williamson. Williamson briefly reviewed the recent events, including the results of McMillan's meeting and hallway conversation with Myshkin. He continued, "We believe Singapore's Initiative will easily garner the two-thirds vote necessary to pass in the General Assembly. A vote on a parallel Decision by the Security Council would certainly get the votes of more than the necessary fourteen of the twenty-one members of the enlarged Council.

"Either Russia or China could try to veto the Singapore Initiative. We will insist that the Singapore Initiative is procedural and therefore not subject to a veto, but we would rather have a unanimous consensus on it.

"Initial reports from Beijing and gossip at UN headquarters in New York give us no reason to think China would veto the Initiative. Abstention by a Permanent Member would not prevent passage. Russia has never responded to McMillan on ending the Russian operation, or on the proposed US amendments to Russia's draft Decision. Our proposed amendments are generally consistent with Singapore's draft General Assembly Resolution, but McMillan has told Ambassador Tan that the prohibition on 'weather modification' must include an exception for 'extreme, urgent situations.'

"Meanwhile, our global surveillance systems and other intelligence indicate that the Russian flights are continuing and have no orders to stand down."

The President's shoulders hunched forward anxiously. "What do you suggest we do? I'm not ready start shooting down Russian planes. Are we really at the end of the diplomatic path?"

"Not quite, sir. First, McMillan should try to meet again privately with the Russian Ambassador, ask for answers to our inquiries, and point out that Russia will be completely isolated if it continues its weather modification flights, opposes the Singapore Initiative in the General Assembly, or tries to veto it in the Security Council.

"Technically, the US will join with about sixteen others on the UN Security Council, including Britain, France, and India, to sponsor a text that combines the elements of the Singapore Initiative with the Russian Security Council draft Decision, since Singapore is not a Security Council Member. It will not include any of the Russian language about violation of sovereign rights or Article 51 self-defense. We will have the votes to support a ruling that our proposed Decision is procedural and therefore not subject to a veto, in accordance with UN Charter Article 27. We can hope that Putin will come to his senses."

The President frowned. "I don't think that's likely. But let's try it. We can always take military action later. A few more months of Russian flights will not have irreversible effects."

Williamson responded, "I hope you are right, sir. But it's also possible that we will soon or have already passed a tipping point unless we take drastic action ourselves. The climate scientists in Secretary Sheppard's DNR are becoming more apocalyptic with every month's new scientific insights on reduced oceanic absorption of carbon, declining agricultural productivity, and shrinking fishery stocks around the world.

"If Russia doesn't reverse course, we could start by just shadowing the Russian flights and recording their actions. And we could make the Russian program public. Russia would be in an awkward position to protest anything we do, since it has just taken military action in almost identical circumstances that it justified as an exercise of its inherent right of self-defense.

"At that point, maybe Putin, and certainly the Russian bureaucracy, will realize what an awkward and difficult position they are in. Starting immediately would put some muscle behind McMillan's demands to Myshkin."

The President thought for a moment, then said, "Okay, but certainly we can wait two weeks and give Myshkin a chance to answer first. Military gestures too often bring startling consequences. As for releasing information about the Russian program to the public, that's only valuable as a threat—once you release it, the damage is done, and we no longer have anything to threaten."

"Yes, sir."

Chapter 30

NEW YORK

The President's desire to continue quiet diplomacy without public disclosure of the Russian program was shortly upended by events beyond his control. Monday, October 24, was United Nations Day. The *New York Times* seized the occasion to headline the essence of leaked documents it had received from unnamed sources and claimed to have verified with other unnamed sources:

> The *Times* has obtained documents containing persuasive evidence that Russia has been secretly engaged in a massive climate alteration program to accelerate the melting of the Arctic ice cap for at least three years. Their purpose is to accelerate the opening of Arctic shipping lanes on a year-round basis.
>
> The change in Arctic shipping caused by the Russian climate modification program is intended to provide President Putin with a justification for an unprecedented suite of major infrastructure development

projects along Russia's Arctic coast, boosting economic development in the region.

Rumors in Moscow suggest that this massive economic development program could also serve as the catalyst for an amendment to the Russian Federation Constitution to allow Putin to serve additional terms as president, effectively making him president for life.

This revelation is particularly significant considering Russia's condemnation of the secret effort by Singapore and other small states to create an atmospheric veil over the Arctic that had the opposite goal. The Singapore project appears to have succeeded in slowing the retreat of the Arctic ice cap and restoring historical weather patterns.

Professor Noah Rothman of the University of Chicago Law School has pointed out that Russia's weather modification activities violate its own statement of the legal principles governing atmospheric geoengineering that it presented to the UN Security Council last June:

Following the logic of the Russian legal analysis, any other Arctic Coast State, including the United States, Canada, or the Scandinavian countries, is legally entitled to shoot down any Russian aircraft dispersing chemicals over the Arctic Ocean, as a defense of its sovereign right to protect itself against foreign aggression.

Climate scientists familiar with the documents are shocked and outraged at the irresponsible character of the Russian program. They believe it largely explains the unexpected and dramatic acceleration of the deleterious warming effects on the entire global ecosystem.

The Russian Foreign Ministry immediately issued a statement denigrating the allegations:

The *New York Times* fabrications are outrageous lies. The *Times* is well-known as the mouthpiece of the US government, the CIA, and the capitalist establishment. Obviously, the US government instigated the publication of these fantastic tales. We note that the UN Secretariat has disclaimed any knowledge of these fake "leaked documents" and refuses to verify their contents.

The fact that the US concocted these allegations strongly suggests that it was complicit in the Indonesian flights into Russian airspace from the beginning. The story is a barefaced attempt to distract the world from that American-inspired, secret, unauthorized atmospheric climate modification project, nominally funded by Singapore and operated out of Indonesia. It is a pathetic attempt to change the subject. It will fail.

Within hours, the *New York Times* story and the Russian denial were headline news around the world. Anti-Russian demonstrations erupted in major capitals. Activists and many scientists asserted that Russia's program was the cause of crop failures, heat waves, floods, forest fires, droughts, and disruption of the traditional agricultural cycles. Several Arctic States and AOSIS Members either recalled their Russian Ambassadors or presented diplomatic protest notes to the Russian Foreign Ministry.

The UN General Assembly quickly adopted an amendment to the Singapore draft Resolution, calling on the Russian Federation to release full information about, and halt, all Arctic weather modification and geoengineering programs until the UN General Assembly and Security Council approves them. The only opposition came in the form of the vociferous objections of Russia, Belarus, and Tajikistan.

Ambassador McMillan immediately asked for another meeting with Ambassador Myshkin. At first Myshkin indefinitely postponed meeting because of "unavoidable scheduling conflicts." But as the worldwide chorus of attacks on Russia's behavior grew stronger, he found time on his calendar.

After a rather formal greeting, McMillan began by asking if there was any answer to his suggestions at the last meeting. Myshkin's face quickly contorted into a grimace. "Forget that," he growled. "I presumed we had an understanding that you would not publicize the alleged Russian program, at least until I responded to your request. That was just three weeks ago. Did you really expect I would be able to turn around President Putin and the entire Russian government in three weeks? I can't trust anything you say anymore."

McMillan had anticipated Myshkin's anger. He tried his best to defuse the situation.

"You have my word that the US government did not release any information about the Russian program. We are more eager to see the end of your project without undermining our cooperation on other matters than to score a public relations coup and embarrass Russia.

"Just this week the President reiterated to me his intention to pursue quiet diplomacy with Russia on this matter. Do you think I would have been pressing you for a meeting if that were not the case?

"At the same time, I must tell you that powerful officials in the President's Administration are pressing for initiation of a military response, beginning with tracking your flights and eventually destroying them if they do not stop. They are relying heavily on the same legal arguments you used to justify destroying the Sky Enterprises drone.

"I was hoping you could tell me that your flights are stopping, and you will support the US amendments to your draft Security Council Decision. The alternative is frightening."

McMillan had spoken softly, but his message only made matters worse. Myshkin was livid.

"You think President Putin cares about world opinion or some UN resolutions? In his view this global attack on Russia merely proves the need for strong Russian confrontation of the US and its cronies. It also shows that this is no time for Russia to consider changing presidents. How do you expect me to overcome that eminently reasonable analysis?"

McMillan, recognizing the impossible position that Myshkin found himself in, paused for a long moment. *I need to let Myshkin catch his breath,"* he realized, *We must remain on speaking terms, or we will both lose what little influence we have over this situation.*

Finally he spoke, choosing his words carefully.

"I understand Russia's frustrations, but I don't think your President has run this movie far enough forward. If I report no progress, our air force will begin shadowing your flights next week. If your flights don't stop within two weeks, the US will begin shooting down your planes. I wonder whether your air force is eager to respond with force against US fighter jets over the Arctic. Are you confident that your air force will win?

"If your air force is not successful, not only will your flights need to stop, you may lose one or more fighter jets in the process. Your air force will be defeated and embarrassed. If your initial defense *is* successful, which I doubt, the US will feel compelled to take even more aggressive action to demonstrate its strength and stop your flights, perhaps by destroying the base of your weather modification operations.

"Either way, the world will proclaim the US a savior. We will of course provide a full report to the UN Security Council on everything we are doing and everything we know about the Russian program. We have learned a great deal now that we have analyzed our data on your flights, which have continued for at least the last five years. I don't see any way that continuing your flights can lead to a happy outcome for Russia."

Myshkin stared at McMillan in silence. Finally, he spoke, struggling to keep his anger under control, as calmly as he could muster.

"This is an unacceptable threat against Russia's sovereignty. We might very well respond militarily. Putin is not that concerned about the opinion of people outside Russia. The Russian people will rally around their leader, and the conflict will give President Putin yet another justification for extending his presidency. Is that the result you are looking for?"

McMillan had already recognized that risk. His reply was equally controlled but unyielding. "We have lived with your President for over twenty-three years now, and we have survived. For all we know a new Russian president could be worse for US-Russian relations.

"But destroying the Arctic ice cap and undermining the planet's habitability are unacceptable threats to the US and the entire world. The flights must stop now. I have been instructed to demand your answers within seven days."

Myshkin sat in silence for a moment, then stood up. "Ridiculous. I think there is nothing more to say. Good day." McMillan stood and offered his hand; Myshkin refused it.

The next morning, McMillan reported to Williamson and the President that the meeting with Myshkin did not go well. The President, recognizing the gravity of the situation, scheduled a meeting of the NSC for that afternoon. McMillan rushed to catch the next Amtrak Acela to Washington. He wanted to participate in this meeting in person.

CIA Director Williamson felt strongly that the US had no choice but to proceed with shadowing the Russian flights if they did not stop within seven days. Ambassador McMillan had drawn a red line at the President's direction, and now the new Administration's credibility was at risk. The meeting was tense, but no one advocated any other course of action. The President gave his approval.

Ironically, among the NSC members, Williamson was the most uncomfortable about this decision. He had the most war-related experience of the NSC members. He never forgot General Eisenhower's words that while military planning is essential, the moment the battle begins, the plans are meaningless. Battles rarely proceed as planned or predicted.

Ten days later, around 2 p.m., Williamson received a call from Robert Schwartz at Defense. "As instructed, our fighter planes began shadowing the Russian flights three days ago. They were, in turn, continuously shadowed by Russian fighters, sometimes a little too close for comfort, but without incident so far.

"Today our flight reports and radar and satellite data indicate that the Russian weather modification flights stopped yesterday morning. We don't know if this is a real change in policy or just a mechanical or logistic pause. But it's a hopeful sign."

"That's excellent news," Williamson replied. "There's no need to continue sending our military aircraft into the Arctic once we know the Russian flights have stopped. Please make certain that instruction is clear to the base commanders."

Williamson still worried that one side or the other would do something provocative, intentionally or by accident. The Russian Air Force had shown again in June it was still a little trigger-happy. And on the American side, some overzealous "top gun" pilot or commander might try to show up the Russians just for fun.

"Definitely," Schwartz replied, "I'll make certain the instructions are clear. And I'll update you if anything changes." Williamson called McMillan to inquire about any further diplomatic contacts or other response to the American requests.

None.

After another forty-eight hours, Schwartz called again. "The flights appear to have stopped completely, and no US fighters are patrolling the Arctic. I would say 'mission accomplished,' with respect to this aspect of our strategy."

Williamson called the President's office and left word for him to call. Fifteen minutes later, the President emerged from a White House celebration and photo op with the Texas Rangers, his home team. He was congratulating them on their first-ever World Series victory, a dramatic five-game triumph. Their victory this fall would help him carry Texas again in next year's election.

Williamson's upbeat call brightened the President's mood appreciably. "This is the most important news I've received this month. It won't help me get reelected as much as the Rangers' victory, but it's certainly more significant. How do you think this news will emerge publicly?"

Williamson answered at length.

"We're not absolutely sure the flights are permanently over yet, sir. McMillan hasn't received any verbal confirmation. But let's assume they are. If Russia doesn't make its own announcement, the news is likely to leak out one way or another within a week or so. Russia will probably continue to deny there ever was a Russian Arctic climate modification program.

"In any case, the Russian media will likely make Putin a hero with enough sense to avoid a military confrontation with the US—a wise, far-sighted world leader, properly cautious in the face of American recklessness. Either way, I suppose Stan Marshall at State should begin preparing our response. I suggest that we express appreciation to Russia for its responsible decision and express hope that it will either support, or refrain from attempting to veto, the draft Decision on geoengineering proposed by the majority of the Security Council's Permanent Members.

"You might even call Putin yourself, Mr. President, congratulate him on his decision, and encourage him to support our amendments. Be sure to reaffirm that the US did not leak the October 24 story to the *New York Times*. That's true as far as I am aware. However the Russian press tries to spin it, Putin won't be happy, and you will need to deal with him or one of his puppets on a range of issues for as long as you are President."

Williamson could feel the President's smile through the phone. "Yes, let's try to make him feel good about the decision and about us as negotiating partners. I hope we can keep our own arm-twisting out of the papers. Please get Stan up to speed on what's happening and how we want to characterize the US and Russian actions. Tell him I told you to relay my message."

"Yes, sir. We can't ensure that the *New York Times* won't carry a back story on how we achieved these results, but I'll talk to McMillan about avoiding any unauthorized comments from the US UN Mission. And congratulations on your diplomatic success!"

Suddenly, the *New York Times* found itself without sources about how Russia was persuaded to abandon its weather modification program. In New York, McMillan again requested a meeting for an update from Myshkin. They met that afternoon at the US Mission office.

McMillan began delicately. "Thank you for coming over. We've seen changes in the Russian flight patterns in the Arctic. I hope you can confirm that these changes are permanent. We haven't given information to the media and we won't in the future, but if the changes are permanent, Russia may want to say so.

"We are prepared to compliment Russia on its responsible course of action and say nothing about the events leading up to it. Our President might call your President to say so if that would be welcome."

Myshkin smiled slyly and replied,

"There are no flights now, and I'm not sure there ever were any geoengineering flights, despite the inflammatory and misleading reports in the US press. As for the future, I certainly cannot make any predictions. I also cannot agree that the US threats were or ever will be acceptable.

"Nevertheless, I believe we have successfully resolved an unpleasant situation. With the help of Defense Minister Boris Ivanov and Foreign Minister Nickolas Tretyakov, we were able to avoid a collision course.

"Your President probably should wait for another occasion for any high-level telephone calls. Our President is not entirely reconciled to this turn of events."

McMillan responded with a smile of relief. "Thank you. That's excellent news, and I congratulate your government on its wise decision."

Myshkin rose to leave. He offered his hand, and McMillan took it in a warm handshake. Myshkin leaned closer and confided, "I'm sorry this business has been so difficult. We are both professionals. Sometimes we find ourselves in impossible positions, defending the indefensible or entirely without instructions. We are each only the voice of a much larger set of institutions."

McMillan, equally aware of the difficult role diplomats must sometimes play, wordlessly nodded to indicate his understanding. Myshkin departed.

The UN Security Council reconvened at the end of the week. Ambassador Myshkin expressed Russia's understanding of the institutional concerns behind the new draft and announced its support:

> Russia recognizes that an active SRM program may indeed become necessary at some point. We cannot let any one Member, not even a Permanent Member the of Security Council, hold the international community hostage while it seeks concessions on other, perhaps completely unrelated, issues.
>
> Russia cannot accept any language in the Security Council Decision or Singapore's General Assembly Resolution that singles out Russia's modest weather modification program or implies that it was more of a threat to the global climate than the many similar programs of other

states. We are pleased that the draft provides a practical exception to the prohibition on all weather modification programs without UN approval.

We note that no international registry of weather modification projects currently exists, and no formal international scientific evaluation of their individual or collective impact occurs.

We believe the UN Secretariat should promptly set up a registry managed by UN Environment, a UN subsidiary, and require real-time access to information from all States. When we have all the data, we can see whether additional steps are needed to ensure that such programs do not interfere with the rights of other States.

If Singapore and the other sponsors agree to these changes in its draft General Assembly Resolution, the Russian Federation will also vote for Resolution A/78/413.

Singapore immediately modified its Initiative to excise the offending language, add a provision directing the Secretary-General to create the registry, and exempt weather modification efforts "extreme, urgent situations."

Within a week, the General Assembly unanimously adopted Resolution A/78/413. A week later, the Security Council adopted the majority's version of the proposed Decision on atmospheric geoengineering, which included the amendments proposed by the US.

Ambassador Myshkin announced that Russia was abstaining, citing the failure of the revised draft Decision to exempt a broader range of legitimate weather modification programs, and expressing misgivings about the dilution of the veto power. The vote was 20-0, with one abstention.

—◦—

On December 24, 2023, after his re-election and the approval of the Singapore Initiative at the UN, Prime Minister Li announced a "Christmas present to the world"—another two dramatic steps to delay the effects of climate change.

First, Singapore requested the UN Security Council to approve a Singapore Project for an experimental SRM tropospheric veil program, built upon the model of the SE project. It would be operated by a new international entity and overseen by UN Environment.

After two years, if the UN Secretariat and UN Environment concluded that the program produced favorable information of sufficient quantity and quality, the

Secretary-General could transform it into an operational program.

The UN Security Council could overrule the Secretary-General's decision to go ahead, or end the program at any time, by a two-thirds majority of Council Members, again without a veto.

Second, Singapore introduced an Additional Measures Resolution that called on all Members to take other specific steps to increase the earth's albedo in their own territories. To encourage prompt action on the Singapore Project and Additional Measures, Singapore offered to place an additional $20 billion into a fund to support the SRM project and the State "albedo projects," on the condition that other States, foundations, and individuals collectively match that contribution during the year 2024.

This offer sent shock waves around the world. It was generous, but most governments were locked into budget cycles that would make it difficult to pledge funds by the deadline.

Inevitably, the United States was expected to contribute the largest share. That would require action by Congress, which might not agree with the President's decision to participate, for partisan or policy reasons. Support from the President himself was not even certain.

To almost everyone's surprise, several private parties promptly stepped forward to provide matching funding. At Al Gore's instigation, Microsoft founder Bill Gates,

Warren Buffett's foundation, and Amazon founder Jeff Bezos each pledged $4 billion. With their encouragement and example, billionaires from a handful of other major economies, including China, Germany, India, Korea, and Singapore, jointly promised to contribute most of the remainder necessary to match the Singapore contribution if the UN Security Council approved the Singapore Project and Additional Measures. The balance was subscribed within two months.

Some scientists and environmental activists remained opposed on principle, fearing that even the experiments might do irreversible harm. But most accepted the reality that an experimental program under UN auspices was an essential step, if only to avoid more unilateral national or clandestine private efforts if the UN remained paralyzed.

After a brief private conversation, Ambassadors McMillan and Myshkin requested and obtained an understanding from the UN Security Council President and Singapore that consideration of the Singapore Project and Additional Measures would be postponed until March 31, 2024. Neither government was yet prepared to proceed without careful consideration of the alternatives and consequences. And both countries were holding elections in 2024.

Returning to New York after celebrating the December holidays with their families, Panday, Doyal, and Ibrahim met for dinner. They toasted and savored their amazing, and surprising, success. There was much to celebrate, and there were smiles and reciprocal congratulations all around. The SE project had succeeded sufficiently to provide enough data to support further efforts to design a safe and effective veil for the globe, and Singapore was leading the way toward an officially-approved veil program.

Politically, they had initiated the SE project without exposing their personal roles or the involvement of the Indonesian Prime Minister. No domestic political figure of consequence in either Singapore or Indonesia attacked the incumbent government for countenancing this secret project. Prime Minister Li had even built his re-election campaign around his visionary approach to climate change.

The Ambassadors' mood came back to earth as Panday addressed the challenge ahead.

"We're not done, you know. Our little adventure was a success, but that was all just preliminary. The commitment of funding for the Singapore Project makes it likely that the Security Council will vote to approve an experimental, globally-supervised geoengineering project. But the crucial provision in the Project is automatic transition to a long-term, operational veil if and when the Secretary-General, not the Security Council Member Governments, concludes it is feasible and desirable. Only that will prevent massive human misery and death while our species tries to work its way out of this self-inflicted carbon-dependent box.

"Even with that authority in the hands of the Secretary-General, the decision process for an operational SRM veil will necessarily be public, transparent, and subject to political influence. It will face enormous opposition from those who think it will inevitably do more harm than good and from those with a strong economic stake in the status quo, not to mention unbalanced people like that Margaret Taylor woman or various fanatical religious groups.

"We will need real scientific support, displayed and advocated in public, and subject to the pressures brought by Security Council Members whose governments have vastly differing interests. We know at least one major power has a substantial investment in hastening year-round ice-free shipping through the Arctic. Do you think prominent Russian climate scientists will support the Singapore Project?"

Ibrahim shook his head in disbelief. "I can't imagine that the world would go backward after all that has been accomplished over the last three years."

Doyal was even more skeptical.

"Ibrahim, my friend, that is how the real world works. Even when the talk is most promising, the results are often disappointing. Most important, we don't know yet what the US will say. President Gonzalez has been pretty good on climate change, but he is up for re-election in eleven months. Will he backtrack during his campaign?

"Even if the UN Security Council votes in favor of the Singapore Project in some form, it might only include the experimental program and reserve the operational decision to itself. Will Singapore and the private donors still fund the experiment in that case? Moreover, two years is a long time. We were convinced the US was committed and locked into a strong climate change program before the 2016 election. We were wrong. Who knows what the 2024 elections will bring?

"I fear we may find ourselves reverting back to the endless debates and stalemate that have bedeviled all our climate change efforts so far. AOSIS shouldn't expect that it will be smooth sailing from here on. And nothing anyone can do will slow the sea-level rise for many years yet."

On that somber note the dinner ended, with a commitment to continue working together.

But Panday decided he'd had enough. On February 15, 2024, he announced his retirement from the Trinidad & Tobago Foreign Service. At his retirement ceremony, he said simply, "I have been deeply honored to serve my country in many capacities around the world. I hope I have contributed to our safety and security, and perhaps a bit to the prosperity and health of the entire world.

"Now I step aside to allow younger, better qualified individuals in our Foreign Service pursue these goals with more energy than I can muster at this stage in my life. I look forward to spending my remaining years with my wife, my children, and my grandchildren. I thank you all for your friendship and support through my many years of service to our country."

Chapter 31

WASHINGTON

On January 22, 2024, the President called Ambassador McMillan and Director Williamson to the Oval Office to review the status of developments on the new Singapore Project and Additional Measures. He began enthusiastically.

"First, thank you for your good advice, and congratulations on your effective execution of our strategy for defusing the Russian ice-free Arctic project. We have quietly resolved the military and political confrontation over the Russian Arctic weather modification program with a minimally provocative military action and no appreciable change in Russia's cooperation, such as it is, on Korea, Iran, and Afghanistan.

"In the coming months, I really need to turn my attention to other domestic and international crises and, of course, preparations for the 2024 election campaign. But Singapore's proposed Project for an experimental and operational tropospheric veil program calls for a crucial and highly visible decision on international climate policy.

"Unlike the original Singapore Initiative, which was ultimately just about procedures for approving atmospheric geoengineering, the Singapore Project and Additional Measures would result in real programs to increase the earth's albedo. It will mean taking a gamble with potentially dramatic human consequences, not just abstract principles and processes. I need your most thoughtful advice.

"Where do we go from here?"

Ambassador McMillan's Memorandum, parts of which he read aloud, expressed admiration for Singapore's bold leadership and dramatic financial offer. He then offered his analysis from the US UN Mission's perspective:

> Neither the US nor the international community has ever even debated the desirability of a UN-approved, large-scale, long-term tropospheric veil program. The Singapore Initiative made novel structural changes in UN governance and the Secretary-General's authority. Now Singapore is advocating new substantive climate programs with its Project and Additional Measures.
>
> The Singapore Project authorizes an experimental program, but it goes well beyond that point in both substance and procedure. If the Secretary-General concludes that the results of the experiment justify proceeding, he can automatically

transition to a full-scale, operational tropospheric veil to slow global warming.

It would take a two-thirds majority to override the Secretary-General's decision. With this structure, the decision to go forward would likely be entirely out of our direct control. The AOSIS States, being desperate, would certainly support the Secretary-General's decision, and that alone would probably rule out a two-thirds override in the General Assembly, and perhaps in the Security Council as well.

The Additional Measures resolution designates other projects designed to increase the earth's albedo everywhere, along with much more aggressive steps to substitute wind and solar power for fossil fuels. These projects are not part of the Singapore's Security Council Project. But the veil is only desirable if we use the time to implement other climate protection actions. While it is likely that the General Assembly will approve the Additional Measures resolution, there is no obligation or assurance that all Member States will implement them.

The political rhetoric supporting the Singapore Project and Additional Measures leans heavily on Dr. Hartquist's 'drowning man' metaphor; namely, that the veil is essential but not sufficient, any more than throwing a drowning man a life preserver is sufficient when a rope or a lifeboat is also available.

China, the EU, Japan, and India, who are well along on these transitional paths and see business opportunities in this policy direction, are supporting it. At the same time, India and China are seeking to minimize binding commitments. Many smaller States will implement the Additional Measures only on the condition that the requirements are accompanied by economic and technical assistance to transform their relatively inefficient fossil-fuel energy systems into something cheaper and more self-sustaining.

Finally, the Singapore Project text does not designate an end point or review period, nor does it include any incentives for States to address climate change permanently by drastically reducing almost all industrial and agricultural human emis-

sions of carbon. I think we can negoti-
ate some amendments to address these
weaknesses.

Politically, I believe we have little choice about supporting Singapore's
Additional Measures resolution if we
expect to be world leaders on climate
change. How quickly we live up to the
proposed obligations is something for the
Congress and the President to determine.

Director Williamson summarized the conclusions of
his own Memorandum, laying out the CIA's reading of the
situation.

Ambassador McMillan has clearly
articulated what could be called the
'inside the UN' view on the impact of
the Singapore Project and Additional
Measures. Let me briefly sketch some
broader foreign policy implications.

First, despite your phone call to soothe
President Putin's ego, he is still firmly
committed to building the infrastructure
for year-round Arctic Ocean navigation.
It would be a signature accomplishment
for his presidency and the linchpin of

his hopes to extend his term in office. He won't give up on it, with or without continuation of his weather modification escapade. After all, the natural effect of climate change on Arctic ice cover still favors his vision of an Arctic future, even without any artificial enhancement.

Second, Russia is pinning its hopes on the idea that the US, facing an election in November and still struggling to reverse the previous Administration's pro-fossil fuel and know-nothing climate policies, will refuse to support the Singapore Project and Additional Measures. Without US or Russian support, they will die, whatever the General Assembly vote.

If the US supports them, Russia will be completely isolated on this highly visible international initiative. If the US opposes the Singapore Project and Additional Measures, China and its allies will have every reason to support them. China would then stand as the most forward-looking Great Power.

Third, as a practical matter, real implementation of the Additional Measures will be difficult without US financial, logistic, scientific, and technical support. Russia can't afford to do much, and China is doing what it can. So the future of these measures depends entirely on the American position.

The CIA believes that on balance the US position in the world will be significantly enhanced if we support both the Singapore Project and the Additional Measures, which will reestablish US world leadership on climate policy. Climate policy will become increasingly important in the coming years, and US leadership will pay dividends in international relations in a variety of ways.

I won't speculate on the domestic economic or political implications, which you already know as well as anyone.

The President was indeed well aware of the domestic political implications. He could see that this decision was his alone. The answer could determine his future for the next four years and world's future for much longer.

Recognizing the importance of unity within his Administration, he scheduled a two-hour Cabinet meeting devoted solely to the American position on the Singapore

Project and Additional Measures. His opening remarks expressed his concerns.

"I've assembled you to let every Cabinet Department present its views and hear each other's views. We can't afford to have a divided cabinet on this subject, which will inevitably be a prominent issue in the campaign. I need everyone to listen as well as talk, and then accept and support my decision from here on in."

After McMillan and Williamson summarized their analyses, Secretary of State Carmell spoke. He saw the decision as an easy choice.

"I agree with the strategy proposed by Alex and Harold. Isolating Russia and undermining its influence is almost always desirable from the US point of view. It highlights to everyone that only the US can provide the leadership the world seeks. No one expects Russia to lead, and the outrage over its secret Arctic weather modification program will not be forgotten.

"If the US votes no, we will be blamed for impeding this thoughtful attempt to mitigate the effects of climate change, which is already causing widespread hardship. China will vote for the Project and Additional Measures and emerge as the most responsible Great Power and a world leader in the eyes of most nations. We have here an opportunity to demonstrate our willingness to lead on a vital global commons issue. We can't afford to pass it up."

Defense Secretary Admiral Clarissa Radford expressed a very critical practical concern. Her Department's vast arsenal still relied on fossil fuel.

"We cannot afford to weaken our military capability in such a crucial respect. We have been working for more than two decades to transform our military's dependence on fossil fuels, but we are still a decade away from reaching that goal both in manufacturing and operating our weapons systems. Russia will never comply with a requirement to abandon fossil fuels in its military operations, whatever the UN recommends or mandates.

"If we and our allies limit our capabilities, Central and Eastern Europe will be exposed to a greater danger of invasion. Even President Trump recognized that if we don't come to their defense, we will be acting in bad faith and damage our credibility for a century. This red line was drawn decades ago, and we cannot retreat from it, either explicitly or implicitly."

Energy Secretary Tyler Watson also strongly opposed the Singapore Project and the Additional Measures. "We'll be giving away America's leading role as a global oil, coal, and natural gas exporter, with severe negative consequences for some of our most basic industries. It would hurt our balance of trade and the value of the US dollar.

"If the Additional Measures are adopted, the US will inevitably be forced to come up with funds to update our existing infrastructure and aid others to do so—funds we don't have in the budget." He was joined by the Secretaries of Commerce and Treasury, who also opposed the Singapore Additional Measures resolution on economic grounds.

Watson also warned of adverse political consequences. "Agreeing to a global takeover of this crucial field could be fatal in the election for you and the Democratic Congressional ticket. We Democrats cannot afford to open ourselves up to a charge of 'weakening our defenses' or 'sacrificing our sovereignty,' whatever the reality."

The last Cabinet Member to speak was again Natural Resources Secretary Kristi Sheppard. Recognizing this discussion as a crucial turning point in climate policy, she read at length from her Memorandum.

> Mr. President and my Cabinet colleagues, DNR strongly believes that both the substantive and the political consequences of failing to give whole-hearted support to the Singapore Project and Additional Measures would be a disastrous mistake.
>
> DNR agrees with much of the international political analysis offered by the Department of State, Ambassador McMillan, and the CIA. Isolating Russia as a global outcast pursuing its narrow

self-interest will add to our image as a strong, generous world leader at a time when China's attempts at global leadership are being undermined by its economic and ecological imbalances and its insistence on regional hegemony at the expense of its neighbors.

Substantively, DNR's scientists are no longer just concerned about the long-term impacts of climate change. They now believe we are more likely than not to see catastrophic worldwide famines and flooding in our lifetimes. These dramatic adverse impacts will be felt here at home as well as abroad. Rising temperatures, droughts, and more intense storms in the Midwest will reduce US agricultural production and exports. A one-meter rise sea level—that's more than three feet—would permanently or frequently submerge the downtown areas of coastal cities in Virginia, Florida, Louisiana, and Texas, and damage many other coastal cities along the Eastern and Southern coasts.

The US Gross Domestic Product could fall measurably because of these impacts, and our quality of life would suffer even more as our labor and material resources go to protecting and rebuilding what we have instead of improving our living conditions. Creating jobs that do not give people more useful goods and services is an illusory gain.

Our international economic influence could also be impaired. The economies of many other countries, like Vietnam, India, and Indonesia, are more primitive than ours, but their more modest infrastructure makes them more resilient in some ways. And the EU is well ahead of us in investing in its transition to renewable energy and planning for catastrophes.

Yes, there will be adverse ramifications for current fossil fuel-based energy production and delivery, for military operations, for trade, and perhaps for balance of payments. But let's not forget that agricultural products and renewable energy equipment are also important exports, especially now that American companies are producing and exporting more electric vehicles, batteries, wind turbines, and solar panels.

With all due respect to Secretary Radford, the Defense Department is understating its progress to ensure it will be the best fighting force in the world for decades to come even without fossil fuels, though its fuel costs will be somewhat higher. The obstacle is budgetary limits, not a technical barrier. Meanwhile, there is no sign that any foreign military force is interested in testing our military capabilities.

The US, like everyone else, needs a tropospheric veil to protect us from, or more precisely, reduce the odds of, devastating nonlinear impacts from global warming. We must recognize that we are gambling with irreversibility every day we allow the current climate momentum to continue. On substance, there is only one justifiable answer.

The other argument I hear is that it's political suicide to address the climate change issue before the election. I agree that losing the election would be a catastrophe in many respects, for climate policy as well as other vital matters. But I think the political reality is that the public is hungry for strong leadership and progress. The voters chose President Obama in 2008 expecting dramatic change, and they were disappointed with the resulting paralysis. Then they tried President Trump, who promised to 'drain the swamp' and 'make America great again,' but he and the Republican Congress turned out to be largely incapable of governing.

The people elected you in 2020, Mr. President, in the hope that they would finally have the kind of forward-looking, optimistic, inclusive leadership they have sought for a dozen years. And you have made solid progress on many domestic issues. But your image as a leader on international matters is still vague.

The polls show that the public wants action on climate change more than ever. The extensive media coverage of Dr. Hartquist's death and the Singapore Initiative and its Project and Additional Measures recommendations have raised public hopes of a breakthrough to progress, not continued fatalism and fear. Taking the lead will demonstrate that you aren't afraid of addressing the hardest international problem we face, you aren't going to pretend we can ignore it, and you aren't going to kick the can down the road to some other president in 2025 or 2029.

I believe supporting Singapore's bold initiatives will put you in the strongest position from which to campaign for re-election. I have no doubt it will help you win in November. The results of Singapore's election two months ago show what voters will do when they see active leadership.

President Gonzalez sat back in his chair. He had been thinking carefully about this decision for some time. He had read memoranda prepared in advance of this meeting by several departments.

Should I announce a decision right now, or think more about it? Should I at least appear to weigh the comments I've just heard? Allow for post-meeting side conversations to satisfy Cabinet Members' egos?

At the end of the discussion, he explained how he intended to proceed:

"Given the importance of this decision and the range of views expressed, I intend to take some time to mull over our course of action. As I noted at the outset, I trust we can present a unified front to the media and the public, and stick to our message this coming year, whatever it turns out to be. Thank you all for your sincere, thoughtful, concise, and articulate presentations. I will have a decision for you soon."

Within five minutes after they adjourned, Secretary Sheppard was on the phone to the President. "I do hope, Mr. President, that you really have no doubt about the right answer. Truly the fate of humanity and civilization, not to mention your re-election, hangs in the balance."

The President had expected this call. He was not ready to answer her yet, even privately. "Kristi, you were very articulate in the meeting, as were most of the others. I promised I wouldn't decide immediately. If I do decide your way, our public statement will track your comments, and our background analyses will emphasize how we are simultaneously leading action on climate change and reducing Russia's standing in the world.

"I would appreciate a draft speech text briefly explaining the merits of the US position along the lines you described. I will probably want to give some visibility to the decision, precisely for the reasons you suggested. Thank you again for your invaluable assistance."

Kristi muttered, "Yes, sir, Mr. President. I'll start work on a draft right away." The President ended the call. Kristi's head filled with angry emotions. She muttered, *Four years ago, when we were both Senators, he was Edwardo and I was Kristi, and he never uttered bromides like 'Thank you again for your invaluable assistance.' Now he's 'Mr. President' and I'm still just 'Kristi' to everyone, even though I'm also a Cabinet Secretary. And now I'm writing material for his speeches instead of my own. Will he also ask Secretary Watson for a draft speech?*

I wonder if he's decided on his course of action. I can't believe he would listen to that same old oil industry flimflam. Maybe it would be time to quit if he did. But that might tilt the election to one of those nativist, 'America First' Republican presidential candidates, which would be the worst result of all.

She gritted her teeth and called in a staff speechwriter to turn her Memorandum from the Cabinet meeting into a polished draft speech, which she revised and delivered to the White House a week later.

The next Monday, at the regular Cabinet meeting, the President discussed the climate issues again.

"The State Department, the CIA, and DNR, the agencies most directly involved, argue strongly for supporting the Singapore Project and Additional Measures. It may be our only hope to save humanity, and it is very unlikely to do any irreparable harm. If we vote yes, American scientists and civil servants will take the leading role in cooperation with scientific experts from around the world. We will marginalize and isolate Russia if it opposes or even abstains on these proposals. If we voted no, our failure to lead would enhance China's status and reputation as the Great Power most concerned about the future.

"Nevertheless, I believe it would be unwise to announce a final decision right now. The Singapore Project and Additional Measures are a dramatic alteration in the world's approach to climate change and the role of the UN. We need to hear from industry, the scientific community, and the public about this issue—both those in favor and those opposed—and deliberate carefully before announcing a conclusion. I have asked Ambassador McMillan to seek a delay in the UN Security Council vote to allow the US and other interested parties to analyze and consider the ramifications of this landmark decision."

Secretary Watson was visibly distressed at the news. He too had called the President. He had been left with a comfortable feeling the President agreed with his position, which now turned out to be wishful thinking.

Secretary Sheppard took some comfort in the defeat of Secretary Watson and the oil industry. At least she hoped that was the reality. But with every day that passed, she saw the opposition building the case for the status quo. And even after the Executive Branch was on the right track, it would still take precious time and effort to persuade the Congress to support the policy and appropriate the necessary funds.

Ambassadors McMillan and Myshkin requested a further indefinite delay in the consideration of the Singapore Project and Additional Measures. Singapore acquiesced, hoping its initiatives were not about to die. Ambassador Tan was heartened by McMillan's request for a meeting to discuss some further "adjustments" to the Project. She hoped they would be minor.

Chapter 32

OMAHA

President Gonzalez read over Secretary Sheppard's draft speech and put it in a drawer in the Oval Office. He had no doubt she was right on the merits, but he was worried about the depth of the opposition from the Departments of Energy, Commerce, Treasury, and most of all, Defense.

Their positions foreshadowed the public debate, which began in earnest after the news that Ambassadors McMillan and Myshkin had officially requested an indefinite delay in the UN Security Council vote. It was a signal to all interested parties that the United States and Russia were not aligned, and their votes on the Singapore Project and Additional Measures were still unsettled.

In the United States, the lobbying efforts were intense on all sides. In addition to personal meetings with the President, several Senators and Representatives introduced draft Resolutions expressing the sense of the Senate or House. Some supported the Singapore Project and Additional Measures, while others opposed them for the assorted reasons the Cabinet Secretaries had argued to the President.

Some Cabinet Secretaries discreetly gave technical assistance to friendly Members and lobbyists and quietly supported draft Resolutions that espoused their views and the views of their constituencies. The media made the topic a regular subject of updates, interviews, and "in-depth" background reports.

The President noted which Secretaries were being helpful and which were more concerned with their standing with their geographic or interest group constituents. *This is turning out to be a useful exercise for evaluating which Cabinet Secretaries deserve to be reappointed or receive some other reward in my second term, if I get one,* he mused.

The President was in no rush to announce his decision. In public, he listened attentively to all opinions. He kept an eye on the public opinion polls and activist demonstrations and asked his campaign pollsters to analyze the demographics and intensity of feelings of those for and against the Singapore Project.

He was waiting for an appropriate occasion. The public at large wasn't very excited about climate change in January and February, though the climate scientists reported that weather conditions in 2023–24 were already reverting to the trend lines that had prevailed before 2022–23. In March, as temperatures rose prematurely, higher levels of rain and snowmelt caused increased flooding, and climate change rose on the list of public concerns.

Republican party leaders were widely scattered on the issue, which also made it wise to delay. Some Republicans now sought to take a forward-looking position on climate change, while others still insisted it was a Chinese hoax or a conspiracy among scientists to get more funding. The President foresaw how the politics of the issue would unfold. *The moment I announce a position, the Republicans will coalesce around an opposing position. At that point, the multiple opinions and open-minded discussion will collapse into a Democrat-Republican polarity.*

April brought more destructive storms and unpredicted weather conditions. Members and lobbyists representing farm communities began to think maybe the scientific community's conclusions on climate change should be taken seriously after all. In May, a series of unusually strong tornadoes in the Midwest again aroused public concern.

The President decided to announce his decision before the hurricane season. If he waited until late summer, it might appear that the weather events and the state of the campaign were forcing him into a decision on political grounds. He preferred to adopt a more statesman-like stance well before then.

On May 18, the President traveled to the Midwest to inspect the widespread damage caused by a series of tornados that decimated upscale residential and commercial areas near 102nd Street and Dodge Road in Omaha, Nebraska. Eleven lives were lost, and the extensive property damage in this well-to-do neighborhood made for dramatic visuals on television. These images were ideal for attracting the attention of middle-class white suburban Americans who often vote Republican.

When a White House Pool Reporter asked the often-repeated question about the President's position on the Singapore Project, the President did not say, yet again, that he was still studying the issue.

Turning to the cameras and doing his best to look strong and decisive, he answered, "As you know, I have consulted extensively with my Cabinet Secretaries, and I have heard the views of a variety of economists, climate scientists, foreign policy experts, and interest group representatives.

"We have just seen the damage caused by extreme weather events, which have become so much more common in recent years. I have made my decision, after careful consideration of the benefits and costs, on the Singapore Project and Additional Measures. I will speak on this subject in a brief television address to the Nation when I return to Washington."

On May 21, the President addressed the Nation, and the world, from the Oval Office. He had reviewed Kristi's draft several times. Aside from a topical introduction, he was happy with the substance, but he felt it was somehow too "soft." He needed his policy to signify something stronger.

After much thought, he called Kristi with a single question.

"In this draft speech of yours, suppose I change the words "tropospheric veil" to "solar shield"? Doesn't solar shield sound a lot stronger than tropospheric veil? Would that be too much of a distortion of the reality?"

His finely tuned political ear told him that a "shield" to reflect the sun's rays suggested something much more effective than a "veil," with its connotations of translucence and femininity.

Kristi paused to consider the implications. *What would the climate change scientific community, in my own Department and in the world at large, think of this new term? Could I say 'Solar Shield' in my speeches and still sound like a thoughtful, informed Cabinet Secretary, rather than a political apologist for the President?*

Finally, she answered, "Mr. President, you are the President of the United States and the most powerful leader in the world. Of course you can call it a Solar Shield. 'Veil' is just a metaphor anyway.

"I don't think my climate scientists will laugh condescendingly or demean your choice of words. And yes, I think the public will find those words more reassuring than the obscure term 'tropospheric veil.' I reserve the right to refer to the Singapore Project as calling for a 'tropospheric chemical veil' in testimony before Congressional committees, but millions of people will hear your words for every one who hears mine. In short, go for it."

The President changed his draft speech by altering the one phrase—for "tropospheric veil," he substituted "Solar Shield." His short and specific speech text was ready, and he delivered it forcefully.

> This weekend I visited Omaha, Nebraska, where I saw firsthand the devastation that nature is wreaking on our homes, our farms, and our cities, more frequently than ever. Immediately after my inauguration as President, I directed my Administration to carefully study the threat of a climate change disaster in the immediate future, not just the next century.
>
> What I saw in Omaha was another demonstration of the dangers of nature on a rampage. We cannot risk the possibility that such events will be an increasingly frequent experience in our daily lives and the lives of our children.
>
> With that in mind, I have thoroughly evaluated the advantages and disadvantages of approving the Singapore Project pending before the UN Security Council. I have met with representatives of every serious point of view.

The Project would initiate a global effort to create a Solar Shield high over the polar regions of the earth. Specially designed aircraft carrying calcite powder, an environmentally safe constituent of limestone, will release it high in the atmosphere, far above the altitude where commercial and most military planes fly. The powder will stay in the upper atmosphere for over a month after release. These aircraft will replenish the powder on a continuous basis.

This Solar Shield will reflect a small percentage of the sunlight that is currently melting the polar icecaps back into space. The objective will be a restoration of the cooler climate conditions that our planet has enjoyed since before the rise of human life on earth.

Although there are a few dissenters, the vast majority of the scientific community believes that a carefully designed, scientifically managed Solar Shield will give us our best hope for a healthier present and a more stable future for ourselves and our children. The Solar Shield, along with other vigorous efforts by the US and other governments, will reduce the risk of the encroaching devastation that could otherwise engulf us.

Our full participation in implementing the Singapore Project and Additional Measures will require funding from Congress, as well as technical support from the Executive Branch, and most importantly, the support and cooperation of each of you, both at the ballot box and in your everyday lives. I hope we can finally all agree that climate change is real and happening now, that it threatens our health and welfare, and that we must act before we do irreversible damage to our only home, the Earth.

Accordingly, I have directed our Ambassador to the United Nations, Alexander McMillan, to ask the UN Security Council to meet promptly on the Singapore Project and Additional Measures. I will personally offer some amendments to the Singapore Project and Additional Measures, which will enable the US to support the creation of a Solar Shield. This vote will not be subject to a veto by any Council Member, and it is my fervent hope that it will pass unanimously.

Every person and every nation on the planet will inevitably share the consequences of our action or inaction. In my opinion, any nation that opposes the Project and Additional Measures is obliged to explain in full the reasons for its vote and the alternative remedies it proposes to ensure the survival of civilization as we know it.

God bless the people of the United States, and the entire world.

Except for the "Solar Shield" substitution, the prepared text was about 95 percent Secretary Sheppard's. The President's speech didn't give her any credit for shaping his decision or even mention her name. She was not on the ballot in November, he was.

The speech was greeted with effusive praise by the leading Democrats and mild criticism from various Republican senators and presidential candidates. Most environmentalists everywhere celebrated the decision.

Opposing political interests remained quiet and began revising their political strategies for the coming election. Corporate leaders, many of whom had not predicted the President's decision, reviewed their long-term plans to see how to prosper in what would be a different economic environment.

The next morning, after watching the favorable media commentary on his speech, the President called Secretary Sheppard. "Kristi, I'm just calling to thank you for your articulate and insightful policy and political analysis. Your persuasive presentations at our Cabinet meetings have been extremely valuable to me. I hope you are happy with the speech. And I believe you are right on both the substance and the politics of this matter. I'm betting on your judgment."

Kristi Sheppard smiled and said, "Thank you, Mr. President. The entire world is betting on you. And I really like your phrase *Solar Shield*. It has a much more solid feel to it."

After the call, Kristi took a few moments to let herself relax and savor her triumph. *Moments like this make all the years of struggling with politics and bureaucracy worth the effort*, she reminded herself.

It was time to prepare to meet the media, which would want her views on the President's decision for the evening news and the daily interview programs. *I suppose I could just say 'the President said everything I would have wanted him to say,'* she thought, *or 'he took the words right out of my mouth,'* laughing to herself.

◦◦◦

On May 27, a week after his climate change speech, the President attended the UN Security Council meeting in person to reinforce the American commitment to support the Singapore Project and Additional Measures. The almost unprecedented attendance of the US President at a UN Security Council meeting made headline news, with live coverage on television around the world, followed by videos posted online.

The President repeated essentially the same speech, with more emphasis on the hopeful, cooperative, forward-looking action the US and the UN were about to take, reflecting its staunch support around the world.

Based on the General Assembly votes on Singapore's Project and Additional Measures resolutions the previous day, the Project would have more than enough votes to obtain the necessary two-thirds majority in the Security Council. The only vocal opposition came from Russian allies who were not members of the Security Council. At first, President Kartawijaya had been leery about supporting the Singapore Project and Additional Measures, but in the end he told Ambassador Hendra to vote yes, joining the General Assembly's overwhelming majority.

After his opening speech, President Gonzalez explained the majority draft Decision's changes to the original Singapore Project. They comprised four additions:

- Before making the decision to transition from an experimental to an operational Solar Shield, the Secretary-General will hold open hearings in every region of the world on the desirability of that step. (Echoing the President's speech, the phrase *Solar Shield* now appeared throughout the draft Decision.)

- The approval of an operational program will be contingent on significant global progress to implement the Additional Measures.

- The UN Security Council will receive a formal report on the impact of both the Solar Shield and the Additional Measures and place the subject on its agenda for discussion at least as often as every three years.

- Advance UN Security Council approval would not be required for weather modification operations that are necessary in "extreme, urgent situations", but they must be immediately reported to UN Environment and narrowly limited to the urgent circumstances. They must stop if a majority of the Security Council disapproves.

In accordance with the Decision on the earlier Singapore Initiative, the veto power had been waived. The only question was whether the vote would be unanimous. Aside from Russia, almost all Council Members wanted to be on the right side of history and on the right side of the American President.

Only Iran, currently one of the rotating Members of the Council, might vote no, reflecting its reliance on oil and the firm belief of its influential mullahs that Allah would never allow the destruction of humanity. In the end, Iran was more eager for full acceptance in the international community. It voted yes, despite its belief that the program was unnecessary.

The Singapore Project was adopted 20-0, with one abstention, Russia.

President Putin never obtained a constitutional amendment that would allow him to run for re-election in March 2024. He endorsed Foreign Minister Tretyakov, who was elected with a large majority. Putin once again became "the power behind the throne," as he had been during President Medvedev's term over a decade earlier.

In June, President Tretyakov reiterated the plans for a massive infrastructure program to support year-round Arctic shipping, giving former President Putin full credit for his vision and groundwork. But the target dates for starting and completing construction were left ambiguous.

In the United States, June 2024 national polls showed substantial improvement in President Gonzalez's approve/disapprove margin and in his image as a farsighted world leader. Both Republican and Democratic commentators predicted an easy victory in the upcoming election. Some leading potential Republican contenders withdrew, postponing their ambitions to 2028, when the odds would be better.

Singapore's Prime Minister Li found himself riding a continuing wave of popularity after the UN adopted his bold initiatives to protect the planet.

Some journalists, after intensely studying the SE documents, concluded that IFC and Wijaya must have played a key role in the SE project. But the thread was too tenuous to support a front-page news story. Wijaya did not acknowledge any personal or governmental role in the SE project. *Perhaps in my memoirs,* he fantasized.

Chapter 33

NEW YORK

After the Security Council vote, Doyal invited Ibrahim to dinner to celebrate the latest AOSIS triumph. Having noted the surprisingly stiff and formal professional interactions between Ibrahim and Wang Shu at various UN meetings, he hesitated to invite Wang to join them without asking Ibrahim.

"Definitely, invite her," Ibrahim responded. "She did more work and took greater professional risks than any of us to accomplish this result. She deserves our deepest thanks."

"Good. I'll call her immediately. What about inviting Ambassador Tan?"

"I think we shouldn't. She did an extraordinary job, but we will inevitably talk about things that only we should ever know."

"Yes, that's certainly true," Doyal agreed.

Doyal thought he detected some discomfort concealed under Ibrahim's generous praise of Wang, but he took the words at face value. He invited Wang; she accepted. Ibrahim steeled himself for the evening ahead. He hoped it wouldn't be too awkward for either of them.

That evening, the three were seated in a relatively secluded alcove in The Palm Too restaurant, a few blocks from UN Headquarters. They drank a toast to their success and a second toast to Wang Shu, Ambassador Tan, and Prime Minister Li for their indispensable, courageous, and farsighted actions for the benefit of humanity. In return, Wang offered a toast to the three Ambassadors for their creativity and daring, so atypical in diplomats. Then a fourth toast to President Kartawijaya and IFC for their willingness to provide the physical platform at great risk, and to President Gonzalez for his willingness to address the real threat of climate change for the United States and the world's coastal and island nations.

Doyal was particularly effusive about Wijaya's willingness to execute the project on its territory and with its people. "I wasn't at all confident he would take the gamble for a project whose outcome was far from obvious and whose immediate effects on Indonesian exports would likely be negative. It could have turned out very differently. I don't know if we can ever give him the public credit he deserves."

Wang filled in some of the blanks about the execution of the SE operations, to the extent she knew them. Some things, like source of the computer software, she learned only after the fact by listening to the Security Council proceedings and poring over the SE documents that were given to the UN Secretariat.

"It all went smoothly from the outset," Wang continued. "I don't know why Martioto and IFC were so cooperative, but it seems clear from their histories that Wijaya and the IFC leader have a strong personal connection. I'm not sure he had any choice but to grant Wijaya's request. But there were significant political, professional, legal, and physical risks for both of them.

"Fortunately, nearly all the SE planes were flown as drones, without pilots or observers aboard, or we might have had a death on our hands. The records delivered to the UN show that SE had decided to acquiesce to the Russian pilot's demand, but he was a little too eager to attack. Had he waited another fifteen seconds he might have seen the drone turn around. In that case, Russia might never have brought this matter to the Security Council. So maybe it was all for the best."

The conversation turned to more topical political matters, including Prime Minister Li's use of the project to strengthen his political position. Perhaps Wijaya could do the same? Or would his close connection to IFC turn the project into a liability? They mooted comparable questions with respect to President Gonzalez, though his performance appeared to result in smooth sailing for the fall election.

Seeing Wang in person and watching her lively personality and crystalline brilliance, Ibrahim was once again entranced. He longed for the chance to speak to her alone. But what exactly could he say?

Eventually Doyal was ready to depart. Ibrahim carefully delayed finishing his tea, seizing his chance for a few personal words with Wang. When they were finally alone, he uttered the words he had been formulating and revising during the last half of dinner.

"I want you to know I miss you terribly. Your voice, your quick intelligence, your smile. I know I wasn't as attentive as you wanted after we went our separate ways. I didn't know what else to do. I had to shut you out of my mind to live at home without the prospect of seeing you again. I hope you would be willing to spend a little time with me here in New York."

Wang paused. She wasn't sure if Ibrahim even knew that Mahmood was living with her. And did she want to renew a relationship with Ibrahim in any case? Now that some sort of resumption seemed possible, she needed more time to think.

"I'm pleased to know your feelings, which I reciprocated for a long time, more intensely than you know. I was miserably alone in Setitor until I made some new friends there. Let me think about it."

Ibrahim tried to smile in the face of these painful words, but failed. He wanted to plead, to say "please," but he was afraid to seem a person to pity rather than love. Instead he whispered, "I understand. I will be leaving for

Malé tomorrow and return in three weeks. I hope I can see you then. In any case, thank you for making this such a pleasant evening for me. I hope you also enjoyed it." Then he rose and quickly walked away, afraid that otherwise he would say something more foolish.

Wang remained at the table, finishing her espresso, and struggling to make sense of the situation. *What do I really want? Participating in meetings with him and now at dinner reminds me why I loved him so much in the first place and why it hurt so much to be without him. He is smart, charming, physically attractive, and excellent conversation, an ideal diplomat—and lover.*

But our careers, his family obligations, and the cultural divide make a lifelong or public relationship impossible. Do I want to repeat the joy and misery that was the result of our secret affair?

And what about Mahmood, now that the work of analyzing the SE documents is essentially finished, and his second six-month visa is about to expire? I rarely saw him at work. He was analyzing documents in the Singapore Mission and the Secretariat offices while I was conferring with the Ambassadors and staff of other Members.

He seems to be quite isolated from the frenzy of the Singapore UN Mission these days. He never complains, but I wonder if he is happy. Maybe he has his own opinions about his future. How can I broach the question of separate futures without hurting him deeply?

Burdened by these concerns, Wang returned to her apartment, where Mahmood was waiting for her with a glass of wine in each hand. He was his usual warm, compliant self, something she did not take for granted this evening.

"How was dinner?" he asked.

"It was delightful. We celebrated our triumph and recognized all the ways the project might have failed. You were an important part of my success, and I owe you a debt of gratitude. We should also celebrate. A toast to our success, and a 'thank you' to you. I could not have accomplished my mission in Setitor or here in New York without you, both professionally and personally!"

Mahmood smiled awkwardly. "I appreciate those kind words. I've been thinking a lot about the future lately. Can we talk about it?"

"Of course," Wang replied, relieved that she would not have to be the one to raise the subject. "Let me get comfortable and sit down." She put away her briefcase, took off her shoes, and joined him on the sofa.

Mahmood began with what was obviously a well-prepared statement:

> You know how much I love you and enjoy being with you every day and night. You are kind and affectionate and considerate. But here in New York, I'm what the Americans call 'a fish out of water.'
>
> I've done all I can for you in analyzing the SE documents. I'm not a diplomat

or an international civil servant, nor do I aspire to be one. Though I have learned a lot over the last six months, I realize I have too little skill with language and too little knowledge of the bureaucratic and diplomatic worlds to make a career at the UN.

I could probably go to work for an Indonesian airline in New York and get a long-term visa that way, but then I would see even less of you than I do now, and we would be leading completely separate lives. We don't know when or where you might be transferred next, or whether it would be feasible for me to come with you.

I don't make small talk with these diplomats and bureaucrats easily. I would only be welcomed by them informally as your companion, never at formal occasions. Marriage to me is probably out of the question for you. And from my family's point of view, it is certainly out of the question for me as well.

It is wonderful to be your companion and lover. A child's fairy tale dream come true. I cherish every minute of it. But I think the end of my visa marks the time for me to get back to my reality, to my home and family in Jakarta, to my Muslim, airplane mechanic world. Living here with you, I've been able to save enough of my salary to give me a good head start on a new life back home. Wang, I know you care about me, but I've no illusions that you will wither and die without me. It's time for me to go.

Wang recoiled at the bluntness, and truth, of these last words. Having spoken them, Mahmood began to cry. Wang took him in her arms. They embraced and cried together. The suddenness of her impending loss overwhelmed her. *Will I ever again find such a supportive, helpful, tolerant, loving companion? Who else would ever be waiting at the door for me at home?*

She tried to say how important and valuable he was to her, but the words would not come. She knew there was a certain disingenuousness about her emotions. His departure, which seemed inevitable eventually, would simplify everything for her. But she would miss this reliable and supportive partner terribly.

Unable to speak, she took his hand and gently led him to the bedroom. They made love with the special tenderness and intensity that comes with consensual farewells and slept in each other's arms. The next several days flew by, as he packed his belongings and arranged his departure. Wang took the days off, and they spent most of the time together seeing the sights of New York—a world she had barely explored, and Mahmood would never inhabit or perhaps even visit again.

A week later he was aboard an Emirates Airbus 380, flying business class for the second time in his life, en route to Dubai and on to Jakarta. Wang asked the Singapore Embassy there to provide a car and driver at the airport to take him wherever he wished to go. Mahmood first said that was unnecessary. But when Wang replied it was a token of the depth of her appreciation for all he had given her, he graciously accepted. It made for a dramatic arrival at his parents' home.

For the first month, they exchanged emails frequently. He sent pictures of his home, his parents, and his siblings, who were all thrilled to have him back. He soon reported with excitement that he had been hired as a mechanic supervisor at Garuda Indonesia, the national airline, in Jakarta. The linguistic and bureaucratic skills he had acquired from Wang and his work at the UN were much appreciated by his new employer, and his career prospects were good.

Before long, his parents identified a prospective bride that he found attractive and pleasant. His experience with Wang had taught him how to be a caring and supportive husband. The marriage was a happy one. Over the years the occasional emails to Wang became photos of Mahmood's wife and children, typically on vacation.

Wang always offered supportive and congratulatory replies. Looking at his photos, she sometimes felt a pang of regret. *What a comfortable, stable life I could have chosen! Perhaps I should have abandoned diplomacy and found enough challenge and opportunity working for a Singapore bank in Jakarta. I could have been the wife and mother in those pictures.*

But that was a fantasy, considering their families' cultural differences. Anyway, it was too late for that, and deep in her heart, she knew it was not the life she wanted.

⌐◦⌐

In July, Ibrahim returned to New York from his home in Malé to make arrangements for his family's arrival in August. He renewed his invitation to dinner by email, too fearful of outright rejection to ask by phone or in person. Wang accepted. They met at Marseille, on 9th Avenue, a short walk from Times Square, a restaurant that serves traditional food from its French namesake, including both classic French and Middle Eastern cuisine.

They talked for hours about the prospects for a permanent Solar Shield, the necessity for a comprehensive, global programmatic response to climate change, and other more urgent but existentially less critical issues pending in the UN. The old chemistry was there, more powerfully than either had anticipated.

Late in the conversation, Wang alluded to her now past relationship with Mahmood and how it had changed her life. Ibrahim took the information in stride. He had surmised that Mahmood had been living with her. A check on Mahmood's address in the UN records had shown only a post office box near Wang's apartment. Ibrahim knew he had no grounds whatever to object, regardless of his pain.

They were both wiser now, and the obstacles to a life together were even more insoluble than before. Ibrahim now held the highly visible position of Maldivian Ambassador to the UN. His family would be joining him in a month so the children could begin school in New York. He and Wang could never live together. The professional sacrifices and emotional pain for Ibrahim and his family would be far too great.

Wang was deeply ambivalent about renewing a relationship that had brought her so much pleasure, but also so much heartache. But at this moment, she could not imagine simply saying good night and taking a taxi to her empty apartment.

She invited Ibrahim to accompany her home, and the night of conversation and passion lived up to their expectations. They met a few more times in July. Neither one said anything about ever meeting again.

Chapter 34

HAVANA

The February 2025 AOSIS conference took place in Havana, Cuba, for the first time. The availability of frequent flights from New York and Washington and elimination of cumbersome visa re-entry procedures in the United States now made Cuba an ideal meeting place for the many delegates whose other assignments included the UN or their government's US Embassy.

The mood was noticeably more upbeat than in previous years. The decisive re-election of President Edwardo Gonzalez, inaugurated just a few weeks earlier, ensured continuity in US foreign policy in many areas, but particularly with respect to climate change and related global commons issues.

The elections also produced a US House and Senate that would be likely to support the President's climate change policies. After the surprising outcome in the US elections in 2016, leaders around the world welcomed the continuation of a predictable American government.

In addition to his home state of Texas, Gonzalez had carried Florida, providing Electoral College votes that far exceeded the votes lost in the "rust belt" states of Ohio and

Pennsylvania. Commentators generally attributed his wide margin of victory in those states to the votes of Latinos, and increasingly settled Millennials, who were attracted by his message of hope, action, and inclusiveness.

Kristi Sheppard had been widely mentioned as the perfect 2024 Vice-Presidential candidate, but she assured President Gonzalez she preferred to remain in her present position as Secretary of DNR. The possibility of her own run for office, either for Governor of California in 2026 or President in 2028, was more appealing than four years as Vice-President, with no independent decisionmaking role in the Government.

The first order of business at the AOSIS Conference was choosing a new Chair. The Honorable Anarood Doyal, the Ambassador of Mauritius, was the only nominee, and he was elected by acclamation.

Doyal had been aiming for a more permanent and more powerful position: Executive Director of UN Environment, succeeding Erik Solheim of Norway. UN Environment is headquartered in Nairobi, Kenya, relatively close to Doyal's home in Mauritius. It would be the perfect match for his diplomatic skills and interests, coordinating environmental programs involving multiple UN agencies.

But Russia opposed his appointment after concluding he was one of the SE conspirators. Putin was no longer President, but his influence ensured that no one suspected of involvement with the SE project would ever be appointed to a leadership position in any UN-related agency.

The AOSIS Conference Chair position was Doyal's swan song. He soon followed Panday's example and left the Mauritius Foreign Ministry. He took a position in the Bank of Mauritius as its representative to the International Monetary Fund, International Bank for Reconstruction and Development, and various Asian regional banks, voting on the distribution of billions of dollars of international project money.

After the usual opening welcome, Doyal called on Delegate Wang Shu of Singapore to explain the recent decisions of the UN Security Council and General Assembly. His introductory remarks were extensive and laudatory.

"The optimism and enthusiasm we feel at this Conference is very largely the product of the far-sighted leadership of one of our own Members. Singapore's initial generosity in funding the Sky Enterprises project, and its courage in taking public responsibility for doing so and defending the necessity for prompt initiation of an experimental Solar Shield, were indispensable.

"We have made great progress over the past two years, thanks to Singapore's vision and generosity. Ambassador Rachel Zhu Tan, ably assisted by Delegate Wang Shu, played a vital role in achieving these dramatic results. I have asked Delegate Wang Shu to explain the amazing events of this past year."

Wang deftly described the SE project and the UN General Assembly and Security Council decisions on the Singapore Initiative, the Project, and the Additional Measures. Doyal called Ambassador Tan forward to receive an Appreciation Award from AOSIS to Singapore. She accepted with a few felicitous diplomatic remarks, including a thanks to Wang, and returned to her seat.

And then, to Wang's surprise, Doyal announced a special AOSIS Award to Wang Shu personally for her efforts. Presenting the award, Doyal briefly described her involvement in the SE project.

"Wang Shu was deeply involved in the execution of Singapore's original project to test the viability of a Solar Shield. Her task was to ensure that the project was being executed honestly, effectively, and efficiently.

"To do so, Ms. Wang gave up her comfortable UNESCO assignment in Paris to live in a remote, primitive area of Asia. When the project abruptly ended, she was transferred on short notice to New York to lend support to Ambassador Tan on Singapore's UN initiatives.

"Others who were involved are keeping their roles secret. But Ms. Wang could not complete her mission by remaining invisible. She gambled her life and career for the good of humanity."

Wang Shu was surprised by the award. She offered a few simple words of thanks to the AOSIS delegates for their commitment to protecting a livable world, and to her parents for their unconditional love and support over the years.

After Wang left the stage, Doyal announced that he had more awards to present.

"We all know how much Dr. Ilsa Hartquist contributed to the thinking and strategy of AOSIS. Tragically, she is not here to accept an award. The AOSIS Board concluded that instead two awards should be given. The first is to Dr. Hartquist's parents, who gave us this brilliant, dedicated, and politically savvy but incorruptible scientist. Their daughter can take as much credit as anyone in history for promoting the survival of the human species."

Dr. Hartquist's parents accepted the award with tears in their eyes as the audience stood and applauded. They responded with a brief "thank you," and left the stage, overcome by their emotions.

After a suitable pause, Doyal continued.

"The final award goes to two Royal Canadian Mounted Police investigators, Marie Veronique Roy and Jon Martin Wolfe, who brought Dr. Hartquist's murderers to justice. These agents, by their diligence, perseverance, and creative investigative skills, solved what was considered a hopeless case. They not only tracked down the murderer, they found the source of the money that paid for the murders. It is professional investigators like these two who make it possible for us all to sleep more easily at night."

Marie came on the stage with Linda pushing Jon's wheelchair. Jon's children and Marie's husband, Chris Roy, were seated in the front row as honored guests. Though Jon had survived, his physical mobility was limited. Fortunately, his mental facilities and ability to speak had largely recovered.

Marie spoke first. "Thank you for this award, which Jon and I will always remember. It is a source of enormous satisfaction for us and the Royal Canadian Mounted Police to receive this recognition of our work. We are not extraordinary RCMP agents. We simply did our job to the best of our ability, as others do, only this time on a case of global interest. We are accepting this award on behalf of all the RCMP agents who do their difficult, tedious, and sometimes dangerous work every day.

"As you can see, Jon was seriously injured by one of the murderers, who thought if he silenced us he would never be captured. The murderer is now in prison, probably for life. Justice has been done."

Jon read his remarks, haltingly, but articulately. "Thank you for this award. Marie, who was my able superior throughout our work on this investigation, was the persistent, creative, and determined prime mover in its resolution.

"While I suffered serious physical wounds, Marie narrowly escaped injury or death on three occasions, once meeting the murderer face-to-face with a gun in his hand, only saved by the presence and good judgment of armed Montreal police officers. Otherwise she might have been shot in her apartment house the same day I was. We both thank you for this award and for your recognition of the important work of the RCMP."

The audience again stood and applauded, as Marie stood impassive, fighting back her tears. She had hardly seen Jon since he was shot, and his damaged physical presence, combined with the knowledge that they would never work together again, was overwhelming. After leaving the dais, she and Chris immediately retreated to their hotel until she could emerge without being surrounded by the media.

<hr />

When the Conference adjourned, Wang began a long-overdue vacation at the Bravo Arenal Hotel, on the beach just east of Havana on the Playa Santa Maria del Mar. The Havana region was still suffering from the Category 3 hurricane that struck in 2021, but the tourist infrastructure had largely been rebuilt. She had informed Ambassador Tan of her vacation plans but told no one else. She was allowed just two weeks before she must return to work in New York.

Wang had a lot on her mind. She felt she had finished this chapter in her career, and it was time to contemplate her future in a systematic manner. The questions were fundamental. She relaxed each day by the pool for the first time in years, drinking a margarita, mulling her options.

I could continue as a career diplomat, but have I exhausted that experience? Is staying at the UN in New York City the life I want, even though the work is often demanding, and at the same time tedious and frustrating?

As a college student she had read *The Education of Henry Adams* to learn about diplomacy and how to parse complex English sentences. She remembered Henry's struggle to find a career after serving as Assistant to his father, Charles Francis Adams, the US Ambassador to London during the American Civil War. Henry's autobiography reports that his father and friends recommended that he not pursue a career as a diplomat. It would be a life of disappointment:

> For diplomacy, I already knew too much. Anyone who had held, during the four most difficult years of American diplomacy, a position at the center of action, with his hands actually touching the lever of power, could not beg some future president for a post of Ambassador at Vienna or Madrid in order to bore himself doing nothing until the next president should do him the honor to turn him out.
>
> For once, all his advisors agreed that diplomacy was not possible.

Like Henry, Wang Shu realized it was unlikely that she would ever again find herself in the center of so many crucial challenges on such an important matter as she had just experienced—obtaining funds directly from the Prime Minister, observing and reporting on the operations of SE, and then working feverishly to generate support in the UN General Assembly and Security Council for a radically new approach to climate change and reshaping the UN Security Council voting, all embodied in the Singapore Initiative, Project, and Additional Measures. Of course, there was follow-up work to do that would stretch for decades, but that could never be as exciting as the original struggle.

Besides, she was fully aware of the fate of Doyal's attempt to become Executive Director of UN Environment. *If Russia opposed him merely on suspicion of his involvement in the SE 'conspiracy,' what would they do to me, given my highly visible role in Singapore's involvement in the plot? Panday wisely retired. Doyal was denied his ambition and left diplomatic service. Maybe I should learn from these examples. I'll never be a visible senior official. Russia doesn't forget its enemies.*

So what other choices do I have now? she asked herself. She tried to let her imagination run free. *Maybe it's time to return to Singapore. I could find a senior position in a bank or insurance company and settle down with a husband to share my life.*

She paused. *Too tame, perhaps? A career in Singapore politics would be more challenging and exciting. The Prime Minister has given me the support and public exposure I need to start down that road if I'm interested. I'd need to choose that path soon while the public recognition lasts. Can I imagine myself being comfortable in the Prime Minister's political party?*

How would I earn a living in Singapore? Henry Adams, apparently comfortable financially, had become a history professor at Harvard and later lived in Washington without a paid job, writing several widely acclaimed books on American historical figures.

Perhaps the Prime Minister could arrange a professorship for me at my alma mater, the National University of Singapore. I might be able to combine teaching with a political career that leads to a position in Parliament or the Cabinet, maybe even Foreign Minister!

Two hours later, while still contemplating options for her future, she found herself facing a more immediate decision. A text from Ibrahim.

> Hi! I'm staying at Il Convento, just down the beach from you. Would you be interested in dinner?

She was surprised and intrigued to learn he was also in Cuba, staying in a hotel not too far away.

Is this a coincidence, or was it planned? she wondered. *How does he even know where I am? Did Ambassador Tan tell him? What exactly does she know, or suspect?*

The text said nothing more, but Wang had little doubt about how dinner and the evening would unfold.

The romantic attentions and supplications of a man that I once loved so deeply may be exactly what I want this week. Can I manage to enjoy him without falling into the painful trap of unrealistic dreams?

This might be our last time together, she reflected, *or maybe not. Perhaps we will meet occasionally, as the opportunity arises. Our relationship will never be anything like what I once wished. But it seems neither of us can bear to say goodbye forever.*

She accepted the invitation with the anticipation of a pleasant evening, the hope of rediscovering some of the joys of those first days with him in Paris a decade ago— and no illusions about the future.

The End

About the Author

S am Bleicher is currently an Adjunct Professor of Law at Georgetown University in Washington DC. From June 2014 to November 2018 he served as a Member and Vice-Chair of the Virginia Air Pollution Control Board. He is a graduate of Northwestern University, Phi Beta Kappa with Honors in Economics, and Harvard Law School.

His novels draw on his experience as a law firm partner and lobbyist; a senior official in the Ohio EPA, National Oceanic & Atmospheric Administration, and Department of State; and a law professor in the US, Russia, and China.